P9-CRP-967

"WHAT DO YOU HAVE THERE?"
BROGNOLA ASKED

"A wild card out of left field," Tokaido responded. "You aren't going to believe it."

"At this point, I'd believe just about anything," Kurtzman said.

"It's from Striker," Tokaido stated. "He and the CIA ops he was working with just cracked that terrorist cell they were tracking in Jordan."

"That's good news," Brognola said. "But how does that fit in with the situation in Spain?"

"They got a guy into interrogation," Tokaido reported, "and get this—he says the Iraqis had an agent fly into northern Spain earlier this week to meet with the BLM. They're trying to get their hands on some nukes and maybe even the supertank."

"That's out of left field, all right," Kurtzman muttered.

"I don't like the sounds of new players," Brognola said. "It puts everything in a whole new light."

DON PENDLETON'S

STONY

AMERICA'S ULTRA-COVERT INTELLIGENCE AGENCY

MAN

ROLLING THUNDER

A GOLD EAGLE BOOK FROM

WORLDWIDE.

TORONTO • NEW YORK • LONDON
AMSTERDAM • PARIS • SYDNEY • HAMBURG
STOCKHOLM • ATHENS • TOKYO • MILAN
MADRID • WARSAW • BUDAPEST • AUCKLAND

First edition August 2004

ISBN 0-373-61956-1

ROLLING THUNDER

Special thanks and acknowledgment to
Ron Renauld for his contribution to this work.

Printed in U.S.A.

ROLLING
THUNDER

This book is dedicated to Feroze Mohammed,
for patience, support and understanding
far beyond the call of duty

PROLOGUE

Nacional Parc Guell, outskirts of Barcelona, Spain

With a faint snap, the thick limb of a towering beech tree tumbled down from the forest canopy and crashed at Angelica Rigo's feet. More than a dozen other branches, all festooned with dark green leaves, lay in a growing mound at the base of the tree. Rigo, a thirty-year-old, ruddy-skinned woman wearing khaki shorts and a matching sleeveless top, wiped the sweat from her brow and checked her watch, then looked up at the handful of men trimming the other branches in the tree above her. She barked at them in Euskara, native tongue of the Basques.

"Can't you work any faster?"

One of the men glanced down from his perch and waved his small, curved handsaw. "Let us use chain saws instead of these toys, and we'll have this tree down three times as fast."

"And you'd be ten times as loud doing it," Rigo countered, fighting back an urge to shout. "How many times do I have to tell you we need to do this quietly?"

"You keep telling us that," the other man called down, "but what is the point? We're miles from anywhere. Who's going to hear us except the birds and squirrels?"

A few of the other men in the tree laughed lightly and murmured among themselves. Staring up at them, Rigo fumed. What had happened to the days when those who joined the movement could be counted on to work with dedication and without complaint? Why was it that she always found herself saddled with slackers and malcontents?

"Just keep working!" she told the men. She hesitated a moment, then grudgingly added, "Have this tree down by sunset and there will be wine with rations tonight!"

As expected, the promise of drink motivated the men, and they began to lay into their work with increased vigor. Rigo lit a cigarette as she watched them. They still needed to clear away another three beeches over the next two days to make the site ready. They would be cutting it close.

Another limb soon tumbled to the ground. Rigo side-stepped it and moved away from the tree, her boots treading softly on the wild grass and trailing vines that carpeted the forest floor. They were in a remote corner of Nacional Parc Guell, a densely treed nature preserve ten miles northeast of Barcelona. The nearest hiking trails were half a day's walk away, so there was little chance that anyone would stumble upon the group illegally falling the beeches. And because the trees were being taken down with minimal disturbance of the overhead canopy, it was just as unlikely that anyone flying overhead would be able to spot the small clearing being carved out of the woods. That would be important come Friday, when the plan was to be carried out.

Rigo made her way through the trees, walking another twenty yards before coming to the edge of a steep-pitched slope that led to a broad, verdant valley. Blowing smoke from her cigarette, she stared out across the valley. Far off in the distance, barely visible through a faint afternoon haze, she could see the rising, honeycombed spires of La Sagrada Familia. The old church, designed more than a century before by infamous Barcelona architect Antoni Gaudi, was still unfinished, and Rigo saw a construction crane poised atop the highest spire like a gigantic metallic grasshopper. Provided the skies were clear on Friday, it would be easy to use the church as a frame of reference while drawing a bead on the intended target, the newly constructed Barcelona civic center, located a few miles southwest of the towers. The trajectory had already been calculated and would be assisted further by GPS readings from a surveillance drone; all that remained was to prepare the launch site and see to it that the FSAT-50 could be delivered on schedule without complications.

Once she'd finished her cigarette, Rigo unclipped her cell phone and, for the third time in the past half hour, checked to make sure it was turned on. It was, and there were still no messages. The woman slipped the phone back in its holder and retreated from the edge of the forest. The mound of trimmed branches at the base of the beech tree was growing higher. Rigo called up a few words of encouragement to her men, then went to check on the other preparations. To her right, a dozen or more smaller saplings had already been flattened, creating a corridor that soon led the woman to the banks of the Avignon River. The river, extending all the way from the uppermost reaches of the Pyrenees, formed the easternmost border of the national park and eventually drained into the Mediterranean near the Barcelona suburb of Sardana. For most of its course, the river ran deep—as much as ninety feet in places—but here there was a fork, with some of the water diverting into a shallow lagoon. The lagoon was also fed by a mountain stream carrying high levels of iron, which gave the water a faintly reddish hue. Another five men stood knee-deep in the water at the lagoon's edge, scooping out spadefuls of mud and pitching them up onto the embankment. The mud, like the water, was rich with iron and the color of sienna.

"How goes it, Xavier?" Rigo called out to the man closest to her.

"Slow," called back Xavier Golato, a tall, broad-shouldered man with massive arms and a shaved head glistening with perspiration. "But we are making good progress."

"We'll have one of the trees down by sunset," Rigo told him. "I want to be able to cut the trunk into sections and use it for a ramp."

"We will be ready," Golato assured the woman. "You'll be able to lay the trunks below the waterline like you wanted."

"Excellent."

Golato took in Angelica's voluptuous figure with a faintly salacious gaze. "I have a trunk of my own waiting for you later tonight," he whispered suggestively.

Angelica returned Golato's gaze with one every bit as lecherous. "Just be careful not to cut it into sections first," she taunted. "I'll be wanting all of it."

The lovers' suggestive banter was interrupted when they saw several of the men stop their shoveling and glance upstream to a fork in the river. Rigo followed their gaze and saw a boat entering the lagoon. Instinctively she reached for the 9 mm Walther pistol holstered on her right hip. She relaxed her grip, however, when she recognized the craft, a small, weathered fishing boat propelled by a pair of outboard motors. There were several men on the deck. One of them waved a greeting as the boat drew closer.

"Looks like they brought company," Golato murmured.

Rigo nodded, eyes on a man's body sprawled out across the foredeck. A few feet from the body was a woman, gagged and bound at the wrists and ankles. Even from this distance, Rigo could see that the woman was terrified. She could also see that the woman, like the dead man, was white.

"Americans?" Angelica called out to the man who had waved to her from aboard the boat.

The other man nodded. "We came across them a quarter-mile upriver," he replied, pointing to a small red kayak lying on the deck near the captive woman. "They were acting suspicious."

Rigo told Golato to have the shovelers stop their work and help guide the boat to a suitable mooring spot ten yards from the section of embankment they had been excavating. After pausing to light another cigarette, she flipped open her cell phone and tried to get in touch with her brothers. Miguel and Jacque Rigo were a few hundred miles away in Bilbao, carrying out the other part of the mission. Neither of them responded. Rigo checked her watch again and frowned. She was supposed to have heard from Miguel ten minutes ago. Had something gone wrong?

Fighting back her concern, she put the phone away and strode along the bank to where the boat was being tethered. Once she'd leaped aboard, she took a closer look at the dead man and saw that he'd been shot once in the head at close range.

"He said they were just tourists, but they have sophisticated camera and radio equipment," the captain of the boat told her, staring down at the corpse. "They were armed, too."

Rigo looked from the body to the other woman. The prisoner eyed her beseechingly, tears streaming down her cheeks. She looked to be in her late twenties, blond haired with a sprinkling of freckles across her cheeks. She tried to say something, but her words were muffled by the gag.

"I'll get to you in a moment," Rigo told her in flawless English.

Then, shifting back to her native tongue, she asked the boat's captain, "What did the sonar come up with, Enrique?"

"The readings were all good," the captain responded. "The depth is acceptable all the way up to Catalia, and there are only a few areas where there are obstacles on the river bottom, but we should be able to maneuver around them."

The woman smiled flatly. It was nice to have some good news for a change. Of course, Enrique had also brought back a problem with him. He knew it, too, and was quick to anticipate Rigo's concerns. Gesturing at the woman prisoner, he said, "After I shot the other one, I told her that she would have one last chance to tell the truth once we got here. She knows she will be next if she doesn't cooperate."

Rigo nodded and unholstered her Walther. She stepped over the body and crouched before the other woman, eyeing her calmly as she reached for her gag.

"I'm going to take this off," Rigo explained calmly, "then you will quietly tell us the truth, yes?"

The other woman nodded fearfully. Slowly the gag was unfastened. The prisoner gasped for air, then began to sob.

"We didn't do anything!" she insisted. "I swear it! We're working on a film, and we were just getting some second-unit footage of the river! That's all we were doing! You have to believe me!"

Some of the other men on the boat brought over a crate filled with two handguns, as well as several high-priced film cameras, tape recorders and a slew of accessories. Rigo inspected the guns first. They were both small, standardized Ruger P-4 .22s. Neither had been fired. Rigo set the guns aside and picked up a telephoto lens, then looked back at the other woman.

"CIA?" she asked. "Or NATO maybe?"

"We aren't spies!" the blonde pleaded. "I'm telling you, we're just working on a film. A documentary about the Avignon River. We only had guns to warn off wild game whenever we came ashore. We weren't doing anything wrong!"

Rigo ignored the outburst and looked through the crate, inspecting the woman's passport, as well as the one taken off the corpse. Both documents seemed on the level, but Rigo knew that meant nothing. She had a dozen seemingly legitimate passports of her own back at the safehouse in Barcelona, and none of them listed her real name or the fact that she was a high-ranking member of the Basque Liberation Movement.

She turned back to the other woman. "One look at what you've filmed and we'll know you're lying."

"Look all you want!" the prisoner said. "Go ahead! I'm telling you, it's just nature footage! That's all you're going to see!"

"They tossed some film into the river when they saw us coming after them," Enrique stated.

"That's not true!" the blonde cried. "It wasn't film!"

"No? What, then?"

The other woman hesitated, then said, "It was just some pot. Some marijuana and a pipe. We know about the laws here, and we didn't want to be caught with it."

Rigo was weighing the woman's words when a young Basque with a wild mane of dark hair poked his head out of the boat's cabin. "A call for you on the radio," he told Rigo. "It's your brother."

"Which one?"

"Miguel."

Rigo shared an expectant glance with Golato, then stood. It looked as if she were going to walk away from the prisoner, but suddenly she turned, casually took aim at the woman's head and fired a round into her face, killing her instantly. As the woman slumped to the deck, Rigo holstered her gun and told Golato, "Once night falls, take them downriver to Sardana and get rid of them, along with the kayak. Make it look like they were robbed by river pirates."

He nodded. "Done."

Rigo excused herself and went to the cabin. The young man directed her to the transceiver, then stepped outside so that she could take the call alone.

"Miguel," she said into the microphone, "I was beginning to worry."

"It took longer than we'd planned, that's all," came the crackly response from the woman's older brother.

"You got your hands on it, then."

"Yes," her brother assured her. "We have the tank."

CHAPTER ONE

Stony Man Farm, Virginia

Rosario Blancanales jogged higher up into the foothills surrounding Stony Man Farm. It was his favorite time of day, just past dawn with the sun yet to break through the early-morning clouds. There was a briskness in the air and the valley below him was quiet and tranquil. He'd passed a few small animals—rabbits and chipmunks—and the occasional bird flapped overhead, but otherwise he felt as if he had the winding dirt path to himself.

Soon Blancanales came upon a rocky escarpment affording a panoramic view of the Shenandoah Valley. From this perspective, Stony Man Farm looked much like any number of other isolated ranch estates scattered throughout pockets of the Blue Ridge Mountains. The main house and surrounding buildings were only faintly ostentatious, seemingly part of a modest farming enterprise that included the raising of seasonal crops and, off to the north, some harvesting of wood. Behind the unassuming facade, however, the sprawling valley enclave served as the command center for the covert Sensitive Operations Group, made up of not only Blancanales's Able Team comrades, but also the warriors of

Phoenix Force and a centralized support group that rarely left the Farm's confines.

From his vantage point, Blancanales could see a few scattered farmhands laboring in the orchards. To his right, standing atop the crest of the nearest mountain, another two men busied themselves inspecting the high, barbwire-topped cyclone fence that encircled the Farm's perimeter. The men, like those working down below, weren't mere hired laborers, but rather highly trained, combat-ready members of the facility. The blacksuits.

Like the security force, Blancanales was a man of deceptive appearance. With his prematurely gray hair and well-tanned Hispanic features, he looked less like a battle-trained commando than a successful businessman out for a quick jog before heading into the office at some high-rise in Washington, D.C. In fact, Blancanales had resorted to such a role while on a recent assignment, using his white-suit savvy to infiltrate a shell company fronting for an Asian gun-running operation. One moment he'd been wheeling and dealing with the company's CEOs at a business office; the next he was fighting alongside Able Team cohorts Carl Lyons and Gadgets Schwarz, trading gunfire with a goon squad at the warehouse where the black-market guns were stored. Before the dust had settled, the men had been forced to resort to hand-to-hand combat, and Blancanales had used his mastery of *bo jitsu* to neutralize a pair of thugs who together outweighed him by more than one hundred pounds. Blancanales had emerged from the skirmish with only a few aches and bruises, but Schwarz had been put out of commission for a few weeks with a stress fracture of the right leg, and while Lyons had quickly recovered from a flesh wound to the shoulder, he'd been subsequently laid low by a particularly virulent strain of the flu.

Now, for the first time in weeks, Blancanales had been presented with a reprieve from the field. Once he was finished with his jog, he planned to get a ride to Dulles International so that he could fly out to California for a long overdue visit with his family in East L.A. It'd been nearly a year since he'd been home, and he was looking forward to the trip and the inevitable backyard barbecues that were always thrown together at a moment's notice once word spread that he was coming home.

As it turned out, however, Fate had other plans in store.

Blancanales was about to start back when he heard a rustling in the brush twenty yards downhill from where he was standing. Someone was heading up the path he'd just taken.

"Yo, Pol," a familiar voice called out. Seconds later, Blancanales spotted Akira Tokaido on the trail. The young Japanese American was a key member of the Farm's cybernetic team. He wore his black hair up in a topknot and, as usual, was chomping away at a few sticks of bubble gum. He popped the pink balloon he'd just blown, then called out, "¿Que pasa?"

"Since when did you speak Spanish?" Blancanales asked.

"That's about all I know," Tokaido confessed. "But you better brush up on yours."

"Why's that?"

"Barbara sent me to fetch you. Something's going down in Spain, and she wants you and Jack Grimaldi to hook up with the guys over there to check it out. Or, as Yoda might put it, 'May the Force be with you.'"

"I think that was Obi-Wan Kenobi."

"Whatever," Tokaido said.

"Isn't Phoenix on assignment in Korea?" he asked Tokaido.

"They wrapped things up there earlier this morning. They're already on their way to Bilbao."

Blancanales sighed. So much for downtime. "What are we up against?" he asked.

"Something about a stolen supertank. Briefing's in ten minutes, or whenever the chief gets back from D.C. He'll fill you in."

As if on cue, the two men suddenly heard the faint droning of an approaching helicopter. Blancanales glanced back out over the valley and saw an unarmed OH-58D Kiowa Warrior drift over the mountaintops and begin its descent toward the Farm's camouflaged airstrip.

"Speak of the devil," Blancanales murmured.

"I won't tell him you said that." Tokaido blew another bubble, then turned and started back down the path, calling over his shoulder, "Last one down's a rotten egg."

Blancanales shrugged and began to lope behind Tokaido, muttering to himself, "I've been called worse."

THE CHIEF WAS Hal Brognola. Also known as the head Fed, he was Stony Man's liaison with the powers-that-be in Washington. Working under the guise of a functionary with the Justice Department, Brognola had been on a first-name basis with the past five presidents, and during that span he'd probably sat in on more meetings of the Joint Chiefs of Staff than any other person.

"I'll try my best to keep this brief," he began, pacing before those assembled in the basement War Room of the main house. Akira Tokaido wasn't present; he'd gone off to join his colleagues at the computer facilities, located in the Farm's Annex. Blancanales was there, however, seated alongside Brognola's top aides, mission controller Barbara Price and Aaron Kurtzman, head of SOG's cybernetic operations.

"I'm sure you're all familiar with the FSAT-50," Brognola said, launching into the briefing.

"Some kind of supertank, right?" Blancanales said.

The big Fed nodded. "We were building them in conjunction with Spain until last spring, when the Defense Department pulled the plug on any further U.S. financing."

"But Spain's kept up production," Kurtzman recalled. "I believe they're calling it the tank of the future. If I remember correctly, they're rigging it to double not only as a war boat but also as a modified submarine."

"Correct," Brognola said. "FSAT stands for Fully Submersible Amphibious Tank. Last time it was tested underwater, it proved functional at a depth of more than a hundred feet. That's six times deeper than you can go in a snorkel-equipped T-72. And that's just the tip of the iceberg as far as the advancements they've incorporated into the design. For starters, they've plated the tank with some kind of lightweight armor that's every bit as strong as DU."

"They're keeping a tight lid on the armor specs," Price interjected, "but we suspect they're using a combination of titanium and plastic along with some variant of the depleted uranium used on the Abrams. Whatever the mix, they've brought the weight of the tank down to under thirty tons. That's roughly half the weight of an Abrams, but it still has an RHA rating of over 1000. On top of that, apparently the frame has built-in pockets that act as ballast tanks when they're filled with gas."

"Let's not get bogged down with too many specifics," Brognola suggested. "That's not the issue."

"Thank God," Kurtzman deadpanned. "You're starting to lose me."

"Amen," Blancanales said. "Let's cut to the chase. Akira

says somebody's snatched one of these tanks. My guess is that's where we come in."

"Right you are," Brognola replied. He moved to one of the monitor screens built into the wall behind him. Kurtzman had already cued up a detailed map of northern Spain. Using one of his signature cigars as a pointing stick, the head Fed indicated a spot along the coast of the Bay of Biscay. "Gamuso Armorers were building the FSATs here in Zamudio, an industrial sector on the outskirts of Bilbao," he went on. "They were field-testing one of the prototypes yesterday afternoon when there was a raid of some sort on the test grounds. We have conflicting reports, but somewhere between twenty and thirty people were killed, most of them members of Gamuso's training crew. Bottom line—the prototype is now missing and assumed to be in the hands of the perpetrators."

"Who's that?" Blancanales asked.

"The Basque Liberation Movement," Price interjected. "They're a splinter group of Euskadi Ta Askatasuma. The ETA."

"Can you shorthand that a little?" Blancanales asked.

"I'll try," Price said. "The ETA is Spain's answer to the IRA. They've been clamoring for a separate Basque state for years, and they've racked up fair-sized death toll in the process, mostly through car-bombings and kidnappings. The Navarra cell is the most violent of the batch, and apparently they splintered off last year because they thought the ETA was going soft."

"Specifically," Brognola added, "there was a falling out after the head of the Navarra cell was gunned down by a Basque counterterrorism unit known as the Ertzainta. We don't need to focus on the Ertzainta right now."

Price nodded and resumed. "The head of Navarra's cell was

Carlos Rigo. He was a widower with two grown sons and a daughter. The children took over the cell and demanded that the ETA drop everything it was doing and go after the men who killed their father. When the ETA balked, they decided to go it alone and formed the BLM. They managed to get their revenge, then they dropped out of sight."

"Until last night," said Brognola. "Now they're back in business, and if they've got their hands on this tank like we think, they've just turned themselves into a force to be reckoned with."

"Assuming they know how to use it," Blancanales said.

"I think that's a safe assumption," Brognola countered. "They were off the radar more than six months, and my guess is they spent most of that time planning this heist. Why would they go to all that trouble unless they were sure they'd know what to do with the tank once they got their hands on it?"

"Fair enough," Blancanales conceded, "but still, it's only one tank, right? I don't care how high-tech it is, it's not like they're suddenly armed to the teeth."

Brognola shook his head. "That's where you're wrong, Pol. You see, one of the upgrades Gamuso made when they took over the development program was a retractable missile launcher. A modified Scud system to be exact. Only it's not restricted to your usual HEAT or AA rounds."

Blancanales sat upright in his seat, already dreading the worse. "Nukes?" he murmured aloud. "It can fire nukes?"

Brognola nodded gravely. "I'm afraid so."

"But it wasn't armed with warheads when they stole it, was it?" Kurtzman asked.

"No," Brognola said, "but there's a small item that's been kept classified since the raid. At roughly the same time the raid was carried out, there was a power brownout inside the Gamuso facility. During all the commotion, somebody managed to gain access to the arms depot. They only had a three minute window of opportunity, but they made the most of it. Once the power was back on and security checked the premises, they came up two missiles short."

"Both of them nukes," Blancanales guessed.

"Yes," Brognola confirmed. "Both missiles had nuclear warheads compatible with the tank's launch system."

"Inside job," Kurtzman speculated.

"That seems a lock," Brognola concurred. "Spain's AMI already has the place barricaded and is interrogating all personnel. They also have the militia laying a dragnet within a hundred-mile radius of the test grounds. And their counter-terrorist forces are honing in on all known BLM strongholds throughout Navarra."

"Sounds like they're covering all the bases," Blancanales said. "And I hate to say it, but, bad as this all sounds, it seems like an internal problem. Why are we being brought in?"

"Good question." Brognola turned his attention back to the monitor, this time pointing his cigar at the northeast coastline of Spain. "This Friday there's a NATO conference being held in Barcelona. Dealing with the ETA and BLM is near the top of the agenda, and both Spain and France have already gone on record asking the other member nations for help. The President has already promised our support."

"So the Basques want to retaliate by heaving a nuke at the conference?" Blancanales said, his voice tinged with skepticism. "Sounds like overkill, don't you think?"

"We can't rule it out," Brognola insisted. "Put yourselves in their shoes a minute. Say you've got some global heavyweights about to gang up on you. Are you going to sit back and wait for them to make the first move? Or are you going to strike first, figuring it's now or never?"

Blancanales nodded. "I'd go with Plan B."

"There you have it, then," Brognola said. "The President was on the phone all night trying to have the conference canceled or at least moved out of Spain, but he's been overruled. Apparently the other countries feel they can't run from these separatists and then expect to sound credible when they talk about standing up to them."

"True," Blancanales said, "but what's the population of Barcelona? A million? Two million? Three? That's putting a hell of a lot of people at risk for the sake of posturing."

"Like it or not, that's the hand we've been dealt," Brognola said. "Phoenix Force will probably be landing in Bilbao within the hour. They're going to scope out the best plan of attack there and await orders. Pol, I want you and Jack to fly to Barcelona and see what you can come up with there. If we turn up any leads on the tank's whereabouts, we'll change focus and move inland in hopes we can head it off."

"And if we aren't able to head it off?" Blancanales asked.

"I think you've already touched on the consequences," Brognola said. "If they get that tank close enough to lob a nuke at Barcelona, we could have casualties in the millions...."

CHAPTER TWO

Cordillera Cantabriea Mountains,
Vizcaya Province, Spain

"Looks like we're gonna hit the ground running, big time," T. J. Hawkins said as he double-checked his parachute gear.

"Fine by me," replied Rafael Encizo, who was preparing to roll open the side door of the MC-130H Combat Talon that had transported Phoenix Force from North Korea. They were flying at less than twenty-five hundred feet over the easternmost fringe of the Cordillera Cantabriea Mountain Range, some eighty-five miles south of Bilbao. Standing alongside Hawkins and Encizo was former SEAL Calvin James, the group's medic. He, too, was suited up and ready to jump once the Talon reached their hastily determined insertion point. The other two members of the commando force, Gary Manning and David McCarter, were up front in the plane's cockpit. It was Manning, the big Canadian, who several minutes before had fielded the call from Spain's Agency of Military Intelligence about the sighting of a twenty-man BLM force moving through the mountains. Ground troops were reportedly on the way to the area, but Providence had given Phoenix Force an opportunity to have the first crack at the purported masterminds behind the recent theft of the top-secret

FSAT-50 battle tank. According to AMI, this particular group didn't have the tank with them, but there was a chance they were in possession of the twin nuclear warheads stolen at the time of the tank heist.

"All set?" James called out to Hawkins and Encizo.

Hawkins nodded as he slung an M-60 machine gun over his shoulder. James and Encizo were both armed with M-4 carbines, the latter's rifle supplemented with a submounted 40 mm grenade launcher. For backup, all three men had M-9 Berettas tucked in shoulder-strap web holsters.

"Let's do it," Encizo said.

James yanked the door along its rollers and staggered slightly as wind howled its way past the opening. He leaned forward and stared down through a smattering of thin-ribboned clouds at the rolling green mountains below. Their insertion point was a broad meadow flanked on three sides by mountain peaks. The BLM was reportedly three miles away, trekking a path downhill from the northernmost mountain range; the peaks would likely block their view of the parachutists as they made their drop. James hoped their luck would hold out. If they could land undetected, it would give them an opportunity to position themselves before the enemy reached the meadow. In a situation like this, it was crucial to make the best of any advantage.

Manning's voice suddenly crackled through the small speaker mounted over one of the cargo holds. "We're there, guys. Give yourselves a ten-count, then go give 'em hell. We'll hook up with you as soon as we set this bird down."

The three paratroopers lined up before the open doorway. James counted down, then lunged out of the plane. He immediately paralleled his body with the ground below and extended his arms and legs outward, slowing his fall. It felt for a moment as if he were flying. Glancing over his shoulder, he saw Encizo and Hawkins were airborne as well, framed against the sky above him, similarly spread-eagled. The Talon had flown on and was already banking to the right, ready to dip behind the nearest mountain peak and begin its descent toward a remote, long-abandoned airstrip dating back to days when there had been plans to develop one of the neighboring valleys into a resort community. There, according to plan, McCarter and Manning would rendezvous with the arriving Spanish militia. There were supposedly a few mountain-worthy Jeeps in the convoy, and Manning had been told that a pair of AH-1Q Cobras were additionally being diverted to the site from a military air base in Bilbao. Using Jeeps and choppers, it would hopefully be possible to move quickly and have the ETA forces surrounded by the time they reached the meadow. The trick, obviously, would be to capture or neutralize the enemy without detonating its lethal cargo.

As he drew closer to the meadow, James spotted a few dozen sheep grazing in the tall grass fifty yards to his right, watched over by a young boy and a large black sheepdog. He tugged at his shroud lines, trying to veer as far away from them as possible. The boy had already spotted him, however, and soon the dog had turned and begun charging through the grass toward him, barking loudly.

"Beat it, Lassie," James muttered under his breath as he prepared to touch down. "You're blowing our cover."

The dog continued to yelp, but the moment James hit the ground, it stopped in its tracks, apparently intimidated by the size of James's quickly collapsing chute. James tumbled expertly and was already unhitching the chute harness when he rose to his feet. He jerked at the lines and hissed at the dog, sending it chasing after Hawkins and Encizo.

Once he'd gathered up the chute and bunched it into a ball, James stuffed it beneath a nearby bush, then strode quickly toward the young shepherd, putting a finger to his lips. The boy, no more than eleven years old, took a tentative step back. A black beret was cocked at an angle on his head, and his hands were clenched around an old Steyr SBS Forester rifle. The weapon was nearly as big as he was, but James had the sense that the boy knew how to fire it.

James had learned to speak Spanish while growing up in a Chicano neighborhood on Chicago's South Side, but he knew that the boy most likely spoke Basque, a language as dissimilar from Spanish as it was from English. Still, he needed to say something to calm the boy. The last thing he wanted to do was to have to draw on him.

"*¡Hola!*" he called out softly, holding his hands out at his sides. Continuing in Spanish, he said, "Don't be afraid. We come as friends."

The boy's expression remained unchanged and he continued to aim the rifle at James. Finally he spoke, not in Spanish or Euskara, but in English.

"Why should I believe you?"

James was momentarily taken aback. By now Hawkins and Encizo had landed and were headed toward him, the sheepdog barking at their heels. The boy took another step back, fanning his rifle back and forth to keep all three men covered.

"He doesn't trust us," James told the others out of the side of his mouth.

"I gathered that much." Encizo stopped alongside James and sized the boy up, then offered a disarming smile. "Your papa taught you well," he said. "*Atzerri otserri,* eh?"

It was the boy's turn to be surprised. He kept his rifle aimed at the men but slowly lowered the barrel as he called out to his dog. The dog fell silent and scampered to the boy's side, then sat on its haunches, tongue trailing from its mouth as it caught its breath.

"Where the hell did you learn how to speak Basque?" Hawkins asked Encizo.

"There was a Basque janitor at my high school," Encizo said. "We got to know each other with all the time I spent in detention. I picked up a few phrases."

"What was the one you just ran by him?"

"'The alien's land is a land of wolves,'" Encizo said.

"Well, tell him the wolves he ought to be worried about are gonna be here any second."

Encizo turned his attention back to the boy, who'd clearly been listening to the conversation.

"What other wolves?" he asked. "BLM?"

Encizo nodded. "Yes," he explained. "There are perhaps two dozen of them, and they're armed. You need to get out of the way and take cover while we—"

Encizo's voice was drowned out by the thundering echo of a single gunshot. A split second later, the sheepdog howled and toppled onto its side briefly. As it tried to get back on its feet, blood began to glisten on its fur where it'd been shot. The boy stared down at the dog and was crying out its name when another shot ripped its way through the nearby grass a few feet to his right.

James instinctively lunged forward and pulled the boy to the ground as he cried out to the others, "Ready or not, here they come...."

PEERING OVER the boy's shoulder, James stared past the scattering flock of frightened sheep. More than a dozen BLM gunmen, all wearing trademark red berets, had appeared at the edge of the meadow. Four of them walked carefully alongside a slow-moving ATV, each holding a rifle in one hand while they used the other to steady the vehicle's cargo, a large, rectangular wooden crate loosely tethered in place by shock cords. Given the crate's dimensions, James could understand why AMI suspected it might well contain the missing warheads.

THE OTHER SEPARATIST fighters had fanned out and were scrambling up into the nearby foothills, which were strewed with rocks and boulders. The terrain provided ideal cover; in fact, it was the same area where Phoenix Force had planned to take up position in hopes of pinning down the BLM forces once they reached the meadow. Now, unfortunately, the Basques had beat them to the higher ground, and it was Phoenix Force that had been placed at the disadvantage.

The gunner who'd fired the first shot was crouched on a low promontory thirty yards up the mountainside. He was lining up James in his sights, but before he could get off another shot, James hurriedly brought his M-14 into play and fired an autoburst across the meadow, driving the man to cover.

As he scanned the foothills for another target, James noticed, for the first time, a small stone hut concealed in the shade of two large chestnut trees less than fifty yards from where the BLM was swarming. A split-rail fence encircled the hut, and a rusting metal water trough sat near the pen's open gate. Just beyond the corral's perimeter, a crude knee-high wall of stacked boulders had been erected behind the house to act as a barrier against rockslides from the mountain.

"Is that where you're staying?" James whispered to the boy.

The boy nodded fearfully. James ducked as another shot whistled past, then asked the boy, "Is anyone inside?"

"My papa," the boy replied. Tears began to well in his eyes. "He's sick. I was tending the sheep so that he could sleep."

James looked over his shoulder and quickly passed the information along to Encizo and Hawkins, who'd both taken cover behind a cluster of boulders rising up through the grass a few yards behind him.

"I'll try to get to him," Hawkins replied. He fired his carbine into the foothills, then split away from Encizo, rolling down into a shallow ditch. Once he'd crawled back up to where he could see the enemy, he called back to James.

"I don't know, Cal. They're a hell of a lot closer to the hut than we are. Getting there ahead of them's gonna be tough."

"We need to try." James turned to Encizo. "Give them a grenade or two but stay clear of that crate they're hauling."

"Sure thing."

Encizo leaned back as a spray of gunfire chipped the boulders he was crouched behind, then countered with a round from his M-14 before turning his attention to the carbine's submounted grenade launcher. James, meanwhile, huddled close to the boy, whose gaze was still fixed on the sheepdog, which now lay still in the grass.

"I'm sorry," he told the boy, "but there's nothing we can

do for him now. You need to get down in the gully with my friend, okay? Crawl all the way and keep your head down. I'm going to check on your father."

The boy sobbed faintly and wiped back a tear, then grabbed his rifle and followed James's instructions. As small as he was, he still presented a target for the enemy, and bullets began to slant down toward him from the foothills.

"Hurry!" Hawkins called out to the boy as he rose and fired back at the enemy. One of his rounds found its mark and a would-be sniper sprawled forward, dropping his rifle. His beret snagged on the lower branches of a nearby shrub and came off as the man hit the ground and rolled a few yards before coming to a rest. Hawkins didn't waste any time admiring his handiwork. He reached out and grabbed the boy's right arm, helping him into the ditch.

"Stay low, amigo," Hawkins told him.

The youth was still crying, but his expression had turned from fear to anger. He crawled lower into the ditch, but stayed put only for a moment. Once Hawkins had turned his attention back to the gunmen in the hills, the boy rose to crouch and raised his rifle into firing position. He quickly took aim and fired off a single shot.

"Hey!" Hawkins cried out. "I told you to stay down!"

The boy ignored Hawkins and fired off another shot. Hawkins look toward the foothills and saw, to his amazement, that the boy had connected with both shots, dropping two men who'd been making their way toward the stone hut.

"I'll be damned," Hawkins murmured under his breath.

He turned to grudgingly compliment the boy's shooting, but the youth had broken into a run, bent over as he followed the ditch's meandering course toward the distant hut. Enemy gunfire slammed into the earth around him, but he refused to stop, much less turn back.

"That kid's trying to get himself killed!" Hawkins called out to James. But James didn't hear him; he was already on the move himself, zigzagging through the grass, sidestepping several of the startled sheep.

Behind him, as promised, Encizo covered James's advance by firing the first of his 40 mm grenades. He'd followed James's warning and aimed away from the ATV, targeting instead a group of gunmen firing from positions among the heaviest concentration of boulders in the foothills. The strategy paid off. The grenade's initial blast quickly took out one gunman, and two others were brought down soon after by a combination of shrapnel and flying rock.

"Way to go, Rafe," Hawkins called out to him.

"We've still got our work cut out for us," James shouted back. As he readied another grenade, he glanced back at the trailhead by which the terrorists had entered the meadow. The driver of the ATV shut off the engine and joined the men who'd been escorting the wooden crate. All five of them huddled on the far side of the vehicle, using it for cover. A stand of chestnut trees blocked their view of James and the young shepherd, so they directed their fire at Hawkins and Encizo.

James put on a burst of speed and was about to catch up with the boy when spotted two guerrillas scaling the retaining wall behind the stone hut. They boy saw them, too, and he cried out in horror as they circled the hut and disappeared behind the structure.

"Papa!"

"Get down!" James yelled as he caught up with the boy. "Let us handle this!"

The boy, however, shook his head determinedly without breaking his stride. "Papa!" he screamed again. "Wake up!"

They were rushing together through the open gateway of the pen surrounding the hut when gunfire erupted inside the enclosure.

"Papa!" the boy wailed yet again.

James lengthened his stride and outraced the boy to the hut. The building was less half the size of a one-car garage, and it looked to James as if the front doorway was the only way in. Figuring the gunfire had likely been directed through a rear window, he bypassed the doorway and approached the far side of the hut, carbine at the ready. As he turned the corner, James froze. Less than ten yards away, one of the Basques stood facing him with a 9 mm Uzi subgun held out before him, finger on the trigger.

Both men fired simultaneously.

James winced as three rounds slammed into his side like jabs from a red-hot poker. He staggered to his right, crashing into the side of the hut. The other man had taken a volley to the chest. Dropping his gun, he pitched forward, landing face-first in the dirt.

Grimacing, James stepped over the body and inched toward the rear of the hut. His side felt as if it were on fire, and he could feel blood seeping from his wounds, but he tried to put the pain out of his mind. He'd taken a few steps when he heard scuffling out near the retaining wall. Whirling, he spotted yet another gunman crawling over the barrier. He emptied the rest of his magazine, bringing the man down, then tossed his carbine aside and backtracked to the man he'd killed moments before, snatching up his Uzi. He was beginning to feel light-headed from the loss of blood, but he forced himself to move on. Rounding the back of the hut, he was about to let loose with the Uzi when he saw another Basque lying in a pool of blood just below a small rear window. James approached cautiously. Once he was sure the man was dead, he peered in through the window.

The shepherd boy had entered the hut and was embracing his father, who held in his right hand the old Smith & Wesson revolver with which he'd apparently shot the man lying at James's feet. The old shepherd was clearly weak on his feet, but it didn't look as if he'd been shot. He spoke to his son reassuringly, but James couldn't make out what the man was saying. There was a odd thundering in his ears, and soon a field of stars began to cloud his vision. When he felt his knees buckling beneath him, James grabbed at the windowsill for support, but his fingers wouldn't cooperate. As he began to fall, his world faded to black.

CHAPTER THREE

Encizo was concerned by all the gunfire that had taken place after James had disappeared behind the stone hut, but he was in no position to investigate. The gunmen stationed behind the parked ATV had him pinned down in the middle of the pasture. He fed another grenade into his M-14's launcher as bullets caromed off the boulders he crouched behind. Encizo figured a well-placed shot could take out the gunmen, but he couldn't run the risk of blowing up the crate still tethered to the vehicle. He had to try another way.

He waited for a lull in the shooting, then took aim at the stand of chestnut trees to the left of the ATV.

"Get ready to wrap this up!" he shouted out to Hawkins, who was still lying prone at the edge of the nearby ditch.

"Go for it!" Hawkins shouted back, rising to a crouch.

Encizo triggered the launcher. The M-14's stock bucked sharply against his shoulder as it sent a 40 mm grenade hurtling toward the trees. Encizo's aim couldn't have been better. The grenade detonated as it struck the base of one of the trees, obliterating most of the trunk.

With a wrenching snap nearly as loud as the explosion itself, the tall chestnut teetered to one side, then came crashing down, its upper branches slapping across the top of the ATV. By then, Encizo and Hawkins were both on their feet and charging through the meadow.

The ploy worked, flushing the enemy from the ATV. Once Encizo reached another crop of boulders, he dropped to one knee and blasted away with his carbine. Two men dropped from view into the tall grass. Judging from the way they'd gone down, Enzico doubted they'd be getting back up. Hawkins had similar luck, firing through the branches of the fallen tree and nailing a gunman seeking out cover behind the shattered trunk.

As Hawkins continued to race toward the chestnuts, however, he was nearly broadsided by a stream of gunfire coming down from the mountains to his right. He dived to the ground and rolled to one side until he reached one of the sheep, which had been caught up in the cross fire and lay dead in the grass. Peering over the carcass, Hawkins spotted two snipers up in the foothills near the rocks where Encizo had fired earlier. He trained his sights on the man who presented the best target. It took three shots, but he finally managed to send a killshot through the man's skull. The other gunman returned fire, missing Hawkins by inches with one shot and stirring the dead sheep with another.

"Got a stray to take care of!" Hawkins called over his shoulder to Encizo. "I'll take him out, then circle around!"

Encizo nodded. He stayed put a moment, eyes on the fallen tree, waiting for another separatist to show himself. None appeared. He stole a quick glance at the stone hut but could still see no sign of James or the shepherd boy. He was about to go have a closer look when he heard the sound of the ATV's engine revving to life. Shifting his gaze, he saw that one of the

Basques had climbed into the driver's seat and was brushing away the branches draped across the steering wheel. Once he'd shifted gears, the man began to back the ATV up, pulling away from the fallen tree.

"Not so fast," Encizo muttered.

He quickly fired off a few rounds, managing to hit the vehicle's framework but not the driver. The ATV separated itself from the tree and began to turn. Encizo realized the driver was hoping to retreat the way he'd come. Cursing, he broke from cover and began to sprint after the vehicle. His carbine was slowing him, so he cast it aside. Without breaking stride, he yanked the 9 mm pistol from his web holster. There was no point in firing, however; the crate blocked his view of the driver.

By the time Encizo reached the fallen tree, the ATV had left the meadow and begun to head down a narrow dirt path that threaded its way between outcroppings and a scattering of tall mountain pines. After a couple turns the vehicle had disappeared from view.

Rather than take the trail, Encizo bounded onto the closest outcropping and followed it, leaping from rock to rock, hoping he wouldn't lose his footing. He could still hear the ATV and tried his best to head in the same direction. Behind him, he could hear intermittent gunfire back in the meadow and figured Hawkins still had his hands full.

After sixty yards, Encizo was forced to come to a stop. The outcropping had not only narrowed to a point, but it had also come to an abrupt end, leaving him poised at the edge of a sheer, forty-foot precipice.

Another stream of expletives spilled from Encizo's lips as he sized up his situation. He had two options: he could either backtrack the way he'd come or try to make his way down the sheer face of the cliff. In terms of catching up with the ATV, either way seemed futile. He could no longer even hear the vehicle, much less see it. Like it or not, it looked as if the enemy had gotten away.

"Way to go, Rafe," he chastised himself.

Encizo was still deliberating his next move when he heard a rustling behind him. He whirled and saw that a mountain goat had appeared atop the outcropping twenty yards behind him. He wasn't sure how it'd gotten there, but Encizo had a feeling the animal wasn't about to let him pass. The goat, a full-grown male weighing more than two hundred pounds, stared intently at Encizo, then lowered its head slightly, tipping its horns forward.

"I don't think that's a good sign," Encizo whispered to himself. He was inching closer to the edge of the precipice when the goat suddenly lunged forward, lowering its head still further.

Just as quickly, Encizo lowered himself over the side, seeking out the first available niches and protuberances for support. He'd make it a few yards down when the goat appeared at the edge of the precipice and stared down at him. Encizo stared back momentarily, then glanced over his shoulder, watching a handful of loose stones clatter down the side of the cliff before crashing against the hardpan below.

"Not good," Encizo muttered. "Not good..."

"HELL, I FEEL like I'm trying to fly that damn supertank," David McCarter groused.

"It's no Cobra, that's for sure," Gary Manning conceded.

When the two men had landed at the airstrip two miles from where they'd jettisoned their teammates, they'd discovered that the two promised Cobra gunships had been deployed elsewhere. In their place, McCarter had found himself at the controls of a Sikorsky CH-54S Tarhe. Better known as the S-64 Skycrane, the Sikorsky was a forty-year-old hand-me-down that had first seen service in the early years of America's involvement in the Vietnam War. In fact, beneath its sun-faded layers of paint, the Skycrane still bore the insignia of the U.S. 478th Aviation Company. One of the largest helicopters ever built, the S-64 was an unarmed workhorse, designed primarily for lifting of up to ten tons of cargo: anything from 155 mm howitzers to the 4536 kg long-fuse bombs used create instant LZs in the Vietcong heartland. In this case, the chopper's tailboom was rigged with a service pod containing a surgical operations facility. Also riding in the pod were six well-armed members, not of the militia—which was on its way up into mountains by foot and Jeep—but rather Spain's special forces. Weighed down with such a heavy load, the chopper lumbered slowly through the air.

Manning had his M-14 at the ready as he scouted the ridgeline of the mountain range they were flying over. In their haste to drop to their insertion point, none of the other Phoenix Force commandos had brought along communications gear, so McCarter and Manning had no idea what kind of situation they would find once they reached the meadow.

"I'm glad we've got some backup in the belly of this sucker," McCarter said, "but I'd trade them in a second for some bloody rocket pods and a nose gun."

"Maybe next time," Manning said.

Soon they cleared the peak and were within view of the meadow. At first, the only signs of disturbance they could see were the slain dog and a couple bullet-riddled sheep lying in the tall grass. Then Manning noticed several bodies lying amid the rocks on the south side of the mountain they'd just flown over.

"Over there," he told McCarter, pointing at the bodies.

The Briton nodded, banking the chopper and coming in from a closer look. "Looks like our guys have been busy."

"Yeah," Manning said, "but where are they?"

The Skycrane's shadow drifted across the meadow as Manning continued to scout for other signs of activity. He was about to point out a few more bodies near the fallen chestnut when the young shepherd boy raced out into view from beneath the canopy of the other trees. He waved wildly as he stared up at the chopper.

"What the hell?" Manning murmured.

"Let's check it out," McCarter said, slowly easing the Sikorsky downward.

The boy backpedaled as the chopper's rotor wash swept over him, flattening the grass around him. Even before the Skycrane had set down completely, the pod doors swung open and the Spanish troops crowded the opening. Once the landing wheels had touched ground, the men piled out, crouching over as they made their way clear of the rotors. Two of them beelined to the boy and began to question him; the others, most of them armed with MP-5 subguns, quickly fanned out in all directions, seeking out the enemy.

"Those lads don't waste any time, do they?" McCarter deadpanned as he killed the engines and unstrapped himself from the pilot's chair.

"Reminds me of us," Manning observed, still scanning the surrounding meadow. "I still don't see the guys."

"I don't like it," McCarter said, worry creeping into

his voice. He reached for his holster, drawing a 7-round, .380 ACP EA-SA Compact.

Once they'd deplaned, McCarter and Manning made their way to the two soldiers interrogating the shepherd boy. One of the men was the unit's leader, Captain Raul Cordero, a tall, ruggedly handsome officer with dark eyes, thick brows and an equally thick mustache that only partially obscured his pronounced harelip. He was fluent in seven languages, including Basque and English.

"He says they fought off the BLM, but one of your men was shot a few times in the side," he reported to McCarter. "He says his father is ill, as well."

"Where are they?" McCarter wanted to know.

"There," the boy interjected, pointing in the direction of the shaded stone hut.

"The wounded man," McCarter asked the boy. "What does he look like?"

"He is African," the boy responded. "He was shot in the side. We can't stop the bleeding."

"Go ahead and check it out," Manning told McCarter. "I'll get a couple stretchers."

Cordero told his subordinate to lend Manning a hand, then followed McCarter and the boy toward the hut. On the way, McCarter had the boy once again describe what had happened. He found out that Hawkins was with James, but that Encizo had last been seen chasing after an ATV carrying some kind of large wooden crate.

"I'll take the bird back up once we check on things here," McCarter told Cordero.

Once they reached the hut, the boy led the two men around back. There, Calvin James lay at the base of the rear window, several yards from the man the boy's father had shot. Hawkins was crouched behind James, pressing a blood-soaked towel against the black man's rib cage. Nearby, the old shepherd sat with his back to the stone wall, hunched over slightly, his ashen-faced glistening with perspiration. He fanned himself with his beret, barely able to muster the strength to look up at his son.

"I'll check the old man," Cordero told McCarter.

McCarter nodded, then crouched alongside Hawkins. James was unconscious, lying on his side, arms and legs stretched out at odd angles.

"How does it look?" he asked Hawkins.

Hawkins shook his head. "He got nailed twice, maybe three times. Must've hit something, because he's bleeding out on me. We need to get him looked at, quick."

"Maybe being stuck with that Skycrane was a good thing after all," McCarter muttered.

"What's that?"

"I flew in in a Sikorsky," McCarter told him. "It's outfitted with one of those OR pods."

"Decent," Hawkins said. "Did a medic come with you?"

McCarter called over to Cordero. "Is there a medic in your unit? My guy needs surgery. Probably a transfusion, too."

Cordero nodded, removing his palm from the old shepherd's forehead. "Yes, we have two medics. One is the best field surgeon you could ask for."

"Good," McCarter said. "I have a feeling he's going to get a chance to prove it."

CHAPTER FOUR

Rafael Encizo slowly extended his right foot toward the base of a scrub brush growing out of the side of the cliff. Once he made contact, he eased his weight onto the limb. It felt capable of supporting him, so he lowered himself a few more inches, transferring his right hand to a narrow crevice.

He was moving at a snail's pace and had only been able to climb ten yards down the sheer incline. The mountain goat had long since retreated from the cliff's edge, but Encizo was committed to his downward course. Several times he'd heard the ATV, and though it was hard to judge its whereabouts given the acoustics of his gorgelike surroundings, he held on to the hope that he'd managed to outdistance it earlier and would be able to intercept the driver should he come his way.

As he continued his gruelling descent, sweat stung Encizo's eyes and blood began to trickle from a score of places where he scraped himself against the rock. His hands and wrists were beginning to ache, and he could feel blisters forming along his fingertips. But he kept on, maintaining his focus, taking care not to rush and risk falling.

Finally he'd made it halfway down the precipice. Pausing to catch his breath, he listened intently. Suddenly his spirits rallied. The ATV now sounded as if it were headed his way. Reinvigorated, Encizo moved sideways along the cliff face, seeking out the concealment of shadows cast by a stand of tall pines lining the mountain ridge behind him. Once he reached the shade, the Cuban stayed put and waited.

Moments later, he spotted the vehicle, raising a cloud of dust as it slowly navigated its way downhill toward him. The driver's attention was on the trail, which was barely visible beneath a layer of loose rock and wild grass.

Encizo remained still, clinging to the rock with both hands and feet. Reaching for his gun was out of the question; it would only blow his cover and make him an easy target. He was faced with another dilemma, as well. The ATV was coming to a fork in the trail. If the driver kept to his right, he'd pass directly under Encizo. If he went left, however, he'd disappear behind another outcropping and likely make his getaway before the Phoenix Force commando could reach the ground.

"Come on, baby," Encizo whispered as the driver slowed to a stop at the fork. "Come to papa..."

Encizo's plea, however, went unanswered.

After a moment's hesitation, the driver of the ATV turned left and soon passed from Encizo's view. The sound of its laboring engine began to fade, as well.

"Dammit," Encizo cursed.

Disheartened, he once again resumed the arduous task of making his way down the cliff. Once he reached the bottom, he figured he'd have no choice but to retrace the Jeep's course back to the meadow. Provided James and Hawkins had managed to neutralize the enemy, they'd have to wait and hope McCarter and Manning would swing by in time to try to intercept the ATV before it came down out of the mountains.

Encizo hadn't gone far when he stopped again. He glanced over his shoulder and stared incredulously at the split in the trail. For whatever reason, the ATV had backed up and reappeared at the fork. After shifting gears, the driver slowly turned right and headed Encizo's way.

The Cuban was no longer in the shade. He froze in place, woefully exposed, as the vehicle approached. Thankfully, the driver was too busy trying to steer his way around fallen rocks to look up. The man was in his late twenties, with shoulder-length hair spilling out from beneath his red beret. He cursed loudly as one of the front wheels rolled over a large rock, jostling the crate behind him. The container had already shifted more than a foot to one side, and the driver had to put the ATV in Neutral momentarily, then rise up in his seat and shift the load so that it was more evenly balanced. He tightened the shock cords slightly, then got back behind the wheel and drove on, eyes once again focused on the trail.

Encizo tensed and readied himself as the ATV passed directly below him.

It was now or never.

He drew a quick breath, then pushed away from the cliff and plunged.

The driver spotted him, but by then it was too late. Encizo dropped onto the crate feet first, bending at the knees to absorb the force of his landing. In the same motion, he shifted his weight forward, flattening himself against the crate's lid. Reaching past the container, he grabbed at the driver's neck.

The driver cried out and reached up one hand to claw at Encizo's fingers. He drew blood, but Encizo refused to release his grip. Encizo shouted in Spanish for the man to stop the vehicle, but the man either didn't understand him or wasn't about to comply. Instead, he eased off on the gas and jerked hard to the right. The crate shifted, and Encizo felt himself sliding sharply to one side. His left leg dropped over the side of the crate. As he tried to reposition himself, the driver suddenly slammed on the brakes, taking Encizo by surprise. He was forced to let go of the driver's neck and grab at the crate to keep from falling off.

Gasping for breath, the driver reached for an Uzi lying in the seat next to him.

"Not a chance," Encizo growled.

Scrambling forward, he tackled the driver and forced him to release the brakes. The ATV began to drift off the trail, but the men were too busy grappling for the subgun to do anything about it.

As they scuffled, the driver lashed out with his elbow and caught Encizo squarely across the bridge of his nose, almost knocking him out. Blood began to flow through his nostrils and wave of nausea passed over him, but Encizo persevered and countered with a blow of his own, kneeing the driver sharply in the ribs. The man let out a howl. He'd managed to get his hands on the Uzi, however, and rammed the barrel in Encizo's right thigh.

The moment he felt the gun against his leg, Encizo kicked outward, slamming his ankle against the underside of the dashboard. The Uzi fired harmlessly to the side. Encizo wasn't about to let the driver get off another shot. Twisting to one side, he freed one arm and lashed out with a karate chop. He caught the other man squarely just below the temple with enough force to knock him out.

By now the ATV had left the trail completely and begun to bound wildly down a steep incline, crashing through several small pines. It glanced off the trunk of a larger tree and swerved sharply to one side. The next thing Encizo knew, he was headed straight for the lip of a deep ravine. The ATV lurched forward, bounding over a sprawl of rocks as large as bowling balls. Behind him, the crate slid forward, as well, striking him between the shoulderblades. Encizo let out a cry of pain. Finally he managed to find the brakes. The ATV brodied sideways and went into a slide before coming to a stop.

One of the front wheels had slipped over the edge of the precipice, however, and as he shut off the engine, Encizo felt the vehicle begin to teeter precariously. He hazarded a glance and saw that the ravine dropped off as sharply as the cliff he'd encountered earlier. The drop-off here, however, was more than twice the distance; it was a good hundred yards straight down to the rock floor.

When Encizo tried to move, the ATV slowly pitched forward. He quickly leaned the other way, stabilizing the vehicle. The driver lay limply beside him, one leg dangling over side. The crate now extended halfway across the driver's seat, forcing Encizo to lean forward. He was wary of trying to push the container back. One false move and he knew he'd find himself plummeting to certain death.

He was trapped.

CHAPTER FIVE

"Let's move it!" McCarter shouted irritably at Manning and Hawkins, who were working to detach the OR pod from the Sikorsky. McCarter stood a few yards from the chopper, holding a flag-sized strip of heavy canvas out before him to block the sun from falling on James and the shepherd boy's father, who both lay on stretchers on the ground. Sergeant Tatis, the medic Captain Cordero had referred to earlier, was crouched over James, tending to his gunshot wounds. The boy, meanwhile, knelt at his father's side, wiping his brow with a damp cloth.

"Hold your horses," Manning told McCarter, "we're almost there."

A power generator grumbled to life inside the pod and moments later Cordero emerged. He lent Manning and Hawkins a hand with the last few couplers, then moved back and reached out to take the tarp from McCarter.

"You should be able to take off now," he said. "Once you're clear, we'll get your man into surgery and do what we can for him."

"Good." McCarter turned to Manning and Hawkins.

"Come with me," he told the big Canadian. "T.J., stay here and keep an eye on things."

"Got it," Hawkins said.

McCarter and Manning quickly boarded the Sikorsky. Cordero tossed aside the canvas, then grabbed hold of one end of James's stretcher. Hawkins took the other.

"Move him very slowly," Tatis told him, stepping back to give them room.

The Skycrane's engines soon drowned out the generator and buffeted the meadow with its rotor wash. The detached OR pod rattled in place slightly as the chopper lifted off. Cordero and Hawkins waited until McCarter had guided the Sikorsky away from the pod before lifting James and hauling him into the portable chamber. The medic was right behind him. Inside, there was an OR table already set up in one corner. Even as Cordero and Hawkins were transferring James from the stretcher, Tatis was probing the wounded man's arm for a vein to tap into with an IV line.

"What is his blood type?" he asked Hawkins.

Hawkins told him. "Are there any units here?"

Tatis shook his head. "No. And he is going to need at least a couple units."

"Can't help," Hawkins said. "He's not my type."

"I'm a match," Cordero said, rolling up his left sleeve. "You can start with me."

The unit's other medic arrived moments later; he and the boy were carrying the stretcher bearing the older shepherd.

"It's too crowded in here." Tatis turned to Hawkins. "Take the boy out with you. Try to find one of our men, tall with a scar down his right cheek. His name is Umiel. Tell him we need him."

"He's got the right blood?" Hawkins said.

"Yes," Tatis confirmed. "Now, go..."

"What about my papa?" the boy asked.

"He will be fine," the medic assured him. "We will give him antibiotics and fluids and he will be fine."

The boy seem unconvinced, but when Hawkins put a hand on his shoulder, he grudgingly kissed his father on the forehead and then followed T.J. out of the pod.

"He'll be okay," Hawkins assured the boy. "Keep the faith."

The boy frowned and looked up at Hawkins. "What does that mean?"

"It means you have to believe things are going to work out." Hawkins glanced northward, looking for the Sikorsky. The chopper had cleared the mountains, however, and dropped out of sight. He turned his gaze back at the OR pod a moment, then told the boy, "Sometimes keeping the faith is all you can do."

After searching the meadow and the area around the chestnut trees, Hawkins spotted Umiel halfway up the mountainside behind the rock hut. He and another soldier had dragged four bodies from the rocks and lined them face-up, side by side, on a level patch of ground. As Hawkins and the shepherd boy approached, the two soldiers finished photographing the dead men's faces, then set the camera aside and drew Kolvan fighting knives from sheaths strapped to their thighs. With studied nonchalance, the men began slicing off the ears of the fallen ETA warriors.

"Hey!" Hawkins shouted, rushing forward. Once he caught up with the soldiers, he grabbed Umiel by the collar and jerked him away from the bodies. Umiel staggered, off balance, then fell to the ground, dropping his knife. Hawkins grabbed it, then glared at Umiel and the other soldier, who'd momentarily stopped his grisly handiwork. When the boy caught up with Hawkins, he took one look at the butchered corpses and turned away.

"What the hell's going on here?" Hawkins demanded.

Umiel didn't understand what Hawkins was saying, but the other man knew a little English and replied, "It is something we learned from the Ertzainta. We take pictures, then check files and find their families. We send ears along with pictures to show what happens if you join BLM."

"I don't know who the Ertzainta is," Hawkins said, "but this is bullshit!"

"The Ertzainta are rogue police," the other man said. "A death squad that puts more fear into these separatists than we're allowed to. We will give them credit for this."

Hawkins stared at the severed ears with disgust, then turned back to the soldiers. "And you don't think that makes them just more determined to keep fighting you?"

The officer smiled menacingly. "If they fight back, we let the Ertzainta come in and kill someone in their family. Soon they will understand we mean business."

This wasn't the first time Hawkins had heard of such tactics used in counterterrorism circles, and there was a part of him that understood the gruesome logic. Still, he couldn't condone the butchery. It was one thing to gun a man down because he was the enemy. Carving him up for souvenirs, regardless of one's rationale, went against everything he'd been taught growing up in a military family with a tradition for valor in the battlefield. This was wrong, and he wasn't about to stand by and watch it happen.

"Sergeant Tatis wants you back at the OR," he told Umiel. Stretching the truth, he turned to the other soldier, as well. "Both of you."

"When we finish," the other soldier said. He was about to slit the ear off another of the dead men when Hawkins yanked out his pistol and thumbed off the safety. The soldier hesitated with his knife and glanced up, finding Hawkins's gun aimed at his head.

"Now," Hawkins said.

The soldier hesitated, glaring at Hawkins.

"Americans," he snapped, spitting at the ground. "Always big shots."

Before Hawkins could respond, he detected a blur of motion to his right. Umiel was lunging toward him, scooping up a handful of gravel. Hawkins reflexively threw his forearm before his face, deflecting the stones as they came hailing toward him. Umiel reached him before he could fire his gun, however, and the two men tumbled to the ground.

The other soldier was about to join the fray when a rock suddenly glanced off his forehead. He dropped to his knees, stunned. Before he could recover his senses, the shepherd boy rushed forward and shoved him in the shoulder, knocking him to the ground. The boy then rushed over to the bodies of the slain Basques and grabbed one of their subguns. He turned it on the Spaniard and fired a blast into the dirt a few feet in front of him, then raised the barrel, pointing it at the man's chest.

By then, Hawkins had managed to overpower Umiel, pinning his arm behind him in a full Nelson. As he wrestled the man to his feet, he grinned at the shepherd boy and told him, "Something tells me your father taught you a few things besides how to tend sheep."

The boy grinned back. "He taught me to always be prepared," he said, adding, "That way, it is easy to keep the faith."

CHAPTER SIX

"There he is!" Manning shouted, pointing at the gorge he and McCarter were flying over in the Sikorsky Skycrane.

McCarter glanced down and spotted the terrorists' ATV, still tilting precariously at the edge of the drop-off where it had come to a stop earlier. Encizo remained trapped in the front seat, shouldering the large wooden crate to keep it from sliding forward any farther. The driver hadn't yet regained consciousness and continued to lie sprawled next to the Cuban, who glanced up and waved faintly with one hand once he spotted the chopper.

"This could get tricky," McCarter said, holding the Sikorsky stable in midair. "If we go down to try to help, the rotor wash is liable to push him over the edge."

"I think you're right," Manning said. "We've got to do something, though."

McCarter shifted his gaze to the route the ATV had taken once it had left the trail. When he spotted a half-fallen, lightning-charred pine tree twenty yards uphill from Encizo's position, he thought he might have stumbled on the solution.

"Check and see if there's any rope around here," he told Manning.

"What for?"

"Just do it!" McCarter snapped.

"Since you asked so nicely," Manning said with a grin.

The big Canadian swiveled his seat around and snapped open a large footlocker mounted over the rear windshield. The locker was filled mostly with tools and emergency gear, but there was also a large spool of heavy link chain. Manning grunted as he hoisted the spool free.

"Will this do?" he asked McCarter.

"That might work even better. How much do you think is there?"

Manning tried to gauge the length of the chain without unwinding it from the spool. "I don't know, ten yards. Maybe twenty."

"Let's give it a shot," McCarter said. He jockeyed the controls, pulling the Sikorsky away from Encizo's position. As he dropped toward the far side of the charred pine, he spelled out his plan. "I'll get you as close to the ground as I can so you can hop down and hook the chain up to the crane hook. Then run a line under that pine and find a way to secure it to the ATV."

"So you can winch it," Manning guessed. "Good idea."

"That's why they put me in charge instead of you."

Manning let out a snort. "And here I thought it was your charm."

"That, too," the Briton replied. "Now hop to it."

"Yes, sir!"

McCarter brought the Sikorsky to within ten feet of a reasonably flat escarpment. The rotor wash raised a cloud of leaves and pine needles, revealing the bare rock Manning would have to land on. The big Canadian manipulated the boom's remote controls, releasing the winch hook mounted under the fuselage. Once he'd unwound six yards of cable, he locked the winch in place and swung his door open.

"Wait for a thumbs-up," he told McCarter.

McCarter nodded. "Good luck."

Manning stepped out onto the cockpit ladder and lowered himself to the last rung, then reached out and let the chain spool drop with a loud clatter onto the escarpment. Once McCarter had lowered the Sikorsky another couple feet, Manning pushed free and dropped to the ground a few feet from the spool. He grimaced as a flash of pain raced up both legs, but there was no time to dwell on his discomfort. He quickly affixed one end of the chain to the winch hook, then limped faintly as he made his way to the toppled pine, feeding out the length of chain behind him. He was rolling the spool under the pine when Encizo called out to him.

"That you, Gary?"

"Stay put," Manning called back. From where he was standing, the tethered crate blocked his view of Encizo.

"Don't have much choice."

"We're going to tug you back to solid ground." Manning quickly relayed the plan as he continued to unroll the spool. He was halfway to the ATV when he ran out of chain. Staring up at the Sikorsky, which was still hovering in position above the charred pine, he signaled for McCarter to feed out more cable.

As he was waiting, Manning detected a glint of refracted light to his right. He looked over his shoulder and traced the glint to a mountain ridge a hundred yards away. As quickly as it had appeared, the flash disappeared.

"Anyone else in these hills that you know about?" he called out to Encizo.

"Wouldn't surprise me," Encizo called back. "Why?"

"I think I caught some light bouncing off a pair of binocs," Manning said.

"Maybe it's reinforcements," Encizo replied. "Wasn't the militia supposed to be on its way up here?"

"Yeah," Manning said, "but they were coming the other way."

"We better get the show on the road, then," Encizo said. "Last thing we need is another warm BLM welcome."

By now McCarter had let out another twenty yards of cable. Manning tugged at the spool, pulling the chain until he'd reached the ATV. There was no trailer jack and he doubted the rear bumper would hold up, so he dropped flat against the ground and reached under the vehicle, knotting the chain to the chassis. Doing so, he nudged the ATV slightly and it groaned, inching farther over the edge of the precipice. One of the rear tires began to rise off the ground.

"Shit!"

Manning quickly scrambled out from under the vehicle and grabbed at the bumper, pressing down with his full weight.

"Push the crate back!" he shouted to Encizo.

"I don't know about—"

"Push it back!" Manning repeated.

Manning shifted his weight and began pulling at the bumper. He was in no position to signal for McCarter to start reeling the ATV in, but the Sikorsky nonetheless began to move upward, taking in the chain's slack. It was going to be close; Manning could feel the ATV slipping forward, pulling him toward the precipice.

"Faster, David!" he muttered, gritting his teeth as he pulled harder on the bumper. He felt his hamstrings and lower back straining from the effort but he refused to let up.

Encizo, meanwhile, had thrown caution to the wind and crawled up out of the driver's seat and begun to scramble across the top of the crate, trying to rebalance the ATV's load so it wouldn't go over the side. Manning stared up at him, his face red, the veins in his neck bulging from his exertion.

"I think we're gonna make it," Encizo said. Now that he'd moved from the front to the rear of the ATV, both the vehicle's rear wheels were back on the ground and it had stopped its forward slide. Moments later, the ATV jerked back a few inches from the precipice. McCarter had taken up all the chain's slack and was now starting to pull the vehicle from the brink of the abyss.

"Almost there," Encizo murmured, preparing to jump to the ground once all four wheels were back on firm ground.

Suddenly a muffled blast echoed from up in the hills, followed seconds later by a larger explosion, this one in the air just above the toppled pine. Manning and Encizo looked up simultaneously.

"David!" Encizo cried out.

A mortar shot had just struck the Skycrane's tail rotor. Destabilized, the chopper had begun to spin around eerily as it dropped toward the ground, taking McCarter down with it.

MCCARTER HAD NO TIME to react. Not that he could have done anything to prevent the Skycrane from crashing. One second he was lurching to one side from the force of the explosion; the next he found the ground rushing up to greet him. All that saved him from being killed on impact was the Sikorsky's manic air dance; just before striking the pines, it had pirouetted and tilted upward so that the damaged tail section touched down first. When the front end followed suit, the branches of the charred pine helped cushion the landing. Still, the impact was jarring enough to throw McCarter against the front windshield. The glass cracked but held in place as he bounded back into his seat, dazed, blood streaming down his face from a scalp gash.

The Sikorsky had come to rest at an odd angle, tilting slightly upward and sideways just enough to throw off McCarter's equilibrium. When he tried to stand, his head began to spin. He grabbed for the copilot's seat to steady himself, but his legs gave out underneath him and he keeled forward, dropping the carbine and toppling to the cockpit's floor. He struck his head again, this time against the instrument panel. The blow was forceful enough to render him unconscious. The last thing he recalled was the smell of leaking engine fuel.

MANNING STARTED to rush toward the fallen chopper, but his strained hamstrings refused to cooperate, slowing him to a quick hobble. Compounding matters, the ground around him came to life as a stream of gunfire chewed at the dirt and the now-slack length of chain reaching from the ATV to the charred pine. Driven back, he took shelter behind the ATV, kneeling beside Encizo, who'd already retrieved the driver's Uzi subgun.

"Bastards," Encizo growled. "Some of them must've veered off before they reached the meadow."

"That or they've got a camp around here somewhere," Manning speculated. He ignored the fiery sensation in his legs and drew his 15-round M-9 Beretta from its shoulder holster. He could no longer see the downed Skycrane, but he could smell smoke and the rank odor of fuel.

"We need to get David out of that chopper before it blows," he told Encizo, speaking above the gunfire.

"I know," Encizo said, "but how? They've got us pinned down."

"What about the jalopy?"

"After what it's been through, I doubt it's running," Encizo said, "but let's give it a—"

Encizo pitched forward, suddenly attacked from behind. The vehicle's driver had regained consciousness and sprang forward from the front seat armed with a combat knife. The blade bit sharply into Encizo's shoulder as the Basque knocked him to the ground.

The Basque quickly pulled the knife free and was about to stab Encizo a second time when Manning intervened, instinctively lashing out with the butt of his pistol. He caught the other man just below the right cheekbone, breaking a few teeth. Stunned, the man dropped his knife and his eyes began to roll up inside his head. Before he could collapse on top of Encizo, Manning grabbed hold of him and jerked him back to his feet with so much force the driver reeled backward. He was still trying to catch his balance when he ran out of ground and vanished as quickly as if a trapdoor had just opened under his feet.

Leaning against the ATV for support, Manning slowly limped forward to the edge of the precipice. With both hamstrings out it felt as if his legs had turned to jelly, and each step was an agony. By the time he reached the edge and peered downward, the driver had landed in a contorted, bloody heap at the base of the cliff.

"That's one down," Manning murmured.

He turned and headed back toward Encizo. The Cuban had pulled himself to his feet. His shirt was soaked with blood where he'd been stabbed. He ripped the fabric aside and inspected the wound. "He took a nice chunk out of me."

"Let me take a look," Manning said.

"Later." Encizo moved past his teammate and slid into the front seat of the ATV. "Come on, let's go get David."

"Easier said than done," Manning replied, struggling to pull himself into the passenger's seat. Encizo reached out with his good arm and helped him up.

"Hammies?"

"Yeah," Manning groaned. "Messed them up playing tug-of-war with the truck here."

"That sucks," Encizo told him. "What happened to the good old days when we came through these firefights without a scratch?"

"Times change, I guess," Manning said. He started to tell Encizo about the gunshot wounds Calvin James had sustained in the meadow when the next stream of gunfire rained on them from the mountains. The crate blocked most of the shots, but a few bullets found their way to the front hood, leaving navel-sized holes. The men knew if they didn't move they would end up sitting ducks.

Encizo quickly keyed the ignition. The engine turned over several times but wouldn't catch.

"Come on, you freaking piece of garbage!"

He tried again; this time the engine turned over.

Encizo was shifting into Reverse when their attackers fired another mortar round their way. Manning caught a fleeting glimpse as it whizzed by, missing the ATV by a few yards. It wound up exploding in the gorge behind them, and the sound of the blast echoed through the mountains like a death knell.

"I guess the good news is we must not be carting those

nukes after all," Encizo speculated. "Otherwise they wouldn't be trying to blow us up."

"In other words, they don't have to pull any punches going after us," Manning replied.

"That's the bad news," Encizo said. "Hang on. Here goes..."

The ATV's front end had been knocked out of alignment during its downhill plunge, and as Encizo guided the vehicle backward, it crabbed sharply to one side. He worked the steering to compensate, and with each turn his wounded shoulder felt as if it were about to fall off.

Encizo backed up the ATV a few more yards, then put on the brakes, bringing the vehicle to a stop several yards short of the pine tree Manning had used to winch the ATV from the edge of the precipice. One of the Sikorsky's main rotor blades extended out over them, and smoke drifted past the front of the vehicle.

"Okay," Encizo said, shifting the ATV into neutral. "Let's try to get to David before he gets fried."

Manning tried to climb out of his seat. He couldn't. "No good," he told Encizo.

"Take the wheel, then," Encizo said. "I'll go."

"I can manage that," Manning stated.

Encizo climbed out of the driver's seat, leaving it drenched with blood, then disappeared from view. Manning drew in a deep breath, then braced himself and struggled to duck under the front end of the crate. The effort drained him.

Beretta in hand, Manning scanned his surroundings, looking for signs of the enemy. The gunfire, which had stopped, at least for the moment, had all come from behind him, and all he could see to his right were rock formations, trees and the occasional shrub. As he was turning to his left, he rammed his cheekbone into the crate's front end.

Muttering an epithet, Manning grabbed the top of the box and pulled himself up until he was sitting on the seat's headrest. He could see Encizo now. The little Cuban had grabbed hold of the downed chopper's rotor blade and was swinging his way, hand over hand, toward the cockpit, feet dangling just above the limbs of the charred pine. The tree had been set aflame by burning debris and the flames were crawling along the trunk, racing Encizo toward the aircraft. Manning could see fuel leaking from a rupture in the boom tank. It would take a miracle for Encizo to get to the cockpit and rescue McCarter before the flames reached the fuel and turned the chopper into a fireball.

Manning knew he had to do something. He prepared to fling himself to the ground, hoping he could crawl to the flames and hopefully smother them. Before he could dive forward, however, another volley of gunfire ripped through the pines and pinged along the side of the ATV, forcing him to crawl back behind the cover of the crate. In the process he wrenched his back and a fresh wave of pain shot through his lower torso.

"Son of a bitch!" he growled, pounding the crate with so much force the lid jarred open slightly.

Manning eyed the lid, then glanced back at the fire. It was a long shot, but he figured if he could pry to lid off and heave it far enough, it might be able to snuff out the fire, or at least divert it away from the chopper.

The lid was nailed shut, but Manning had opened a wide enough gap for his fingers, and he tugged upward, ignoring the pain in his back, as well as the bullets slamming into the far side of the ATV. After a few agonizing seconds, the lid finally came free.

Manning glanced into the container, then whistled low and muttered, "I'll be damned."

ENCIZO WAS as mindful of the creeping flames as Manning, and when bullets began zipping past his head, he finally let go of the rotor blade and dropped down onto the burning tree. He tore at his blood-soaked shirt, ripping it from his back and then using it to slap at the flames. It worked at first, putting out the part of the fire closest to the fuel spill. He couldn't get any other of the burning branches without putting himself back into the line of fire, however, and soon it became clear that he was fighting a losing battle.

Pressing the shirt against the gash in his shoulder, Encizo made his way back toward the chopper, half climbing, half stepping over the brittle branches of the pine. Finally he reached the Sikorsky's ladder and climbed up to the cockpit. Peering in, he saw McCarter struggling to get to his feet, still bleeding from his scalp wound.

"Over here!" Encizo called out.

McCarter glanced up, a quizzical expression on his face.

"Come on!" Encizo jerked the door open and reached out to McCarter. "We've got to get out of this firetrap, quick!"

McCarter hesitated, then took Encizo's hand. The Cuban pulled hard, helping the Briton to the doorway.

"They really pulled the rug out from under you that time, didn't they?" he wisecracked.

"Rug?" McCarter said dully.

"Let's go," Encizo told him. "Gary's waiting in the ATV."

"Gary," McCarter repeated.

Encizo climbed back down the ladder, then dropped to the ground. He was waiting for McCarter to catch up when he heard a loud crash behind him. Turning, he saw the wooden crate tumble over the side of the ATV, spilling its contents onto the ground. Instead of the missiles and warheads the men had been concerned about, the crate had been filled with weapons: LAW rocket launchers, assault rifles, submachine guns and boxes filled with ammo clips. As for Manning, he was beside the vehicle's rear cargo bay, in the process of setting up a Barrett .50-caliber machine gun on its tripod stand.

"Thought I'd lighten our load," he called out as Encizo and McCarter made their way to the ATV. "Let's get the hell out of here before we get toasted!"

"I'll drive," Manning told McCarter, pausing to snatch up one of the assault rifles. He handed the gun to McCarter. "You can ride shotgun."

McCarter stared at the rifle, entranced, as Encizo bounded into the driver's seat and started the engine.

"Come on, David, dammit!"

McCarter looked up, then moved around the ATV and took a seat next to Encizo.

"Glad to see you in one piece, David," Manning called out from the rear of the vehicle.

As soon as McCarter climbed in, Encizo geared the ATV and popped the clutch. The vehicle lunged forward, still listing to one side as it raced clear of the downed Sikorsky. Moments later, there was a resounding explosion and shards of flaming shrapnel erupted in all directions. Manning ducked low in the vehicle, aiming the Barrett into the hills. Triggering the gun, he sent an autoburst streaming at their attackers. He couldn't see if he'd hit anyone, but there was yet another lull in the gunfire coming their way.

Encizo veered the ATV sharply to the right, heading up a slope that led back to the trail it had strayed from earlier. Just as they reached the path, a pair of fleeting shadows passed over the ATV. Glancing up, Encizo and Manning spotted a pair of Cobra gunships heading toward the enemy positions in the hills.

"Hot damn!" Encizo said. "It's about time we got some help!"

Once he reached the trail, Encizo quickly realized the ATV's front wheels were so misaligned he was in danger of crashing into the rocks flanking either side of the path. After a few yards he gave up trying and brought the vehicle to a stop.

"Stay put," he told Manning. "David and I'll go help mop up, then we'll come back to get you."

Manning nodded.

Encizo was halfway out of the ATV when he noticed that McCarter was still in his seat.

"David?" he asked. "Are you all right?"

McCarter stared at Encizo. He looked confused. "David," he said. "Is that my name?"

CHAPTER SEVEN

Stony Man Farm, Virginia

"Amnesia?" Carmen Delahunt was floored by the news Akira Tokaido had just delivered after a briefing with Aaron Kurtzman. "David has amnesia?"

Tokaido nodded. "All these times we've accused him of being out of his mind, who'd have thought we'd wind up being right?"

"Not funny," Delahunt snapped. Anger flushed her cheeks just a shade lighter than her fiery red hair.

"Hey, just a little gallows humor, all right?" Tokaido countered.

"I repeat," Delahunt said. "It's not funny. What's next? Are you going to start making wisecracks about Calvin being a holey man because he took three bullets?"

"Okay, I got it."

Tokaido shrugged and pitched his bubble gum into a trash receptacle as he made his way to the far corner of the Annex Computer Room, where steam rose from Kurtzman's legendary coffeepot.

Along with Tokaido and Huntington Wethers, who was due to arrive any moment, Delahunt rounded out Kurtzman's cybernetics team. The members of the group had never joined Able Team or Phoenix Force on the battlefield, yet within the confines of the Computer Room they played an equally important role in helping to stem the tide of global terrorism and high crime both at home and abroad.

Both Tokaido and Delahunt had been on duty for the past ten hours. Carmen had planned to go on break as soon as Wethers arrived, but in light of recent developments, she figured her usual midday catnap would have to wait. Stifling a yawn, she cursored across her screen, calling up a messaging program that would allow her to stay on top of any communications coming in from the field teams. There was one new message, from Rafael Encizo, under the heading "Med Update." Delahunt was opening up the message when a cup of coffee suddenly materialized at the edge of her desk.

"Peace offering," Tokaido said when she glanced up. "You were right. I shouldn't have been smarting off like that."

Delahunt picked up the cup and offered a tentative smile. "If this stuff's fresh, you're forgiven."

"The spoon didn't get stuck when I was stirring the cream," Tokaido said.

"Close enough."

Delahunt was taking a sip when the doors behind them opened and in walked a tall, crisply dressed black man with traces of gray in his short-cropped hair.

Huntington Wethers, a former cybernetics professor at Berkeley, had the most analytic mind of anyone working at the Farm, and when it came to sorting through the constant stream of information filtering into the Computer Room, Wethers was more often than not the first to glean the patterns and connections that transformed raw data into useable intelligence.

"I just heard Phoenix Force ran into some difficulties in Spain," Wethers said to Tokaido and Delahunt as he made his way to his workstation.

"There's an understatement," Tokaido said.

Delahunt shot him a warning glance, then quickly told Wethers about the ill-fated mission outside Bilbao.

"Terrible," Wethers said once Carmen had finished. "What's everybody's medical status?"

"I was just working on that," Delahunt said. "Give me a second."

Wethers and Tokaido stood by watching as Carmen read through Encizo's e-mail. "Actually, David's in the best shape of them all, at least physically," she reported. "He's got a mild concussion and needed some scalp stitches where he struck his head. They'll be giving him a CAT scan soon so they can come up with some kind of prognosis on his amnesia."

"Hopefully it'll be only short-term," Wethers said. "That's usually the case in situations like this."

"That's what we're banking on," Delahunt said. "As for Calvin, he's still in surgery. A field medic managed to stop the bleeding from his gunshot wounds, but they're going back in for one of the bullets because it's positioned too close to one of his arteries."

"But he's going to pull through, yes?" Wethers asked.

Delahunt skimmed through the rest of Encizo's note, then said, "Rafe says it's touch and go. The surgeons told him it was a miracle they were able to bring Cal in alive, given all the blood he'd lost. He got a couple units from two of the guys in that commando outfit that flew in with David and Gary."

"And Gary? How's he?"

Delahunt shook her head. "Partial tear in his right hamstring, and a strain in the left. That plus he pulled the muscles in his lower back. He can barely move.

"And with Rafe, the knife nicked a tendon and sliced into his right deltoid. He'll be in a sling and full-arm cast for at least a few weeks."

"Bottom line," Tokaido interjected, "is that they're all out of commission except for T.J."

"This is quite a blow," Wethers said. "First we lose two guys from Able Team, and now this."

"I know," Delahunt concurred. "And what's really upsetting is that it looks like this was just a wild-goose chase."

"Not entirely," Tokaido reminded her. "I mean, we did manage to take out an BLM cell that was trying to set up a base in the mountains there."

"Maybe so," Delahunt conceded, "but if you ask me, I think the Basques deliberately tried to make it look like they were carting those stolen missiles."

"Diversionary ploy?" Wethers queried.

"Exactly," Delahunt replied. "Look at all the manpower that went into that mission. Not just on our part, but Spain, too. With everybody focused on those mountains, it gave the BLM a better chance to smuggle the missiles out of the area. Not to mention this supertank."

"The needles have left the haystack, you're saying," Wethers replied.

"That would be my guess," Delahunt said. "And the more time that passes without us finding them, the wider the search area's going to get."

"And on our part, we're down to Pol and T.J.," Tokaido said. "And Pol's not even expected to reach Spain for another few hours. The trail's just going to get colder."

"Fortunately, it's not up to just us," Delahunt reminded Tokaido. "The Spanish are pouring as many resources into this whole thing as they can, and they're getting help from the French and NATO, too."

"Yeah, but they're not as good as us," Tokaido said. "You're talking boys going out to do a man's job."

Delahunt managed a smile. "Do I detect a little home-team prejudice?"

Tokaido grinned back. "Hey, if you can't root for the home team, what good are you?"

Wethers was in no mood for comic relief. He glanced across the room at one of the monitors depicting a sat-link photo of the mountainous terrain that stretched between Bilbao and Barcelona. He asked the others, "What have Hal and Barbara had to say about all this?"

"The chief's back in Washington conferring with the Joint Chiefs of Staff," Delahunt responded. "Barbara's back at the main house. She said she was going to go over the backgrounds on some of the blacksuits and see if we can patch together a backup team to send over."

"Won't be the same," Tokaido said. "There's no replacing the guys in Phoenix Force or Able Team."

The cybercrew was interrupted as the door behind them opened a second time. This time, it was a tall, blond-haired, blue-eyed man who strode purposefully into the room. His face was pale and his forehead glistened with sweat.

"I'll take that as a compliment," he told Tokaido.

"Carl?" Delahunt called out, startled to see the Able Team leader up and on his feet. "What are you doing here?"

Carl Lyons snapped a salute and flashed a menacing grin. "Reporting for duty, what else?"

"You've got the flu, for God's sake," Delahunt protested. "Look at you, you're sweating like you just came out of a steam bath."

"Flu schmoo," Lyons snarled. "I just got done talking with Barbara. We've got work to do, so quit gawking and track me down a jet so I can get my ass to Spain, pronto."

CHAPTER EIGHT

Facaros Pass, near Bilbao, Spain

Luis Manziliqua awoke with a start. He thumbed his wrist-watch to light up the LED display. It was almost midnight, when meant he'd dozed off for nearly two hours. With a groan, he slowly rose to his feet. He'd fallen asleep sitting between two large boulders near the peak of Mt. Facaros and he was stiff. He stretched for a moment, then wearily grabbed a pair of binoculars from the ground and trudged a few yards uphill to his post atop the mountain.

Night had fallen over the area. There was a crescent moon overhead, and the cloudless sky was sprinkled with a scattering of bright, winking stars. It was cool up here at the higher elevations, and Manziliqua turned up the collar of his shirt to fend off the chill of a faint breeze. He was stationed thirty miles inland from the Bay of Biscay, and yet he could smell the sea in the air, a briny scent that brought to mind his previous life as a fisherman plying the waters near the coastal town of San Sebastian. How much simpler life was then, he mused. He'd found the daily routine stifling and couldn't wait to leave it behind, but there were times now when he wished he'd never listened to the prattling of his cousins and got it into his head that there was romance and glamour to be found as a revolutionary. Hah! Where was the romance and glamour in pulling sentry duty night after night, first in the mountains overlooking the Gamuso proving grounds and now here atop the highest and loneliest peak of the San Madrillo Mountains? His job was to stay put and scour his surroundings for any noteworthy activity. Only once—last night at the proving grounds—had there been anything worth reporting. The rest of the time, from dusk to dawn for three weeks running, he'd had little to look at but the activity of wildlife and the occasional traipsing of planes through the heavens. His biggest challenge, night after night, was to stay awake and try to keep from driving himself crazy humming the same songs over and over as he tried to dispel the boredom. Some revolution.

Of course, it could be worse, he figured. He could have been among those who were killed earlier that afternoon twenty miles to the south. He hadn't heard all the details, but apparently they'd lost nearly twenty men. That put things into perspective. He'd take boredom over death any time.

Yawning, Manziliqua put the binoculars to his eyes and lapsed into the tedious ritual of panning the terrain below. From his position, he had a view of two mountain roads leading inland from Bilbao. There was little to see of the first road; it was almost completely veiled by a blanket of fog, one of several cloudlike pockets obscuring much of the lower elevations. As he shifted his gaze, Manziliqua spotted a herd of elk crossing a dimly lit meadow valley. He wished he were down closer to them. He'd lugged a 50-caliber Barrett SWS up into the mountains with him, and with a rifle like that he could easily take out at least one of the elk once he was within eighteen hundred meters. True, it wouldn't do much to advance the cause of the BLM, but at least he'd have something to show for his night in the mountains. And roast elk sounded a hell of a lot more appetizing than another ration of hardtack and canned meat.

Manziliqua watched the elk until they disappeared into the fog, then turned his focus to the second mountain road. A sudden curse spilled from his lips.

Nearly a quarter-mile stretch of the winding road was il-luminated by headlights and taillights. Several dozen vehicles were idling in place, trailing clouds of exhaust into the night air. He traced the line of cars and trucks with his binoculars, then held his focus on the head of the line. There, two army transport trucks were parked off on the shoulder. Three armed soldiers blocked the road while more than a dozen other men circled the first two vehicles, searching the interiors and scru-tinizing its occupants. After a few moments, the vehicles were waved through and the troops closed around the next two cars. Manziliqua was too far away to hear any of the activity, but soon he heard the faint droning of rotors and, glancing up, he saw the lights of a helicopter approaching the roadblock.

Lowering his binoculars, Manziliqua scrambled downhill to the boulders where he'd fallen asleep earlier. Next to the Barrett .50 was an AN/PRC-126 radio. He snatched up the transceiver and hurriedly patched through a call. He was wide awake now, pulse racing. The roadblock had clearly been in place for some time. How was he going to explain not hav-ing reported it earlier? Miguel was going to be furious. Manziliqua had seen him pistol-whip men for lesser trans-gressions. What would happen to him if Miguel figured out he'd fallen asleep at his station?

Think fast, Manziliqua murmured to himself. Think fast....

"IDIOT!" MIGUEL RIGO switched off his microphone and slammed it back on the cradle of a transceiver mounted under the dashboard of the Mack truck he was riding in. "He'll pay for this!"

Zacharias Brinquel, a rotund Basque in his midfifties, was behind the wheel of the big rig. He'd overheard enough of Miguel's angry exchange with Luis Manziliqua to know the problem they'd run into.

"We're headed for a roadblock?" he said without taking his eyes off the narrow mountain road before him.

"Yes. Three miles from here," Miguel muttered. The clean-shaved, thirty-year-old leader of the Basque Liberation Movement pounded his fist against the dashboard, then popped open the glove compartment and pulled out a well-worn top-ographical map. "He claims the fog kept him from spotting it earlier. Pah!"

Brinquel took a final drag on his small cigar, then flicked the cheroot out his window. "More likely the only fog was between his ears," he guessed.

"I'll teach him to fall asleep at his post!"

Miguel quickly unfolded the map across his lap and shone a small penlight on the area they were driving through.

"Slow down," he told the driver. "There should be a spot around the next bend where we can turn."

Brinquel frowned. "Turn? Up here in the mountains? Not with our load."

"We don't have a choice."

"I'm not a truck driver, Miguel," Brinquel protested. "It's hard enough for me to keep us on the road. I've never backed a truck up and turned it around."

"Now is a good time to learn," Miguel countered. "Put on your flashers."

Brinquel shook his head wearily and switched on the emergency lights. He checked his rearview mirror, but it was impossible to see if there was any traffic behind them. The truck was hauling a forty-foot-long prefab trailer home, and the structure extended out more than ten feet on either side of the flatbed it was resting on, blocking Brinquel's view, as well as taking up a good portion of the oncoming lane. Twice already the trailer had been nearly clipped by traffic coming the other way, and as he slowly rounded the next bend on the mountain road, he again took up both lanes.

As Miguel had predicted, once they'd cleared the bend, they came upon a straightaway where the road was flanked on either side by a good twenty yards of level ground. To their right, just beyond the wide shoulder, a flimsy guardrail marked the edge of a precipitous drop into a deep, narrow gorge. Turning the truck without going over the side would be a chore, even for an experienced driver. Brinquel weighed his predicament and shook his head again.

"I can't do it, Miguel," he said. "It's too dangerous."

Miguel reached to his side for a 9 mm Walther pistol similar to the one his sister had used earlier in the day to execute the woman who'd been picked up near the BLM's worksite in Barcelona. He pressed the gun's barrel to Brinquel's head and barked, "Try!"

Brinquel didn't so much as flinch. His eyes went cold, as did his voice.

"Who do you think you're talking to, Miguel?" he asked calmly.

Miguel held the pistol in place a moment, then slowly

pulled it away. He averted his gaze from the driver and busied himself attaching the Walther's sound-and-flash suppressor.

"I apologize, Zacharias," he finally murmured.

"You and your brother. Such hotheads." Zacharias sighed. He managed a faint smile. "Just like your father, rest his soul."

"Don't forget Angelica."

"Yes, your sister, too," Brinquel said.

"I guess none of the apples have fallen far from the tree."

His point made, Brinquel dropped his smile and told Rigo, "Your father never pulled a gun on me."

Miguel was given pause. His father and Brinquel had been best friends since the early years of the ETA, and Zacharias had been at Carlos Rigo's side the day, just over a year ago, when he'd been gunned down by the Ertzainta. By all rights, Brinquel had been next in line to take over as the head of the Navarra cell, but power held little interest for him and after he'd helped avenge Carlos's death in an assault against the Ertzainta, he'd turned the organization over to Miguel, his friend's elder son, who'd promptly broken with the ETA. Still, Miguel continued to rely on Brinquel's experience and quiet wisdom as a counterpoint to their impatience and hardheadedness. He looked up to the man and the more he thought about it, the more Miguel regretted having taken his frustrations out on him.

"It won't happen again," Miguel promised.

"No, it won't," Zacharias responded calmly. "Now, are you sure there is no other way around the roadblock? What about San Marcos Pass?"

Miguel inspected the map again and shook his head. "The road is too steep," he said. "Besides, if the traffic is backed up as far as Luis says, we would be seen. No, we need to turn around."

Brinquel chuckled. "Somehow I knew you were going to say that."

"I have confidence in you, Zacharias," Miguel assured the driver. "Just take it slow."

Brinquel nodded. "With this load, I couldn't take it fast if I wanted to."

Halfway through the straightaway, the older man eased the semi off onto the shoulder and headed toward the guardrail. Once he was within a few yards of it, Brinquel turned the wheel sharply and headed back toward the road. He'd hoped that by some miracle there would be enough shoulder on the other side of the road for him to turn the truck without having back up, but once he crossed the median, he quickly ran out of room and was forced to put on the brakes just shy of the mountains. The truck was now completely straddling both lanes of the road.

"So far, so good," he said, putting his foot on the clutch and reaching for the gearshift knob rising up from the floor. "Now is when we need to say our—"

Brinquel's voice was drowned out by the sudden bleating of a car horn. A pair of headlights switched to high beam and bathed the truck's cab with a harsh glow.

Miguel squinted past Brinquel and saw a small sports car in the road. He couldn't tell the make of the car, but from the sound of the horn he guessed it was a Fiat. Its driver continued to work the horn, giving off a series of short blasts, then settling on a prolonged, one-note wail that echoed off through mountains.

Miguel cursed to himself and opened his door. "Back up just a few yards, then turn the wheel and inch forward. Keep doing it until we're turned around."

"Where are you going?" Brinquel asked.

"To have a talk with our friend about his horn," Miguel said.

"Best make it a short talk," Brinquel said. "They can probably hear that horn all the way from here to the roadblock."

Miguel got out and circled the front of the truck, holding the gun behind his back as he approached the car. He was right. It was a late-model Fiat. The driver was a man in his forties, wearing a designer shirt and white slacks. He looked to Miguel like some sort of businessman, but when he raised his voice and shouted for the truck to move, the driver cursed at him like a longshoreman. All the while, he kept the heel of his right palm planted against the car's horn.

"I'm running late, damn you!" he shouted. "Get out of my way or I'll report you to the—"

The man suddenly fell silent. Miguel had brought his pistol into view. Before the man could react, Miguel pulled the trigger, putting two rounds into the driver's face. The man's head snapped back from the force of the rounds, then he slumped to one side.

Miguel holstered his gun, then leaned into the car, reaching past the driver and shifting the Fiat into gear. As the car began to move forward, Miguel turned the steering wheel, then backed away. The Fiat quickly veered off the road and headed for the guardrail.

When the car hit the barrier, there was a dull crash and the sound of snapping wood. The railing's uprights gave way, and seconds later the Fiat disappeared over the side. A series of small explosions marked its swift descent to the bottom of the gorge.

Miguel turned and headed toward the rear of the truck. Brinquel had already backed the rig up once and moved forward, but he was still nowhere close to completing the turn.

"Back up again!" Miguel called out. "I'll tell you when to stop!"

As Miguel moved toward the partially collapsed guardrail, one of the trailer home's windows opened. Two men peered out. Like Miguel and Brinquel, they both wore berets. One of the men brandished an M-14 carbine and bore a close resemblance to Miguel, though he was bearded and wore his hair longer. It was Jacque Rigo, Miguel's younger brother.

"What's happening?" he called out.

Miguel quickly explained the situation, then said, "Close the window and stay put."

"Are you sure we can get around the roadblock?" Jacque asked.

"Let me worry about that," Miguel snapped.

Jacque was about to retort but thought better of it and withdrew inside the prefab along with the other man.

Miguel moved back to the guardrail, then signaled to Brinquel, who slowly backed up. Once the truck was again within a few yards of the barricade, Miguel waved his arms and shouted for Brinquel to stop. The older man put on the brakes, then shifted gears and pulled forward. He had to repeat the maneuver a second time, but finally he'd managed to complete the turnaround.

"What did I tell you?" Miguel said as he got back in the cab and slapped Brinquel on the shoulder. "You're more of a truck driver than you thought."

"Maybe so." Brinquel's face had broken out in a sweat. He wiped his brow with the back of his hand, then pulled a fresh cheroot from his pocket. Miguel lit it for him, then they drove in silence, heading back the way they'd come. Brinquel had to steer wide several times to avoid oncoming cars, then, after a quarter mile, Miguel pointed out the windshield.

"Turn up there."

Brinquel frowned. "That road dead-ends at Lake Pabal. What is the point of going there?"

"You'll see," Miguel told him. "I've come up with a better plan. The roadblock wound up working in our favor."

"Are you sure?" Brinquel sounded skeptical.

"Positive," Miguel responded. He quickly divulged what he had in mind, concluding, "This way it will be even more difficult for them to realize we've pulled a switch on them."

Zacharias still wasn't convinced but he wasn't about to argue. He drove on, and once he reached the turnoff, he guided the rig onto an even narrower dirt road that led down a steep, winding incline. He had to downshift to keep the vehicle under control, and soon there was yet another obstacle to contend with.

They were entering a fog bank.

Brinquel slowed the truck to a crawl and leaned forward in his seat in hopes of getting a better view of the way before him. It helped a little, but soon his visibility had been reduced to less than five feet.

"Maybe Luis was telling the truth about the fog," Brinquel murmured.

"I doubt it," Miguel said.

After another few yards, the road straightened and began to level off. Suddenly Miguel held his hand out, motioning for Brinquel to stop.

"Turn off the engine and kill the lights," he said.

"Why?"

"Just do it!"

Brinquel obliged, planting his foot on the brakes to keep the truck still. In the wake of the engine's constant roar, the sudden silence seemed almost deafening. But soon Brinquel was able to make out the sound Miguel had apparently heard moments before. It was a mechanical droning, sounding from overhead.

"A helicopter," Brinquel whispered.

Miguel nodded, putting a finger to his lips. He had his gun back out, and he reached to the floor of the truck, then handed Brinquel a 30-mm AGS-17 grenade launcher. The weapon, with its thick stock and barrel, had the look of a futuristic rifle out of a science-fiction movie.

As Brinquel cradled the launcher on his lap, a faint beam of light appeared ahead of them, probing into the fog from above. The fog was so dense, however, that the beam was barely able to penetrate it. As the shaft of light swept toward them, Miguel kept an eye on the hood of the trunk. If light reflected off the hood, it would likely mean the truck had been spotted, forcing their hand.

Seconds crept by slowly, then the beam washed faintly over the truck. The fog blunted the light before it could reach the hood, however, and soon after the light disappeared, the sound of the helicopter began to fade, as well.

"They missed us," Brinquel whispered.

"I hope so," Miguel responded. He quietly opened his door again. "Wait here. I'll be right back."

Brinquel was about to ask where Miguel was going, but the door closed and Miguel vanished from view into the fog. Brinquel's cheroot had gone out. He reached for some matches, then changed his mind and contented himself with chewing on the end of the cigar.

Less than a minute later, Miguel appeared out of the fog

and returned to the truck. He'd left the door open and he reached in, pulling the transceiver from under the dashboard as he spoke to Zacharias.

"Shift into Neutral and point the wheels straight," he said. "When I tell you, take your feet off the brakes and make sure the truck keeps going straight until it reaches the water."

Brinquel couldn't hold back his reservations any further. "I can't believe you talked me into doing this."

"You'll be fine," Miguel insisted. "Just remember to keep your window down and lay down across the seat once you hit the water. After the explosion, wait a few seconds, then you can go ahead and swim out through the window. We'll be waiting for you ashore."

"You make it sound so simple," Brinquel said. "Maybe we should trade places."

"If that's what you want," Miquel offered.

Brinquel thought it over, then shook his head. "No, I'll do it," he said warily. "But I have to tell you I don't swim very well."

Miguel grinned. "You said you couldn't drive a truck, either. Maybe you'll surprise yourself again."

Miguel clipped the transceiver to his belt, then took the grenade launcher before closing the door and stepping back from the truck.

"Good luck, Zacharias."

Brinquel smiled wanly. "I'll take all the luck I can get."

The older man sat back behind the wheel, lit his cheroot and took a few slow puffs and listened to Miguel as he spoke with his brother and the other men inside the trailer home. Then two of the men got out and climbed up onto the prefab's roof. Brinquel knew the men were placing small plastique charges along the middle of the roof, as well as on the front and back seams that held the two halves of the trailer home together.

The work went quickly. Once it was finished, Brinquel took a final puff on his cheroot and was tossing it out the window when the sound of gunfire suddenly ripped through the night air. Alarmed, Brinquel glanced to his left.

Forty yards away, two armed commandos had materialized out of the fog, carbines blazing. There was a thump up on the roof of the trailer home, then Brinquel heard one of the men rolling over the side to the ground.

"Bastards," Brinquel muttered. He realized the commandos had to have rappelled from the helicopter. They'd spotted the truck after all.

Outside the truck, Miguel returned fire with his pistol, as did the other gunman still on the roof. The two commandos dropped in their tracks. They weren't alone, however. More gunfire streaked out through the fog, glancing off the side of the truck, as well as the trailer home.

"Go!" Miguel shouted to Brinquel as he holstered his Walther in favor of the grenade launcher. "Now!"

Brinquel let his foot off the brakes and ducked in the cab after a round of gunfire took out the front windshield. The truck began to pick up speed as it rolled downhill through the fog.

Miguel, meanwhile, dropped to a crouch, peering into the fog where the shots were coming from. When he spotted a faint muzzle-flash, he fired the ASG. Seconds later, a 30 mm grenade exploded loudly, drowning out the pained screams of at least two men who'd been nailed by the projectile's shrapnel. The Basque who'd leaped from the roof stood alongside Miguel and fired in the same direction, hoping to take out anyone not killed by the grenade.

Miguel quickly readied the launcher with another round, but as the din of the explosion faded, so did the screams. Miguel waited a moment. When no further shots came his way, he set the launcher aside and rushed over to the man who'd been shot when the commandos had first attacked. The man was lying facedown where he'd fallen from the roof of the pre-fab. Miguel knew it couldn't be his brother, but still he held his breath anxiously as he turned over the body. The dead man turned out to be one of the newer recruits. No great loss, Miguel thought to himself.

He was soon joined by the other gunman, Guillermo Blanca, a slight, lean man whose large brown eyes were magnified by the thick lenses of his glasses. He'd put his gun away and was now holding a small remote-control device.

"Let's get down to the lake," Miguel told him, rising to his feet. "Hurry!"

As the men jogged along the road, following the same path taken by the truck, Blanca held the remote out before him. "As soon as the truck hits the water, yes?"

"Yes," Miguel told him, "and not a second before. We want to make sure everything sinks."

As the men neared the lake, the fog began to dissipate, allowing a glimpse of the truck's taillights. Brinquel had managed to keep the vehicle on a straight course, and it was within twenty yards of rolling into the lake.

Blanca slowed to a stop and poised his thumb over the largest button on the remote. He waited until he saw the truck splash into the water, then pressed the button.

Miguel stopped running, as well, and watched as a quick series of small explosions rocked the joint seams of the trailer home. As it began to sink below the waterline, the prefab split in two. Both sides fell away from the flatbed, revealing for a brief moment not the inner walls and home furnishings one would have expected, but rather two identical-looking battle tanks.

In a matter of seconds, the tanks—along with the truck carrying them—disappeared from view beneath the surface of the lake. The prefab partitions continued to float momentarily, then were slowly pulled underwater, as well.

"Good work, Guillermo," Miguel said as the two men continued to view the results of Blanca's handiwork. "It couldn't have gone more perfectly."

The explosives expert seemed less sure all had gone well. "I hope Zacharias is all right," he said.

"He'll be fine," Miguel replied, eyes on the lake. There was a trace of concern in his voice, however. He could see a few small pieces of debris from the trailer home floating on the surface of the lake, but there was no sign yet of the truck's driver.

"Come on, come on," Miguel muttered impatiently.

Moments later, Brinquel finally surfaced, gasping for air. He glanced around momentarily, then thrashed through the water toward shore. Miguel waded out to meet him.

"Are you all right?"

Brinquel nodded and spit out a mouthful of water, then told Miguel, "It goes down nearly twenty meters. Unless the water is crystal clear, no one will be able to see anything down there."

"Good," Miguel said. "They'll have to send down a diving crew. That will take time."

Blanca greeted Zacharias, then asked Miguel, "Should I set off the last explosion?"

"Not yet," Miguel told him, unclipping the field radio from his belt. "First let me check in with my little brother."

JACQUE RIGO WAS ten years younger than his brother and eight years younger than his sister. Miguel and Angelica had figured out early on that Jacque was an unplanned child and throughout Jacque's childhood they rarely passed on an opportunity to remind him that he was an "accident." Jacque had weathered the abuse as well as possible, but he spent his growing years dogged by feelings of inferiority, feelings he tried to overcome by applying himself hard at school and in sports. As a consequence, he excelled academically and was the first and only of the Rigo children to graduate from high school and receive a college degree. He was also the first of the children to follow in the footsteps of their father and join the ETA. The move had endeared him to his father and earned the envy of Miguel and Angelica, who had quickly followed suit, teaming up to insure that they regained their father's favor at Jacque's expense. By the time of Carlos's death, the original pecking order had been restored, with Miguel and Angelica taking over the reins of the ETA's Navarra cell and its offshoot, the BLM. Jacque had resented the turn of events, but there was little he could do about it. He was consoled, somewhat, however, when the plan to seize the FSAT-50 was first hatched, because his collegiate background in computers and his natural affinity for weapons systems made him the logical choice to head up the team that commandeered the amphibious tank and was now responsible for seeing to its safe passage from the Gamuso proving grounds to Barcelona. If only by default, he'd made himself indispensable, and though Miguel and Angelica still had a tendency to talk down to him, their condescension was now tempered by a measure of respect. And if he succeeded on his end with the mission, Jacque hoped that at long last his brother and sister would come to treat him as a peer.

When Jacque received his first call from Miguel after the FSAT-50 had been driven into the depths of Lake Pabal, he was hard-pressed to suppress a smile. Instead of "little brother," Miguel had called him Jocko, a nickname Jacque had received from his father soon after joining the ETA.

"All is well on our end," Jacque reported. "We've pulled free of the truck and all of the tank's systems are operational."

"And the decoy is still in place?"

"Yes," Jacque said. "It's still strapped down to the flatbed. Once we're further across the lake, I'll call back with an 'all clear.'"

"We'll be ready," Miguel told him. "Keep up the good work, Jocko."

Jacque clicked off his microphone, beaming with pride. He was standing in the middle of the FSAT-50's control compartment. For a tank, the area was surprisingly large, with room for four men, as well as the array of equipment and weapon controls needed for the tank to function. With him was another member of the BLM, Geraldo Carreon, as well as two members of the Gamuso training crew who'd been taken prisoner during the seizure of the tank. Carreon had a gun to the head of Rey Hespera, who was at the controls. The other man, weapons expert Matteo Bainz, sat in the gunner's seat, his arms tied behind his back.

Over the past four months, Carreon and Jacque had both extensively studied spec sheets on the FSAT-50's operating systems, but until they were sure they could take over the running of the tank on their own, they planned to keep their captives alive, holding out the false promise that at some point they would be freed.

As for the tank, it plied the depths of the lake with ease, its position in the water carefully regulated by the controlled release of a helium-derivative gas into ballast chambers located beneath the tank's armor plating and below the floor of the watertight, pressurized compartment. There was none of the constant jostling that came with driving a tank over rough terrain. Instead, the FSAT-50 moved more like a submarine in still waters, the drone of its engines muffled by the ballast chambers.

"Where are we going from here?" Rey Hespera asked Jacque as he continued to navigate across the lake.

"Once we're halfway across the lake," Jacque told the captive, "change course to northeast until you come to the mouth of the river."

"And after that?"

"That's not your concern at the moment," Jacque responded.

"What are your plans for the tank?" It was perhaps the twentieth time Hespera had asked the question since being taken hostage.

"Not your concern," Jacque repeated.

To emphasize Jacque's point, Carreon pressed the barrel of his gun closer against Hespera's skull. "If you need something to worry about," Carreon told the commander, "worry about doing your job right so that you'll be able to see your family again."

Matteo Bainz called out to his colleague from the gunner's seat. "Stop antagonizing them, Rey. Just do what you're told and shut up about the rest!"

Jacque smiled at Bainz. "I see you're still the wise one of the group."

Bainz met Jacque's gaze, then looked away.

Jacque walked back and forth in the compartment, idly fingering the control panels mounted to racks that lined the walls on either side of him. He couldn't wait until they'd reached the river and moved on to a point where they could stop long enough for him and Carreon to take over the controls and see if they could successfully handle the tank on their own. The prisoners were getting on his nerves, and they would continue to be a distraction so long as their services were needed. He and Carreon would be better off once they had the tank to themselves.

Another few minutes passed, then Hespera called out, "We're halfway across the lake."

Jacque exchanged a glance with Carreon, then reached for the transceiver and placed a call back to his brother.

"All clear, Miguel," he said. "Go ahead."

MIGUEL HAD LED Brinquel and Blanca into the foothills overlooking the lake. The hills were lush, providing them with better cover than the flatland where they'd engaged with the helicopter troops. From their vantage point, they could see that the chopper had circled and was heading across the lake toward them, sweeping the area before it with its probing searchlight.

"Ready?" Miguel whispered to Blanca.

Blanca double-checked his remote-control device and nodded. "Ready."

"Then let's give our guests something to look at," Miguel replied. "Now!"

Blanca thumbed the remote's detonator button. Seconds later, a faint rumbling sounded from deep inside the lake. The force of the underwater explosion was strong enough to disrupt the glassy surface of the lake. There was a violent splashing, in the wake of which a concentric band of rippling waves radiated in all directions.

"Good. Now they'll know right where to look," Miguel whispered.

In setting off the explosives that had been rigged inside the second tank, Blanca had only been following orders. He was still in the dark, however, as to why Miguel had arranged to have the tank destroyed in such a matter.

"How is that good?" he asked, eyes on the chopper, which had veered toward the spot where the underwater charge had gone off.

"Come morning, they'll send divers down to investigate," Miguel explained, "and when they see all the debris, they'll figure we lost the tank trying to smuggle it cross-country."

"Okay, I understand," Blanca said, "but I thought the plan was to blow up the decoy on land."

"Obviously there was a change in plans," Miguel told him. "But think about it. Underwater, it will be even more difficult for them to tell we blew up a decoy than if we'd done it on land. This will buy us even more time. By the time they figure out we've fooled them, hopefully the tank will have reached Barcelona."

Out over the lake, the helicopter hovered above the dying ripples, illuminating them with its searchlight. Miguel suspected that at some point they would make another sweep around the lake's perimeter.

"Let's go," he told the others. "We'll lose them in the mountains."

As the Basques made their way farther uphill through the dense fog, Blanca stayed close to Miguel. "Something has been bothering me," he told the group's ringleader. "Do we really plan to use nuclear warheads on Barcelona?"

Miguel exchanged a look with Brinquel, then told the explosives expert, "Only as a last resort. If all goes well, we will be able to make do with a conventional warhead."

"That means there is some other plan, right?" Blanca ventured. "What is it?"

"You'll find out soon enough," Miguel responded. "And you'll play an important role."

"We're going to set off a bomb inside the civic center?"

Miguel was evasive. "Just take my word for it," he told Blanca. "One way or another, we will bring down that convention hall and our enemies inside it."

CHAPTER NINE

Barri Gotic Quarter, Barcelona, Spain

When the alarm on the nightstand beside her began to bleep, Angelica Rigo awoke with a start. She quickly untangled herself from Xavier Golato's arms and turned it off. It was 4:00 a.m. and still dark inside the top floor of the loft building that for the past three months had served as the BLM's base of operations in Barcelona. Angelica had hoped she'd gotten to the alarm in time to keep from waking Golato, but he stirred slightly, then groaned and opened one eye, taking in Angelica's nude body as she climbed out of bed.

"Where are you going?" he asked her sleepily.

"I need to meet Cristofer," she reminded him, "to get the plans."

"Cristofer." Golato spit the name contemptuously. "I'll be glad when we're done with him."

"You're just jealous because he has a crush on me," Angelica teased.

"Ha! What's to be jealous of? He's nobody." Golato propped himself up in the bed and reached out for Angelica. "Come here. We have a little time."

Angelica stepped clear of his reach.

"Business before pleasure," she told him. "Go back to sleep. We have a full day ahead of us. I'll be back in awhile."

"Just remember," Golato said. "Cristofer gets paid in euros, not personal favors."

Angelica laughed lightly. "Sounds like jealousy to me." She moved back to the bed and kissed Golato atop his bald head, then on the lips. "Don't worry," she assured him. "No matter what Cristofer might hope for, my relationship with him is strictly business. Now go to sleep."

Appeased, Golato slumped back down on the bed. By the time Angelica had decided what she was going to wear for her rendezvous—a nondescript department store blouse and skirt—Golato was snoring peacefully. She dressed quickly, then put up her hair and donned a wide-brimmed straw hat and a pair of cheap, large-framed sunglasses. After stepping into a pair of sandals, she regarded her reflection in a full-length mirror hanging from the back of the door.

"Tourista," she murmured, satisfied that once out in the streets she would pass for just another face in the crowd.

Once she'd slipped her Walther pistol into an oversize purse, Angelica left the bedroom and negotiated her way through the clutter of the loft's main area. The loft was located in an isolated, run-down industrial section of Barri Gotic, one of the more unsavory neighborhoods in all of Barcelona. Other loft complexes on the block had been taken over by artists and fledgling bohemians, and at one time there had been plans to renovate this building, as well, as evidenced by a twenty-foot-high scaffolding rig that dominated the middle of the loft. It had been decided that the building was too decrepit to salvage, however, and the project had been abandoned a few weeks before the BLM had moved in. As drab and run-down as the loft was, it was a luxury suite compared to the lower floors, which were in such a squalid state of disrepair that their only tenants were rat colonies and transients. In a few weeks the structure was slated for demolition to make way for the warehouse and distribution center of a major Barcelona toy manufacturer. By then, Angelica and her cohorts would be long gone, their mission accomplished.

Some of the men who'd been helping to prepare the tank site at Nacional Parc Guell had come into town for the night along with Angelica and Golato. They were spread out across the floor, sleeping on cots and old mattresses. In the dark it was hard to see them, but like Golato, most of them were snoring, and to Angelica their combined racket seemed louder than the chain saws they kept wanting to use on the beech trees back near the river. At least the noise kept away the rats, she thought to herself as she made her way to the kitchen area.

Angelica opened a can of soup into a saucepan, then set it over one of the stove's burners. The soup would take a while to heat up, so she moved over to a bank of grimy windows overlooking the city. Staring past the moonlit rooftops and upper floors of downtown office buildings, she could see the shadowy outline of the same bottlelike cathedral towers she'd eyed yesterday from the forest. Now she was looking at them from the other side and they were much closer, only a few miles away. In fact, if the tank were to overshoot its mark on Friday, the loft building would likely find itself spared the need for a wrecking ball.

Of course, if all went according to plan, Angelica mused, the tank's accuracy would be a moot point. If all went according to plan, she and the others would be able to bring down the civic center without having to use the tank, much

less either of the stolen nuclear warheads. As valuable as they
were as contingency options, Angelica and her brothers hoped
to retain the weapons for sale on the black market, where they
would earn enough money to help the BLM expand its operations and notch up its efforts to create an independent Basque
state. There was already an offer on the table for one of the
warheads, and in a few hours Miguel would be meeting with
an Iraqi agent to close the deal.

Behind Angelica, the saucepan slowly began to rattle on
the stove. She hurried over and turned down the heat, then
added a couple ice cubes to the soup, cooling it so that she
could quickly drink it down. She didn't want to be late for her
rendezvous with Cristofer.

Once finished with the soup, Angelica grabbed her purse
and got on the freight elevator located at the far end of the loft.
The elevator was as old as the building, with a folding gate instead of sliding doors. As it began its slow, creaky descent, she
took the Walther from her purse and tried her best to hold her
breath. Floor by floor, the stench of urine, feces and rotting
garbage grew stronger, assailing her nostrils. When they'd
first moved into the building, it had amazed Angelica that anyone would choose to live in the squalor of the lower stories.
But having crossed paths with most of the transients at one
time or another, she realized they were all either half-mad or
so enslaved to their drug addictions they'd become indiffer-
ent to their living conditions. Several times, she'd been ac-
costed by these denizens, but much as she was grateful for the
way they deterred curiosity seekers from venturing up to the
top floor, she wasn't about to subsidize them and whenever she
rode the elevator now she always had her gun out in plain view.

This morning, the gun came in handy.

Angelica had made it as far as the second floor when the elevator ground to a stop and she found herself staring through the gate at a grizzled, wild-eyed man who stank of tuna and cigarettes. When he reached out to open the gate, Angelica leveled the Walther at his chest and told him, "Sorry, this one's taken."

The man wasn't about to argue. He stepped back, all but vanishing into the darkened hallway behind him.

Angelica continued down to the ground floor and quickly made her way outside, grateful for a breath of fresh air. Within three blocks, she had left behind the loft quarter and found herself in a more tourist-friendly section of Barri Gotic. It was still dark out and the streets were quiet. A few minutes passed before she was able to flag down a cab.

"The civic square," she told the driver as she got in.

"The square's closed off," the cabbie responded. "Something about security for that NATO conference."

The news didn't come as a complete surprise to Angelica; Cristofer had forewarned her it might happen. It would make their job a little more difficult, but if Cristofer came through, they would have no problem bypassing security and carrying out their plan.

"Then just take me to the Croissanterie del Pi," Angelica told the driver. The breakfast shop was three blocks from the civic square. She figured she could walk the rest of the way.

The taxi pulled away from the curb and headed north on Carrier d'Avinyo. The driver wasn't the talkative type, which suited Angelica. She contented herself to staring out the window at the sidewalk vendors who were setting up their wares for the day ahead.

The drive took less than ten minutes. Angelica stopped at

the breakfast shop for a cup of coffee, then sipped it as she made her way up the street to her destination.

The Barcelona Civic Square encompassed what, only a few years ago, had been squalid cluster of run-down shops and apartments. After the city had seized the land by right of eminent domain, they'd leveled the area and started from scratch, erecting a monolithic, five-story civic center that tried to meld the old and new along with the whimsical, amorphic architectural lines of Gaudi's Casa Battlo. Surrounding the center was a sprawling, cobblestoned plaza. Normally, the plaza was a crowded gathering spot teeming with thousands of sightseers and local residents idling away the long afternoons that broke up the Barcelona workday into two distinctive shifts. This day, however, traffic cones encircled the periphery of the plaza and armed soldiers stood guard near posted signs declaring the area off limits for the next four days. The area was eerily deserted save for a few scattered flocks of pigeons and work crews reinforcing the cones with concrete traffic barriers. More troops were positioned twenty yards south of the unfinished entrance to a subway station that, by year's end, would link the center with two different subway lines. The soldiers were guarding a four-lane driveway that led to the center's underground parking garage. Now and then they would scrutinize vehicles attempting to gain entry to the facility. Most were turned away, but a few catering trucks and cars driven by workers at the building were waved through after presenting credentials and undergoing a rigorous search that included the use of two bomb-sniffing dogs. The dogs were handled by two local police officers.

One of the officers was Julio Cristofer.

Angelica remained across the street from the plaza, pretending to show interest in a pair of bronze sculptures flanking the entrance to Hotel de la Portaisse, a modest two-star establishment where many of the journalists covering the NATO conference would be staying. Opening her purse, Angelica reached past her gun for a small camera and a tourist guide to Barcelona. By now the first, faint glimmer of dawn had appeared on the horizon, providing just enough daylight for Angelica to look convincing as she snapped a few photos of the statues. Once she'd finished, she flipped open the tourist book and thumbed to the index. By the time she'd tracked down a description of the statues, as well as the hotel, Cristofer had crossed the street. Angelica could see him out of the corner of her eye as he came up behind her. The officer walked past without acknowledging her other than offering a quick whisper that she was barely able to pick up.

"Seven twelve," he murmured.

Angelica committed the number to memory, then took a moment to finish reading the entry in the tourist book. Afterward, she put the book and camera away. Unlike the civic square, security was lax at the hotel, and Angelica had no problem charming her way past the doorman. By the time she reached the lobby, Cristofer was nowhere to be seen. Angelica crossed to the elevators, got in and pressed for the seventh floor. Room 712 was halfway down the hall. Angelica knocked on the door.

"It's open."

Angelica let herself in. Cristofer smiled at her from the living room. He'd already taken off his holster and was in the process of unbuttoning his shirt. He was a tall, handsome man in his late fifties with a full head of auburn hair.

"I almost didn't recognize you," he told Angelica.

"Let me take care of that."

Angelica took off her hat and sunglasses, then set her purse on the coffee table and moved into Cristofer's waiting embrace. Their lips met and, contrary to what she'd told Xavier Golato, Angelica clearly had no interest in withholding her affection.

"How's that, my love?" she purred in the officer's ear.

"Much better," Cristofer responded. "But let's do something about that hair."

He unclipped Angelica's barrette and grinned as her hair tumbled to her shoulders. Angelica helped undo the last buttons on Cristofer's shirt, then stroked his bare chest.

"You got your hands on everything?"

"Everything you asked for," Cristofer replied. "Blueprints of the civic center and the parking garage."

"And the schedule for all the night workers?"

Cristofer nodded. "It's all in the bedroom."

"Why am I not surprised?" Angelica laughed playfully, letting her fingers drop to Cristofer's waist. As she began to unfasten his belt buckle, she asked, "How long are you on break?"

"Long enough," Cristofer said. He took her hand and began to lead her to the bedroom. "Let's go and make ourselves comfortable."

CHAPTER TEN

Aeropuerto del Prat, twelve kilometres south of Barcelona

The sun was just beginning to cut through the early-morning haze that blanketed the airport as Rosario Blancanales stood on the edge of the tarmac near one of the airfield's remote hangars. He peered through the haze at the USAF B-1B Lancer taxiing down the runway toward him. Once the sleek bomber came to a stop, he ventured forward, eager to greet the first passenger to deplane.

"Lookin' pretty chipper, there, Ironman," Blancanales told his colleague as the men shook hands. "Especially for somebody who looked like death warmed over a couple days ago."

"Fever broke somewhere over the Atlantic," Lyons confided. "I was so soaked I needed to change clothes twice."

Lyons was now wearing a pair of lightweight chinos and a white T-shirt. He'd lost ten pounds to the flu but was still an imposing presence, standing over six feet tall and boasting a muscular physique to rival that of pro athletes half his age. He carried an overnight tote, and slung over his shoulder was a satchel filled with weapons and ammunition. Like Blancanales, who'd arrived in Barcelona a little over an hour before, he'd been cleared by the Spanish military to enter the country without having to contend with customs officials.

"What's the word on Phoenix Force?" Lyons asked as the men strode away from the jet.

"Except for Hawkins, they're still all pretty banged up," Blancanales reported. "The only real good news is James pulled through that second surgery in fine form."

"They got the bullet?"

Blancanales nodded. "Yep. I just got off the phone with T.J., and he says Cal's already talking about getting back into action."

"Fat chance," Lyons said.

"Yeah, well that's what everybody was saying about you," Blancanales told him. "Are you sure you're back up to fighting speed?"

"Hell, yes," Lyons insisted. "Look, the whole way out here I was either sleeping or downing fluids. I'm ready and rarin' to go."

"Spoken like a true Ironman."

"What about David?"

"He's still got amnesia."

"They do that CAT scan on him yet?"

Blancanales checked his watch. "Even as we speak. Probably be a while before they have any results."

Once the men entered the hangar, Lyons saw five Spanish soldiers in full camou gear attending to their gear near an L51 Galicia helicopter. A couple of the men glanced up at the Americans, then shifted their focus back to their gear. Along with MG-3 machine guns, the group was armed with a bulky 105/30 mm light gun.

"They're with UOE," Pol explained. "Unidades de Operations Especiales."

"My Spanish sucks," Lyons says, "but I think I heard 'special ops' in there somewhere."

Blancanales nodded. "They're Spain's version of Delta Force. Same outfit Phoenix Force got teamed up with."

"Looks like they're getting ready to party."

"Apparently we're close to pinpointing an ETA safehouse somewhere in the city," Blancanales reported. "Once we get the word, we're going in."

"All right," Lyons said. "That means I don't have to sit through some damn briefing."

"There's one other thing," Blancanales said. "A couple U.S. citizens just turned up dead over in some subdivision on the other side of the city. Man and a woman, both shot in the head. Word is they were here doing a nature documentary on the Avignon River for some cable channel."

"How do they figure into this?" Lyons wanted to know.

"We're not sure they do at this point," Pol said. "At first it looked like they were taken out by some street gang that's gotten into river pirating. Only thing is these gangbangers apparently tend to stick with switchblades or Saturday night specials. According to the coroner, the woman got whacked with a Walther pistol."

Lyons shrugged. "So maybe one of these punks got his hands on a bigger pop gun."

"Maybe," Blancanales conceded. "But the coroner says they also weren't killed where they were found. They were dumped there. What's more, it looked like the woman had been bound and gagged before she was shot."

"Could be a lot of explanations for that," Lyons said. "I still don't get the terrorist connection."

"Then try this on for size," Pol responded. "The woman was Patricia Brigada."

"Sorry," Lyons said. "That doesn't ring a bell."

"Her father's Patrick Brigada. Undersecretary of the Treasury. He's been the main force behind our freezing assets of ETA-related businesses with accounts in the U.S. The past couple months he's widened the net and gone after some BLM fronts, as well."

Lyons frowned. "And he's coming to this NATO conference?"

Blancanales nodded. "He's already here. He was going to meet with his daughter and see a few sights before the conference got under way. Instead, he's making arrangements to send her home in a box, along with her boyfriend."

"That's rough," said Lyons.

"So, needless to say, whether there's an ETA link or not, Washington wants the killers found."

"Got it," Lyons said.

The men were circling the helicopter when the cockpit door swung open and a tall, wiry American with close-cropped curly hair bounded to the ground, beaming at the sight of Lyons.

"Hey, hey!" he called out, "Look what the cat dragged in!"

"G-man," Lyons responded, trading high fives with the other man. "I figured you'd be around here somewhere."

Stony Man pilot Jack Grimaldi had been shuttling the men of Able Team and Phoenix Force on missions ever since the founding of the Sensitive Operations Group. Though slighter in build than the commandos, he knew his way around a weapon or two and had logged his share of time in the battlefield.

"Nifty little bird they've got here," Grimaldi said, gesturing at the Galicia. "I'd rather have an Apache, but it'll do in a pinch."

"Then I take it you'll be doing the honors once we fly out of here," Lyons said.

Grimaldi smiled. "Won a coin toss with their guy."

The three men continued to the mechanics' station and were helping themselves to coffee when one of the UOE commandos jogged over to them. Blancanales spoke with the man briefly, then nodded and turned to the others.

"Better make those coffees to go," he said. "We've found the safehouse."

CHAPTER ELEVEN

Barri Gotic Quarter, Barcelona

After she'd showered and changed back into her tourist garb, Angelica Rigo emerged from the bathroom, looking forward to the breakfast Cristofer had ordered up to the room.

"Smells wonderful," she said, eyeing the service tray set on the edge of the unmade bed.

Cristofer had his back to her. He'd already dressed and was on the phone. He held a hand up, gesturing for her to be quiet. Once he'd finished the call, he hung up and slowly turned. One look at the expression on his face and Angelica knew something was wrong.

"Do you know anything about an American couple that was shot somewhere around here yesterday?" Cristofer asked.

Angelica was stunned. She hadn't mentioned the shooting to Cristofer, figuring it was none of his business. Now that he'd put her on the spot, she wasn't sure how to respond. Her hesitation, however, told the officer all he needed to know.

"The woman," he said. "Did you know who she was?"

Angelica went to the bed and picked up a croissant, doing her best to appear nonchalant as she buttered it. "She was in the wrong place at the wrong time," she said, still not about to volunteer any more information than necessary. "We assumed they were CIA."

"Not quite," Cristofer said, "but you've got the right country. Her name was Patricia Brigada. Her father's with the U.S. Treasury Department."

Angelica closed her eyes a moment and cursed. Cristofer strapped on his holster and donned his service cap, then poured himself a cup of coffee. Whatever passion the two of them had shared a few moments had quickly fallen by the wayside. After he'd taken a sip, he broke the uneasy silence.

"Let's be grown up about this," he told her. He reached past the tray for an envelope filled with the money Angelica had delivered in exchange for the information about the civic center. "We're using each other here, and a nice roll in the sack here and there is icing on the cake. I don't have a problem with that, and you don't need to fill me in on everything your people are up to. As a matter of fact, the less I know, the better."

Angelica stared at Cristofer. "That's one thing I like about you. You know how to get to the point."

Cristofer let the compliment slide. "You've really created a situation for yourself with this one. You've stepped on the giant's toe. If you think you had your work cut out for you before, that's nothing compared to what you're going to find yourself up against from now on."

"I see that," Angelica responded evenly. She'd lost her appetite and set down the half-eaten croissant. "What's done is done. We'll deal with it."

Cristofer finished his coffee and checked the time.

"I need to get back to work."

"I'll leave first," Angelica said, grabbing her purse. She'd already put away the information Cristofer had gotten his hands on for her.

"Before you do—" Cristofer kissed Angelica, then stepped back and regarded her with a look of sadness mixed with regret "—I'll finish the job once you're ready, but this is our last rendezvous. I can't see you again."

Angelica nodded slowly. "I understand."

She was on her way out the door when Cristofer called out to her.

"Be careful."

By the time she reached the elevator, Angelica was trembling and fighting back tears. She wasn't sure why. Cristofer meant nothing to her. Like he'd said, they were using each other. And as for the woman, it was a stroke of bad luck. They'd get past it.

Angelica did her best to compose herself on the ride down to the lobby. Once she left the hotel, she turned her back to the civic center and walked the other way. Even in her disguise, she felt suddenly exposed and vulnerable. Wary now of taking a taxi, she instead made her way to the nearest subway station. The morning rush was under way, and she took comfort in the crowded lines. She took the uptown route to the Liceu exit, then returned to the streets. By now she was feeling a little better.

Two blocks from the loft complex, Angelica stopped at a park and lit a cigarette as she punched out a number on her cell phone. The phone was rigged with a scrambler, cutting down on the chances that her call might be intercepted. Her older brother picked up on the fourth ring.

Miguel had much to report. He related the close call in Facaros Pass, explaining that he and the others had managed to elude a helicopter search and make their way clear of the area. As for the tank, their brother was aboard along with Geraldo Carreon and they were taking it downriver toward Zaragoza, where efforts would be made to smuggle it back aboard some sort of trailer rig. A ground force of twelve men would follow the tank's course as closely as possible in a disguised panel truck, ready to lend whatever support might be needed.

"Have the authorities discovered the decoy tank yet?" Angelica wondered.

"Not yet," Miguel responded, "but I've spoken with our contacts and it sounds like they'll be sending down divers and a bathyscaphe later in the day. They will be lucky to find anything before sundown."

"That's not necessarily a good thing," Angelica responded. "Until they spot the decoy, they'll still be on the lookout for the tank."

"Don't worry, we'll play it safe," Miguel responded.

"What about the warheads?"

"They were delivered to Pamplona as planned," Miguel said. "I'm on my way there now to meet with the Iraqis."

"Good."

"How goes it in Barcelona?"

Angelica drew in a breath, then sighed and broke the news about identity of the woman she'd killed the day before. Miguel was furious at first, but quickly put things into perspective. In doing so, he ironically relied on the same phrase Angelica had used on Cristofer—a saying they'd heard their father use countless times when coming to grips with a setback in his life.

"What's done is done," Miguel said. "Now, tell me some good news."

"We have all the information on the civic center," Angelica said. "I could use Guillermo's expertise for planting the explosives."

"He's already on his way," Miguel said. "He'll fly there from Burgos, probably sometime tonight. I will pass along his arrival time once I have it."

"Good."

The siblings spoke a while longer, doing their best to assure themselves that they'd successfully dealt with the hurdles that had come their way and would still be able to carry out their objectives. After they ended the call, Angelica put the phone back in her purse, overcome with a sense of relief. Yes, they had run into a few complications, but things were, on the whole, going along better than could be expected. She thought back to one of her father's other favorite sayings. No guts, no glory. Well, she thought, it certainly took guts to try to pull off what they were attempting. Glancing heavenward, she imagined her father looking down on her with pride. She smiled to herself.

Angelica's gaze was still focused on the clouded sky overhead when a helicopter droned into view, flying low over the nearby rooftops. Angelica knew enough about aircraft to know it wasn't a civilian chopper, and as she watched, she saw the side door of the copter's hold slide open, revealing armed soldiers in camou gear. Worse yet, there could be no mistaking but that the men were headed for the industrial area where Angelica's colleagues were hiding out.

In an instant, Angelica's smile faded and her fleeting euphoria gave way to alarm. She grabbed for her cell phone and quickly dialed another number. The phone rang. And rang. And rang.

"Pick up!" Angelica seethed under her breath. "Pick up, Xavier, before it's too late!"

As Jack Grimaldi guided the L51 Galicia toward the industrial park, Carl Lyons stood alongside Rosario Blancanales in the open cabin and stared out at the loft building where the BLM was reportedly holed up. A bank of skylights rose at pitched angles, and several air-conditioning units and antennas cluttered the rooftop.

"Jack's not gonna be able to pull a Santa here," Lyons told Blancanales. "Hell, a pigeon would have trouble landing down there."

Blancanales nodded grimly. "You got that right."

Two of the UOE commandos standing alongside the Able Team commandos quickly conferred with each other, then began to feed a thick length of rope out through the open doorway. Another of the soldiers backtracked to the doorway leading to the cockpit. He knew just enough English to tell Grimaldi to get the chopper as close to the roof as he could and hold it steady.

"Looks like we're going to rappel our way down," Lyons surmised.

Blancanales stared down past the dangling rope. Down on the ground, an unmarked panel truck had just pulled into the parking lot next to the loft building. Pol had been on enough raids to know what the truck was carrying.

"Some ground support," he murmured. "That'll help matters."

Lyons, like Blancanales, had armed himself with a Colt M-4 outfitted with a submounted grenade launcher. He slung the rifle over his shoulder and was about to grab the rappel line when one of the Spaniards angrily waved him away.

"You go after us," the man admonished.

Lyons shrugged and stepped back. "Fine. Knock yourself out."

"Age before beauty," Blancanales wisecracked over the drone of the rotors.

Once the rope had been extended down to within a few yards of the roof, the lead soldier checked the pulley system and locked the line in place, then took hold and began to lower himself, hand over hand, toward the building. The other UOE troopers followed suit, forming a human chain along the length of rope. Down on the ground, meanwhile, the panel truck rolled to a stop twenty yards from the building. The rear doors flew open and more armed soldiers emerged, quickly fanning out.

Suddenly a blast of machine-gun fire burst up through one of the skylights, shattering glass. Two of the men on the rappel line screamed in agony as bullets dug into them. One soldier dropped lifelessly to the roof while the other fell through another of the skylights and disappeared from view.

"They're on some kind of scaffold!" Lyons shouted, spotting two BLM gunners through the broken glass. He leveled his M-4, but before he could get off a shot, a third UOE commando took a round to the head and dropped from the rappel line. He landed on one of the antennas, impaling himself on the upright shaft. He flailed briefly, then went limp, dangling at an unnatural angle like a half-toppled scarecrow.

Up in the chopper's cockpit, Grimaldi saw what was happening and quickly banked the Galicia away from the rooftop. Blancanales, meanwhile, dropped to the cabin floor and reached out to the surviving Spanish commando. As he pulled the man back up into the cargo hold, Lyons fired away with his M-4, dropping the two gunmen on the scaffold. Another terrorist quickly replaced him, however, and fired back, skimming the chopper's fuselage.

"I think I saw a fire escape on the south side," Lyons shouted over his shoulder to Grimaldi. "Let's try that!"

"I'm on it!" the pilot responded.

As the Galacia drifted away from the rooftop, Lyons emptied the last rounds from his M-4 at the skylights, then quickly reloaded. Beside him, Blancanales bounded back to his feet along with the remaining Spaniard. Glancing at the ground, the men saw a handful of bedraggled-looking men fleeing from a side doorway, hands raised high in the air as they encountered soldiers looking to enter the building.

"Something tells me those aren't the guys we're looking for," Lyons said.

"I think you're right," Blancanales said. "Squatters is more like it."

"If that's the case," Lyons said, "they have to be wondering why we thought we'd need this much firepower to force an eviction."

Once the Galicia had cornered the building, Lyons saw that he'd been right about the fire escape. It clung to the south facing like a metallic vine, extending from the second story up to a window on the top floor. Lyons unlocked the pulley and fed out another ten yards of rope. When he grabbed the line and began to lower himself, he was spared the assault the Spaniards had faced earlier.

Blancanales wanted to make sure they weren't taken by surprise again, so before he climbed out of the cabin, he pointed out the MG-3 machine gun lying on the floor and told the surviving Spaniard, "Keep us covered from the air."

The Spaniard was in shock and Blancanales had to repeat the command before the soldier nodded and began to unfold the MG-3's stand so he'd be ready to fire should any enemy forces appear on the roof.

Once Lyons was within a few yards of the fire escape, he let go of the rappel line and dropped to the landing, then veered to one side, giving Blancanales room to land beside him. As the chopper pulled away, Lyons tried the window. It was locked from the inside, so he shattered the glass with the butt of his rifle and reached inside to flip the latch. He yanked the window open and crawled into the building. Blancanales followed.

They found themselves in a dark, narrow corridor. They weren't alone. Four men were running toward a stairwell at the far end of the hallway, and a fifth terrorist stood before the freight elevator. He turned on Lyons and Blancanales, aiming his 5.56 mm FAMAS subgun. He and Lyons fired simultaneously.

Bullets bore into the ceiling and walls around the Able Team commandos. Lyons's rounds were more on the mark, ripping through the other gunman's chest. He keeled to one side, slamming into the elevator gate, then slumping to the floor. That didn't put an end to the terrorists' resistance, however. At the end of the hallway, one of the Basques glared hatefully at Blancanales and Lyons, then unpinned a grenade clutched in his fist.

"Down!" Lyons shouted to Blancanales.

Both men dived to the floor.

In his haste, the terrorist lobbed the grenade too high and it glanced off the ceiling halfway down the hall, well short of its intended targets. The corridor rocked with a deafening explosion as the grenade went off, blowing out the walls around it and bringing down a section of the false ceiling. Smoke and dust began to cloud the hallway, obscuring Lyons's and Blancanales's view of the fleeing terrorists. Their next move was obvious, however.

"They're heading downstairs!" Lyons shouted as he scrambled to his feet. His ears were ringing from the explosion and he could barely hear himself.

Blancanales was right behind him as he charged down the corridor. They'd made it as far as the elevator when a second explosion rocked the building. This time the blast came from one of the lower floors. More smoke began to roil up through the elevator shaft.

"They took out the elevator," Lyons guessed.

He and Blancanales pried open the elevator gates. The rising smoke quickly engulfed them, but they were able to see that there was nothing in the shaft but the elevator's taut cables. Across the way, however, they could see the loft through the elevator's other gate, which had been jarred opened by one of the explosions.

"Go ahead and check it out," Lyons told Blancanales, reaching through the smoke for the cables. "I'm going to see if I can get down a floor."

"Got it."

Lyons grabbed hold of the cables and began to lower himself down the smoke-filled shaft. Blancanales waited until his teammate had disappeared into the smoke, then crouched a moment at the edge of the shaft gauging the distance to the other side of the shaft. However far it was, Blancanales knew it'd take one hell of jump to avoid coming up short and falling down the shaft.

In a few seconds, the smoke had thinned, giving him a better view of the shaft. He crouched a little lower, drew in a breath, then exhaled as he lunged forward, arms stretched out before him. He might have made it all the way across if he hadn't struck one of the elevator cables with his left thigh. It was only a glancing blow, but it was enough to foil his attempt. Instead of reaching the opening, he crashed chest first into the shaft wall just below it. Fortunately, his reflexes were quick enough for him to grab hold of the other gate, breaking his fall. With considerable effort, he was able to wriggle his way up to the opening and then into the loft.

Before him, two men lay dead on the floor near the scaffolding, one a downed BLM gunman, the other the Spanish commando who'd fallen through the skylight. A third man lay atop the uppermost scaffold, his right arm and leg dangling over the side. There was no sign of life save for a few rats who'd been driven out into the open by all the commotion. They scampered about the base of the scaffold, bounding over the bodies of the two men on the floor.

Smoke was beginning to fill the loft, but it wasn't coming from either of the earlier explosions. Apparently the Basques had started a fire before fleeing from the loft, and flames were quickly devouring a heap of fast-food wrappers and newspapers set near the scaffolding. Blancanales went to investigate, hoping there might be some valuable documents worth rescuing from the blaze. The fire was growing too fast, however, and the intense heat drove him back. He quickly surveyed the loft, but there didn't seem to be anything worth salvaging, so he quickly backtracked to the elevator.

Before he could reach it, however, he was knocked to the floor by the force of a third explosion. Plaster from the ceiling showered down on him. He shook off the debris and scrambled to his feet. The blast had come from the stairwell area a floor down from him. He quickly slung his carbine over his shoulder and reached into the elevator shaft. Grabbing the cables, he followed Lyons's route down to the next level. Lyons was there waiting for him, having fired a grenade round from his M-4.

"I think I got a few more of them," he told Blancanales.

The two men stormed down the corridor to the far stairwell. The grenade had blasted through the outer wall, and they could see sky through the opening. Two men lay dead at the top of the steps, half-buried in debris. Another lay wounded on the landing, surrounded by trash. It was Xavier Golato. The bald man groped through the garbage for his handgun, but before he could reach it Lyons bounded down the steps and overcame him.

Blancanales rushed past them to the next floor. By now the ground troops had made their way up to the same level, and Blancanales had to duck back into the stairwell when they fired at him, mistaking him for one of the terrorists. He shouted to them in Spanish, telling them to hold their fire.

For the first time since the siege began, the building fell silent. Blancanales could hear the chopper outside the building as he backtracked to where Lyons had hauled Golato to his feet.

"They set the loft on fire," Blancanales told Lyons. "We'd better get out of here."

"Fine by me," Lyons said.

Moments later, the ground forces reached the stairwell. Blancanales passed along the warning, and together they hurriedly made their way down to the ground floor, taking their prisoner with them.

Once outside, Lyons and Blancanales glanced up and saw smoke pouring out of the top floor of the building.

"Not much chance of tracking down any evidence now," Blancanales said.

"No shit," said Lyons. "I take it they didn't have a shredder."

As the Galicia floated down toward a patch of asphalt near

the panel truck, Blancanales eyed Golato, then told Lyons, "He doesn't match up with the mug shots of the Rigo family."

"Figures," Lyons said. "That would've made things too easy for us."

"Well, if they're still inside, maybe we'll smoke them out."

ANGELICA RIGO KNEW it was foolhardy to approach the burning shell of the loft building, but she couldn't help herself. She had to find out if any of her men had managed to escape.

Police had already arrived on the scene had begun to cordon off the area, but they were hard-pressed to hold back the throng of onlookers drawn by the commotion. Angelica pulled the brim of her hat lower as she waded into the throng. A pang of dread crept over her as she watched flames pour out of shattered windows on the top three floors. It was a windless day, and grim-looking clouds of black smoke rose up from all sides of the building. Soon a pair of fire trucks howled their way onto the scene, but Angelica doubted they would be able to do much. She suspected the upper floors would collapse shortly, taking the rest of the building down with them. The only hope for Xavier Golato and the rest of her men was that they'd somehow managed to reach the ground floor and sneak out ahead of those who'd come to raid the building. And even that hope began to fade as Angelica inched closer to the head of the crowd and saw the number of troops encircling the building. She wasn't surprised to see members of the UOE, but she was taken aback by the sight of two men who looked to be Americans, or at least members of some NATO force. Cristofer was right; they'd stepped on the giant's toes.

Angelica was weighing the repercussions when she caught

a glimpse of a prisoner being escorted to the panel truck by the Americans and several UOE commandos.

"Xavier!" Angelica whispered to herself. He was still alive!

More curiosity-seekers were flocking around the building, and Angelica had to jockey her way through the crowd to keep an eye on Golato. He was directed into the back of the panel truck, and after the two Americans had followed him inside, the doors were closed and the vehicle began to pull away, threading its way past the firefighters and police. Nightsticks raised, the police warned spectators to back away and let the truck by. Once it reached the street, the truck was flanked by a convoy of motorcycle cops as it sped from the scene. At the same time, another police car approached from the other direction, and as it drew closer, Angelica saw that it was the Barcelona Police Department's K-9 squad. Cristofer was behind the wheel. Angelica guessed he'd been called on the chance his dogs would be needed to sniff out the loft for explosives.

Angelica was watching Cristofer pull to a stop alongside the other police vehicles when there was a loud, sudden rumbling behind her. She turned and saw a large portion of the loft building's west wall break away from the main structure. The ground troops quickly scattered clear as the wall collapsed upon itself and crashed to the ground with so much force that a cloud of smoke and soot billowed toward the crowd like some malevolent fog. There were screams and shouts, and Angelica was elbowed and jostled as the crowd around her fled from the onrushing cloud.

Angelica took advantage of the distraction and cut sideways through the throng, making her way toward the parked police cruisers. Regardless of what Cristofer had told her earlier, she had to see him.

JULIO CRISTOFER had known early on that it was a mistake to have gotten involved with Angelica Rigo, but by then it had been too late. The money the BLM was throwing his way was too hard to turn down, as was the sex between them; he'd never known a woman who could make love with such passion. But with Americans nosing around the city, enough was enough. He'd been relieved when Angelica had agreed that they should stop seeing each other. She could have made it difficult for him. After all, one anonymous phone call to internal affairs and he would be ruined. And that might have been the least dire of possible consequences. He suspected the BLM routinely executed allies who had outlived their usefulness, and despite their amorous times together, who was to say Angelica wouldn't turn around and put a hit on him now that he'd said he wanted out? That, of course, was still not out of the question, and at least for the next few days Cristofer knew he'd have to watch his back even more than usual.

As he helped his partner unload the dogs from the back seat of the squad car, he thought it was ironic that so soon after his tryst with Angelica he'd find himself here at her base headquarters. He doubted she'd had time to get back before the raid, so he was sure she hadn't been caught up in the shootout. The last thing he expected, however, was to spot her in the crowd flocked around the crumbling ruins of the loft building. And yet there she was, three rows back in the mob swelling its way toward him and the dogs. He couldn't believe it.

Cristofer handed his leash to his partner, Trabor Nadra, a young man half his age. "Go ahead and take the dogs," he said. "I'll help keep this crowd in check."

Nadra nodded and led the dogs away. The animals were jittery, and he had to hold the leashes tightly to keep them from lunging at the crowd.

Drawing his nightstick, Cristofer advanced on the mob. "Move back! Keep this area clear!"

For the most part the crowd complied, turning back on itself. Angelica, however, inched forward, working her way to the front. Cristofer made his way to her. Once he was close enough, he whispered, "What are you doing here? Are you out of your mind?"

"I know what you said," she replied, keeping her voice low. "But I need your help!"

"Here?" Cristofer said. "Now?"

"Please!" Angelica pleaded.

Cristofer was furious. He wanted nothing more than to turn his back on her and walk away, and yet he found himself glancing around to make sure none of the other police were watching, then grabbing Angelica while shouting at her, "All right, you! You're under arrest!"

He hauled her clear of the mob and led her brusquely over to his squad car, whispering to her, "Play along!"

Cristofer motioned for her to stand spread-eagled against the side of the car, then leaned close as he pretended to frisk her.

"They took Xavier hostage!" Angelica whispered back urgently.

"What do you expect me to do about it?"

"I can't let them interrogate him!"

Cristofer finished frisking Angelica, then whirled her around and eyed her savagely. "This is more about him being your lover," he accused.

"I need your help," Angelica insisted. "I need to free him somehow!"

"I can't help you!" Cristofer snapped. "You shouldn't have come here. Now go, before somebody recognizes you!"

"You need to help me," Angelica told him.

"I can't!" Again Cristofer glanced around. A handful of police officers stood less than twenty yards away, but they were busy with the crowd and had their backs turned to him. He looked back at Angelica and told her, "You can walk away and nobody will be the wiser. Write off your boyfriend and move on!"

Angelica's eyes hardened. "Don't force my hand, Julio."

There it was. Cristofer didn't have to ask her to elaborate. He knew a threat when he heard one. He knew, too, that Angelica wasn't bluffing.

"The Americans have him now," Cristofer told him. "What do you expect me to do?"

"You're resourceful," Angelica told her. "You'll think of something. And I'll make it worth your while."

Cristofer stared hard at the woman, trying to muster his resolve. It was no use, however. Angelica had him where she wanted him, and they both knew it. Cristofer cursed himself for having gotten into this situation, then grudgingly told the woman, "I'll do what I can."

CHAPTER TWELVE

Gamuso Armorers, outskirts of Zamudio, Spain

Located in the mountains some twenty miles from Bilbao, Gamuso Armorers was an eight-building complex spread out over twenty acres. Half of those twenty acres—a parched, isolated valley parcel bisected by a branch of the Vizcaya River—was used as the weapon maker's proving grounds. It was there that the FSAT-50 amphibious battle tank had been seized by the Basque separatists two nights earlier. The seizure had taken place at the river's edge, and when T. J. Hawkins arrived at the site along with an investigatory party that included UOE commander Raul Cordero and two members of Spain's Agency of Military Intelligence, the ground was still littered with bullet casings and mottled with pools of dried blood. The tank's tread marks were visible, as well, trailing all the way down from the manufacturing plant—a hundred yards uphill from the valley—to the embankment of the river.

"By the time I brought reinforcements down, they had already taken control of the tank and gone into the river," explained Oswaldo Lopez, a middle-aged member of Gamuso's security detail. He pointed toward a gorge at the end of the valley and went on. "Just around the bend there is a service road. From the looks of it, they had a truck waiting there and loaded the tank onto it. We searched the area by helicopter, but..." The man shrugged and raised his palms into the air. "Nothing."

"Obviously they tried to transport it overland," Cordero said, "and when they learned about the roadblock at Facaros Pass, they detoured to the lake, thinking they could take to the water again and sneak past us. Something went wrong and the tank blew up on them."

"A terrible loss," Lopez said, "but better that than having them be able to use it."

"We have divers searching through the wreckage at the lake," said AMI Senior Agent Gregorio Valentino, a short, wiry man in his early fifties. "It looks as if they had the tank concealed inside the shell of a mobile home. Very ingenious."

The men were speaking in their native tongue. Hawkins, who knew little Spanish and no Basque at all, could only stand by and listen impassively. He'd come to come to Zamudio without the other members of Phoenix Force, who were being treated for their injuries at Santa Maria Regional Hospital, a facility located just outside Bilbao. It had taken some badgering for him and Cordero to join the investigators, and Valentino, who already felt his territory was being encroached upon by the CIA and NATO intelligence, had retaliated by conducting the interview with Lopez in Euskara. Hawkins felt the older man was being petty, but he'd played along patiently thus far. Cordero, in turn, had kept him abreast of things, translating at least the gist of what was being said.

Once he'd been filled in on latest exchange, Hawkins glanced at Valentino, then told Cordero, "Ask him if the divers have found the warheads yet."

Valentino clearly understood what Hawkins was asking but continued to force Cordero to play middleman, waiting for the commando to translate the question into Basque, then responding in kind.

"He says no, they haven't," Cordero told Hawkins afterward, "but they're still looking."

Hawkins grinned back at Valentino and told him, *Gracias, muchacho.*

Valentino's partner smirked, but the senior agent wasn't amused. He turned away from Hawkins and preoccupied himself for a few moments taking in the surrounding valley. The Spanish militia had stationed armed guards around the site the morning after the raid, and a dozen men were still positioned at strategic points along the river. They watched the investigatory team with bored detachment, assault rifles slung.

"If the grounds here had been as well guarded the night of the raid," Valentino finally remarked, turning his focus back to Lopez, "we probably wouldn't be in this predicament."

"Hindsight is golden," Lopez retorted. "And, just so you know, we had a security detail down here for the test. They were the first to die when the raid began."

"And the BLM, where did they attack from?" Valentino queried.

"I've already answered these questions a dozen times at least to a dozen other investigators," Lopez protested. "Don't any of you people take notes?"

"You know how it is," Valentino replied calmly. "Everyone likes to conduct their own investigation. Now it's our turn. So, if you don't mind..."

Lopez fumed and paused to light a cigarette. Cordero took

advantage of the break to translate for Hawkins. Afterward, the Phoenix Force commando shook his head.

"It sounds like America hasn't cornered the market on bureaucracy."

"There's something to be said for a friendly rivalry between agencies," Cordero countered. "Competition can force people to put forth the extra effort that sometimes makes a difference."

"Maybe so," Hawkins muttered, "but for every time it helps, there are ten times that you wind up wasting manpower and giving an edge to the enemy."

Cordero shrugged. "We live in an imperfect world."

"You can say that again."

Once he'd lit his cigarette, Lopez blew smoke Valentino's way and said, "All right. You want to know how the raid went down. I'll tell you, as best I know.

"Except for here at the attack site, we found no vehicle tracks or footprints other than those made by our own men. So we are thinking they were lying in wait here on the river, probably in a boat or a raft. They waited for the tank to come to them, then they made their move. For our men, it was like stumbling into an ambush. Of all those killed, nearly half went down without firing a shot—it happened that quickly."

"To stage such an ambush, don't you think they would need some help from the inside?" Valentino wondered.

"I've already explained that a dozen times, too!" Lopez snapped.

"Make it thirteen," Valentino said.

"All personnel at Gamuso have been interrogated and found to be beyond suspicion, with only three exceptions," Lopez said tiredly. "There are two men who were working at the depot where the warheads were kept who disappeared immediately after the brownout. They are still missing, so, yes, it is likely they had a hand in the theft."

"And the third person?" Valentino asked.

"Timo Ibanez," Lopez said, "who's with our research-and-development team. He is more knowledgeable about the FSAT-50 than anyone. He had already checked out for the day by the time of the raid, and he failed to report for work yesterday. His home has been searched, and his relatives are being questioned as to his whereabouts."

"And we are looking into his cell phone records," Valentino said.

Lopez threw his cigarette into the dirt and glared at Valentino. "Then you do know all this information already!"

"It never hurts to double-check," Valentino said.

Lopez spit at Valentino's feet and made an obscene gesture with his right hand, then turned and stormed off.

Hawkins turned to Cordero and murmured, "I don't think you need to translate that."

"I'll go see if I can calm him," Cordero told Valentino. He jogged off after Lopez, leaving Hawkins with Valentino and the other AMI official, whose name was Martin Zamara.

"Excuse us a moment," Zamara told Hawkins, speaking up for the first time.

He led Valentino from the American, then told his superior, "I wasn't aware that we were running a check on phone records."

Valentino nodded. "I put through the order just before we came down here, while you were off talking to the people at the munitions depot."

"I see," Zamara replied.

"Is there a problem?" Valentino asked.

"No," Zamara said. "It is just that I am on good terms with the leader of the team that handles cell traces. I was thinking that perhaps I should talk to him, to make sure that we are given priority."

"I already told him as much," Valentino responded.

"Perhaps," Zamara said, "but there is priority, and then there is top priority, if you catch my meaning."

Valentino shrugged. "If you think it will expedite matters, feel free. I don't think we'll get much more out of our Mr. Lopez, anyway."

"I'll make the call right now," Zamara said.

The junior officer, a native of Bilbao who had entered AMI from the ranks of the military, once again excused himself to Hawkins and strode off toward the river. Once there, he turned his back to Valentino and the others and pulled out his cell phone. Like most cells used by AMI, the phone was equipped with a scrambler to reduce the chances of calls being intercepted or traced. He dialed, then stared out at the river as he waited for an answer. After six rings, someone came on the other line. It wasn't anyone from the Agency of Military Intelligence, however.

It was Miguel Rigo's right-hand man, Zacharias Brinquel.

Zamara quickly identified himself, then told the other man, "Have you reached the safehouse yet?"

"No," Brinquel replied, "but I should be there in a few minutes. Have you heard about what happened in Barcelona?"

"No," Zamara said. "What happened?"

Brinquel quickly told the AMI officer about the raid on the loft building and Xavier Golato's apprehension by the authorities. "We have a mole with the Barcelona police," he concluded. "He's been trying to reach you for some help pulling strings to get Xavier released."

"I've been out in the field all day," Zamara said. "I'll do what I can, though. For now, though, we have another situation here in Navarra. Concerning Timo Ibanez, the technician from Gamuso."

"What about him?"

"As soon as you reach the safehouse," Zamara told Brinquel, "check with Ibanez and see if he has his cell phone with him."

"And if he has it?"

"Tell him not to use it under any circumstances," Zamara said. "Tell him not to so much as turn it on."

CHAPTER THIRTEEN

White House briefing room, Washington D.C.

"This is definitely good news," Admiral Reese Solter remarked, glancing over the computer dispatch being passed around the room.

"It would certainly appear that way," the President replied. His voice, however, lacked Solter's conviction.

The dispatch continued to make its way around the room. The entire Joint Chiefs of Staff was on hand, save for Army General Howard Wadsworth, who had begged off in favor of seeing through a troop exercise down the coast in Norfolk. As was customary, Hal Brognola was sitting in on the meeting in his long-standing capacity as special presidential adviser from the Justice Department. Of course, his real purpose was to steer any decision-making in a way that would best utilize the services of SOG. Before entering the meeting, he'd already conferred with Barbara Price back at Stony Man Farm and had been apprised of Lyons's and Blancanales's part in the raid on the BLM safehouse in Barcelona. Neither man was mentioned in the dispatch, which credited Spanish UOE commandos with taking down the cell purportedly behind plans to wreak havoc on the upcoming NATO conference. Like the President, he was concerned by the relative ease with which the BLM had been dealt with over the past two days. It didn't smell right to him.

CIA Director Mosely Pearson shared the sentiment. The oldest man in the group, Pearson was still an imposing presence, his six-foot-four, two-hundred-pound frame tautly filling out his tailored, charcoal-gray suit. He rubbed his fingers through his silver hair as he skimmed the dispatch, then passed it on to Keith Jarlewski of the Department of Defense.

"It's all too pat for me," Pearson boomed in his deep, stentorian voice. "I've dealt with these Basques in the past, and they're crafty bastards. It'd be just like them to sacrifice a few pawns hoping to get us to drop our guard."

"I have to disagree," said Jean Viraque, the only non-American in the group. As head of NATO intelligence, he'd been invited by the President to sit in on the meeting. He was a short, plainly dressed man with small eyes and large, bushy mustache. He stared across the table at Pearson and went on, "We've had our share of dealings with the BLM, as well as their ETA counterparts, and, with the exception of a few dealings with the IRA a few years back, they've restricted themselves to a strictly domestic agenda. And their expertise doesn't go much beyond car-bombings and your run-of-the mill assassinations of local politicians. When it comes to going up against NATO and trying to make use of nuclear warheads and high-tech tanks, I think they're simply out of their league. They have no experience in these kinds of matters."

"There's always a first time," Pearson said. "And, as you well know, nearly every terrorist organization starts out small but eventually sets its sights on bigger targets."

"Yes, yes," Viraque conceded. "But let's keep our perspective. True, the BLM was crafty enough getting its hands on the tank and these warheads, but look at what has happened since. First they were trounced soundly in the mountains outside Bilbao. Then, that same night, they had the tank blow up on them, and most likely the warheads, as well."

"The divers still haven't found any trace of the warheads in that lake," Pearson reminded the Frenchman.

"Not yet they haven't," Viraque responded. "But they have at least another two days of searching to go. I'm confident the bombs will be accounted for."

Brognola glanced at the President and saw him shake his head as he scribbled notes on the pad set out before him.

"To continue," Viraque went on, gesturing at the dispatch, "we've clearly knocked out the cell that was planning to carry out the attack on the NATO conference. That is three strikes against them, and, as you Americans say at your baseball games, 'Three strikes and you're out.'"

"Unless the catcher misses the ball," Brognola corrected.

Viraque stared at Brognola. "What is your point?"

"My point," Brognola said, "is that if we miss something or give them a chance to regroup, they might still carry out the attack."

"Not likely," Viraque said.

"What I think my colleague is suggesting," the President said intervening, "is that we consider postponing the conference and moving it to another country. And I still think it's an idea worth considering."

Viraque shrugged. "We've already been through this. I have already spoken with Prime Minster LaMierre, who in turn has spoken to most of the other delegates. They refuse to be intimidated by these upstarts. They intend to have the conference go on as scheduled."

"Then I'll just need to have a talk with Mr. LaMierre," the President responded.

Viraque smiled. "As you wish. But I would remind you that the United States has only one vote in this matter. By my count, even if you change LaMierre's mind, you will still be vastly outnumbered."

The President smiled back at Viraque. "Then I guess I'll have to make more than just one phone call."

There were a few suppressed chuckles throughout the room. Viraque's face reddened and he looked down at his notes, no longer in the mood to contend with the others. Marine General Carson Medavoy, head of the Armed Forces, as well as the Joint Chiefs of Staff, waited for the murmuring to subside, then spoke up for the first time in several minutes.

"I believe this is the last item on our agenda, gentlemen," he said. "Unless anyone else has some other business to bring up, I move we adjourn."

Secretary of State Izzy Donnells raised his hand. "There is one matter," he said. "Concerning the murder of my colleague's daughter."

"Of course," the President said.

He turned to Pearson and Brognola. "Anything new to report?"

"We're still investigating," Pearson responded.

"Actually," Brognola said, "there is a new development." He turned to the CIA director and whispered, "I just got word as I was flying in. You probably have a message waiting for you."

Pearson grinned. This wasn't the first time Brognola had scooped him, and he doubted it would be the last. Most other heads of intelligence would likely have taken affront, but although Pearson was not privvy to the doings of SOG, he'd benefited enough from Stony Man assistance in assignments over the years that he felt he could afford to be magnanimous.

"Let 'er rip," he told Brognola.

Brognola told Donnells and the others, "I'm sure you all know that the undersecretary's daughter was killed outside Barcelona yesterday in what at first appeared to be a gang-related shooting. It's since come to our attention that the woman was killed with a 9 mm round from a Walther pistol. It's not the sort of weapon the gangsters there tend to use."

"Maybe they've had an upgrade," Admiral Solter wise-cracked. "Like the ETA with this tank."

"Let me finish," Brognola said. He glanced at the computer message he'd received from Aaron Kurtzman while en route to Washington earlier. "We've just received coroner's reports on some of the men killed at the Gamuso proving grounds during the seizure of the supertank. Two of them were gunned down by a 9 mm Walther."

"The same gun?" Donnells asked.

"We don't have ballistics reports yet," Brognola admitted, "but it's the same make of gun. Granted, it could be mere coincidence, but if there's a connection, we're looking at the BLM being responsible for executing an American citizen."

Pearson turned to Viraque. "Which would mean they're widening their agenda beyond just trying to carve out some land to call their own."

"Whatever the case," Brognola concluded, "I don't care how soundly we've trounced the Basques since they grabbed those warheads and that tank. I still say they're out there somewhere and that they've got a lot of fight left in them."

Rio Ebna, forty miles south of Pamplona, Spain

LIKE THOUSANDS of other wandering Basque nomads who had forsaken poor-paying jobs in small villages in favor of life in the wild, Alberto Birstas and Willem Franco made a point never to stray too far from the nearest river. The river, after all, wasn't only a place to bathe, but it was also a source of food and drinking water. Early that morning, after filling their canteens and starting a fire at their campsite along the banks of the Rio Ebna, Birstas and Franco had assembled their fishing poles and tossed lines into the gentle current. They'd picked a good spot, because in the time it took each man to smoke two hand-rolled cigarettes, they'd pulled five gleaming trout from the river.

Now, while the gutted fish sizzled in a frying pan set over the dying embers of the fireplace, the two men stripped down to their skivvies and dived into the cold, rushing water. Once they'd washed themselves, they lapsed into their daily contest of seeing who could stay the longest underwater. The loser would have to clean the skillet once they'd had breakfast.

The men had been evenly matched until a week ago, when Birstas had struck upon a winning strategy and beaten his friend four days in a row. It was a simple enough ploy: Birstas would merely swim until he reached the river bottom, where he would take hold of a sunken tree or some other object and force himself to stay put until he felt his lungs were about to burst. By the time he surfaced, he would inevitably find Franco headed toward shore, cursing his bad luck and wondering aloud how his friend had managed to beat him yet again.

This day, Franco was determined to find out. Instead of merely taking a deep breath and dropping below the waterline for as long as he could, he opened his eyes once he was underwater and began to swim after Birstas. The water grew colder and darker the deeper they went. Soon, he saw his friend grab hold of a long metal pipe rising up from the depths at a slight angle.

So that was his secret!

Two could play that game, Franco thought to himself, diving lower into the river behind Birstas. He figured he'd hold on to the pipe, as well, and even the playing field. Then they would see who truly had the strongest lungs!

Before Franco could catch up with his friend, however, Birstas suddenly recoiled from the pipe and began to swim away from it, a look of horror on his face. Spotting Franco, he gestured wildly toward the surface, then moved past the other man, clawing at the water as if trying to pull himself up a rope in his haste to flee the depths. Puzzled, Franco stayed in place and stared toward the river bottom. Then, suddenly, he, too, was overcome with fear. Before his eyes, the shaft was rising up from the river bottom toward him, and for the first time Franco realized it wasn't a pole at all, but rather the barrel of a cannon. And it was more than a mere cannon; it was attached to a large and dull-colored turret.

A tank!

Franco stared at the FSAT-50 in disbelief. He had no idea how the tank had floundered into the river, but by all rights he knew it should have sunk to the river bottom and stayed there. And yet there it was, rising toward him as if it were no heavier than a piece of driftwood that had dislodged itself in the current. How could it be?

Terrified, Franco turned from the tank and swam quickly toward the surface, letting the air escape from his lungs. The moment his head was above the water, he gasped and swam after Birstas, who was already halfway to the riverbank.

"Wait for me!" he cried out.

But his friend was in no mood to remain in the water any longer. Once he'd reached the embankment, he scrambled ashore and rushed toward the campsite, where he began to hurriedly gather his belongings. The trout were ready to be turned, but food was the last thing on the nomad's mind.

"Hurry!" he shouted to Franco as his friend emerged from the river.

"What was that?" Franco cried, rolling his things inside his sleeping bag. "It couldn't be a tank!"

"I don't know," Birstas responded, "and I don't want to find out!"

The men were hurriedly pulling on their clothes when they heard a loud splashing behind them. Turning, they stared dumbfounded as the FSAT-50 rose into view and began to roll onto the embankment like some one-horned beast.

Shrieking, the men scrambled away from their campsite, leaving behind the now smoking frying pan. A meadow stretched away from the river and the men bolted through the tall grass, desperate to reach the winding, two-lane dirt road that ran parallel to the Ebna. Birstas was overjoyed when he drew near to the road and saw a truck bearing the insignia of Spain's Forestry and Agriculture Ministry. The vehicle had just pulled off to the shoulder and the driver was staring his way.

"Help!" Birstas shouted, waving his arms frantically. A few steps behind him, Franco echoed the plea.

The driver turned away from the men for a moment, then opened his door and stepped out of the truck. He was carrying a Mossberg 835 Ulti-Mag shotgun.

"That won't be enough!" Franco shouted. "There's a tank down there! It came up out of the river and..."

Franco's voice trailed off and he ground to a sudden stop alongside Birstas, who'd also frozen in his tracks when the driver had raised the shotgun into firing position. He was aiming at them.

Before the nomads could react, the driver pulled the trigger. The shotgun's blast echoed across the river as Birstas took the round in the stomach. He doubled over and dropped to his knees, spilling his bloody, riddled entrails into the tall meadow grass. Franco started to reach out but saw that his friend was beyond help. Casting aside his bedroll, he dived to the ground and began to crawl on his belly through the grass, hoping against hope there was somewhere out of this nightmare that had befallen him. The bending grass gave him away, however, and he hadn't gone far when the 12-gauge barked again. He grunted as buckshot plowed through the back of his skull, then collapsed, dead in the grass.

As the driver strode through the grass toward his victims, ten more BLM separatists piled out of the truck's cargo hold. Some paused to stretch while the others made their way toward the river, where the FSAT-50 had come to a stop a few yards from the dead men's campfire.

Jacque Rigo was the first one out of the tank. He remained on the turret, his 9 mm Walther aimed at the hatch. Rey Hespera and Matteo Bainz crawled out next, followed by Geraldo Carreon.

"Climb down, then put your hands on your head," Rigo told the two prisoners.

Hespera and Bainz meekly followed orders. The tank's commander had been pistol-whipped at some point, and the right side of his face was swollen. Once Rigo and Carreon had clambered down to the ground, they were joined by the truck's driver, whose name was Salvador Jobe. Indicating the campsite, Jobe told Jacque, "A couple vagrants. I took care of them."

Jacque stared past Jobe and saw Birstas and Franco being carried toward him by some of the men from the truck.

"Weigh them down and toss them in the river," he told the men. "And while you're at it..."

He took aim with his Walther and calmly shot Hespera through the heart, then shifted his aim and killed the tank's gunner, as well. The men dropped to the ground alongside each other, just missing the campfire.

Jobe regarded the bodies, then glanced up at Jacque. "I take it you and Geraldo had a chance to try your hand at the controls," he said flatly.

Jacque nodded. "All those weeks of preparation paid off."

"Did you bring more fuel?" Carreon asked Salvador. "We're running low."

Salvador nodded. "Back in the truck. I'll get it for you."

"In a minute," Jacque interjected, reaching over and pulling the frying pan from the campfire. "Let's eat first."

CHAPTER FOURTEEN

Pamplona, Spain

It had been dark when Miguel set out from the BLM's mountain hideaway in the mountains near Faracos Pass. Driving a hot-wired Land Rover stolen from the closest national campground, he'd driven the country back roads to Pamplona. Once there, he parked on a side street just off Vanguas Y Miranda, two blocks from the city's main bus terminal. The morning sun was up but still low in the sky, cloaking the streets in long, dark shadows. Miguel was reminded of paintings by DeChirico he'd seen during a trip to the museum in his childhood. In the paintings, however, he recalled the streets evoking a sense of dark foreboding. Such was not the case this morning in Pamplona. The city was in the midst of its annual festival honoring its patron saint, St. Fermin, and as he walked past Plaza Principe de Viana, there was a carnival-like spirit in the air. The screeching pipes of the *dianas* had already announced the beginning of the day's festivities, and colorfully dressed *zaldikos* pranced down the street, pretending to ride the ornately decorated cardboard horses sprouting from their waists. They were surrounded by costumed dancers cavorting to the shrill melodies of *gaiteros* and *txisularis* players.

Other celebrants wore large, papier-mâché masks bearing the likeness of St. Fermín, and every few steps Miguel spotted another one, each with the same short goatee and dark, noble eyes. For Miguel, who was already paranoid, the cumulative effect was unnerving. He felt as if he were being watched and followed. He'd taken care to arrive in Pamplona unnoticed, and, like his sister in Barcelona, he'd forsaken his normal Basque attire for that of a tourist, but still he felt uneasy. If the authorities had been able to sniff out their safehouse in Barcelona, who was to say they weren't similarly on the scent of the BLM's quarters here in Pamplona? Miguel wanted to conclude his business as quickly as possible so that he could return to the country, where he felt more secure.

Angelica had called Miguel after the raid in Barcelona, tempering the bad news with hopes she could free Xavier Golato and still carry out the bombing of the civic center, with or without the aid of the supertank. Miquel hoped his sister was right, but he had his doubts. With some help from their contacts within the IMA and the Barcelona police force, springing Xavier from custody might not be a problem, but the effort would take focus and resources away from the master plan, which, even before the raid on the safehouse, had been a long shot. And now, given all the setbacks they'd faced since getting their hands on the FSAT-50, they had lost their margin for error. From here on in, everything would have to fall into place according to plan.

Difficult as it was to put all this from his mind, Miguel tried. It was important that he concentrate on the matter at hand, the reason he'd come to Pamplona in the first place.

His meeting with the Iraqis.

For now, at least, that was all he had any control over.

As he headed up Avenue de San Ignacio toward Plaza del Castillo, Miguel noticed that those masquerading as St. Fermin were becoming outnumbered by men—and a few women—dressed in white with red sashes around their waists, each carrying a rolled-up newspaper. The runners. They were all making their way toward the narrow, cobblestoned streets of Cuesta de San Domingo, Mercaderes and Estafeta, where soon the legendary bulls of Pamplona would be charging, bound from their pens at the edge of town for the Plaza de Toros, third-largest bullring in the world. There, by day's end, the beasts would meet their deaths at the hands of matadors and toreadors.

Miguel had participated in the running of the bulls years ago when he was young and foolish with no sense of purpose. Now, for him, the run seemed trite and insignificant. If one was going to risk his life, he figured, it might as well be for a higher, more worthwhile cause, like that of the Basque Liberation Movement.

Miguel's paranoia flared anew when the howl of sirens suddenly cut through the sounds of merriment. The crowds in the street parted to make way for a pair of ambulances, and, up ahead at the next intersection, three police cruisers began to cut around traffic, roof lights flashing. Soon all five vehicles were headed down Paseo Tejeria, the street where Miguel had arranged to meet up with some of his men before rendezvousing with the Iraqis. Miguel hesitated, heart racing. As a swarm of revellers began to head toward the commotion, he warily followed, taking care to stay near the periphery of the crowd so that, if need be, he could readily flee.

The squad cars and ambulances came to a stop two blocks up the road, just past the office of tourism. As he drew closer,

Miguel saw the reason for all the excitement and began to relax slightly. Apparently too many people had crowded onto a second-story balcony overlooking the street and the structure had collapsed under their weight. The police were doing their best to keep the crowd away from the accident site, where more than a dozen people lay amid the rubble of the balcony. Most of them were moving, but it looked to Miguel as if there were at least a few fatalities. A handful of civilians ignored the police and insisted on helping paramedics trying to free victims trapped under a large section of the balcony. Several women and children cried out as they watched the grim proceedings.

Much as he felt a passing sympathy for the victims, Miguel figured the accident could work in his favor. True, the area would likely be crawling with even more police any minute, but they would not be scouting the crowd for terrorists; their attention would be on the crowd and the wounded. To be safe, however, Miguel spent a few moments playing the part of a curious onlooker before breaking away from the crowd and continuing up the block.

Zacharias Brinquel had arrived in Pamplona well ahead of Miguel, and when the two men met up near a newspaper kiosk two blocks from where the bulls would be running, Brinquel had with him two other men, both tall and muscular, wearing loose shirts to conceal the guns sheathed in their shoulder holsters. The two larger men stood back and watched the commotion around the accident site while Miguel stood alongside Brinquel and picked up a magazine and idly flipped through the pages. The older man was already pretending to be engrossed with the front section of the morning paper. Neither man looked at the other, and even as they began to speak in soft whispers, they continued to stare at their periodicals.

"Did you see the accident?" Miguel asked.

"No," Brinquel replied, "but I heard it. We were worried for a moment that we were under attack."

"Understandable." Miguel quickly changed the subject and asked Brinquel about Timo Ibanez's cell phone.

"I took it from him as soon as I reached the safehouse," Brinquel replied. "Unfortunately, he'd already used it once."

"When?"

"Last night, when he arrived here. He called his bank in Switzerland to set up the money transfer."

Miguel shook his head faintly. "So eager to be paid off he didn't think about the risks."

"I made him aware of his stupidity," Brinquel said.

"He's lucky he's still valuable to us. Did you get rid of the phone the way I told you?"

Brinquel nodded as he flipped the newspaper open to another page. "We stopped by the bus terminal and I planted it in the cargo bay of a bus heading for Biarritz. There's enough of a charge to keep the phone running most of the way. Anyone tracing his call will think he's left Pamplona for the coast."

"Let's hope so," Miguel said. "Now, what about the Iraqis? Are they here?"

"Yes." Brinquel stared blankly at the newspaper as he continued to speak to Miguel out of the side of his mouth. "I recognized Abtaj. He has five men with him that I could see."

"He brought an entourage?" Miguel could barely contain his rage. "What was he thinking?"

"Maybe he doesn't trust us," Brinquel deadpanned.

Miguel shook his head with disgust and set down the magazine.

"Let's go," he murmured. "Keep a safe distance."

"Of course."

Brinquel lingered at the kiosk a moment as Miguel strode off, passing the other two men without acknowledging them. He walked away from the accident scene and turned down a side street. A small horde of beggars latched on to him, pleading for alms, but he ignored them and they finally gave up, turning their attention elsewhere.

At the end of the block, Miguel came upon a large parking lot filled with tourist buses. Throngs of vacationers milled around the buses and the inevitable array of souvenir and food stands set up on the nearby sidewalks. Others paraded off on foot up the street toward the city's cathedral, whose looming spire rose into view above the surrounding rooftops. Miguel surveyed the crowd and finally spotted the Iraqis. They were standing a few yards away from a raggedly dressed street performer who stuck a blazing torch into his mouth, then looked skyward and blew a dragonlike gout of fire into the air. The Iraqis paid little mind to the performer; they were scanning the crowd, no doubt looking for Miguel. They were all dressed casually in civilian clothes, but there could be no mistaking their Middle Eastern features. Miguel muttered a curse under his breath, then nonchalantly strode up to the men, singling out the oldest, a tall, gaunt man with a pencil-thin mustache and dark, horn-rimmed glasses.

Bansheh Abtaj.

A one-time member of Saddam Hussein's Republican Guard, Abtaj had in recent years ingratiated his way into the upper echelons of Iraqi intelligence. He was Miquel's contact. They'd spoken by phone several times over the past two weeks, but this was the first time they'd met face-to-face.

Abtaj nodded a greeting to Miguel, then tossed a few coins into a hat set at the fire-eater's feet and walked off. His men followed close behind, dogging Miguel's steps, still scanning their surroundings like Secret Service agents guarding the President during his morning walk through the Rose Garden.

"You stick out like a sore thumb," Miguel whispered hotly to Abtaj. "Why don't you all just go ahead and wear sandwich boards telling everyone who you are?"

Abtaj smiled indulgently. Two of his front teeth were gold.

"We are innocent tourists, like yourself," he replied calmly. "It is a free country, no?"

"You might at least have had the sense to have brought some women and children along with you," Miguel countered. "Even then, you'd look suspicious."

Abtaj's smile faded. He stopped walking and faced off with Miguel. "I did not come here to be critiqued on the way I conduct my operations."

"If you want to talk business, we will do it man to man," Miguel told him evenly. "Have your goons spread out and make themselves less conspicuous."

"And you expect me to believe you came here alone?" Abtaj glanced briefly over Miguel's shoulder. "I see at least three men who are undoubtedly covering you."

"They're covering me from a distance," Miguel said. "I don't have them lapping at my heels."

Abtaj sighed. "You're every bit as short-tempered as I feared you'd be. But if you insist..."

"I do."

The Iraqi turned to his men and gestured subtly with his hand. The others pretended not to notice, but within moments they had dispersed, splitting off into three separate groups.

Miguel led Abtaj down the block, then motioned at a vacant table outside a small sidewalk café overlooking the cathedral grounds. He took a seat allowing him a view of the street. Abtaj calmly sat across from him. Before they could talk further, a waiter appeared before them. They ordered tea, then waited for the server to leave before speaking in earnest.

"Now, then," Abtaj began, "I assume you have the tank and the warheads."

"Not with me, obviously, but yes, I have them," Miguel said. "Along with the plans for both."

"Here in Pamplona?" Abtaj queried.

Miguel was evasive. "Provided you meet our price, I can have the plans and one of the warheads in your hands by the end of the day."

Abtaj raised an eyebrow. Their waiter reappeared long enough to set a tea service before the men, then just as quickly drifted off toward another table. The Iraqi tore open a packet of sugar and added it to his tea, then reached into his shirt pocket for a slip of paper with a series of numbers scrawled across it. He slid the paper across the table.

"We will give you this much for the plans, the tank and both warheads," he said.

Miguel didn't bother to look at the paper. He glared at Abtaj. "That was not the arrangement we discussed. You said you wanted only the plans and one warhead."

"Our needs have changed," Abtaj said.

"How so?"

"You are well aware of what has been going on in our country the past few weeks," the Iraqi told Miguel. "We are up against formidable enemies within our borders."

"As the government here is with us," Miguel reminded the other man.

"I don't think we need to get into that," Abtaj said. "In any event, given the situation, we no longer feel we have the luxury of time on our side. We need a way to track down the enemy in their mountain lairs and snuff them out. Decisively, in a way that will give them second thoughts about rising up against us again."

Again, Miguel felt as if he were hearing about his own predicament with the Spanish government, albeit from the other position. This time, however, he held back from alluding to his support for the rebel forces trying to bring down the current Iraqi regime. He contented himself to listen as Abtaj continued to make his case.

"It would take time for us to build a tank from plans," the Iraqi said, "just as it would take time to build a second warhead. Better we get our hands on everything up front."

Miguel didn't respond at first. He glanced out at the street. He could see Brinquel and another of his men, as well as three of Abtaj's underlings. They were scattered among the crowd, but both sides were clearly watching each other's moves. Miguel could only hope the face-off didn't seem so obvious to others as it did to him.

He was still watching the men when, moments later, the squeal of sirens once again filled the air. The crowd was forced to scramble clear of the streets as the two ambulances raced past, bearing those wounded in the collapse of the balcony. As soon as they had repositioned themselves, however,

Miguel's and Abtaj's men resumed their almost comical surveillance of one another.

Miguel waited until the ambulances had passed, then turned back to the Iraqi. "All we have to offer you are the plans and one warhead," he said.

"Is that so?" Abtaj responded.

"That is what we told you when we agreed to meet."

"Yes, I know," Abtaj said. "But what you tell us and what our sources tell us are two different things. Our sources tell us you have the tank and two warheads."

Miguel was taken aback but tried not to show it. He continued to stare at Abtaj, holding his ground. "All we have to offer you are the plans and one warhead," he repeated.

"And what are you going to do with the tank and the other warhead?" Abtaj asked.

Miguel refused to answer.

"Let me take a guess, then," Abtaj responded. His smile returned. "The NATO conference in Barcelona."

Miguel did his best to keep a poker face. "If you don't want the plans and the warhead, we have other offers."

Abtaj went on as if Miguel hadn't spoken. "As I said, we have our sources. We know about the raid on your safehouse in Barcelona this morning, just as we know about the attack on your men yesterday in the mountains outside Bilbao. We also have word that you ran into problems trying to transport the tank and wound up losing it in an underwater explosion."

It was Miguel's turn to smile. "If you thought the tank was destroyed, you wouldn't be trying to buy it."

Abtaj nodded faintly. "We feel the tank that was destroyed was a decoy, in hopes the authorities would become less diligent about trying to track it down while you moved it across the country."

Miguel eyed the Iraqi impassively but felt a grudging sense of admiration. Abtaj might be a buffoon when it came to arranging a rendezvous, but he was clearly masterful at gathering intelligence. Still, Miguel wasn't about to give the man what he was asking for.

He pulled a pen out of his shirt pocket and glanced at the slip of paper Abtaj had given him. He crossed out the number scribbled on it and wrote in a new figure, then slid the paper back across the table to Abtaj.

"For this much, we can give you the plans and one warhead," he said. "Our original agreement."

Abtaj eyed the counteroffer, then glanced up at Miguel. "The NATO conference will be over in a week. Perhaps by then the tank will have served its purpose and you will be more inclined to part with it."

"If you want to discuss some other deal in a week's time, so be it," Miguel said. He pointed at the slip of paper. "This is the only offer on the table at the moment. Take it or leave it."

Abtaj reached into his pocket again, this time withdrawing a gold-plated cigarette case and a matching lighter. He opened the case and held it out to Miguel, who shook his head. Abtaj helped himself to a cigarette, then held the slip of paper over the lighter's flame. Once it caught fire, he set it in the ashtray. At that same instant, a skyrocket suddenly exploded high in the air over the city. Startled, Abtaj sat up in his chair and reached inside his shirt.

"Relax," Miguel told him. "They're just announcing the bull run." Sure enough, in the wake of the explosion a thunderous roar began to echo through the streets south of where the men were sitting. Miguel couldn't be sure, but he thought he could hear, above the clamor, the pounding of the bulls' hooves as they charged down the side streets.

"You Spaniards have some foolish customs," Abtaj remarked.

"We are Basques," Miguel corrected, "and our customs are no stranger than some of yours."

"Perhaps," Abtaj conceded.

Miguel pointed to the ashen remains of the burned note. "I take it you have decided to renege on your offer."

"On the contrary," Abtaj replied, "I was merely destroying evidence." His golden smile returned as he told Miguel, "We have a deal."

THE MEN ARRANGED to meet later in the day to make the transaction. Afterward, Miguel stayed put and paid the bill as he waited for Abtaj and his entourage to leave the area. Even after he'd lost sight of the Iraqis, Miguel was wary Abtaj had left someone behind to trail him, so he took a circuitous route back to the safehouse. First he, Brinquel and the two other strongmen headed back to Avenue de Estafeta, arriving just as another skyrocket announced the end of the bull run. From there, the men split off in separate directions. Miguel took a cab north for three blocks, then got out and hopped a bus heading east to the outskirts of town. He got off after several stops and walked two blocks to Camara de Comptos. Though by now he was convinced he wasn't being followed, he took the added precaution of taking a taxi back to Plaza Principe de Viana, then walked the final two blocks to where he'd parked the Land Rover. He'd already switched plates when he stole the vehicle, but he went ahead and made a second switch before driving off. Wanting to avoid the revelry in the streets as much as possible, he looped around the city to Media Luna, which led him along the Arga River to an upscale residential neighborhood located high on a bluff less than a mile from the bullring.

Large, ostentatious mansions lined the cul-de-sac, each home surrounded by a wall or fence and meticulously landscaped grounds. Miguel, as a rule, found such blatant displays of wealth abhorrent, but he'd made an exception of Dr. Ruben Dupentiez, whose sprawling estate took up nearly the entire end of the cul-de-sac. Dupentiez, a renowned Pamplona plastic surgeon, was a longtime public supporter of the conservative PNV party, which years ago had helped create the Basque Autonomous Region, but privately the doctor's sympathies lay with the separatist movement, and over the years he had funneled millions of dollars to the ETA and, more recently, their BLM offshoot. Six months ago, when the U.S. Treasury Department began its latest crackdown on shell corporations with ties to both organizations, Dupentiez had been forced to curtail his financial support, prompting the BLM's plan to seize the FSAT-50 and nuclear warheads for sale on the black market. To compensate, however, the plastic surgeon had recently purchased a second home—a villa across the border in Biarritz—and moved there, allowing the BLM to use his Pamplona residence as a base of operations. The only condition was that the separatists refrain from any activities that might draw suspicion from the neighbors. The Rigos had complied, and it was the understanding of everyone on the block that Dupentiez had leased his home to an architect who was overseeing the construction of a new guest house and jai alai court on the property. The construction crew was made up BLM members skilled in the building trades, and consequently their comings and goings—usually timed with the beginning and end of normal workdays—seemed nothing out of the ordinary.

When he reached Dupentiez's estate, Miguel pulled into the driveway, which was barricaded by a tall wrought-iron gate. He pressed the speaker button located above the key-pass slot and spoke briefly to someone inside the grounds. Moments later, the gate slowly opened. Rigo passed through, following the horseshoe driveway to the front of the mansion. Parked directly ahead of him was the black Lincoln Town Car Zacharias Brinquel and his henchmen had driven into town earlier. They had to have returned only a few moments before Miguel, because he could hear the engine still cooling under the hood. Off to his left, two men were out on the lawn tending to a flower bed. Miguel didn't recognize them, but he knew they were doubling as guards and likely had submachine guns near at hand. He nodded to them as he headed up the front walk. Brinquel was waiting for him in the doorway. Behind the older man, Miguel could hear the sound of someone playing piano inside the mansion.

"The Iraqis tried to follow us, but we lost them in traffic," Brinquel stated.

"Good," Miguel said. "If they were tailing me, I lost them, as well."

Inside, the mansion was sparsely furnished but filled with expensive artworks. Miguel recognized a Miro print on one wall and, hanging over the fireplace mantel, a large, framed Picasso painting of a bullfighter.

"Our host has good tastes, eh, Miguel?" Brinquel observed.

Miguel nodded absently. He was in no mood for small talk. He still had a number of things to attend to before his second rendezvous with Abtaj later in the day.

"Where is Ibanez?" he asked.

"That's him playing the piano," the older man responded, gesturing through the living room. "In the den."

"What about the others?"

"Out sunning by the pool."

"And Luis? Is he with them?"

Brinquel eyed Miguel warily and shook his head. "No, he isn't."

"Where is he?" Miguel asked.

"You're not going to like it."

"Where is he?" Miguel repeated.

Brinquel hesitated, clearly uncomfortable at having to be the bearer of bad news. Finally he said, "He decided to run with the bulls."

"He did what!" Miguel's face flushed with anger. Bad enough Luis had nearly foiled their plan by falling asleep while on watch in the mountains the previous night. Now, instead of making an effort to amend for his mistake, the fool had gone off to take part in the run. No doubt he'd been just down the block from Miguel as he was meeting with Abtaj.

"He thinks we came here to play?" Miguel fumed. "I suppose afterward he's going to put on one of those big heads and go parading around like St. Fermin!"

"He said he'd be coming straight back after the run," Brinquel said.

"Then where is he?"

Brinquel shrugged. "I assume he will be here shortly."

"I want to see him as soon he gets here!" Miguel snapped. "I'll be out back. Meet me there in a few minutes with the men who came with you for the rendezvous with the Iraqis."

Brinquel nodded.

Miguel turned and crossed the living room into the den. Timo Ibanez, the missing director of research and development for Gamuso Armorers, was a short, burly man with thick glasses and a receding hairline. He sat hunched over the piano, engrossed in his playing, unaware that Miguel had entered the room. The terrorist leader had to clear his throat twice to get the man's attention.

"A nice piece," Miguel said.

"Rachmaninoff. It helps to relax me," Ibanez replied, quickly adding, "I apologize for using my cell phone earlier. I wasn't thinking."

"It's been taken care of," Miguel told him. "Now, much as I hate to take you from your piano playing, I need you to arrange for the warheads to be moved. One of them in particular needs to be placed in as small a container as possible. One that will not draw suspicion."

"What do you plan to do with it?"

"That is not your concern," Miguel replied. "Just have it ready by five o'clock. If you need some incentive, think of the money that will be waiting for you in that Swiss bank account of yours once we are finished."

Ibanez nodded but didn't seem consoled. "If you use the warhead in a way that kills innocent civilians, it will be blood money."

"Money is money," Miguel responded.

Ibanez sighed and slowly closed the lid on the piano keys. There was a part of him that felt that by continuing to abet the Basques he was covering up his conscience, as well. Troubled, he changed the subject.

"Speaking of money, Paulo and Juan are concerned that they have not been paid yet."

"I'm on my way to take care of them right now," Miguel assured Ibanez.

Ibanez stared at Miguel. "I don't like the way you said that."

"Take care of the warheads," Miguel told the other man. "That is your only concern. Do you understand?"

Ibanez was about to say something but thought better of it. He nodded meekly and rose from the piano bench.

Miguel watched him head off into another room, then turned and used the French doors to let himself outside onto the back terrace. The terrace overlooked the grounds, and off in the distance there was a panoramic view of the entire city of Pamplona. Two high-powered telescopes had been set up on tripod stands near the far railing. Miguel went to them and peered through one, focusing on the Plaza de Toros, located just downhill of the bluff the Dupentiez estate rested on. He found himself looking at the upper rows of the bullfighting ring, where the high-priced seats were located. The stadium was empty now, but after sundown, as the bullfights began, he would be down there with the extra warhead, meeting with Abtaj to trade the weapon for cash. Someone would be watching the transaction from up here on the terrace, on the lookout for any sign of a double-cross by the Iraqis.

Miguel was adjusting the position of the second telescope when Brinquel stepped out onto the terrace, holding a cell phone. He waited for Miguel to finish his task, then passed along the bad news.

"Luis won't be back any time soon."

"Why not?"

Brinquel folded the cell phone into his pocket and sighed. "He was injured in the run," he said. "A bull gored him in the side."

Miguel couldn't believe it.

"I wished it had killed him and saved me the trouble," he muttered. "Did he have any identification on him?"

Brinquel shook his head. "No. He said he'd give them a phony name and address."

"That's what he says," Miguel retorted. "If I know Luis, he'll do a poor job of lying and wind up being interrogated. They'll have him singing like a bird."

"What should we do, then?"

"Do you really have to ask?" Miguel replied. "Which hospital did they take him to?"

"We have a problem there," Brinquel said. "The hospitals here are overcrowded from the balcony accident. Luis is being airlifted somewhere outside the city."

"Where?"

"I'm not sure yet," Brinquel said. "I'm waiting for a call. We'll know then."

Miguel closed his eyes a moment, trying to rein in his anger. What else could go wrong for them?

"Once we know where he is," Brinquel offered, "I can see to it that he's taken care of."

"That would help matters," Miguel said. "I have my hands full."

"I will head out the minute I hear."

Brinquel excused himself and headed back inside. Miguel remained on the terrace, still fighting the rage that had come over him. He was pacing to and fro when he heard the sound of laughter coming from the grounds below. He moved to the railing next to where the telescopes had been set up. A roll of tall cypress pines blocked much of his view, but to his right he could see the construction crew laboring around the site where the guest house was to be built. The ground had been dug out and a large concrete truck had backed up to the edge of the cavity, ready to pour the foundation. The crew was working diligently. None of the men were laughing. No, the laughter was coming from somewhere else, somewhere closer.

Miguel moved along the railing until he was clear of the pines. Then he saw them: Paulo Ortiz and Juan Veres, the two men who'd facilitated the theft of the warheads from the Gamuso facility two nights earlier. They were sitting in chaise longues at the edge of a large, kidney-shaped pool. Both men wore only swim trunks and were sipping cocktails as they basked in the sun, joking to each other as they watched the workers.

Miguel was about to shout down to them, then stopped himself and instead reached into his pants pocket, withdrawing a metal cylinder no larger than a roll of quarters. He then pulled a handgun from the shoulder holster under his shirt. It was a 9 mm Walther pistol similar to ones owned by his brother and sister. The guns had been the last gift any of them had received from their father before his death.

Miguel affixed the sound suppressor to the end of the barrel, then reached behind him and tucked the gun inside his waistband. A staircase led down from the terrace. He took it, and once he reached the grounds, he circled a tall hedge that kept him from view of the construction crew. Once he reached the end of the hedge, he was within ten yards of the concrete deck that surrounded the swimming pool.

Ortiz and Veres had their backs turned to Miguel, and neither man heard him as he approached, striding purposefully across the lawn. Once he was within a few feet of Ortiz, Miguel drew his Walther and pulled the trigger. The man twitched slightly as the bullet tore through his skull. His cocktail glass fell and shattered on the concrete, alerting Veres that something was amiss. When he turned to look, Veres found himself staring down the bore of Miguel's sound suppressor.

"Here is your payment," Miguel said. He pulled the trigger again, placing the round through Veres's forehead. His head snapped back and he slumped in the chaise.

Miguel tucked the gun back in his pants. Behind him, a door opened and the two men who'd accompanied Brinquel into the city earlier came out of the mansion.

"Give me a hand," Miguel told them.

One of the men grabbed Ortiz under the armpits and yanked him off the chaise. The other did the same with Veres. They left a trail of blood as they dragged the dead men across the grass to the work site. The workers stared on impassively as the corpses were flung, one after the other, into the dirt hole. Miguel, meanwhile, stood back and signaled the man behind the wheel of the concrete truck.

"Go ahead!" he called out.

The driver hesitated a moment, then nodded and worked the controls. Two workers guided the sluice over the foundation as the concrete began to flow forth. The grayish sludge slowly spilled out over the two corpses. Rigo watched until the bodies were covered, then turned and told the two strongmen, "Get a hose and wash away the blood."

Miguel headed back toward the mansion. Brinquel intercepted him halfway, once again carrying his cell phone.

"They flew Luis to a hospital just outside Bilbao," he told Miguel. "Santa Maria's."

CHAPTER FIFTEEN

Santa Maria Regional Hospital

David McCarter slowly awoke in his hospital room on the top floor of Santa Maria Regional Hospital. His head ached, and when he tried to open his eyes, the light was blinding and made the pain worse. He closed his eyes and lay still, trying to make sense of his predicament. He'd overheard Rafael Encizo speaking to one of the doctors after he'd been wheeled back into the room after his CAT scan. He'd suffered a mild concussion, the doctor had said, but the CAT scan had turned up no other abnormalities. His prognosis had been upgraded, and in the doctor's opinion McCarter was well enough to be released later in the day.

Well enough?

McCarter didn't understand. How could he be considered "well" when he still had no idea who he was? It made no sense.

McCarter soon realized he wasn't alone in the room. On the other side of the plastic curtain cordoning off his bed area, he heard a man talking on the phone. The man spoke in a low voice, but McCarter was able to pick up a few words here or there. The other man was talking about some sort of tank. There was also mention of Barcelona and some men with strange names like T.J., Pol and Ironman. McCarter suspected he was supposed to know them, but the names meant nothing to him. He also knew he was supposed to be a member of some sort of top-secret U.S. commando group, but the details eluded him. It was maddening.

He'd tried testing his memory earlier and found that he could remember multiplication tables, as well as the names of all fifty states and most of their capitals. He knew it was baseball season back in America. It seemed as if he could recall a million different things, but none of them had to do with who he was or how he'd come to find himself lying in a hospital bed in Spain.

Why? Why couldn't he remember?

The plastic curtain was suddenly pulled aside, and McCarter found himself staring at a tall man with Hispanic features dressed in civilian clothes. He had one arm in a sling.

"Hey, look who's up," Rafael Encizo called out, flashing a smile.

McCarter started at the man, uncomprehending.

"It's me, Rafe," Encizo said. "How are you doing?"

McCarter slowly shook his head. "I'm sorry, I—"

"Still in a fog, huh?" Encizo pulled a chair over and sat alongside the bed. "Don't worry, it'll pass."

"When?" McCarter wanted to know.

Encizo sighed. "I wish I had the answer to that one," he said. "The doctors don't know. A few hours, a few days...they really can't be sure."

McCarter muttered a stream of epithets under his breath.

"I see you haven't lost your vocabulary," Encizo quipped.

"A lot of good that does me," McCarter said. "Where are the other men we were with?"

"Gary is in the next room." When Encizo saw that the name didn't register with McCarter, he added, "Gary Manning. Next to you, he's second in command."

"I guess he's in charge now."

"Calvin James is the other guy," Encizo explained. "He's back in surgery again. Third time. He's doing better, though."

"Tell me again what we were doing," McCarter said. "Maybe it'll help trigger something."

"It's worth a try."

Before Encizo could launch into an explanation, however, they were interrupted when a nurse strode into the room carrying a food tray.

"I have breakfast for you," she told McCarter, struggling with her English. "You are hungry, yes?"

McCarter stared at the food: oatmeal, juice and a foam cup filled with canned pears. "Not really," he said.

"Humor her," Encizo suggested. He stepped back so the woman could place the tray on McCarter's lap.

"First I take your blood pressure," the nurse said. "Very quick."

McCarter extended his arm and let the woman strap the gauge around his bicep. As she inflated the gauge, McCarter heard a loud droning outside the hospital. A shadow drifted past the window. Encizo went to take a look, then told McCarter, "Looks like a medevac chopper. There's a helipad down in the courtyard."

"They come from Pamplona," the nurse told the men. "There were injuries in the *encierro*."

"The running of the bulls?" Encizo asked.

The nurse nodded, then unstrapped the blood pressure

gauge and told McCarter, "A good pulse. Good blood pressure. Everything is normal."

"If everything's normal, then what's wrong with me?" he snapped irritably.

The nurse recoiled from the outburst. "I am only a nurse. I can't—"

"I want to know who I am, dammit!"

"Easy, David," Encizo told him.

"I want some answers!" McCarter demanded.

"I will get the doctor," the nurse said. She quickly scribbled a few notes on McCarter's chart and hurried from the room.

Encizo grinned at McCarter and helped himself to one of the pears. "You haven't lost your way with the women, either."

McCarter took the food tray off his lap and set it aside, then stared hard at Encizo. "Tell me."

"Tell you what?"

"Tell me who I am," McCarter said. "I want to know who I am!"

"I'm not sure we should get into all that right now," Encizo said. "The doctors say—"

"I don't care what the doctors say!" McCarter interrupted angrily. "I want to know who I am!"

Encizo regarded McCarter a moment then sighed. "That's a tall order, David, but I'll give it a shot. Where do I start?"

"Just tell me all you know," McCarter demanded.

"All right, all right. Let's see," Encizo began, "Okay, you were born in London and named after your father. David McCarter, Sr. He was a brigadier in the British army, then went on to serve in Parliament. I don't know all that much about your mother, but I think her name was Mary. Ring any bells?"

McCarter shook his head with frustration. "Go on."

"You went to some state school in London," Encizo went on. "You were expelled once for joyriding, but got reinstated. That's funny, because you wound up test-driving for British Leyland Motors, and by the time you hooked up with Phoenix Force, you could drive just about anything with wings or wheels."

None of it meant anything to McCarter. "What's Phoenix Force?" he asked.

Encizo shook his head. "Sorry, but I have to draw the line there. At least until you get your memory back. It's a security thing."

"Fine," McCarter said. "What else, then? What else can you tell me?"

"Let's see..." Encizo glanced up at the ceiling a moment, trying to recall the chronology of McCarter's life. "You served in the British army. You married a woman you met while you were stationed in Northern Ireland. Colleen was her name."

"Are we still married?"

Encizo shook his head. "No, you were divorced after four years. No kids. You still keep in touch with her, though."

McCarter closed his eyes a moment, trying to envision his wife. Nothing registered. He opened his eyes again. He guessed that Encizo could sense his exasperation.

"Maybe we should wait on this, David," he suggested.

"No," McCarter said. "Tell me something else." He glanced down at his hand and noticed that the pinkie on his right hand was scarred and bent inward at an odd angle. "How did I get this?"

Encizo glanced at McCarter's pinkie, then told him, "In Nam. Laos, actually. You were a special observer as the war was winding down. You got in the way of a grenade. You've got scars on your shoulder and further up your arm, too. Good for a DSO."

"What's that?"

"Distinguished Service Order," Encizo told him. "A medal-of-honor thing."

"I don't remember any of it," McCarter said flatly.

"You stayed in the service, though," Encizo said. "A few years later you wound up in the SAS. You were one of the heroes who busted up a takeover of the Iranian Embassy in London. Operation Nimrod?"

"I don't remember," McCarter repeated. "None of it."

"I don't know what else to tell you," Encizo confessed. "Well, actually, if it'll help matters any, you're a first-class pain in the ass, but when the shit hits the fan, there's nobody else I'd rather have covering my back."

"Is that a compliment?"

"In our racket it is," Encizo said. "Bottom line is, when it comes to being a soldier, you're as good as they come."

McCarter let that sink in, hoping it would register. It didn't. It only filled him with more questions. One in particular troubled him.

"I've killed men before, then, right?"

Encizo was quick with his reply. "Nobody that didn't have it coming to them."

Before McCarter could ask another question, Encizo's cell phone chirped.

"Sorry, but I've got to take this," Encizo said, flipping the phone open. "It's the Farm."

Encizo got up from his chair and moved away from the bed as he took the call. McCarter watched him, wonderingly. The Farm? What Farm? And what was this Phoenix

Force he supposedly belonged to? Was he some kind of hired killer?

McCarter made a fist and weakly pounded his mattress. Dammit, why couldn't he remember?

CHAPTER SIXTEEN

Barcelona, Spain

For Officer Julio Cristofer, it was a case of bad news, good news.

The bad news was that he'd been unable to wrangle Xavier Golato from custody before he was questioned by the authorities. By the time Cristofer had contacted Martin Zamara in Bilbao and arranged for AMI to intervene, Golato had already been taken into an interrogation room, where he was being grilled, not by military intelligence, but rather by the Barcelona district attorney and two police detectives assigned to the suspect's case. None of those men were on the take, at least not to Cristofer's knowledge, and he knew that any request to sit in on the interrogation would only draw suspicion.

The good news, however, was twofold. First, Golato had been taken to Cristofer's precinct station for questioning, allowing him to at least be close at hand to monitor the situation. And when Zamara's faxed paperwork had come in authorizing Golato's transfer to Bilbao for additional questioning by AMI, Cristofer had been able to get himself assigned to drive the prisoner to the airport. There, a military intelligence team would be waiting to accompany Golato to Bilbao. They weren't in collusion with Zamara and the BLM, but that wasn't a problem. Cristofer had no intention of ever reaching the airport.

Now, all that remained was for Golato to be released into his custody. As he waited, Cristofer pretended he was immersed with filling out a backlog of reports at his desk, which afforded him a view of the hallway leading to the interrogation room. In truth, however, he was writing out a note to slip to Golato at some point before they set out from the precinct station for the airport. Cristofer hadn't been able to speak to the prisoner and it was vital that Golato know exactly what was going on and what he would need to do to help regain his freedom.

Cristofer glanced up periodically as he wrote, checking the hallway, but as the minutes dragged on, no one emerged from the interrogation room. Cristofer began to worry. Angelica Rigo had assured him that Golato would refuse to answer any questions, but what if she was wrong? It would be bad enough if Golato started confessing to BLM activities in Barcelona. If he went a step further and began to talk about the terrorist group's connections within the police and military establishment, especially here in the city, it could spell doom for Cristofer. Even if Golato didn't mention him by name, a red flag would be raised and internal affairs would be brought in to investigate. And if there was one thing Cristofer feared as he waited out the last few months before his pension, it was coming under the scrutiny of IA. He knew the men in that outfit, and once they were on the scent of wrongdoing within the ranks, he knew they would be as relentless as bloodhounds until they turned up the necessary evidence to bring down anyone who'd stepped outside the line while in the performance of their duties. And though he'd always been careful to cover his tracks, Christopher had stepped out of line plenty of times during his years as a cop, not only on behalf of the BLM, but also for members of organized crime and a handful of local politicos. He couldn't afford to fall under suspicion. All IA would need to get its hands on was one loose thread and he would see his spotless record quickly unravel before his eyes.

Cristofer was still mulling over his concerns when he sensed someone standing behind him. Before he could react, he heard the stern, deep voice of precinct Captain Armando Otason.

"I need a word with you, Julio."

As nonchalantly as possible, Cristofer shifted a pile of unfinished reports on his desk, using them to cover the note he'd been writing to Golato. He was afraid, however, that it might already be too late. He didn't know how long Otason had been standing behind him. As he turned in his chair to face the captain, Cristofer's heart raced with apprehension.

"It's about this weekend," Otason said. "I know you're not scheduled to work, but I need some men to put in some overtime. They're looking for additional security at the civic center while they're having that NATO conference."

Whatever relief Cristofer felt in realizing that Otason hadn't seen the note was quickly replaced by dread at the thought of being asked to work over the weekend.

"I wish I could help out," Cristofer said, "but I'm taking the family down the coast to Valencia. We've already put a deposit down on a motel room."

"I suspected as much," the captain said. "But you may have to change your plans, anyway. If I don't get enough volunteers, I'll have to draw straws and put a few men on duty regardless."

Cristofer did his best to hide his shock.

"I understand," he responded. Managing a faint grin, he

joked, "I don't suppose officers with seniority could be tipped off as to which straws are longer."

"Nice try." The captain chortled. "I'll get back to you."

As he watched Otason cross over to talk to some other officers, Cristofer unconsciously began drumming his fingers on his desktop. If he wound up being chosen, he would have to dip into his pockets and pay another of the officers to volunteer in his place. Angelica hadn't spelled out exactly why she'd wanted the blueprints for the civic center and all the other information regarding the work crews, but Cristofer knew damn well that it involved something more consequential than a peaceful demonstration in the streets. There was no way he was going to place himself anywhere near the vicinity of the civic center this weekend. One way or another, he was going to stick with his plan to round up his family and get as far from Barcelona as possible before the conference got under way.

As if Cristofer wasn't saddled with enough worries, a few minutes later the front door to the station opened and he saw two familiar figures walk up to the desk sergeant. The Americans. After accompanying Golato to the station earlier, they'd only stayed around long enough to get their hands on the prisoner's booking mug shot. Once they'd left, Cristofer thought he'd seen the last of them. And yet now here they were again. What were they up to? he wondered. Had they somehow circumvented the IMA and come to take Golato?

Cristofer's concern escalated when he saw the desk sergeant wave to another officer, gesturing for him to take the Americans back to the interrogation room.

Cristofer glanced at his paperwork and scribbled away as the Americans were led past his desk. After conferring briefly with Captain Otason, they entered the hallway. Cristofer looked back up. One of the detectives had emerged from the interrogation cell. He shook hands with the Americans, then led them into a room adjacent to the one where Golato was being questioned; the room with the two-way mirror. The Americans would be able to witness the interrogation, but that was all. It seemed like a good sign.

Distracted as he was, Cristofer managed to finish one of his reports. He was starting on another when the captain came back over.

"All right, Julio," Otason told him. "Go ahead and bring one of the undercover cars around front. The prisoner will be ready to go in a few minutes."

"Why are the Americans here?" Cristofer asked.

"They're just here to compare notes with the detectives," the captain said. "You know Americans. They always have to make everything their business."

Cristofer nodded, then asked, "Since we're taking an unmarked car, does that mean there'll be no escort?"

"No, there'll still be an escort," Otason said. "Two motorcycle officers. But they'll be out of uniform, riding regulation street bikes. One will ride a ways ahead of you and the other will trail from a distance. We'll have a decoy escort head out before you in a squad car with a standard cycle formation."

"You think the BLM will try something?" Cristofer asked.

"We want to be prepared for any contingency," the captain responded.

"Of course," Cristofer said, increasingly confident that there was one contingency Otason hadn't considered. There was still one last factor in the plan to take into account. As he got up from his desk, Cristofer asked the captain, "Is it all right if Nadra rides with me?"

"Of course," Otason replied. Grinning, he added, "I don't think you'll be needing the dogs, though."

Cristofer returned the grin. For his plan to work without drawing suspicion, someone in the convoy taking Golato to the airport would have to be sacrificed, and Cristofer couldn't think of a better candidate than his new partner. Trabor Nadra, who'd been on duty with Cristofer earlier in the day when they'd been called from the civic square to the site of the raid on the BLM safehouse, was a vain, arrogant rookie cop overeager to rise up through the ranks. In fact, Cristofer was certain Nadra was the one who had blown the whistle to IA a few weeks ago, leading to the dismissal of Cristofer's former partner. After all, when Nadra had subsequently taken the man's place, he'd upped his rank in half the time it would have normally taken him. Cristofer couldn't stand the man, and he'd been looking for a way to get back at the young upstart and avenge what had happened to his ex-partner. This would be it.

If all went according to plan, for Trabor Nadra the ride to the airport would be one-way.

"HE'S NOT GIVING us anything," Detective Nikola Etixa told Carl Lyons and Rosario Blancanales as the men peered through the large two-way mirror at Xavier Golato. The bald-headed prisoner was sitting back leisurely in his chair, blowing smoke rings in the air as if he didn't have a care in the world. A large wooden desk separated him from Etixa's partner and the city prosecutor, who, in contrast to Golato, both seemed perturbed and agitated.

"I don't understand," Lyons said. "You just told us you've been talking with him for nearly an hour."

"Talking, yes," said Etixa, a lean, impeccably dressed man

with neatly cropped black hair and large brown eyes. "But it is getting us nowhere."

"Sounds like the conversation we're having," Lyons groused.

Etixa eyed Lyons calmly. He wasn't about to let the American get on his nerves. "There was a Hollywood movie a few years ago called *The Usual Suspects*. Perhaps you remember it."

"Yeah, I remember it," Lyons said.

So did Blancanales. "That's the one about the guy who keeps fabricating stuff while he's being interrogated so he can throw the police off the truth."

Etixa nodded. "Our prisoner here is trying out for the sequel. So far he told us that BLM was responsible for 9/11, the assassination of that Russian premier last year and the poison-gas incident last month in Beijing. If we give him enough time, I'm sure he'll eventually take credit for every terrorist act of the past ten years."

"All except the ones they're really responsible for, that is," Blancanales guessed.

"Correct," Etixa said. "We will be glad to be rid of him."

"Now what are you talking about?" Lyons asked.

"You weren't told?" Etixa responded. "He's being flown to Bilbao so that he can have his fun with our military intelligence people."

"When did this come about?" Blancanales asked.

Etixa quickly explained about the requisition order that had been faxed to the station earlier by AMI Agent Martin Zamara. "Normally we would contest the order," he concluded. "At least long enough for us to get some information that would help us on our end. In this case, however, as I said, good riddance to him."

Blancanales stared through the mirror at Golato, who had

put out his cigarette and was now speaking passionately to his interrogators, making dramatic gestures with his hands. From the looks of irritation on the faces of the prosecutor and other detective, Blancanales guessed that Golato was elaborating on yet another of his fabrications.

"Is there any chance I could talk to him?" Blancanales asked. "My Spanish is good and I can speak a little Catalan."

"I can't allow it," Etixa said. "The orders from AMI were that no one but their people were to speak with him once we finished. You'd be wasting your time, anyway."

"Don't be so sure," Lyons interjected. Indicating Blancanales, he went on, "This guy's as good as it gets when it comes to interrogations. If anybody can get this guy to crack, it's him."

"Maybe so," the detective said, "but I have my orders. Believe me, there is no love lost between me and AMI, but they are on good terms with my captain. If I let you in to see Golato, there would be repercussions."

Lyons shook his head. "Goddamn office politics."

Etixa had no interest in pursuing the topic any further, so he quickly changed the subject. "I hope this doesn't mean you're going to withhold the information you said you had for us."

"No, we don't play those games," Lyons said.

He handed over the computer printouts he'd downloaded from the laptop he and Blancanales had brought to Barcelona with their other provisions. After sending Golato's mug shot to Aaron Kurtzman back at Stony Man Farm, the cybernetics staff had gone to work, running their photo through the Farm's massive database, which—at least according to Kurtzman—rivaled that of the National Security Agency. They'd sent back a shorthand dossier tabbing Golato as a midlevel operative with the Basque Liberation Movement. He had a criminal record dating back to his early teens and had served time in a Longrono prison, where, according to the files, he'd converted to the separatist cause.

"We already have most of this information," Etixa said as he skimmed over the dossier.

"Figures," Lyons said. "But it was worth a shot."

"Wait a moment," the detective said. He'd just flipped to the last page. "Now, here is something new."

"What's that?" Pol asked.

Etixa pointed at the printout. "This item about Golato saving Angelica Rigo's life two years ago during a coup attempt within the ranks."

Blancanales remembered the reference. "Golato played human shield, right? Took four bullets meant for Rigo."

Etixa nodded thoughtfully. "We knew about the coup attempt, but we were never able to find out who was shot in the woman's place. If it was Golato, it puts a whole new perspective on things. These Basques have a strong sense of honor among themselves. If Golato saved Rigo's life, she would feel obliged to return the favor."

"Provided she's still alive," Lyons said. "Seems to me there's a good chance she's buried in the rubble of that loft building."

"We've only recovered a few bodies so far, and they were burned beyond recognition," Etixa said. "It will take time for the coroners to make any identifications. In the meantime, we feel it is best to assume that Angelica Rigo is still alive. And, as I said, if she's alive and feels indebted to Golato, it is a good thing we are taking precautions while taking him to the airport."

"What kind of precautions?" Lyons wanted to know.

Etixa quickly told Lyons and Blancanales about the diversionary ploy already in place, then added, "Given what we know now about Golato and the woman, I think we might want to add some helicopter surveillance for each of the caravans. We may need to beef up the ground support for Golato's procession, as well."

"Careful," Lyons said. "If you add too many men, you're going to defeat the whole purpose of the decoy."

"How many more men would you suggest?" Etixa asked.

Lyons shared a knowing glance with Blancanales, then told Etixa, "Two should do it."

CHAPTER SEVENTEEN

Gamuso Armorers, outskirts of Zamudio, Spain

Once they'd finished their business at the testing grounds, T. J. Hawkins and the other members of the investigatory team returned uphill to the manufacturing complex. There they were met by Oswaldo Lopez's superior, as well as two intelligence officers from NATO, Trace Harper from the CIA's Bilbao field office, and two officers from the Spanish Ministry of Defense, which had taken over full funding of development of the FSAT-50 after the U.S. had withdrawn from the program the year before. The meeting was to be conducted in Euskara and Hawkins didn't feel like forcing Cordero to translate the play-by-play, so he begged off, figuring there were better ways to make use of his time. While the others headed into the administration building, he ventured across the central courtyard to a row of vending machines located outside the cafeteria. The selections, as well as the instructions, were printed in Spanish, and Hawkins was still puzzling over how to buy a candy bar when Lopez appeared alongside him.

"Maybe I can help." The security officer's English was limited and he spoke it with a thick accent, but Hawkins had no trouble understanding him.

"Thanks." Hawkins pointed out what he wanted, then held out a palmful of change. Lopez took a few of the coins and fed them to the machine, then pressed a few buttons, releasing a Snickers bar to the bottom tray.

"That is not a very healthy breakfast."

"I'm used to it," Hawkins replied. "Thanks again. I didn't think you'd want to do any of us any favors after what we put you through."

"My problem was with the one from AMI," Lopez said. "He was making trouble for you, as well."

"That he was," Hawkins said.

"I am willing to cooperate if I am treated with some respect."

"I know the feeling." Sensing an opportunity, Hawkins baited the guard. "I'd love a chance to show that guy up."

Lopez looked puzzled. "Show him up?"

"Get the upper hand on him," Hawkins said. "You know, find a way to get to these three missing guys before he can."

"Ah, yes, yes, I understand," Lopez replied. "If there is any way I can help, I would be glad to."

Hawkins smiled. Just the opening he was looking for. "Valentino mentioned that he was trying to trace the cell phone of that person in research and development."

"Timo Ibanez."

"That's the one," Hawkins said. "If I knew his number, I bet my people could find out where he is quicker than Valentino's crew."

Lopez deliberated momentarily, then told Hawkins, "Come with me."

Hoping he was onto something, Hawkins followed Lopez

from the cafeteria to an adjacent two-story building partially shaded by a stand of tall trees that looked as if they'd been well-established long before the weapons plant had been built.

"Security and communications," Lopez explained as he opened the door to the side entrance. "My office is on the top floor. I can access the personnel records and get you Ibanez's phone numbers."

"I was hoping you'd say that."

As they took the elevator up, Lopez told Hawkins, "When they told me Ibanez was a suspect, I wasn't surprised."

"Why's that?" Hawkins wanted to know.

"His personality," Lopez explained. "He was secretive about everything."

"How so?"

"He always ate alone," Lopez said. "Usually in his office, with the door locked. And he liked to come in early and leave late, so that he had the research-and-development building to himself."

"Could be he was just dedicated," Hawkins suggested.

"Dedicated, yes," Lopez said. "But to whom? That is the question."

The two men got off the elevator. Lopez's office was halfway down the hall. The room was small and cramped, filled with filing cabinets and a large, cluttered desk half-covered with computer equipment.

"Our central computers are located at the end of the hall," Lopez said as he booted up, "but I can get the same information from here without drawing as much attention."

"I appreciate it," Hawkins told him.

Once he'd logged on and entered his password, Lopez

quickly called up the firm's personnel records. It took him less than a minute to access the information he wanted. He quickly copied down Timo Ibanez's various phone numbers, then repeated the process with Paulo Ortiz and Juan Veres, the two men who'd disappeared after instigating the brownout at the weapons depot. Once he'd finished, Lopez handed the numbers over to Hawkins.

"Where are your people located?" he asked.

"Back in the States," Hawkins said. He was trying to figure out the quickest way to get in touch with the Farm when Lopez offered a solution.

"If you'd like, I could get you on a secure line," he said, pointing at the computer.

"You just made me an offer I can't refuse," Hawkins said with a grin.

Lopez smiled back. *"The Godfather."* He entered a few commands, then rose from his desk and motioned for Hawkins to take his place at the computer. "I will stay out of your way," he said. "I have some filing to catch up on."

Hawkins sat before the computer and eyed the keyboard hesitantly. Everything had fallen into place so easily with Lopez he was beginning to feel suspicious. Had the guard set a trap for him? If he tried to reach the Farm, would his communications be intercepted?

Hawkins glanced over at Lopez. The man had turned his back and was trying to cram folders into a file drawer already filled to capacity. He finally cursed under his breath and pulled out a stack of papers, pitching them into the trash.

"Everything in triplicate," he muttered in English after apologizing to Hawkins for his profanity. "They want extra copies of everything. For what?"

Lopez resumed his filing. Hawkins decided the man could be trusted, but he hedged his bet just to be safe. Instead of trying to contact the Farm directly, he first accessed the Internet and logged onto a high-security instant messaging service, then entered a coded message. On the surface it seemed he was innocently asking another party about plane arrivals on the Gulf Coast of Florida. In fact, however, he was querying the cybercrew back at Stony Man Farm to run a security check on the line he was using and make sure it was safe to use for communications.

Within twenty seconds of sending his message, Hawkins received a coded response from Carmen Delahunt, telling him to stay on the line and type something innocuous. Hawkins obliged and began typing, over and over again, "The quick brown fox jumped over the lazy dog."

"Any luck?" Lopez asked, calling over his shoulder.

"Getting there," Hawkins said.

After another forty seconds, a coded message from Delahunt gave Hawkins the green light to proceed. He gave the fox and dog a rest and quickly updated the Farm on the situation in Spain, then passed along Ibanez's numbers, as well as those of the other two missing men. Delahunt responded that they would get back to him in a few minutes.

While he waited, Hawkins thanked Lopez again for his help, then got up from the desk and went to the room's lone window, which overlooked the courtyard. He saw Valentino and the other investigators walking across the grounds to a large, hangarlike building. As they approached the structure, a large bay door slowly rolled open, revealing a handful of mechanics and technicians hovering around a tank unlike any Hawkins had ever seen before.

"The FSAT-50," Lopez said, moving alongside Hawkins and staring out the window. "It's not as close to being operational as the one that was stolen, but, at least for now, it's our main prototype."

The tank was smaller than Hawkins had anticipated. It seemed to be only three-quarters the size of an Abrams MBT, with a much lower profile and a protective housing that shielded all but a few inches of the treads from view.

"It almost looks like a spaceship," Hawkins commented.

Lopez chuckled lightly. "The one thing it can't do is fly," he said. "But, who knows, maybe at some point they'll find a way to make it do that, too."

"Wouldn't that be something?"

As the men watched on, the investigatory team entered the hangar. Valentino spoke to one of the technicians, who, in turn, motioned for the others to step clear of the tank, allowing the investigators to have a closer look.

"Technically, it is a light tank," Lopez explained, "only its RHA rating is as high as that of a full-fledged tank. So along with its defensive strength, you have maneuverability and a tank that can be more easily transported than its larger cousins."

"Where's the missile launcher?" Hawkins asked. "Aren't they usually mounted on the turret?"

"Usually, yes," Lopez said. "But with the FSAT, the launcher is retractable. Do you see that hatch door toward the rear of the turret?"

Hawkins looked where Lopez was pointing. "Yeah, I see it."

"Instead of flipping open, it slides to one side and then the launcher rises up on hydraulic lifters," Lopez said. "And once the launcher is in place, the crew can activate a series of spikes built into the tread guards. The spikes drive into the earth and help to anchor the tank in place. That way they can increase their accuracy when they launch their missiles."

Hawkins shook his head with amazement. "That sucker has more gizmos than a Swiss Army knife."

Lopez nodded gravely. "Yes, only I don't know of any Swiss Army knife that can fire a nuclear warhead."

Stony Man Farm, Virginia

T. J. HAWKINS WASN'T the only member of the Sensitive Operations Group contemplating the FSAT-50.

Back from his White House briefing with the Joint Chiefs of Staff, Hal Brognola stood behind Aaron Kurtzman in the Computer Room at the Stony Man Farm Annex, staring over the computer wizard's shoulder at a monitor screen depicting the amphibious tank's schematics.

"What do you think, Bear?"

Kurtzman eyed the schematics as well as the sidebars describing the tank's protective armor. "I think you're onto something, Hal."

Barbara Price wandered over from the adjacent computer stations, where Huntington Wethers and Carmen Delahunt were hard at work running a trace of the phone numbers Hawkins had just turned over to them. Tokaido was on break, napping back at the main house barracks.

"What are you two up to?" Price asked Brognola.

"We just got an update from the divers checking out that lake where the FSAT-50 blew up," Brognola explained. "They're hauling up pieces for reassembly at a warehouse in Bilbao, but from what they've seen so far they're pretty sure the main explosion went off inside the tank."

"No surprise there, is it?" Price said.

"No," Kurtzman interjected, "but we've been looking over the schematics and gauging the firepower onboard when the tank was heisted. Even if a couple rockets had gone off and taken out the fuel tank, the force wouldn't have been strong enough to do the kind of damage they're talking about."

"And there's no sign of radiation," Brognola added, "so that rules out those nukes being the culprit."

"I'm not sure what you're getting at," Price said.

"A few things," Kurtzman explained. "First off, we're thinking the tank had to be rigged with extra explosives. Enough to make sure it was destroyed beyond recognition."

"Why?" Price wondered.

"Hang on, we're getting there," Kurtzman responded. "Secondly, even with extra explosives on board, the real FSAT wouldn't have sustained all that much damage except for the interior." He pointed at the computer screen and elaborated, "The plating is just too damn impregnable. Even in a worst-case scenario, the shell and framework would've remained intact, especially when you consider the water pressure. It wouldn't have just blown to bits."

"Then you're saying it was a stand-in," Price guessed. "Not the real FSAT."

"Exactly," Brognola said. "We're thinking it's a decoy. They want us to think the tank's been destroyed."

"To buy some time while they try to sneak it cross-country to Barcelona," Kurtzman added.

"That's a pretty elaborate ruse," Price said.

"Just gives you an idea of what we're up against," Brognola said.

"Another couple things," Kurtzman told the mission controller. "The truck cab was salvageable enough for them to see that the windows were rolled down when it went into the lake. Add that to the fact that they haven't found any bodies in the lake yet, and it seems pretty likely the driver deliberately drove into the water, then bailed out and made it ashore before the explosion."

"Okay, I follow that," Price said.

"Then there's the truck bed itself," Brognola went on. "It's more than twice the length of the FSAT."

"But that could be because they were carrying one of those pre-fab trailer homes, right?" Price said. "To hide the tank inside of."

"Maybe they were hiding more than one tank," Kurtzman suggested. "And if that's the case, you have to figure the real deal cut loose and moved clear before the explosion, then used its sub capacity to make a run for it underwater."

Price took a moment to assimilate the information, then said, "If you guys are right, we need to get out word and step up the search again."

"Already on it," Kurtzman said. He worked his keyboard and called up another screen showing a topographical map of the mountainous region between Bilbao and Barcelona. He'd already overlaid a mileage grid and circled a five-hundred-mile area due east of the lake. "We've got a call out the AMI and NATO to intensify the search in this area. NSA's going to shift a couple satellites for a bird's-eye view, and there'll be choppers running cross patterns with infrared scanners. If the tank's making its way along the bottom of some riverbed, hopefully we'll be able to pick up a heat signature."

"Can we put any of our people on this?" Price wondered.

"Not many options there," Brognola reminded her. "Hawkins is still tied up at that weapons plant, and both Pol and Ironman are off in Barcelona trailing that prison convoy headed for the airport in Barcelona. Everybody else is pretty much out of commission."

Before the trio could discuss any further strategy, Carmen Delahunt called out, "Bingo!"

"Hang on a second," Brognola called back to her. He told Kurtzman to continue to get the word out about the likelihood that the FSAT was still at large, then followed Price to Delahunt's computer station.

"Got a trace?" Brognola asked the redhead.

Delahunt nodded. "Timo Ibanez. Gamuso's D&R guy."

"Where's he calling from?" Price asked.

"Well, it gets a little tricky," Delahunt said. She pointed to her screen, which depicted a map of the Navarra region of northern Spain, with a number of concentric circles mapping out coverage areas for Ibanez's cell phone provider. Three of the circles were blinking side by side.

"We've got a call originating in Pamplona," Carmen said, "but the signal keeps shifting northward."

"He's on the road," Brognola guessed.

"That's what we're supposed to think," Huntington Wethers called out from his station a few yards away. "But I just locked in on the number he's calling. It's a ski resort in the Pyrenees."

"And...?"

"And it's a recorded message on skiing conditions," Wethers said. "I called in on another line and they only update every hour, so there's no reason for him to be staying on the line as long as he has."

"How long's that been?" Price asked.

Wethers checked his screen. "Thirty-five minutes so far."

"Could be he just forgot to end the call," Brognola suggested.

"Yeah, right," Delahunt said, snorting. "And maybe he's just a harmless ski enthusiast."

Price smiled ruefully. "Another decoy."

"That's what my money's on," Delahunt said. "He wants it to look like he's headed north for the coast somewhere."

"But the odds are he's still back at square one," Brognola concluded.

"Bingo again," Delahunt said.

Brognola reflected on the matter and quickly decided on a course of action. He told Delahunt, "Have T.J. pull stakes and head out for Pamplona, pronto."

"Will do," Carmen replied.

"Not so fast," Wethers called out from his station. He was eyeing a dispatch he'd just called up on his computer. "Before we move T.J.," he told the others, "I think there's a small matter he should look into."

CHAPTER EIGHTEEN

Gamuso Armorers, outskirts of Zamudio, Spain

"Is everything all right?" Oswaldo Lopez asked Hawkins.

The Phoenix Force commando had just logged off the computer and returned to the window overlooking the courtyard. The FSAT-50 had been driven out of its hangar so that the investigatory team could get a better look at it in the bright light of day. Hawkins eyed the team members with growing concern. Instead of answering Lopez, he asked the guard, "How quickly can you get me a helicopter?"

Lopez was taken aback. "There's a helipad on the roof," he said. "There should be two helicopters on standby. But why—?"

"Get one of them up and running and fly it down to the courtyard," Hawkins explained on his way out the door. "I'll meet you there."

Bypassing the elevator, Hawkins took the stairs to the ground floor, his mind racing. He hadn't been all that surprised when Carmen Delahunt had informed him that the BLM had a mole working inside Spain's Agency of Military Intelligence. It helped to explain the ease with which they had pulled off the heist of the FSAT-50 and the two warheads. But if Hawkins were to have guessed who the turncoat was, his money would have been on Gregorio Valentino, the agent who'd given him such a hard time while they were at the proving grounds.

He'd have been wrong.

Once he reached the courtyard, Hawkins beelined to the tank and pigeon-holed Valentino.

"Where's your partner?" he demanded. "And spare me the translator!"

Valentino looked at Hawkins, perplexed. He said nothing. Raul Cordero ventured over to find out what was going on. Hawkins ignored Cordero and shouted again at Valentino, "Zamara! Where is he?"

Valentino shrugged and turned to Cordero with a look of amused condescension. He started to talk to the other man in Spanish, but Hawkins cut him off, whipping out his pistol and aiming it at Valentino's face.

"I said, spare me the translator!"

The other members of the investigatory team recoiled from the altercation. In the background, a trio of security guards raced toward the tank, assault rifles raised. CIA Agent Trace Harper regarded Hawkins as if he'd gone mad.

"Are you off your rocker?"

"This man's partner is a turncoat. He's working for the BLM!" Hawkins explained without taking his eyes off Valentino. "He had a hand in planning the tank heist!"

"You can verify that?" Harper asked.

"We've got it from two different sources," Hawkins said.

"Good enough for me." Harper pulled a gun tucked under his left arm and aimed it at Valentino, as well. Cordero, meanwhile, shouted for the guards to hold their fire. The guards obliged but kept their rifles trained on the two Americans. A pall of silence fell over the standoff, broken only by the mechanical drone of the FSAT-50 and, off in the distance, the sound of a helicopter's rotors coming to life.

Finally Valentino spoke, addressing Hawkins in English.

"If Zamara is a traitor, it is news to me," he said calmly.

"Where is he?" Hawkins repeated.

"He just left," Valentino said. "He had business in Bilbao to attend to."

"How long ago?"

Harper answered for Valentino. "He left right after our briefing in the admin building." Checking his watch, he added, "It couldn't have been more than ten minutes ago."

"There's only one access road between here and Bilbao," Valentino replied. "He's likely still on it. And, again, on my mother's eyes, I have no knowledge of any collusion—"

"I don't want to hear about your mother's eyes!" Hawkins responded curtly. Both he and Harper lowered their guns. The guards followed suit. By now the chopper, a refurbished, unarmed Bell 47G, had lifted off the helipad of the S&C building and was angling its way down toward the courtyard. Lopez was sitting up front next to the pilot. It looked to Hawkins as if there were room for one more person in the rear cabin.

"I'm going after him by air," Hawkins told the others. "With any luck we can take him alive and get some information out of him."

Valentino's face was flushed with anger. For once, it was directed at someone other than Hawkins. "Give me the first crack at him," he seethed. "I'll see to it that he talks."

Cordero, who'd been speaking with two of the tank's technicians, came over and told Hawkins, "We might be able to give you a hand with the tank."

"I don't see how," Hawkins said. "That thing's not fast enough to outrun a car."

"It doesn't have to be," Cordero responded. He pointed to the turret cannon. "Its gun will do the running."

"I want him alive," Hawkins insisted.

"I understand." Cordero gestured at the helicopter. "Go ahead. Leave the rest to us."

Hawkins wasn't about to argue. He started toward the chopper, then stopped and pointed at one of the guards. "I could use a rifle," he said.

Cordero passed along the request. One of the guards stepped forward and handed Hawkins his M-4 carbine.

"Gracias," Hawkins told the man.

Crouching to avoid the rotors, Hawkins made his way to the chopper and climbed aboard, squeezing past Lopez and settling into the rear seat in the back of the cockpit.

"Have him follow the road leading from here to Bilbao," Hawkins told the guard.

Lopez passed along the request. The pilot nodded and lifted off from the courtyard.

"Who are we going after?" Lopez wanted to know.

Hawkins told him, "Hopefully the missing piece of the puzzle."

MARTIN ZAMARA angrily tossed his cell phone onto the passenger seat beside him as he guided his late-model Camry down the winding mountain road leading away from the Gamuso facility. He was on his way to Navarra Regional Airport, where he'd planned to await the arrival of BLM prisoner Xavier Golato. Now, it seemed, his trip was likely to be in vain.

"Damn fool!" he muttered to himself. "'Sense of honor'? What the hell does that have to do with anything?"

Zamara had just finished talking on his cell phone with Miguel Rigo, who'd relayed word that his sister was going to try to free Golato before he reached the airport in Barcelona. Miguel had tried to talk Angelica out of it, but apparently she'd already made up her mind and put a plan into motion. Why? Because she felt she indebted to Xavier for saving her life a few years ago. Oh, yes, and also because Golato was her lover.

What an idiot, Zamara fumed. Couldn't the woman realize how short-sighted she was being? The authorities were close to being convinced they'd crushed the BLM cell in Barcelona. Why give them any reason to think otherwise? All Angelica had to do was let Golato get on the damn plane and he, Zamara, would see to it that the prisoner managed to slip through the cracks once he arrived here in Bilbao. But no, Miguel's sister decided she needed to spring Xavier personally, even if it meant letting everyone know she didn't die in the collapse of the loft building in the Barri Gotti quarter. What chance would she have of carrying out the bombing of the civic center once everyone knew she was still alive? Although, of course, that might not even be the case if she bungled her attempt to free Golato.

"Damn fool!" Zamara repeated.

The AMI agent had the road to himself. The weapons plant was the only destination reachable by the twelve mile, two-lane stretch of asphalt, and since the day shift had already arrived for work, there wasn't much chance of him encountering any traffic before reaching Bilbao. He took out his frustrations on the gas pedal, squealing his tires as he rounded a bend, then headed downhill toward a long straightaway that ran the length of a narrow valley. Much as it seemed pointless to go to the airport, he didn't feel like turning around. Valentino and the others weren't likely to come up with any new leads, and he wasn't in the mood to put up with the squabbling between his partner and the Americans. He figured he'd be better off stopping by the AMI office in Bilbao. There he'd be in a better position to find out quickly just how much Angelica's fool's errand was going to compromise the BLM.

Once he reached the valley, Zamara took one hand off the wheel and fished through his pockets for his cigarettes. He tapped one out and was pressing the dashboard lighter when he glimpsed something in his rearview mirror.

A helicopter.

It was drifting his way across the valley, flying low. He couldn't be certain, but it looked to him like one of the security choppers from the weapons plant. Zamara eased his foot off the accelerator and lit his cigarette, then blew a cloud of smoke before checking the mirror again. The chopper was still headed his way.

A flutter of paranoia came over him. What the hell was going on? He reached under the dashboard and grabbed the transceiver microphone, then quickly put in a call to his partner. Valentino was quick to answer. Trying his best to sound nonchalant, Zamara claimed he was just checking in and wondered if the investigators had come up with anything.

"No," Valentino's voice crackled over the small speaker. "Why do you ask?"

There was something about his partner's tone of voice that put Zamara on his guard.

"Just curious," he said, eyes still on the rearview mirror.

There could be no mistaking it now; the chopper was definitely following him. Zamara tried to fish for some clue as to why. "If you want, I can turn around and come back."

"That won't be necessary," came Valentino's reply. "Go ahead with whatever you're doing."

Zamara signed off, then placed the microphone back in its cradle and flipped his cigarette out the window. He'd worked with Valentino long enough to know when the man was holding something back.

He checked the mirror a final time, hoping against hope that the copter had veered off onto another course. No such luck.

A chill ran down Zamara's spine.

There're on to me, he thought.

By now he was halfway across the valley. On either side of the road there was nothing but open grassland. Nowhere to run, nowhere to hide. His only chance of eluding his pursuers was to beat them across the valley and hope he could lose them in the mountains.

Steeling himself, Zamara once again pressed the accelerator to the floor. The Camry lunged forward.

The chase was on.

BACK AT THE WEAPONS plant, CIA Agent Trace Harper had just received a com-link update from Hawkins. He turned to the other members of the investigatory team.

"Zamara's making a run for it," he reported. "They don't know if they can overtake him before he reaches the mountains."

"Then we have no choice," Raul Cordero said. He turned to the technician he'd spoken to earlier. "Let's go with the first plan."

The technician nodded. He was standing a few yards from

the FSAT-50, which had repositioned itself to a patch of hard ground directly adjacent to the courtyard. On his signal, the tank crew went into action.

First came a rapid series of pneumatic bursts as eight sharp, three-inch-thick steel spikes housed in the tread guards were driven into the earth with so much force the entire tank shuddered.

"What the hell was that!" Harper muttered.

"They're anchoring the tank before it fires," Cordero told the CIA agent. "Now they'll send out a drone so we can line up our shot."

"Drone?"

"Watch," Cordero told the American.

Harper eyed the tank as a mortarlike tube telescoped up from the turret housing. Seconds later, a projectile burst forth from the tube with a dull roar, rocketing into the air.

"It heads out like a standard mortar round," Cordero said, handing Harper a set of binoculars. "But there's a gyroscopic gauge in the nose cone, and once it stops its ascent, the wings are activated and it converts to a surveillance drone."

It took Harper a moment to bring the drone into his sights. Then, as he watched, the aerial projectile leveled off in the air and, as Cordero had just explained, a set of wings fanned out on either side.

"The drone has a GPS sat link," Cordero went on. "Its camera will pinpoint Zamara's car and calculate its speed, then send back coordinates so we can pinpoint our aim."

"We aren't going to take out the car, are we?" Valentino interjected.

Cordero shook his head. "No. We're only looking to keep

it from reaching the mountains. After that, it will be up to the men in the chopper."

"I SEE THE DRONE," Hawkins said, glancing out the rear window of the Bell 47G, "but I think it's going to be too late to help."

"We will see," Lopez replied. His eyes were on Zamara's Camry, which was now within a hundred yards of reaching the mountains, where the road would wind its way through a narrow gorge inaccessible by helicopter. The pilot was flying at full throttle as it swooped down toward the fleeing AMI agent, but, as Hawkins had just told Harper, they weren't likely to catch up with the car, much less get close enough to where Hawkins could try to bring his M-4 into play.

"I suppose we could just fly to the other side of the mountain and wait for him to come out," Hawkins suggested.

Lopez shook his head. "He knows we're after him. Once he reaches the mountains, he'll probably abandon the car. There will be plenty of places to hide, and with all the vegetation, we won't be able to track him by air. He could slip away before we can do a full ground search."

"Dammit!" Hawkins cursed. "So close..."

He was watching the Camry close in on the mountains when, without warning, a 40 mm conventional warhead plowed into the roadway thirty yards ahead of Zamara. The explosion sent dirt and asphalt showering into the air, and through a rising cloud of smoke Hawkins saw that the blast had left a thirty-foot-wide crater blocking off the renegade agent's escape route.

"Get back, Loretta!" Hawkins whooped, marveling at the precision strike. "We've got him!"

FOOT ON THE BRAKES, Martin Zamara tried to stop short of the crater, but he couldn't prevent the shrapnel-riddled Camry from skidding sideways into the raw, smoking maw. The vehicle rolled over once, then righted itself and came to a rest on the far incline.

Zamara had wrenched his shoulder and his forehead was bleeding where he'd struck it on the rearview mirror, but he ignored both injuries and stumbled out of the car, fueled by fear and adrenaline. He coughed his way through the smoke and crawled his way back up to the road. His ears were ringing, but he could still hear the sound of the helicopter overhead. He glanced up and saw it closing in on him. He reached inside his suitcoat and withdrew his pistol. As he raised it and began to take aim at the chopper, however, a round from Hawkins's carbine ripped into his shoulder.

Zamara roared in pain and fired errantly at the chopper, then broke into a run, leaving the road and ducking in the tall grass that flanked the road. It was a futile gesture, however, because as the chopper dropped lower toward him, its rotor wash flattened the grass around him, making him an easy target. Cursing, he tried again to fire at his pursuers, but another volley from the chopper—this time a 3-round burst—stitched across his midsection like jabs from a hot poker.

Wincing through his pain, he weakly raised his arm and fired a few shots that glanced harmlessly off the underside of the Bell 47G's fuselage. The chopper pulled away, but Zamara knew they'd be back.

"Damn them," he fumed. They were planning to take him alive. He wasn't about to give them the satisfaction.

There was only one way out.

Zamara drew in a deep breath, then carefully placed the

barrel of his gun against the underside of his chin. He waited patiently for the chopper to appear above him, then grinned defiantly at the men staring down at him and pulled the trigger.

CHAPTER NINETEEN

La Costa Seacoast Drive, south of Barcelona

Angelica Rigo smiled with satisfaction as she approached the gateway in the long, rambling wooden fence that ran alongside the coastal road leading from Barcelona to the regional airport. For once, things were going her way. Not only was the gate unlocked, but the cattle grazing the thin strip of land between the road and cliff were untended.

"This will be easier than I hoped," she murmured as she let herself through the gate. She was wearing olive-colored Spandex biker's shorts and a matching top, as well as a protective helmet. Her Walther pistol was tucked away in the fanny pack strapped around her waist. Julio Cristofer had suggested she get rid of the weapon, as it was now linked to the shooting of Patricia Brigada, but the weapon held too much meaning for her. Besides, even if the authorities managed to trace it to her, it wouldn't do them any good. It wasn't as if she were about to let herself be taken into custody and have the gun used as evidence against her. No, if they came after her, she would fight them to the death. What was more, if need be, she had already resigned herself to the fact that this might very well be that fateful day.

The cows paid little heed to Angelica as she strode through

the grass to the edge of the cliff. It was a hundred-foot drop down to the frothing waters of the Mediterranean. There was no beach; the surf pounded directly off the side of the cliff, creating clouds of mist that roiled halfway up the precipice. Looking northward, Angelica could see the road stretching out for several miles, following the contour of the coastline. Opening her fanny pack, she reached past her gun for a pair of palm-sized, high-powered binoculars. She brought them to her eyes and focused down the road, watching for the first sign of the convoy bringing Xavier Golato to the airport.

Several minutes passed, but the only traffic she spotted was a sports car and touring van. Angelica began to feel anxious. She checked her watch. What was taking them so long?

Angelica was beginning to wonder if there had been a last-minute change in plans when she finally spotted the lead motorcycle in the convoy. It rounded the bend two miles away, followed a few seconds later by the unmarked car carrying Golato.

Angelica quickly put away the binoculars and circled the cows, then began clapping her hands as she approached them, shouting, "Come along, come along! Let's go now!"

The cattle stirred, then began to move away from Angelica. She kept moving toward them, herding them toward the open gateway. She continued to shout and clap until five of the cows had finally ventured onto the road. She followed them, then partially closed the gate and jogged north to the nearest bend in the road. Instead of a guardrail, there was a thick, waist-high stone wall flanking the edge of the road closest to the cliff. Angelica quickly clambered over the wall and climbed down the other side. There were sufficient hand- and footholds for her to continue a few yards down the side of the cliff. There, partially obscured by a cluster of brush growing out of the side of the rock facing, was a large drainage culvert. The rusting, corrugated pipe, which emptied mountain flood-waters into the sea below, was nearly four feet in diameter.

Angelica crawled into the pipe. Waiting there were two knobby-wheeled mountain bikes she'd carried down after being dropped off by one of her men twenty minutes earlier. Lying next to the bikes was the body of a transient Angelica had killed back in Barcelona. The man's head had been quickly shaven and he'd been changed into a shirt and pants similar to those Xavier had been wearing when he'd been apprehended after the raid on safehouse in Barri Goti. His ankles were shackled and his hands were handcuffed. Up close, he bore little resemblance to Xavier, but Angelica wasn't concerned. If all went well, nobody would know the difference....

As CRISTOFER FOLLOWED the plainclothes motorcycle officer leading the prisoner convoy along the coastal road, he patiently listened to his young partner's ceaseless bantering. Trabor Nadra was talking about his desire to get into motion pictures, and, as Cristofer was expecting, he eventually got around to asking, for at least the dozenth time since he'd joined the force, if his partner could help him out. Cristofer, after all, occasionally worked security on film sites and had moonlighted a few times as a stunt driver in some low-budget action thrillers.

"Have you talked to that director about me yet?" Nadra asked, broaching the topic.

"I already told you, he's out of town until the end of the month," Cristofer replied.

"I know, but I thought maybe you might have talked to him on the phone."

Cristofer shook his head. "You'll have a better chance if I wait until I can talk to him in person," he said.

"Maybe so," replied. He wasn't about to get off the subject, though. "Like I told you, it wouldn't have to be a big part. I can start small and work my way up."

Cristofer tuned the man out as he continued to rattle on. By now they were coming up on the bend in the road where Angelica had said she'd be waiting. Cristofer stole a look in the rearview mirror and saw Xavier Golato eyeing his reflection. He nodded faintly. Golato fingered the shoulder strap of his seat belt and nodded back.

Behind them, Cristofer could see another two plainclothes motor cops following him from a few car lengths back. The Americans were nowhere to be seen, but he knew they were bringing up the rear. Cristofer had been briefly taken aback when he learned they had decided to follow the convoy, but his concerns had since passed. They wouldn't be able to do anything to keep the plan from being carried out.

As he neared the bend, Cristofer gently eased down on the accelerator and braced himself. Up ahead, the motorcycle rounded the turn and briefly disappeared from view. Cristofer had his window rolled down, however, and when he heard the squeal of brakes, he knew that Angelica had come through on her end.

This was it.

GOLATO DIDN'T KNOW exactly how it was going to happen, but he knew that when it did, every second would count. He already had his hand on the clasp to his seat belt when the car rounded the bend. He spotted cows in the middle of the road, then caught a quick glimpse of the motorcycle cop braking to a stop a few yards ahead of them. The next thing Golato knew, Cristofer had swerved the car sharply to the right to avoid hitting the officer. In doing so, he veered off onto the shoulder slammed the car into the rock wall at an angle. Golato was thrown forward by the impact as the front-seat air bags deployed with a sound like shotgun blasts, filling the car's interior with a powdery white cloud.

Though dazed, Golato quickly recovered his wits. Fueled by adrenaline, he quickly unfastened his seat belt and crawled over the front seat. He couldn't tell how badly Cristofer or the other cop had been hurt, but that wasn't his concern. He squeezed past Trabor Nadra and grabbed for the door handle. The stone wall prevented the door from opening all the way, but Golato had enough room to squeeze out of the car. He heard shouting in the road behind him, and as he scrambled up and over the wall, bullets skimmed off the stone and whistled by.

The handcuffs and shackles made the climbing difficult, but Golato managed to scale his way down the rock facing of the precipice. He'd nearly reached the culvert opening when he glanced down and saw Angelica shove the transient over the lip of the drain pipe. The body tumbled downward, striking the cliff several times before splashing into the surf.

"I've got you!" Angelica called out softly, grabbing hold of Xavier's right leg and helping him into the drain pipe. There Golato collapsed, exhausted from his ordeal. He reached into his pocket and pulled out the keys Cristofer had placed under his seat along with the note forewarning of the escape attempt. Angelica took the keys and kissed him quickly, then began to unlock Xavier's shackles and handcuffs.

"You came through for me," Golato murmured, rubbing his

wrists where the cuffs had chafed them. "And I never thought I'd have a good thing to say about Cristofer, but—"

"Quiet!" Angelica whispered, putting a finger to Golato's lips. She had her Walther out. She reached into a tote secured to the seat of one of the mountain bikes and handed Golato a Parkerized Auto-Ordnance .45 ACP. He glanced past the bikes and saw that the drainage pipe ran another fifty yards inland before opening up to daylight.

"There's a path there we can take once we're sure the coast is clear," Angelica whispered. "I brought along some biker gear for you to change into."

Golato grinned at Angelica. "I guess this makes us even, eh? I saved your life, and now you've done the same for me."

Angelica smiled but cautioned, "We're not out of this yet."

"I KNEW THEY'D TRY something," Carl Lyons muttered as he brought his rental car to a stop in the middle of the mountain road. Up ahead, the two plainclothes officers they'd been following had abandoned their motorcycles and rushed forward to the car that had been carrying Xavier Golato.

Lyons and Blancanales got out of the car, guns drawn. By the time they reached the others, the officers had already reached the crashed vehicle Julio Cristofer had been driving. One of them opened the driver's door while the other went to the rock wall and peered over the side. Peering around the bend, Lyons saw the third motorcycle cop standing beside his downed bike, shaking a fist at the stray cows milling about on the road. It seemed pretty clear to Lyons what had happened.

Blancanales, meanwhile, joined the cop at the wall overlooking the Mediterranean. Glancing down, he saw a body floating in the surf.

"I must have got him," the cop said in Spanish as he lowered his gun.

Blancanales asked the man to radio for the helicopter that had been tracking the decoy convoy.

"What's the point?" the officer replied, still staring down at the surf. "He'll be washed out to sea before they can get to him."

"Do it anyway," Blancanales said.

As the officer headed back to his bike, Blancanales went over to the wreckage of the car. Cristofer had been helped out and was sitting on the ground, looking as if he'd just regained consciousness. Trabor Nadra was still pinned between his seat and his air bag, out cold, blood streaming from his nose. There was no one in the back seat.

A farmer soon appeared in the narrow field between the road and the cliff, shouting and waving his arms frantically as he made his way to the half-opened gate.

"He's wondering what happened," Blancanales translated for Lyons.

"He's not the only one," Lyons grumbled.

"Seems pretty obvious," Blancanales said. "The cows got loose and when the lead guy braked for them—"

"I get that part," Lyons said, cutting his partner off. "But the timing's a little hinky, don't you think?"

"I know what you're saying," Blancanales said, "but if it was planned, it didn't pan out." He told Lyons about the body he'd seen floating in the surf.

"Are you sure it was him?" Lyons asked.

"From what I could see, yeah," Blancanales said.

"It's too damn pat," Lyons said. "I smell a rat."

Lyons went to the wall to have a look for himself. Blancanales went with him. The cop who'd shot at Golato was still there. He pointed down at the surf and murmured something to Blancanales.

"He says the body just went under."

"Wonderful," Lyons said. He leaned forward and looked down the side of the cliff. There wasn't much to see but scalloped rock and a few patches of wild brush.

They were interrupted by the sounds of cursing from the other side of the car. Cristofer was the one swearing. He was on his feet, waving away an officer trying to convince him to sit back down until an ambulance arrived. Cristofer kicked the side of the car angrily, still cursing.

"He's pissed that he was following too close to the lead cop," Blancanales told Lyons. "He says if he'd been a few more car lengths back he wouldn't have had to veer off the road."

"Them's the brakes," Lyons deadpanned.

By now Cristofer's partner had come to in the front seat. Trabor Nadra moaned and then let out a cry as he realized where he was. One of the other officers leaned into the car and told him to stay put. Nadra obliged, but once he became aware of the blood flowing down his chin, he dabbed at his nose and pushed the air bag out of his way so he could get to the rearview mirror. His most immediate concern, obviously, was how the crash had affected his looks. Cristofer realized as much and began to harangue him for his vanity.

Lyons and Blancanales moved away from the car and joined the motorcycle officer who'd nearly collided with the cows. He'd calmed down somewhat and was grilling the farmer, who insisted that he distinctly remembered closing the gate earlier after he'd led the cattle across from his main pasture on the other side of the road.

"I doubt he was in on it," Lyons said after Blancanales

briefed him on the interrogation. "My guess is the Basques opened the gate and let some of the cows out, then drove off once they saw us coming."

Blancanales stared up the road, which disappeared around another bend less than a half mile away. "If that's the case, there's not much chance of us catching up with them."

"Probably not," Lyons said. He saw the police chopper fly overhead and dip down toward the water, then told Blancanales, "See about having them head up the road, just in case. They'll have a better chance of spotting somebody than they will fetching that guy out of the sea."

"It's worth a try, I guess."

Blancanales jogged over to the motorcycle cop who'd put through the call to the police helicopter. He was still on the transceiver, and after the Able Team commando told him to have the chopper case out the rest of the roadway leading to the airport, the officer nodded. "While they do that, we have something to check out," he added.

"What's that?" Blancanales said.

The officer pointed toward the chopper and reported, "They're saying there's a drain pipe in the cliff just below where the car crashed. We couldn't see it because there's brush growing over the top side."

"That's it, then!"

Blancanales turned from the cop and darted toward the rock wall. Lyons saw him and rushed over. As he started over the wall, Blancanales told him what he'd just found out.

"Tricky little bastards," Lyons said, following Blancanales over the side.

Both men still had their guns out, and they climbed cautiously down the side of the cliff, splitting off once they reached the brush that had concealed the culvert from view. Lyons climbed down on the right side of the pipe, Blancanales the left. By the time they were within sight of the opening, the helicopter had risen to their level and was hovering in position a few dozen yards away. Lyons could see the pilot. He was shaking his head.

"Damn!" Lyons grumbled. Still, he had to see for himself. Gun in hand, he signaled to Blancanales, then swung into the opening. There was no one there.

A HANDFUL OF BIKE TRAILS led away from the culvert. All of them were marked by recent tread marks. On the faint chance that Xavier Golato was alive and had somehow managed to escape, the helicopter conducted an aerial search of the various paths. Several bikers were spotted and stopped, but none of them turned out to be the missing prisoner.

By the time the chopper finally made its way to the small coastal town of Librizia, two miles from the spot where the convoy had been forced to a halt, Xavier Golato and Angelica Rigo had already arrived and concealed their bikes inside the rear of a panel truck bearing the emblem of Coasta Brava Plumbing Supplies. Carefully stacked inside the truck were cartons containing fourteen kilos of high-yield explosives along with timing devices and remote detonators. The explosives had been secured by Guillermo Blanca, the same man responsible for blowing up the decoy tank and prefab home back at the lake near Faracos Pass. Blanca was at the wheel of the truck, which he'd appropriated shortly after his arrival in Barcelona earlier in the day. He was the one who'd dropped Angelica off on Seacoast Drive along with the two bikes and the body of the slain transient. Afterward, he'd driven into

Librizia, where he'd been waiting for Angelica to show up with Golato.

"All right, we're set," Angelica told Blanca once she'd closed the rear door of the panel truck. "Let's get out of here before they set up any roadblocks."

Blanca nodded and put the truck in gear. They were parked behind a small market at the edge of town, less than two blocks from a country road leading back to Barcelona. If all went well, they'd reach the capital in less than an hour.

As the pair began changing out of their biking gear, Golato eyed the packaged explosives dubiously.

"It doesn't look like there's enough there to bring down the civic center," he said.

Blanca overheard and disagreed. "If the blueprints are accurate and I can get access to the parking garage," he said, "I have enough explosives to bring the place down twice."

CHAPTER TWENTY

Santa Maria Regional Hospital, outskirts of Bilbao, Spain

Gary Manning awoke in his hospital bed and saw that he was now sharing his room with a new patient, a young, bare-chested Spaniard whose entire left side was covered with gauze and tape. The man was asleep, hooked up to an IV half-filled with a unit of blood.

"A bull nailed him in Pamplona," explained Rafael Encizo, standing at the foot of Manning's bed. "The hospitals were all full there so they flew him in."

"Misery loves company," Manning groaned.

"Still hurting?"

The big Canadian nodded. "My back's doing better, but my legs still feel like I'm soaking them in lava."

"We'll get 'em to up your painkillers next time they come around," Encizo said.

"I don't know about that," Manning said, stifling a yawn. "I'm still a little foggy from the last dose."

"So what? It's not like you need to do anything but lie around. Might as well sleep."

"I guess," Manning said. "Any word on Calvin?"

"Great news there. He breezed through his last surgery, and they've got him upgraded now to stable."

"Great news is right," Manning agreed. "What about David?"

"No change there," Encizo said. "I tried jogging his memory, but he's still blocked."

"It's going to take time."

"Afraid so," Encizo said. "I just heard from T.J., though. Turns out one of the guys he went to the weapons plant with was a mole for the BLM."

"You're kidding."

"Nope. Guy from military intelligence," Encizo explained. "Apparently he had a hand in the tank heist somehow."

"We've got him under wraps, then."

"Yeah, but unfortunately the wrap's a body bag." Encizo briefly filled Manning in on the short-lived chase that had ended with Zamara's suicide, adding, "T.J.'s stopping by on his way to Pamplona. Looks like the missing tank specialist might be holed up there."

"Why's T.J. stopping here?" Manning wondered.

"To pick me up," Encizo said.

"Pick you up?" Manning queried. "What about your shoulder?"

Encizo shrugged, patting his sling. "I've still got one arm and two good legs," he said.

"I thought you were under orders to take it easy," Manning recalled.

"Maybe so, but this Florence Nightingale routine's getting old," Encizo said. "If you need somebody to hold your hand, there's a couple hot-looking nurses floating around. Lay on some of that Canadian charm of yours and they might even hold more than your hand."

Manning grabbed a box of tissues and threw it at Encizo, telling him, "Get out of here."

Encizo tossed the box back at Manning, then unclipped his cell phone and set it on the edge of the bed. "If you want to make yourself useful, go ahead and call the Farm. They should be getting an update soon on what Carl and Rosario are up to in Barcelona."

Manning yawned again. "Maybe I'll grab a few more winks first."

"Good idea." Encizo started for the door, calling over his shoulder, "I'll let you know if we turn up anything in Pamplona."

Manning nodded. Once Encizo left, he grabbed the remote and aimed it at a TV mounted to the ceiling across from his bed. He flipped through a few channels but didn't see anything that interested him. He turn the set back off and lay back in bed, closing his eyes. The burning sensation in his legs made it hard to get comfortable. He shifted a few times, trying to find a good position. Nothing worked. Maybe Encizo was right about boosting his pain meds, he thought.

Manning paged the nurse's station, then shifted again. As he waited for someone to show up, he glanced out the window. All he could see were a few mountaintops and a patch of sky dotted with small clouds. For a few minutes he watched the clouds move slowly across the peaks, then he closed his eyes. Within a matter of seconds, he nodded off to sleep.

The next thing he knew, he was awakened by a faint scraping sound. He didn't know how long he'd been out. The sound, it turned out, was that of the plastic curtains being drawn around the patient in the other bed.

Manning was puzzled. He figured it was the nurse he'd called and was about to call out to her when he heard someone cry out on the other side of the curtain. The cry was quickly stifled, replaced by the sound of scuffling. A tray crashed to the floor and the curtain rustled faintly, as if someone had backed into it.

Manning wasn't sure what was going on, but he instinctively sat upright in bed, on his guard. He was throwing off his covers where he heard a muffled retort.

Suppressor, he thought.

The scuffling ceased on the other side of the curtain.

Manning ignored the throbbing of his hamstrings and swung his legs over the side of the bed. Across from him, the curtain swung open and he found himself staring at Zacharias Brinquel. The man was wearing an orderly's uniform, but Manning doubted he belonged to the hospital staff. Behind him, the patient from Pamplona lay dead, bleeding from a bullet wound to the forehead. There was no time for Manning to try to make sense of what had happened.

Brinquel had turned the gun on him.

With as much force as he could muster, Manning pushed away from the bed and dived at his attacker. Brinquel fired a round that tore through Manning's hospital gown, missing his ribs by mere inches, then backpedaled as the Canadian crashed into him. The Basque lost his footing and the other bed rolled away from him as he fell to the tile floor, Manning on top of him.

Manning tried to grab Brinquel's gun but managed only to get his fingers around the other man's wrist. Still, it was enough to keep the weapon pointing away from him, and when Brinquel fired again, the round plowed harmlessly into the wall behind them. Manning jerked hard to his right after the shot was fired, slamming his adversary's hand against the frame of the next bed. Brinquel cursed under his breath as the gun flew from his hand and clattered out of reach.

The two men continued to grapple on the floor. Manning tried to get in a few judo chops, but at such close quarters they proved ineffective. Brinquel shrugged off the blows and fought back. Hampered by his bad legs, Manning had trouble keeping it an even fight, and soon Brinquel had managed to gain an upper hand, freeing one hand long enough to cut loose with a karate chop that caught the Canadian squarely at the base of the skull.

Dazed, Manning fell away from his opponent. The older man quickly scrambled to his feet and snatched up his gun. He turned back to Manning and took aim at his face.

Manning stared down the barrel, conscious enough to wrap his mind around one grim realization.

I'm a dead man, he thought.

As the shot was fired, Manning flinched and closed his eyes, awaiting the fatal round.

Nothing happened.

Stunned, Manning opened his eyes. Zacharias Brinquel stood looming over him, but in a glance the Canadian could see that the man was dead on his feet. His arm dropped to his side and the gun fell to the floor, then he collapsed, pitching forward. Behind him, framed in the doorway, stood Manning's savior, holding the pistol that had brought Brinquel down.

"David..."

McCarter strode into the room, crouching over the corpse to make sure Brinquel was dead. He then turned to Manning.

"You all right, Gary?"

Manning nodded weakly. "Yeah, I guess so."

"Here, let me give you a hand."

As McCarter helped Manning to his feet and guided him

back to his bed, the Canadian wondered, "Where'd you get that gun?"

McCarter gestured over his shoulder. Manning glanced out into the hallway and saw another man lying dead on the floor. Moments later, two security guards appeared, as well, along with Rafael Encizo. The guards leveled their guns at McCarter, but Encizo yelled at them in Spanish and they lowered their weapons.

"I was out waiting for T.J. when I heard all the ruckus," Encizo said as he joined his comrades.

Sitting on the edge of his bed, Manning stared at McCarter. Something had just dawned on him.

"You called me Gary," he said.

"Yeah, what about it?" McCarter replied.

"Your memory," Manning said.

McCarter was taken aback. Slowly a grin came across his face. "I'll be damned," he muttered.

"You got it back?" Encizo wondered.

"I'll be damned," McCarter repeated. He thought back, trying to figure it out. "Hell, I was just lying in bed when I heard all this racket next door, so I got up to check it out and ran into this guy in the hall with a gun. I guess I just went with my instincts, 'cause the next thing I knew he was down and I had his gun."

"Just like that?" Encizo marveled. "No blow to the head or anything?"

McCarter shook his head. "Not that I remember. I'm telling you, it just happened."

"Lucky for me," Manning said.

"Bloody damn miracle," McCarter stated, still incredulous at the suddenness of his recovery.

Encizo glanced over at the security guards, who, in turn, were inspecting the two dead men inside the room.

"Well, I might be wrong," he ventured, "but I think we just had a couple BLM guys fall in our laps."

Manning agreed. He gestured at Brinquel and said, "I think he tried to smother the other guy when he woke up and started fighting back."

"Now neither one of them are going to talk," Encizo said.

"Maybe one of them's the guy we're looking for," Manning suggested. "You know, the tank specialist."

"Could be, but somehow I doubt it," Encizo said. "I got a feeling that guy's still in Pamplona."

"Well, then, let's wrap it up here and get to Pamplona," McCarter said.

"I don't know if they're going to want to release you just like that," Encizo reminded McCarter. "They'll probably want to keep you here while they run a few tests."

McCarter laughed. "Tests, my bloody ass! No way am I staying cooped up here. I'm back in business, lads."

Pamplona, Spain

MIGUEL RIGO CHECKED his watch, then anxiously resumed pacing the terrace patio overlooking the city of Pamplona. He was waiting for two phone calls. It had been nearly an hour since Zacharias Brinquel had checked in from the parking lot at Santa Maria Hospital. Brinquel had promised to call back once he'd silenced Luis Manziliqua. And AMI agent Martin Zamara was supposed to have checked in half an hour ago to pass along any pertinent classified intel regarding the search for the missing FSAT-50 and efforts to quash the BLM in

Barcelona. Miguel also wanted to know if the authorities had picked up a signal from Timo Ibanez's cell phone and jumped to the conclusion that he'd left Pamplona. What was taking them so long? Miguel knew it wasn't a case of no news being good news. The more time that passed without his hearing from either man, the greater the likelihood they'd run into complications.

A sense of foreboding began to overcome Miguel. He tried to fight it off. He lit a cigarette and wandered to the terrace railing. Down on the grounds, workers were screeding the concrete foundation for the guest house, insuring that the two men killed earlier would remain encapsuled in the concrete. Likewise, the bloodstains had been washed away from the grass and the deck around the pool, where Ibanez now sat, his back turned to Miguel, staring blankly at the water. The technician had already secured the two warheads for transport; they were still inside the mansion.

Miguel blew smoke and shifted his gaze to the Plaza de Toros, where, in a few short hours, he was scheduled to exchange one of the warheads and schematic plans for the tank to the Iraqis in exchange for a suitcase filled with enough currency to allow the BLM to further escalate its war for independence. He knew his organization had reached a point of no return. The next few days—perhaps even the next few hours—would determine whether their cause was at long last achievable or doomed to failure. And, much as he tried to shake off his gloom, Rigo couldn't help but feel that the tide was shifting against him.

Given his frame of mind, the last thing Miguel needed to see was an increased police presence at the bullfighting arena. And yet, as he stared down at the facility, he saw a procession of five squad cars pull into the parking lot, joining the dozen or more police vehicles already parked near the main entrance.

Nerves on end, Rigo went to one of the telescopes trained on the arena and peered through the sights, shifting his view from the stands to one of the outer gates. As he feared, the police had set up metal detectors and were beginning to search those waiting in line to attend the bullfights. Further, two bomb-sniffing German shepherd dogs were escorted out of one of the squad cars and led on leashes into the parking lot, where the animals began to circle the first vehicles they came across. Miguel cursed. There was no way now that he could meet the Iraqis at the stadium. The risk was too high.

Miguel was still coming to grips with this latest development when his cell phone rang, startling him. He quickly unclipped the phone from his waist, expecting it to be Brinquel or Zamara. He was wrong on both counts.

It was his sister.

"It's done," Angelica reported. "Xavier's been freed."

Miguel was glad to hear that his sister was alive, but he kept the joy from his voice and instead retorted, "At what cost?"

Angelica hadn't divulged earlier how she'd planned to help Xavier escape, and when Miguel learned the details, he couldn't help but be impressed by his sister's ingenuity. Still, he had his doubts as to whether the authorities believed it was Golato's body they'd seen being carried away by the surf.

"If they thought it was him," he told Angelica, "why did they send that helicopter to check all the bike paths?"

"It doesn't matter what they thought," Angelica countered. "The fact is Xavier's here with me, along with Guillermo.

We're back in Barcelona with the explosives. All we have to do is smuggle them into the civic center."

"You make it sound so simple," Miguel said, staring out at the police activity around the bullring as he spoke. "You don't think they'll step up security even more than they already have?"

"We'll get past them," Angelica promised. "Remember, we have someone on the inside. We can't fail."

"You're right there."

"There's another security matter we need to be concerned about," Angelica told her brother. "My contact here in Barcelona says the authorities have become suspicious about the tank. There is talk that they've figured out we used a decoy at the lake."

Miguel closed his eyes a moment and cursed under his breath. "That explains the helicopters Jacque's men have been seeing."

"Have they spotted the tank?"

"No," Miguel said. "Jacque is taking all the right precautions."

"How far has he gotten?" Angelica asked.

"He's in Alvaro somewhere," Miguel responded. "I just spoke to him a while ago. The river he was taking got too shallow so he's moving the tank overland along the base of the Pyrenees until he hooks up with the Avignon."

"He needs to be careful," Angelica advised. "Even if he's using trees for cover, the helicopters might be equipped to pick up the tank's heat signature."

"Believe it or not," Miguel said, "Jacque already came to that conclusion. That's why he's staying close to the mountains."

"I don't follow you."

"Alvaro is riddled with hot springs, remember? If he can find one that is sheltered enough, he's going to put the tank in the water and wait until dark, when the fog keeps the choppers at a distance."

"The hot springs will mask the tank's heat signature," Angelica guessed. "How clever. Was that your idea?"

"No," Miguel confessed. "It would seem our little brother has a head on his shoulders after all."

Angelica asked Miguel what else was happening back on the other coast. Miguel explained that he was still waiting to hear from Brinquel and Zacharias, then told Angelica about the beefed-up security at the bullfighting arena.

"I'm going to have to meet the Iraqis someplace else," he concluded.

"Watch your step with them," Angelica advised.

"I intend to," Miguel responded. "I intend to."

CHAPTER TWENTY-ONE

Stony Man Farm, Virginia

It was as close as anyone at the Farm was likely to get to having a picnic on the grounds.

Anxious to get some fresh air after twelve hours cooped up in the Computer Room, the SOG braintrust—Hal Brognola, Barbara Price and Aaron Kurtzman—had taken their lunches out to a grassy sward fifty yards uphill from the chipping mill. As they discussed the latest developments in Spain, the trio watched workers haul in another load of newly felled trees.

"I wish bringing in these BLM thugs could be as easy as bringing wood to the mill," Brognola commented.

"Seems to me we're faring all right on that front," Kurtzman said. "We've got them on the defensive, at least."

"Maybe so," Brognola conceded, "but let's face facts. Yes, it's great that we weeded out one of their moles and knocked out that cell in Barcelona, but they still have the tank and the warheads."

"You got me there," Kurtzman said.

"And barring some good news from the coroner's office in Barcelona," Brognola went on, "it seems pretty likely that the Rigo kids are still out on the prowl. All we've killed off are low men on the totem pole."

"With the exception of Zacharias Brinquel," Price corrected, glancing at the notes she'd brought along with her. "They figure he was a senior adviser, maybe more."

"I wonder about that," Brognola said. "If he was so high in the ranks, what was he doing trying to make that hit at the hospital? Something like that's usually farmed out to one of the drones."

Kurtzman grinned at Brognola. "I won't tell Ironman or McCarter you said that."

"Touché," Brognola replied. "Okay, I take it back. Still, the bottom line here is the BLM still has the ways and means to wreak havoc in Barcelona. And no matter how hard we try to get NATO to call off the conference, they aren't budging."

"Then we'll just have to keep at it," Barbara said. "Hopefully Phoenix Force can come up with something in Pamplona, then head out to Barcelona to help Pol and Carl."

"Speaking of Able Team," Kurtzman interjected, eyeing the laptop hooked up to his wheelchair keyboard. "It looks like they might be onto something."

"Like what?" Brognola asked.

Kurtzman quickly finished encrypting the message that had just come in through his wireless, then reported, "It's something from the coroner's office there."

"They IDed the Rigo sister?"

"No, nothing like that," Kurtzman said. "One of the medical examiners pulled a real Sherlock Holmes when he got a look at some of the shoes they took off a few of the guys that got pulled from the rubble of that loft building."

"Shoes?" Barbara said.

"Yeah, I know it sounds crazy," Kurtzman said, "but apparently most of the shoes were caked with this reddish mud the ME says is only found along the banks of some lagoon north the city. It's a few miles from where they found the body of the Brigada woman, but the lagoon feeds into the same river she was filming for the documentary she and her boyfriend were working on."

"Sherlock Holmes is right," Price marveled. "Any mention of why the mud's red there?"

"Mineral runoff from the mountains," Kurtzman said. "But that's hardly the issue. Let's add it all up. Just before we came out here for lunch, I showed you guys that archive photo I found of the Rigo kids flashing Walther pistols like the one that killed Patricia Brigada. So let's assume one of them— probably the sister—pulled the trigger. If she was at that lagoon along with the guys from the safehouse, you have to figure Brigada and her boyfriend stumbled onto some kind of BLM activity and were killed because of it."

Brognola saw what Kurtzman was leading up to. "And if we're assuming they stole that tank to use on the NATO conference," he interjected, "it stands to reason the lagoon's some kind of staging area."

"And if this Angelica Rigo is still alive," Price concluded, "odds are that's where we'll find her. Or at least what's left of her crew."

"Works for me." Brognola turned to Kurtzman. "Go ahead and have Carl and Pol move on this."

Kurtzman nodded and began typing out a return message. Price and Brognola, meanwhile, fell silent and nibbled at their lunches. Downhill, the whine of lumber saws emanated from inside the chipping mill. Even though the mill was enclosed, the cloying smell of sawdust began to carry in the light afternoon breeze.

Price was finishing her sandwich when she saw Akira Tokaido emerge from the mill and break into a jog. He was carrying a computer printout and had a look of urgency.

"If that's the news about the muddy shoes, we're already on it," Brognola called out to the cyber agent.

"Muddy shoes?" Tokaido said. "What are you talking about?"

Price quickly filled him in on the latest word from Barcelona.

"That'll teach them not to wipe their feet," Tokaido said afterward.

"What do you have there?" Brognola said, indicating the sheet of paper Tokaido was holding.

"A wild card out of left field," Tokaido responded. "You aren't going to believe it."

"At this point, I'd believe just about anything," Kurtzman said.

"It's from Striker," Tokaido said, using Mack Bolan's code name for most missions on behalf of the Farm. "He and the CIA ops he was working with just cracked that terrorist cell they were tracking in Jordan."

"That's good news," Brognola said. "But how does that fit in with the situation in Spain?"

"They got a guy into interrogation," Tokaido reported, "and get this—he says the Iraqis had an agent fly into northern Spain earlier this week to meet with the BLM. They're trying to get their hands on some nukes and maybe even this supertank."

"That's out of left field, all right," Kurtzman murmured.

"I don't like the sounds of it," Brognola said. "It puts everything in a whole new light."

"Did we get any specifics on this agent?" Price asked.

Tokaido nodded and read from the computer sheet. "Guy's name is Bansheh Abtaj."

Pamplona, Spain

BANSHEH ABTAJ, too, had just heard about the raid in Jordan. His feelings were mixed. Yes, perhaps his mission had been compromised, especially if the Americans had learned of his whereabouts. But some good had come out of the attack, as well. According to the report he'd received, among those slain by the Americans had been Nujbahl Ahmet, the closest thing he had to a rival within the ranks of Iraqi intelligence. For the past four months, Abtaj had had to watch his back constantly while in Iraq, fearing that Ahmet would try to take him out in hopes of further solidifying his power base. Now the bastard was dead, along with his top adjuncts, and it was Abtaj whose position had been fortified. If he could come through on this deal with the Basques, he would be acknowledged as the Iraqis' most powerful field agent. And anyone who knew the political situation in Iraq knew that the country's next leader could just as likely come from the ranks of intelligence as from the military or an electoral vote. If Abtaj could pull things off here in Spain and capitalize on his increased stature once he was back in Iraq, who was to say that in the coming months he couldn't maneuver his way to the top of his country's political heap?

First things first, though, Abtaj thought to himself as he sipped a glass of mineral water and stared out the living-room window of his penthouse suite at the Pamplona Royale. Like Miguel Rigo, Abtaj had an unobstructed view of the bull-fighting arena, and he, too, saw that the local authorities were going to make it difficult to carry out his rendezvous with the Basques. The situation didn't overly concern him. After all, their meeting point could be changed easily enough. In fact, Abtaj figured it might be possible to take advantage of the "dilemma" and arrange for Miguel to meet someplace where it would be easier to guard against a double-cross. He didn't trust the Basque and wouldn't have put it past him to try to reclaim the warhead and plans for the tank once he'd gotten his hands on the money. Of course, if the opportunity presented itself, Abtaj was just as likely inclined to turn the tables on Rigo, taking back the money and leaving the Basque dead.

Abtaj's ruminations were interrupted by the ringing of a doorbell. The agent wasn't alone. Two of his subordinates stood alongside him at the window, staring out at the city through high-powered binoculars. Another two men were stationed near the door, armed with Uzi submachine guns. One of them glanced through the peephole, then opened the door, admitting a sleek, striking woman in a designer pantsuit carrying an attaché case. With her were two of the men who'd accompanied Abtaj when he'd met Miguel Rigo earlier in the day.

"Greetings, Rena," Abtaj greeted the woman. "You have the money, I see."

"Of course," the woman replied, setting the valise on the coffee table and raising the lid. "It's all here."

Abtaj stared at the neatly stacked rows of bound currency. "And you had no trouble converting the money?"

"Does it look like I did?" the woman retorted.

The other men were taken aback by Rena's tone of voice. It would have been anathema for any of them to address Abtaj so harshly. And this was a woman.

If Abtaj had been offended, it didn't show. He smiled indulgently at the woman. He was used to her insolence and even admired her for it.

Rena Duli was Iraqi born but had been raised in the United States and, obviously, had little use for the traditional Muslim restrictions against women. In America she had earned a Harvard law degree, as well as a Ph.D. in business administration, and since returning to her native country she had been instrumental in helping to finance Abtaj's operations, as well as securing the release of several of his close associates after they'd been arrested on suspicion of terrorist activity in Hamburg and Algiers. For the better part of the past two years Rena had also shared Abtaj's bed on numerous occasions, and though Abtaj would never admit it—either to her or himself—he was in love with the woman. And it had to do with more than her stunning looks and figure. Rena was the only woman who'd ever challenged him, the only woman he'd ever met who was unafraid to look him in the eyes and speak her mind when she disagreed with him. He liked to call her his little whetstone, because she kept him sharp.

"A matter has come up," he told the woman after closing the lid to the valise. "I need to speak to you privately."

"I'd like a drink first," Rena replied, crossing to the wet bar. "It's been a long day."

Again the others were visibly scandalized by the woman's behavior. She paid them no mind, however, and poured herself a shot of whiskey from a crystal decanter, then tipped her head back, downing the amber liquid in one swallow. Abtaj watched her impassively, then directed her to follow him into the adjacent den, a large room featuring a large fireplace and a billiards table.

"You really should show a little more deference when there are others around," Abtaj gently scolded the woman as he closed the door behind him and threw the dead bolt. "No sense giving them reason to question our relationship."

"Who cares what they think?" Duli replied. She kicked off

her pumps, then pulled Abtaj close to her and smiled sultrily as she let her hand wander below his waist. "I think I've found the matter that has come up."

"It's no small matter," Abtaj said, kissing the woman's hair. "As you well know..."

"Let me attend to it," Duli cooed in his ear. She fondled him through his pants, then took a step back, hoisting herself up onto the edge of the billiards table. Leaning back, hands on the green felt, she smiled invitingly. Abtaj stepped forward and was beginning to unbutton her blouse when there was a knock on the door.

Abtaj's eyes flashed with anger.

"What is it?" he shouted over his shoulder.

"We've spotted something," came the voice from the other side of the door. "You might want to take a look."

"In a while!" Abtaj snapped. "Let me finish my business!"

Duli leaned forward and ran her fingers through Abtaj's hair. "Maybe it's important," she whispered.

"Nothing could be more important than this," Abtaj replied, stroking the woman's cheek.

After a pause, the man on the other side of the door called out again. "It's the Basque. We've spotted where he's staying!"

The anger drained from Abtaj's face.

"I stand corrected," he told Duli, kissing her forehead. "I'll only be a moment."

The woman nodded, smiling. "I'll be waiting."

Abtaj took a moment to compose himself, then moved from the den, sternly eyeing the man who'd interrupted his tryst. "You'd best not be mistaken."

"We're sure it's him," the man replied. He pointed to the window, where another of Abtaj's subordinates stood peering out through his binoculars. When Abtaj reached his side, he handed over the field glasses and pointed.

"Atop that bluff on the far side of the bullring," he told Abtaj. "The terrace of the third house on your left."

Abtaj raised the binoculars and stared out the window. He followed the other man's directions and soon found himself staring at a man standing between a pair of telescopes mounted on tripods.

"It's him, all right," Abtaj murmured.

By the time he'd lowered the binoculars, a plan was already formulating in the Iraqi's mind.

"Now I know where to have our little rendezvous...."

CHAPTER TWENTY-TWO

Nacional Parc Guell, outskirts of Barcelona, Spain

Raising clouds of dust along a firebreak traversing the north flank of the park's highest mountain peak, a camou-painted Hummer slowly made its way toward a remote trailhead. Up ahead, a pair of four-wheel-drive SUVs was parked at the site, along with three motorcycles and a handful of mountain bikes. More than a dozen hikers stood near the vehicles, listening to a park docent describe the various sites to be found along the paths that led from the trailhead.

"Looks like we're going to spoil somebody's party," Carl Lyons said, peering out from the back seat of the Hummer.

"Better us than the BLM," Rosario Blancanales replied. He was seated next to Lyons. Behind them, three armed UOE commandos sat pensively, hands clasped tightly around their carbines. Another soldier rode up front next to the driver, UOE Captain Estevan Peidro.

The hikers eyed the Hummer curiously as it came to a stop at the trailhead. When the soldiers emerged, their expressions quickly changed to alarm.

"Forgive us," Peidro called out to the group as he approached them, "but an emergency has come up. I'm afraid we'll need to close off this section of the park."

"What kind of emergency?" the docent asked suspiciously.

"I'm sorry, but that's classified. You'll all have to take the firebreak road back to the main entrance. The sooner you leave, the better."

"If you're here officially, I would have received some kind of notice," the docent insisted.

"I don't have time to argue with you," Peidro snapped. "You can complain all you want once you reach the ranger's station."

"This park belongs to the people of Barcelona," the docent said. "You have no right taking it over for some kind of military exercise!"

"This is no exercise," Peidro assured the docent. "I can tell you that much. Now, please leave the area."

One of the hikers eyed the soldiers, then said, "It's the BLM, isn't it? I've heard the rumors."

"I can't comment on that," Peidro said.

As it turned out, the captain had no need to go into further detail. Once the name of the separatist organization was mentioned, the docent abruptly ceased her protests and echoed Peidro's command for the hikers to evacuate. They needed no further persuasion. In less than a minute, the hikers had gotten onto their bikes or into their vehicles and started a caravan leading away from the trailhead.

"Civilians," Peidro muttered. "They're worse than sheep."

"Let's get on with it," Lyons suggested.

"Of course." Peidro started to unfold a topographical map of the area, then changed his mind when he spotted a larger rendering of the park's layout posted on a bulletin board near the trailhead. He summoned his men over, then pointed to the map as he laid out their strategy.

"From our position here, there are three approaches to the lagoon. Two are through the forest. Mantos and I will circle from the right. Viali, you will take Vincente and Francisco and move head-on through the woods until you reach this spring. Wait there until we signal you.

"As for you two," Peidro concluded, eyeing Lyons and Blancanales, "if you scale this rise to our left, you'll come on a small mountain lake. It feeds the stream that runs down to the lagoon. There's no official trail there, but people venture out there anyway so you'll probably be able to find a pathway down."

"Got it," Blancanales said.

"With any luck, their focus is on the river and they won't have lookouts posted back this far," Peidro went on. "But everyone keep your eyes open just the same. If all goes well, we will have blocked off any path of retreat once the others strike from the river."

"And if we're really lucky," Lyons muttered under his breath, "we'll catch Angelica Rigo in the sweep."

"That'd be icing on the cake," Blancanales agreed.

Peidro finished his briefing and asked if there were any questions. When no one spoke up, he waved over the man who'd been riding next to him in the Hummer. Together, they forged their way into the dense foliage to the right of the trailhead. The three soldiers who'd ridden behind Lyons and Blancanales followed suit and quickly disappeared into the brush.

"Okay, let's take the high road," Lyons told his teammate, indicating the high-pitched slope to their left.

Blancanales led the way. There was no trail and the incline

was covered with loose stone and gravel, making it difficult for them to get a decent footing. Fortunately, thick tufts of scrub brush grew up at regular intervals and they were able to grab hold of branches to assist their climb. Along with their carbines and side arms, Lyons and Blancanales, like the others, had been armed with Spanish-made Sojo-586 crossbows; the latter were slung across their backs along with quivers containing steel-pointed bolts. Except for ammo pouches containing extra magazines for the carbines, they carried no other provisions.

Neither man spoke as they scaled the slope, but they intuitively assisted each other, with Lyons scanning the terrain around them so that Blancanales could better focus on blazing a trail.

The men had the sun at their backs, and as they neared the top of the rise they could see small, fleeting shadows sweep across the mountainside ahead of them. Lyons glanced up and saw a pair of eagles circling lazily overhead. He was about to point them out to Blancanales when a rifle shot suddenly echoed across the peaks.

Both men froze in place. One of the eagles suddenly plummeted from the sky and dropped to the ground thirty yards ahead of them.

Lyons tapped Blancanales on the shoulder and motioned to a crevasse in the ground just to their right. The two men quickly scrambled into the cavity. Lyons had his pistol out, Blancanales his carbine. They waited tentatively, peering through the brush surrounding the rim of the crevasse.

"Hunters?" Lyons whispered.

Blancanales put a finger to his lips. Lyons listened and soon he could hear the sound of two men talking to each other near the top of the rise. He couldn't make out what they were saying, but it sounded as if they were talking in Euskara.

"Basques," Blancanales said. "One guy's calling the other an idiot for taking target practice while they're on sentry duty."

"Blessed be the stupid," Lyons whispered, "for they shall tip their hand."

Finally the two men came into view, standing at the edge of the crest. One of them glanced downhill, looking for the fallen eagle. The other had a two-way radio pressed to his ear.

"I think he's calling the main camp," Blancanales told Lyons. "Telling him everything's okay."

"Good," Lyons whispered back. "Of course, things aren't as hunky-dory as he might think."

Lyons quietly holstered his pistol and unslung his crossbow. Blancanales did the same. Once they'd both fed bolts into the Sojos, they carefully raised the bows into position, targeting the two sentries.

"I've got the one on the right," Lyons murmured.

"On three," Blancanales whispered back.

As he drew the bow taut, Blancanales raised his right pinkie, then lowered it. He did it again, then, on the third twitch, he let his bolt fly. Lyons's shot hissed through the brush in unison.

One after the other, both sentries went down, neither making a sound other than that of their bodies hitting the earth.

Rising up from the crevasse, Lyons and Blancanales quickly rushed forward. One of the sentries was already dead, but the other was struggling to his knees and reaching for the fallen radio. Lyons beat him to it, then finished the man off, skewering him through the heart with one of his bolts.

"That'll teach you to go after endangered species," he said as he watched the life drain from the man's eyes.

Blancanales grabbed the radio and shut it off.

"If they just reported the coast was clear, we're okay," he said. "Still, we better get a move on."

"Right behind you," Lyons said.

RICO COLOMBE, captain of the fishing boat that two days earlier had chanced upon Patricia Brigada and her boyfriend while running a sonar check on the Avignon River, had been left in charge of the crew readying the lagoon site for the arrival of the FSAT-50. Since part of the work crew had been killed in the raid on the BLM safehouse in Barcelona, progress was slow. The embankment ramp made of lashed beech trunks was only half-completed, and men were still up in the trees trying to clear out the area where the tank was to position itself for firing on the civic center. The work would go faster, Colombe figured, if he pulled in the handful of sentries posted around the perimeter of the site, especially now that they were dispelling their boredom by taking potshots at birds flying overhead. Angelica had been right about these men; they were slackers and misfits, the dregs of the BLM. And now, with the separatists coming under increased fire from the enemy, recruiting fresh blood was going to be more difficult than ever. They desperately needed to pull off a major coup over the next few days, something inspiring enough to draw the interest of men who could truly help the movement.

"We need to get this job finished quickly," he said aloud. He was standing on the foredeck of his boat, which was still moored beneath the boughs of some low-hanging trees that lined the edge of the lagoon.

A few yards away, one of the workers, a short, gnome-faced man name Magglio, was squatting on the edge of a footlocker, sharpening machetes and pruning saws. When he overheard Colombe, he glanced up and said, "I know Angelica didn't want us to use chain saws, but she's not here. If we went ahead and used them, we could catch up on our work."

"Chain saws would be too noisy," Colombe said.

"That's what she said, too," Magglio replied, "but if we have sentries shooting off their guns, what's the difference? I say we use the saws and be done with it. If Angelica comes back and sees that everything is in place, she won't have anything to complain about."

Colombe thought it over, then asked Magglio, "How many chain saws do we have?"

The other man smiled and patted the footlocker he was sitting on. "I know there are three in here," he said. "And I think there are more in the hold."

Colombe checked his watch, then glanced up through the trees at the afternoon sun. They could still get in another few hours of work before dusk. With chain saws, they could at least finish the clearing by then. If they worked through the night, they might even be able to tether together the rest of the ramp. It seemed worth a try.

"All right." Colombe sighed. "Let's do it."

"Wise move," Magglio said. "You'll see."

"I'll call in a couple of the sentries to help out."

The other man set aside his sharpening stone and opened the footlocker, taking out one of the chain saws. Colombe, meanwhile, grabbed his two-way radio and tried to reach the men stationed up at the ridgeline. No one answered his call.

"What now?" Colombe muttered angrily. He tried the radio again. Still no answer.

"After the way you cursed them out, they probably left the radio turned off," Magglio suggested.

"How are they supposed to keep in touch without the radio on?" Colombe retorted, shaking his head angrily. "They're worse than useless!"

The other man set the chain saw back, then closed the lid on the footlocker. "Help me carry this ashore," he suggested. "Then I'll run up and get them."

Together, the men lifted the footlocker and propped it on the edge of the boat. Colombe remained aboard, holding the container in place, as Magglio jumped down to the embankment, sinking up to his ankles in the thick, reddish mud.

"All right, I have it," he called up, grabbing the other end of the footlocker.

The captain was about to jump down from the boat when he stopped himself and glanced over his shoulder. Out across the lagoon, an old, weathered fishing trawler, twice the size of Colombe's vessel, drifted into view, heading downriver. There were a few men on deck holding fishing rods over the side of the boat.

"Why wasn't this reported?" Colombe grumbled. "Don't we have any sentries who know how to do their job?"

Before Magglio could respond, the other boat suddenly veered its course, gliding into the lagoon. At the same time, Colombe heard, for the first time, the drone of a helicopter. A few seconds later, a Galicia came into view, sweeping across the river toward the lagoon. On the boat, meanwhile, the men had cast aside their fishing rods in favor of assault rifles.

"Attack!" Colombe shouted at the top of his lungs. "We're under attack!"

He let go of the footlocker and dived to the deck as a volley of gunfire blistered the far side of the boat. Ashore, Magglio quickly reeled backward, letting the locker drop into the mud, then sprinted along the embankment, spreading the alarm. He'd only covered a few yards of ground when he came into the sights of the helicopter's pod guns. No less than five rounds plowed into him, ripping through his chest and ribs. He let out a final cry, then sprawled forward, landing a few yards shy of the partially submerged ramp. His lifeblood seeped into the mud, turning it even redder.

Colombe had fared better, but only for the moment. He managed to crawl along the deck to the main cabin without being struck, but as he scrambled inside and grabbed for a Weatherby Mark V rifle, gunfire from the other boat took out the cabin windows. Colombe howled in pain as flying shards of glass struck him in the neck and shoulders. He did his best to ignore his wounds and whirled toward his attackers, taking aim through the Weatherby's scope. He fired and took out a gunner on the foredeck of the other boat, but two more soldiers quickly took the dead man's place and returned fire before Colombe could line up another shot.

Struck in the face, the Basque dropped his rifle and staggered backward, crashing into the boat's controls before dropping to the floor. Groaning, blood steaming across his eyes, he groped blindly for the Weatherby. He managed to reach it, but his fingers went limp before they could close around the stock.

"Mother of God," he gasped, expending his final breath.

"WE CAME across a sentry, too," Captain Peidro told Lyons and Blancanales, speaking loud over the sound of gunfire emanating from the lagoon. Peidro had rendezvoused with Lyons and Blancanales moments before the shooting had started. They were positioned on an outcropping fifty yards uphill from the clearing the BLM had been carving out of the forest. The rest of the commandos were down on the ground, slowly closing in on the enemy; now and then Lyons and Blancanales caught a glimpse of them stealing through the brush. From their vantage point, however, the overgrowth was too dense for them to see the fighting up ahead.

"I don't know if we're going to pick any more of them off back here," Lyons said. "From the sounds of it, they're making a stand where they are."

"Go ahead if you want," Peidro replied. "I'll stay put and—"

The captain was cut off in midsentence as a round of gunfire tore through the canopy overhead, striking him in the shoulder. Lyons tracked the direction the shot had come from and quickly returned fire with his carbine.

"They've got somebody up in the trees!" he said. "Back up!"

He and Blancanales bolted upright and assisted Peidro to his feet. They retreated from the edge of the outcropping just as another burst chattered their way, glancing off the rock surface they'd just abandoned. They took cover behind the thick, gnarled trunk of an old beech tree growing from the edge of the stream that coursed past the promontory.

"I'm all right," Peidro said with a grimace, pressing a hand against his shoulder wound. Blood seeped up through his fingers. "Go finish them off!"

"In a minute," Lyons said. He leaned away from the trunk and fired blinding into the treetops. "First we need to get these snipers out of their roosts."

Blancanales glanced up the side of the tree they were crouched behind, then slung his carbine over his shoulder and told Lyons, "Give me a boost and I'll try to beat them at their own game."

Lyons looked up, as well, then nodded and cupped his hands together, creating a makeshift stirrup for Blancanales to step into. Pol grabbed hold of Lyons's shoulder, then quickly hoisted himself up. Once he was within reach of the lowest branch, he grabbed hold and pulled himself up into the tree. One of the snipers apparently saw what he was up to and fired a round that chipped bark off the side of the tree.

"I'll try to keep them busy!" Lyons called up.

"That would be nice," Blancanales replied.

He waited for Lyons to return fire, then set his sights on the upper branches and began climbing. At one point he glanced downhill and saw the body of a commando who'd been felled by sniper fire. Off in the distance, the exchange of gunfire continued. Blancanales could also hear the chopper droning overhead, and he proceeded cautiously. The last thing he wanted to have to deal with was having Grimaldi mistake him for one of the enemy.

Halfway up the tree, the trunk began to narrow and branch out. Blancanales stopped climbing and secured his footing, then cradled his carbine in the gap where the trunk forked. He peered through his sights, trying to get a bead on the man who'd been firing at him. With all the trees between them, however, it was no easy task. He spotted a pair of squirrels frantically bounding from limb to limb, as well as a large, untended bird's nest in the upper reaches of a tree directly across from the stream, but otherwise all he could see were leaves and a network of intertwining branches.

Finally he spotted his target. Forty yards away, high up in one of the other beeches, the sniper, like Blancanales, was straddling two branches and leaning against the tree's trunk as he lined up his shot.

He was aiming directly at Blancanales.

Both men fired simultaneously. The Able Team warrior felt the sting of a bullet grazing his right thigh, but he ignored the wound and kept an eye on the other gunman. He wasn't sure if he'd hit him, but the man reeled back slightly and lost his footing. Flinging out one arm, he tried to grab the nearest branch for support but came up short. The sniper's rifle dropped from his grasp as he began to fall. The branches beneath him snapped under his weight, and by the time he cleared the lowermost limb he was falling backward, feet up over his head. His neck snapped when he hit the ground, killing him instantly.

Blancanales stayed, shifting his gaze and searching the treetops for signs of another sniper. When he couldn't see one, he finally took time to inspect his wound. Ripping open his pantleg, he saw that his thigh was soaked with blood. It looked worse than it was, though. The bullet had gone clear through, striking nothing vital. All he'd have to do was stop the bleeding and he was sure he'd be all right.

Slinging his rifle back over his shoulder, Blancanales began to climb back down.

"Nice work," Lyons called up to him. "Looks like he got a piece of you, though."

"Just a nibble," Blancanales assured his partner.

He continued to slowly make his way down, wincing whenever his wound brushed against the trunk or one of the branches. Off near the lagoon, meanwhile, the firefight continued, punctuated now by the occasional blast of high explosives. Blancanales couldn't be sure if they were grenades or mortars, but he was concerned by how deeply the blasts were reaching into the forest.

"Back off, Jack!" he muttered, certain the rounds were coming from the Galicia Grimaldi was piloting.

A few seconds later the tree he was climbing quaked violently, struck by an errant shell. Blancanales managed to grab hold of the trunk and keep himself from falling, but it wasn't enough. Below him, he heard a sickening snap, and the next thing he knew the tree was pitching violently forward, carrying him with it.

THE MOMENT he'd felt the tree being struck, Carl Lyons had instinctively lunged away from the trunk, knocking Captain Peidro flat on the ground and shielding him with his body. When the trunk snapped seconds later, splinters of wood struck his back and thighs with enough force to raise welts. Lyons winced.

"Why the hell do they call it friendly fire?" he murmured.

When he looked over his shoulder and saw the tree falling away from him, he quickly scrambled to his feet, leaving Peidro to tend to himself, at least for the moment.

"Pol!" Lyons cried out.

Blancanales was still perched halfway up the toppling beech, clinging to one of the branches. He didn't have many other options. The tree was crushing every small tree in its path as it toppled toward the mountain stream, and jumping clear seemed just as deadly a proposition as hanging on until he was brought crashing to the ground.

As Lyons watched on helplessly, he saw Blancanales bend to a crouch. Then, a split second before the tree hit the water, Blancanales lunged outward, trying to leap clear. It almost worked. He managed to prevent himself from being impaled on one of the larger branches, but there was no way he could avoid landing in the stream, which, at this point of its downhill run toward the lagoon, was more of a rapids. He disappeared briefly below the crimson-tainted waterline, then surfaced for a moment—just long enough for Lyons to see that he'd been knocked unconscious. The current snatched him up and began to carry him along like so much flotsam.

"Son of a bitch!" Lyons shouted.

He knew that if he didn't get to Blancanales quickly, the man would either drown or wind up being battered against the huge boulders that rose from the deep stream at irregular intervals, breaking the river's flow. There was no easy way down to the stream, however. The safest way would have been to backtrack to the base of the outcropping, then crawl down to level ground. But there was no time for that. Instead, Lyons opted for the most direct approach.

Though the tree Blancanales had been perched in had snapped clear of its stump, once it had landed in the water it had stayed put for the most part, meaning that its splintered base still angled up into the air above the small trees it had crashed through. To reach the tree from the outcropping would require a twelve-foot leap, so Lyons took a few steps back, nudging into Peidro.

"You'll never make it!" the captain told him.

"Just what I wanted to hear," Lyons said. He steeled himself, then bolted forward, getting three full strides in before flinging himself headfirst into the air.

He'd hoped to land atop the fallen tree, but he'd mistimed his jump slightly and came up short. He made the best of it, reaching for one of the splintered ends poking out from the underside of the tree. He managed to grab hold long enough to swing his legs out under him so that when he let go, he landed at the edge of the stream feet first. Without hesitation, he went with his momentum and threw himself into the water.

The stream was cold, so cold that by the time he surfaced Lyons could already feel his fingertips beginning to go numb. He figured that was the least of his problems. He sputtered, treading water and letting the current drag him along as he tried to spot Blancanales. There was no sign of him.

"Damn!"

There was nothing for Lyons to do but start swimming toward where he'd last seen his partner. He plied his way through the water with broad strokes, twisting his body whenever he came upon one of the boulders. For every one he managed to avoid, however, there were two that he bounded off. He felt as if he were swimming through a gauntlet and being struck from either side by a sledgehammer. He continued to keep an eye open for Blancanales, but the farther he was dragged along the watery obstacle course, the more his hopes faded. Worse yet, he could feel his arms and legs going numb on him, as well. If he stayed in the water much longer, he wasn't going to get out alive, either.

Then, after glancing a final set of boulders, Lyons suddenly felt himself dropping as if the stream had suddenly been pulled out from underneath him.

He was being swept over a waterfall.

CHAPTER TWENTY-THREE

Lyons assumed it was all over for him.

There was no sensation of seeing his life passing before his eyes, however, no glimpse of white light from some mysterious other side. In fact, there was little time for any kind of reaction, because just as suddenly as he found himself being carried over the side of the waterfall, his would-be death ride came to an abrupt end as he was deposited into deep pool of water a mere dozen yards below the rim of the falls. The water was a few degrees warmer, and the reddish taint was diluted by runoff from the Avignon River. Once he surfaced and blinked his eyes clear, Lyons realized he'd landed in the northernmost edge of the lagoon.

After drawing in a few breaths, he swam clear of the falls and began looking around for Blancanales. A small peninsula jutted into the lagoon, blocking his view of the combat zone, but from what he could hear, it seemed the firefight was drawing to a close. There were intermittent bursts of gunfire, but the only other sound was that of the helicopter. It was hidden from view by trees growing up from the peninsula, but Lyons could tell it was close by.

The water got warmer the farther he swam from the waterfall, and the numbness began to fade from his arms and legs. Not that he noticed. He scanned the surface of the lagoon for his partner, but all he could see were floating branches and other bits of debris carried down by the stream. A pang of dread began to gnaw at him, and when he finally spotted a body floating facedown a dozen yards to his left, the pang gave way to a sudden feeling of emptiness.

"Goddamn it, Pol," he cursed, furiously stroking his way toward the body.

It wasn't right, Lyons thought to himself bitterly. All these years of facing up to the enemy and living to tell the tale, and now Blancanales had been brought down by his own side. Dammit, it wasn't right.

Once he reached the body, Lyons reached out and started to turn the drowned man over. Even before he got a look at the face, Lyons took note of the man's clothing and felt a stirring of renewed hope. One glimpse at the bluing features of the dead man and Lyons's hope turned to relief and guarded euphoria.

It wasn't Blancanales. The dead man was Basque. He'd been shot twice through the chest. Lyons figured it was a sentry who most likely had been taken out by the commandos on the fishing trawler.

Lyons let go of the body and was about to resume his search when he heard a faint voice behind him.

"Over here."

Lyons turned in the water. At first all he could see was a large, leafy bough floating in the water. Then a hand poked through the leaves and parted a few small branches, revealing a familiar face.

"That was quite a ride, huh?" Blancanales called out.

Lyons grinned as he swam over to his colleague. Blancanales was clinging to the bough with one hand.

"Damn, am I ever glad to see that ugly mug of yours," Lyons stated. "I thought you were a goner."

"You and me both," Blancanales conceded. "I blanked out for second there, and when I came to, here I was, playing rub-a-dub-dub in this oversize bathtub."

"Yeah, well, I think we're soaked enough," Lyons said. "Let's get the hell out of here and help them wrap up the party."

"Gladly."

The men pushed away from the bough and wearily swam toward the nearest embankment.

"How's the leg?" Lyons asked between strokes.

"Hell if I know," Blancanales confessed. "It's still there, I guess."

"I know what you mean," Lyons replied. "I'm ready to hop in a microwave and have them set it on defrost."

Once they reached land, the men straggled up through the red mud, then collapsed, exhausted. A last few gunshots sounded through the forest across from them, then gave way to the throb of the helicopter. Finally the men caught a glimpse of the Galicia. It swept out over the river, then turned and started toward them.

"Shit, not again," Blancanales groaned. He slowly rose to his feet and waved his arms over his head, shouting, "Open your eyes, Jack! It's us!"

The chopper swooped down, fanning the surface of the lagoon as it bore down on Lyons and Blancanales. The men warily stared at the pod guns, then shifted their gaze to the cockpit windshield. Sunlight glanced off the glass, however, and they weren't able to see if Grimaldi had recognized them.

Suddenly the aircraft pivoted sideways, giving Lyons and Blancanales a view of the rear cabin. Lyons breathed a sigh of relief when he recognized Peidro poised in the opened doorway, holding a gauze patch to his wounded shoulder.

"I was hoping we'd find you here," the Spaniard called out. Indicating the cockpit, he quickly added, "I already gave the gunner hell for taking you out of the action."

"Screw it," Lyons said. "All's well that ends well. Just set that whirlybird down so we can get out of here."

"I think that can be arranged."

The Galicia flew past the two men, then set down on a patch of grass twenty yards behind them. Blancanales leaned on Lyons, favoring his wounded leg, and the two men made their way to the chopper. Once they were aboard, Grimaldi wandered back from the cockpit to greet them.

"Guess I blew it back there," he apologized. "I was so busy dodging bullets I couldn't keep an eye on the gunner."

"Ancient history," Blancanales said. "Give the guy a slap on the wrist and tell him to be more careful next time."

"Will do."

Grimaldi returned to the controls. As he lifted off and circled back to the clearing where most of the fighting had taken place, Peidro handed Blancanales the same first-aid kit he'd used to clean his shoulder wound.

"From the looks of it, we were right about this being a staging area for the tank," he said. "So far we've counted a dozen men, counting sentries."

"Is that all?" Blancanales said, swabbing his leg with disinfectant. "They sure put out a lot of bang for their buck."

Peidro nodded. "We lost three of our own."

"Sniper fire?" Lyons guessed.

The captain nodded again, adding, "I don't think they were up there as snipers, though. They all had handsaws and machetes. I think they were up there working on the trees and just brought their rifles along as a precaution."

"What about Angelica Rigo?" Blancanales asked.

Peidro shook his head. "She's not among the dead," he said, "but we're still combing the perimeter. Maybe she'll turn up."

"Somehow I doubt it," Lyons said.

By now they'd reached the main stretch of the lagoon. The commandos had moored their fishing trawler alongside the bullet-riddled boat where Rico Colombe had been gunned down. Close by, Lyons and Blancanales could see the top edge of the half-finished ramp poking up from the water's edge.

"I take it the tank hasn't shown up yet," Blancanales said.

"No," Peidro confirmed. "There's no sign of it, but if this was where they planned to bring it ashore, I think we have a good chance of finding it if we head upriver and keep our eyes open."

"Let's do it, then," Blancanales said.

"And while we're at it," Lyons added, "let's hope they don't find out we just fumigated this rat's nest they're headed for. Otherwise they're likely to burrow in a hole somewhere where we'll never find them."

"I can vouch for my men," Peidro told Lyons. "There's no way any of them would spill information to the enemy."

"Good for them," Lyons said, "but we've already uprooted one mole, and my experience has been that if you find one, you can bet your bottom dollar there are others."

CHAPTER TWENTY-FOUR

Barcelona, Spain

"...and you'll probably have that headache for a while, so make sure to get this prescription filled," the doctor told Cristofer, handing him a slip of paper. "Take two pills right off, then another two before you go to bed if you're still in pain."

Cristofer thanked the doctor and set the prescription on his hospital bed while he changed into his street clothes. It wasn't only his head that hurt. He'd banged his knees on the dashboard when he'd driven the patrol car into the guard wall on Seacoast Drive, and the outward force of the air bag had left him with bruised ribs. They were slight injuries, to be sure, but injuries nonetheless, and in a way he was thankful to have sustained them. If he'd have walked away from the wreck without a scratch, suspicions might have arisen about his possible complicity in Xavier Golato's escape attempt. As it was, he knew it was likely he'd face questioning at some point.

When precinct Captain Armando Otason strode into the room as he was buttoning his shirt, Cristofer braced himself. This is it, he thought to himself.

"So, how's the hero of the day?" Otason greeted him.

Cristofer was taken aback.

"Hero?"

"I was just in talking with Rodrigo," Otason said, referring to the motorcycle cop who'd led the ill-fated caravan. "He says if you weren't so quick behind the wheel, you'd have run into him and he'd be dead instead getting off with just a sprained ankle."

"I just reacted," Cristofer responded modestly, still on his guard. "I barely remember it happening."

"Well, your reactions saved the day," Otason replied. "Your partner was singing your praises, too. When he wasn't complaining about his broken nose, that is." The precinct captain chuckled. "Idiot thinks that air bag ruined his chances of being a movie star."

Cristofer forced a grin. "He's probably right."

"It could have been a lot worse." Otason patted Cristofer on the back. "Good work."

The compliment did little to stem Cristofer's creeping sense of paranoia. He couldn't help wondering if the captain was setting him up by making it seem like he wasn't under suspicion. If internal affairs had been brought in, it'd be just like them to have Otason lure him into a false sense of security, hoping he'd somehow betray himself down the line. Cristofer knew he had to be careful.

"I still don't think I'm any kind of hero," he protested. "I let the prisoner get away."

"For all of five seconds," Otason countered. "He's dead and probably half-eaten by sharks by now, so, in my book at least, all's well."

"But how can we be sure it was him?" Cristofer said, deciding his best course was to play devil's advocate. "The body was washed away before we got a chance to look at it."

"Maybe so," Otason responded, "but when we checked the cliff, we saw fresh bloodstains and broken shrubs where he bounced off the rocks before hitting the water. What more proof do we need?"

"But what about that drainage pipe?" Cristofer asked. "I thought we figured the BLM was waiting there for him after they'd let those cows loose in the roadway."

"If they were there, they must have fled once they saw him fall," the captain theorized. "They had enough time to reach the bike paths and make a getaway before we spotted the pipe. So, yes, we still have some of those bastards on the loose, but that's a whole other matter. The fact is, thanks to you, we didn't lose any men. I'm going to see to it that you get a commendation."

"That's really not necessary," Cristofer said.

"I insist," Otason told him. "And I want you to go ahead and take a few days off. With pay, of course."

This was too easy, Cristofer thought. He eyed the captain, looking for some indication that he was being set up. If Otason was hiding some ulterior motive, however, it didn't show.

"What about the convention?" Cristofer asked. "I thought we were understaffed."

"We'll manage."

Cristofer decided to play the dedication card; he knew what a sucker Otason was for loyalty.

"I appreciate the offer," he told the captain, "but I'd rather get back to work. I can take some time off after the convention."

"Are you sure?"

Cristofer nodded. "You still need me to run the bomb checks on the civic square, right?"

"Good point," the captain conceded. "You know those dogs

better than anybody. Except maybe Nadra, of course, but I'd hate to have to rely on him. Besides, he's insisting that he wants to stay here another day so he can have a consult with a plastic surgeon about his damn nose."

"That's Nadra for you," Cristofer said.

"All right, then," Otason said. "Go ahead and work through the weekend, but then you're getting some time off. That's an order."

"Understood," Cristofer said.

Otason saw that Cristofer had dressed and said, "I'm on my way to the station. Do you need a ride anywhere?"

Cristofer shook his head. "I need to fill a prescription, then I want to get something to eat. I can take a cab home."

"Fair enough." The captain patted Cristofer on the back again, then excused himself and left the room, just as the nurse was coming in with Cristofer's discharge papers. Cristofer took his time signing them, then asked for directions to the pharmacy. As he waited downstairs for his prescription to be filled, Cristofer nonchalantly kept an eye on everyone else in the pharmacy. He wanted to know if he was being followed. No one seemed suspicious, but he remained cautious as he left the hospital. It was dusk outside. Cristofer walked in the twilight to a small restaurant halfway up the block. He ate out on the sidewalk dining area, keeping a watchful eye on traffic and pedestrians passing by on the sidewalk. Again, he spotted no one who looked as if he or she might be tailing him.

Once he was done eating, Cristofer went inside to use the bathroom, then slipped out the back entrance and crossed a back alley to a side street. He saw a bus pull up to the corner and waited until the last second to board it, then rode less than two blocks before getting off and switching to a taxi. It wasn't until he'd ridden halfway across the city to the Drassanes district that he began to relax.

Finally convinced he wasn't being followed, Cristofer got out of the cab and walked another three blocks, then slipped into an alley and circled to the back entrance of a nondescript sheet-metal plant. There was a man standing near the door, and when he spotted Cristofer, he reached inside his coat.

"It's me," Cristofer said, holding his hands out at his sides as he walked within range of the light mounted over the door.

The man was Emilio Carreon, a low-ranking BLM recruit. "We were wondering if you'd show up," he said as he opened the door for Cristofer.

"I didn't want to risk using a phone," Cristofer explained.

Carreon nodded, grabbing a walkie-talkie clipped to his belt. "They're upstairs," he said. "I'll let them know you're here."

Once inside the building, Cristofer took a flight of steps up the second floor. Angelica was waiting for him on the landing, a broad smile on her face.

"You did it!" she whispered, kissing him on the cheek and giving him a slight hug. "We were worried about you."

"I'm fine," he assured her, fighting back an urge to hold her closer. One way or another, he was determined to put the woman out of his life after this evening. Succumbing to her charms wasn't the way to go about it. "Let's get on with it."

Cristofer followed Angelica into a workroom filled with several industrial lathes and other metal-working equipment. Xavier Golato was there, huddled over a workbench next to Guillermo Blanca, the BLM's explosive expert. When he spotted Cristofer, Golato moved over to greet him.

"The wonder worker!" Golato said, shaking Cristofer's hand vigorously. "I'm indebted to you, my friend."

All the praise was beginning to get on Cristofer's nerves. He shrugged off the compliment and told Golato, "Let's just hope the rest of your plans go as well."

"Indeed," Golato said. "Come, have a look at what we've put together."

Once they reached the workbench, Golato and Angelica moved close together, leaving Cristofer to stand across the table from Blanca. Cristofer suppressed his jealousy and turned his attention to the bomber's handiwork.

Blanca had housed slabs of C-5 plastic explosive inside eight different traylike sheet metal compartments, each the size of an attaché case. The slabs in each compartment were connected by wiring to two separate detonators. One featured a LED timer, the other a small transceiver.

"The casings are the same dimensions as these power boxes," Blanca explained, pointing out Polaroid snapshots Cristofer had taken of the receptacles positioned on each level of the civic square's underground garage. "I'll have them rigged with adhesives so you only have to press them into position on the back side. They'll be out of sight, but if anyone happens to see them, they'll look like part of the whole unit."

Cristofer nodded. "I understand."

"The only problem will be securing them in position without being spotted by the security cameras," Golato said.

"That's not a problem," Cristofer said. "I've already timed the cameras."

"What about the dogs?" Angelica asked.

"The dogs will be sniffing for what I tell them to sniff for," Cristofer said. He pointed to the compartments containing the plastique. "They'll ignore these."

"Good," Blanca said. "If all goes well, the timers will set

off the bombs just as the conference is about to open. If for some reason we need to change the time or detonate them earlier, we can do it by remote."

"And you're sure these will bring the whole place down?" Cristofer asked.

Blanca nodded, then unfolded one of the blueprints Cristofer had delivered to Angelica earlier in the day. "They'll weaken these key supports," he said, pointing to the diagram as he spoke. "And the two charges set here will set off the main gas line. That will be the coup de grâce."

"And where does the tank come in?" Cristofer wanted to know.

Golato and Angelica exchanged a look, then Angelica told Cristofer, "You haven't heard?"

"Heard what?"

"They raided the site we'd hope to fire the tank from," Angelica explained. "That is no longer an option."

"Fortunately," Blanca interjected, "we likely won't need it. Even if the square doesn't implode on itself, there will be enough casualties for us to declare victory."

Cristofer was confused. "Then you went to all the trouble of stealing the tank for nothing?"

"It was an insurance policy," Angelica told him. "And even if we can't use it here, we will still be able to cash it in."

CHAPTER TWENTY-FIVE

Alvaro Hot Springs, Pyrenees Mountains, Spain

"It looks like we outfoxed ourselves this time," Salvador Jobe told Jacque Rigo as the two men stood at the edge of the steaming hot springs they'd driven the FSAT-50 into more than two hours earlier.

"Shut up," Jacque snapped irritably. "I don't need to be reminded."

As brilliant as Jacque's strategy for concealing the tank had seemed at the time, there was a variable both he and the engineers who'd helped Timo Ibanez design the FSAT-50 had failed to take into consideration. At least two of the seals meant to waterproof the drivetrain and engine compartment had been unable to withstand the temperature of the hot springs, and when dusk approached and Jacque decided they should resume their cross-country trek, it had become clear that the damage was worse than anticipated. The drivetrain in particular had been rendered inoperative, preventing the FSAT from making use of its treads.

In short, the tank was stuck.

Once Jobe and the backup troops had arrived in the FAM truck, they had helped Jacque and Geraldo Carreon try any number of ways to wrest the tank from the hot springs—everything from running a tow line to the truck to filling the ballast holds in hopes of getting it to float—but nothing had worked. Now, as twilight faded and the first stars of the evening appeared in the night sky overhead, the bulky vehicle remained mired in place, more stubborn than a defiant mule.

"At least no one can see it from the air," Jobe philosophized, gesturing at the canopy of leafy branches that the men had propped over the FSAT-50's turret.

Jacque glanced skyward, past the branches. It had been more an hour since the last helicopter had passed by overhead, but every few minutes he had seen planes streaking through the higher altitudes. So far the planes had all been passenger jets—bound from Paris to Barcelona, no doubt—but he figured that eventually some surveillance aircraft would come along the same air route and sniff them out, provided the enemy's spy satellites didn't beat them to it.

"We can't just stay here and wait for them to find us," Jacque grumbled miserably.

"We still have the truck," Jobe reminded him, pointing to the FAM vehicle parked uphill from the hot springs. "If someone spots us, we can leave the tank behind and make a run for it."

Jacque didn't respond. Leave the tank behind? It was out of the question. As it was, he was sure that his brother and sister would blame him unmercifully once he was forced to break down and let them know what had happened. It was bad enough the tank was stuck. If he were to let it slip out of his hands, as well, he would never hear the end of it. Miguel and Angelica would mock him and second-guess him, not only for driving into the hot springs, but also for prematurely killing the tank's crew. They'd say Rey Hespera and Matteo

Bainz would have known better than to try to use the springs as a hiding place. They'd go back to calling him little brother and making him the butt on their constant jokes. He was determined not to let that happen. No, he wasn't about to abandon the tank. And if it was the last thing he ever did, he was going to figure a way to haul it out of the springs and get it running.

Jobe was still thinking along the same lines. "We could send some men out to look for something," he suggested. "A tow truck with a winch might work."

"A tow truck?" Jacque said. "We're in the middle of nowhere! There's not a service station within twenty miles of here."

"Maybe not," Jobe countered, "but cars break down even in the middle of nowhere and need to be towed. We could take the truck back to the main road and pretend it stopped running. If we could reach someone by phone, hopefully we could get them to send the biggest tow truck they have."

Jacque thought it over.

"All right, it's not a bad idea," he finally conceded. "Take a few men and see what you can do."

Jobe left Jacque and wandered over to a small clearing next to a stand of nearby trees. Most of the other men were sprawled out on the grass. Some were eating rations while others slept. Jobe was rounding up a crew when the FSAT-50's main hatch door swung open. Jacque turned to the tank and saw Geraldo Carreon rise into view, pushing aside a few of the tree limbs obstructing his way. For the past hour he'd been cooped up inside the tank, trying to figure a way to access the drivetrain compartment without flooding the cabin. So far he'd had no luck. All he had to show for his labors was a faceful of grease and sweat.

"A call from your brother," he called out to Jacque. "He says it's important."

Jacque's stomach knotted as he kicked off his boots and waded into the steaming water. Once he reached the tank, he clambered up to the turret and took the radiophone from Carreon, telling him, "Take a break and go get something to eat."

Carreon gladly abandoned the tank, leaving Jacque alone to talk with his brother.

Miguel's first words were ominous. "Geraldo says you've run into some kind of problem with the tank."

Jacque was furious. He cupped his hand over the mouthpiece and shouted to Carreon. When the other man glanced back, Jacque made an obscene gesture and cursed him.

"I'm sorry," Carreon called back, "but I was hot and frustrated and it just came out."

"That's no excuse!" Jacque countered.

"Hello?" came Miguel's voice over the headset. "Jacque? Are you there?"

Jacque turned from Carreon and sighed with resignation. There seemed little point in lying, so he warily passed along the news about the tank. As expected, he was answered by a stream of epithets. Miguel was shouting so loud Jacque finally held the headset away from his ear and waited until his brother had calmed down.

"There was no way we could have known," Jacque said in his defense. "You thought it was a good idea yourself when I first mentioned it to you."

There was a pause on the line, then Miquel, said, "What's done is done. And if it's any consolation, you're not the only one who's run into problems. Someone has cast the evil eye on us."

"What do you mean?" Jacque asked.

"I mean, it doesn't really matter any more whether you can get the tank running," Miguel responded.

Jacque listened with growing alarm as his brother brought him up to date on the spate of setbacks the BLM had suffered the past few hours: the deaths of Zacharias Brinquel and Luis Manziliqua, the loss of contact with Martin Zamara and, most recently, the raid on the lagoon site outside Barcelona where Jacque was to have delivered the tank.

Jacque was shaken by the news. Brinquel's death tore into him particularly. Zacharias had always treated him like a favorite nephew, even before he'd joined the ETA. He found it hard to imagine that the man was dead. But even in the midst of Jacque's grief, he took his brother's advice and was consoled that at least he wasn't the only one who'd been visited by misfortune. It truly seemed as if a curse had befallen the BLM.

"Where does that leave us?" Jacque asked his brother once he'd absorbed all the news. "Do we have to forget about attacking the conference?"

"No," Miguel assured him. "On that front, at least, the news is good." He quickly related the news of Xavier Golato's daring escape from police custody and assured Jacque that the plan to bomb the civic square was still on.

"And you've dealt with the Iraqis already?" Jacque asked.

"Actually, that is the reason I called," Miguel said. "When I met with them earlier, they said they wanted the tank and both warheads. I turned them down at the time, but now I think we might renegotiate."

"I can see them wanting both warheads," Jacque replied, "but given the tank's condition, I can't see them wanting it."

"Of course they'll want it," Miguel responded. "The drivetrain isn't what they're interested in. They want the tank to launch the warheads. We may have to lower our asking price, but at this point I say we sell it to them and let them worry about how to get it out of the country."

As the brothers discussed their options in more detail, another jetliner streaked by overhead, leaving a faint contrail of exhaust in its wake. Miguel could hear the plane through the phone connection and asked Jacque what was making the noise. Jacque explained there was air traffic passing over the hot springs at regular intervals.

There was a pause on the line, then Miguel told Jacque, "I know you said the drivetrain is out, but what about everything else? Are the weapons systems operational?"

"I think so," Jacque said. "We haven't tested them, but Geraldo ran a check and he's sure we have the use of everything in the turret."

"If that's the case," Miguel concluded, "I have a plan."

CHAPTER TWENTY-SIX

Alvaro Hot Springs, Pyrenees Mountains, Spain

Jacque Rigo stood atop the turret of the mired FSAT-50, eyes on the highest mountain peak to the north. The sky was clear and the moon was full enough for him to be able to make out the silhouette of the Pyrenees. He could also see the other men huddled beneath the nearby trees, soaking in the warmth of a gas-fired heater. Salvador Jobe was with them; the plan to get their hands on a tow truck had been abandoned in favor of the new strategy laid out in Jacque's conversation with his older brother.

Jacque's stomach rumbled with hunger and he felt a chill in his bones from the light evening breeze, but he ignored the discomfort. After several minutes, he finally received the signal he was waiting for: the keening hoot of a night owl, or at least the closest the sentry on the mountaintop could come to imitating the nocturnal bird of prey.

"Finally," Jacque muttered.

He climbed down the open hatch to the main cabin of the

tank. Geraldo Carreon was seated before the gunner's console, hands poised over the controls, eyes on a small bank of IVIS terminals.

"We've got our plane," Jacque told him. "Are you ready?"

"I've been ready for the past twenty minutes," Carreon replied.

As Jacque watched, Carreon toggled the controls for the recon drone, then activated the launch sequence. Seconds later, there was a muffled whoosh and the tank vibrated faintly as the drone took to the air.

"Here's the screen to watch," Carreon told Jacque, pointing to the upper right IVIS monitor. The screen blinked momentarily, then a luminous green LED grid appeared, following by a small, blinking cursor that drifted smoothly from quadrant to quadrant.

"That's the drone," Carreon explained. "Once the wings are activated, the light will stop blinking and the sensors will start to send back readings."

"I understand all that," Jacque said impatiently.

Both men continued to watch the screen. Soon, as Carreon had warned, the cursor glowed a steady green and its movement across the grid slowed, meaning the drone had leveled off and was switching over to its recon capacities. Carreon worked the controls, changing the grid display slightly, shrinking the viewing area enough to allow a column of digital readouts to scroll down the right side of the screen.

"Now it's synchronizing its readings with the satellite and GPS coordinates, yes?" Jacque guessed.

"Correct," Carreon replied. He adjusted the contrast on the display, then directed Jacque's attention to the upper left section of the gridwork. "There's the plane."

"They aren't going to be able to detect the drone, are they?" Jacque wondered.

"Not likely," Carreon replied. "Even if it was a surveillance craft, I've got the drone flying low enough to avoid detection."

"What's the information scrolling down the side there?" Jacque wanted to know.

"Observation data on the plane," Carreon said. He turned a control knob, slowing the crawl of information so that he could read it. "We have its size and the speed it's traveling, as well as its altitude and flight course."

"And...?"

Carreon sized up the data and reported, "It's a passenger jet. Either a 737 or DC-10."

"Headed for Barcelona?"

"I'll have to check." Carreon opened up a smaller window within the screen and entered a set of readings, then compared them with those in the right column. "Yes," he told Jacque. "It's heading for Barcelona by way of Paris."

"And it's within target range?"

Carreon checked another set of readings, then nodded. "No problem. All we'd have to do is activate the SAM launcher and synchronize it with the drone. We'd have a five-mile window of opportunity to bring it down with a direct hit."

Jacque was elated. He put both hands on Carreon's shoulders and shook him slightly, "You've done well, Geraldo."

Carreon grinned, but cautioned, "You can congratulate me once we've brought a plane down."

"Soon enough," Jacque said. "For now, though, go ahead and recall the drone."

Carreon nodded again and turned his attention to the task of guiding the drone back to the tank. As he did so, Jacque watched the screen. In moments, the passenger jet had cleared the grid, moving out of target range. This had only been a test. Come tomorrow, when Carreon set his sights on the first passenger jet to come his way before the nine-o'clock news, he would carry through with a missile launch. The downing of the plane would also coincide with the opening session of the NATO conference, and once the news spread, there would undoubtedly be a period of mass confusion at the meeting hall as the authorities tried to grasp what had happened and decide on a course of action. It would be during that interlude that the bombs would go off inside the civic square's underground garage. By the time the dust settled, not just Spain but the entire world would be forced to realize the BLM wasn't going to back down until its demands were met. And Jacque would have played a major hand in the show of force. No longer would he be referred to as merely the youngest of the Rigo siblings. People would now have to utter his name in the same breath as that of Miguel and Angelica.

Jacque climbed back up through the hatch and splashed his way out of the hot springs, filled with renewed vigor and euphoria.

"This will be it," he whispered to himself. "My time has come."

CHAPTER TWENTY-SEVEN

Pamplona, Spain

Bansheh Abtaj gently pulled himself off Rena Duli, pausing to kiss her naked breasts before climbing down from the billiards table.

"You are a goddess," he told her.

Duli smiled. "And you are my big, strong bull."

Abtaj laughed as he reached for his clothes. "I'll take that as a compliment, even if they kill the bulls around here."

"That won't happen to you," Duli told him. "At least not by my hand."

Abtaj quickly dressed, then strode to the window and parted the curtains. Through the glass he could see people celebrating beneath the streetlights, and when he opened the window he could hear their revelry. A few blocks away, at the Plaza de Toros, the bullfights were under way and the stadium was packed. As the Iraqi took it all in, Rena came up behind him and wrapped her arms around his chest, kissing his neck.

"I suppose it's time for me to go," she murmured.

Abtaj nodded and turned to face the woman. "You might want to put some clothes on first."

"I thought you wanted me to cause a distraction."

"Not until you reach the stadium," Abtaj reminded her. "Walk out of the hotel looking like that, you'd never make it that far." He kissed her, adding, "I don't like the idea of those heathens laying a hand on you."

"You want me all to yourself."

Abtaj shrugged. "Who could blame me? Now, hurry and get dressed. I need to check on the other arrangements."

Abtaj finished buttoning his shirt on his way out of the den. Two men were still standing vigil before the living-room window, eyeing the Dupentiez estate through their binoculars. The others were busy changing into brightly colored costumes like those worn by the celebrants in the street. They'd also gotten their hands on several large papier-mâché masks and the same sort of horse costumes Miguel had seen men parading around in earlier in the day. Using duct tape, the men were securing Uzis and MP-5 submachine guns inside the facades. Additionally there were more than a dozen hand grenades set out on the coffee table. They, too, would be concealed inside the costumes before the men set out from the hotel.

Abtaj checked his watch, then told the men, "We'll leave in ten minutes."

One of the men nodded and pointed to the sofa beside him. "You get to be St. Fermin."

Abtaj eyed the costume and oversize headpiece bearing the likeness of city's patron saint. How ironic, he thought. That morning he'd been spooked by the sight of all the St. Fermins roaming the streets. Now he would be one of them.

The Iraqi took a colorful robe from the sofa and was pulling it on over his street clothes when his cell phone rang, startling him. He wasn't expecting any calls. He quickly grabbed the phone.

The call was from Miguel Rigo.

"There has been a change in plans," he told Abtaj.

The Iraqi was at first taken aback, concerned that his own plans would now be thrown into disarray. But as Miquel explained the situation, the Iraqi smiled to himself. Things couldn't be working out better.

Miguel, it turned out, had had a change of heart and decided to sell the tank, as well as both warheads after all. The only caveat was that the tank had incurred some sort of mechanical breakdown in its drivetrain. The Iraqis would have to retrieve it on their own and figure a way to steal it out of the country.

"How can we be sure there is only a problem with the tank's mobility?" Abtaj asked once Miguel had finished.

"We are arranging a demonstration," Miguel told him.

"Explain," Abtaj said.

"Turn on your television tomorrow morning and watch the news," Miguel told him. "You will see what the tank is capable of."

"What are you planning?" Abtaj asked.

"You will see," Miguel explained. "Afterward, we can meet. I'll give you the warheads and tell you where you can find the tank."

"What kind of money are we talking about?" Abtaj wanted to know. "If the tank is stranded somewhere and we need to assume the risk of moving it, the price obviously will have to be considerably less than what I offered you earlier."

"Of course," Miguel responded.

The two men bartered briefly over the phone before settling on a price. Abtaj, however, was still wary that Rigo and his men might leave the safehouse, thwarting his plan. He needed some assurance they would stay put, at least for the next hour.

"We'll meet here in Pamplona to conclude the deal, yes?" he said. "I'll need to make arrangements to secure the rest of the money, and I would prefer to have it delivered here where I'm staying."

"That is not a problem," Miguel told him.

"Good," Abtaj replied. "Now, what time in the morning should I be watching for this 'news'?"

"Nine o'clock," Miguel said. "And I have a feeling you will be able to turn to any channel and see what has happened."

"I am looking forward to it," Abtaj said.

The Iraqi ended the call, then slipped the phone back inside its holder and turned to the other men, who were eyeing him expectantly.

"Let's go," he told them. "I think the festivities here are in need of some more fireworks."

"THERE'S RAFE NOW," David McCarter said, glancing out the window of his rental car, parked just outside Pamplona's main bus terminal. He was talking long distance on his cell phone with Aaron Kurtzman.

"I'll let you go, then," Kurtzman told him, adding, "And, again, it's good to know you're back to firing on all cylinders."

McCarter quickly wrapped up the call, then unlocked the door for Encizo, who'd just come out of the terminal. Encizo had a few photos of the Rigo siblings and other known members of the BLM tucked inside his sling. He'd just shown the photos to employees at the terminal, hoping someone would be able to point out who'd planted Timo Ibanez's cell phone on the bus heading north out of Pamplona earlier in the day. The move had paid off; they had their man.

"It was Zacharias Brinquel," Encizo told McCarter as he

slid into the passenger seat. "The guy you plugged back at the hospital. He must've made the plant on his way to Bilbao. One of the drivers remembers him boarding the bus to San Sebastian for a few minutes. Said he had to drop something off with one of the passengers."

"That adds up," McCarter replied. He started the car and inched out of the terminal parking lot, carefully negotiating his way around the throngs of people spilling out into the street.

"Any news from the Farm?" Encizo asked.

McCarter nodded, turning onto a less-congested side street leading away from the heart of town. "Bear says AMI intercepted the bus and found the phone stashed under one of the back seats."

"Thing is, this really doesn't help us much," Encizo said. "We've got a trail that ends with a dead guy in Bilbao. Meanwhile, Ibanez is out there somewhere with those two nukes and we're not any closer to finding him than we were when we got here."

"Maybe T.J.'s had better luck," McCarter said.

"I sure hope so."

"How's the shoulder holding up?" McCarter asked.

"I'm good," Encizo said, adjusting his sling.

After driving past Parc de la Ciudadela and Plaza de Juan XXIII, McCarter turned left onto Avenida de Bayona. A block past the festive merrymaking taking place at Club Marengo, he pulled to a stop along the curb in front of a row of small stores. There were efficiency apartments located above the shops, and after pressing the intercom at a locked gate, McCarter barked a password, then led Encizo up the steps and down the hall to a flat being used as a temporary base of operations for the CIA. There they were greeted by Agent Trace

Harper, who'd been part of the investigatory team T. J. Hawkins had accompanied to the Gamuso weapons plant. He'd flown to Pamplona earlier with Raul Cordero of the Spanish military's special forces. Cordero was inside the apartment, as well, on the phone with one of his contacts. He nodded to McCarter and Encizo and continued his call.

"We have something on their explosives expert," Harper said after the men from Phoenix Force had relayed the information about the planting of Ibanez's cell phone. He led McCarter and Encizo to the kitchen area and grabbed a sheet containing the same head shots Encizo had shown around the bus terminal. He pointed out one particular photo.

"His name is Guillermo Blanca," Harper said. "He's linked to a string of car bombings and that blast outside the stock market in Madrid last spring. He likes to work with C-5 plastique, the same type they turned up when they dragged that lake for the tank."

"Sounds like our guy, all right," Encizo said, eyeing the photograph.

"Anyway," Harper went on, "I've got a second-hand report through an informant that Blanca got his hands on a few crates of C-5 a week ago. Not only that, but also timers and detonators."

"Great," Encizo said, "but where does that get us? I mean, obviously he used the stuff to blow up that decoy tank and the prefab they found in the lake, right?"

"Some of it, yeah," Harper said. "But if he'd used it all, there wouldn't have been anything left to find. That tank and prefab would've been turned into confetti."

"In other words," McCarter said, "he's got some bigger fish he's still planning to fry."

"Exactly," Harper agreed. "And if I was a betting man, I'd say the target's not in Pamplona."

"Barcelona?" Encizo said.

"That'd be my guess," Harper said. "It might well be they've been planning something in tandem with an attack by the supertank. And if that's the case, knocking out that base of theirs on the Avignon River doesn't mean they're out of the ballgame yet."

"They'll just resort to Plan B," Encizo surmised.

"Exactly," Harper said. "And who knows, maybe they've got a Plan C up their sleeves, too."

"We've got some guys in Barcelona," McCarter said. "I'll see that they get on it."

"Same here," Harper said. Gesturing at Cordero, he said, "UOE and AMI are gonna boost their presence there, too."

"Hell," Encizo said, "while we're at it, we might as well head there ourselves. I mean, you have to figure by now everybody we're looking for has already pulled stakes from Pamplona."

"I wouldn't be so sure," Raul Cordero called out from across the room. He'd just gotten off the phone and had overheard the last exchange.

"What makes you say that?" Encizo said.

Cordero tapped a forefinger on the lid of his cell phone. "I've been checking with my sources, too, and it looks like our Iraqi friends are still here in town."

"Where?" Harper asked.

"I'm not certain," Cordero confessed, "but there was a major cash conversion at the Banco de Lozano this afternoon. Roughly the equivalent of two million U.S. dollars in Iraqi currency converted to euros."

"Down payment on a tank and a few warheads?" Encizo suggested.

"A fair assumption," Cordero replied, "especially if you consider that the woman who made the transaction turns out to be a known associate of Bansheh Abtaj."

"And they just let her waltz out with the money?" McCarter said.

Cordero shrugged. "It was a perfectly legal transaction," he said. "At the time, no red flags had been raised, so there was no reason to scrutinize the woman, much less put a tail on her."

"How do we know for sure that it's her?"

"My contacts found out after the fact," Cordero said, "by reviewing footage from surveillance cameras at the bank."

"Okay, then," Encizo said, "I take it back. Maybe we'll stick around after all."

Cordero nodded. "If they withdrew the money here, it stands to reason they plan to make their transaction with the BLM here, too."

"Yes, but whereabouts here?" McCarter wondered.

The answer came three minutes later when T. J. Hawkins showed up. For the past two hours, he and one of Harper's Basque-speaking colleagues had been playing the long shots. Instead of terrorist-related leads, they'd been combing the city's underworld in hopes of turning up a fluke lead from prostitutes, drug dealers or loan sharks who might have unwittingly done business with the BLM. They'd run into their share of dead ends, but finally they'd struck paydirt.

"You're not gonna believe this one," Hawkins said once he and the other CIA agent had entered the flat. They had with them the same batch of photos the other men had been relying on. Hawkins separated one sheet from the others and directed everyone's attention to the mug shot of a young man staring out at the world with cold, dark eyes. "A couple days ago he was cruising the back alleys behind the cathedral looking to score some cocaine and speed. A prostitute talked him into some hashish and a hand job instead."

Harper eyed the photograph, unimpressed. "This guy's small potatoes," he said. "We don't even have his name. So what if he decided to get his horns clipped."

"Let me finish," Hawkins said.

"Sorry," Harper said. "Go on."

"This woman says they smoked a little and he started rambling on about some construction work he was doing just east of town, near the river," Hawkins said. "Something about a jai alai court and a guest house on some estate owned by a hotshot plastic surgeon."

"We pressed her for specifics, but that was all she could give us," said the other CIA agent, "so I figured we'd stop by the newspaper office and talk to our friend at the city desk."

"Edgar?" Harper said.

The other agent nodded, then told the others, "He's been on the job thirty years and knows this town inside out. With just those few things to go on, he put it together and bingo! We've got ourselves the name and address of a PS who, it just so happens, is staying out of town while he has all this work done on his place."

He handed a slip of paper to Harper, who looked it over and raised an eyebrow.

"Pretty high-priced neighborhood for a BLM safehouse," he said skeptically. "How sure was he about this?"

"Like I said, we told him what we had, and he was right on it. I mean, no hesitation."

"That's my point," Harper countered. "Maybe he jumped to the wrong conclusion."

McCarter wasn't about to waste any more time on debate. "There's one way to find out," he said, pointing at the slip of paper with Ruben Dupentiez's address. "I say we cut the chitchat and take a look for ourselves."

CHAPTER TWENTY-EIGHT

Barcelona, Spain

"Well, that was a bust," Carl Lyons grumbled as he climbed out of the helicopter.

He, Rosario Blancanales and Jack Grimaldi had just spent two hours flying up one side of the Avignon River and down the other, looking for the missing FSAT-50. They'd come up empty-handed. And after checking in with the Farm, they realized their earlier rout of the BLM forces at the lagoon had done little to neutralize the separatists' threat to the NATO conference. Following Lyons out of the chopper, Blancanales summed things up in a nutshell.

"No tank, no one to interrogate, no Angelica Rigo."

Jack Grimaldi bounded out of the chopper cockpit in time to hear Blancanales's remark and added sardonically, "And to top things off, I nearly got you guys killed."

"We're past that, Jack," Blancanales reminded him. "Let it go."

The men had touched down at the private hangar at the edge of Barcelona's Aeroport del Prat. They'd been running on fumes the last few miles, and Lyons had overruled refueling so that they could resume their aerial search. He didn't see the point. Captain Peidro of the UOE had already sent out a pair of special-forces choppers better equipped to handle night surveillance, and given the latest news from the Farm about a possible plan to use explosives on the civic square, Lyons figured their time could be better spent on the ground trying to ferret out the BLM's bomber. The question was where to start looking.

Peidro was waiting for them inside the hangar. Following the lagoon raid, he'd returned to Barcelona in the fishing trawler along with the surviving members of his unit. After having his wounds tended to, he'd showered, changed into a clean uniform and put down a good meal. Unlike the Americans, he looked fresh and reinvigorated. When he suggested that the men follow his lead and take a well-deserved break, however, they declined.

"We like to bop till we drop," Lyons wisecracked.

"You'd function better after some rest," Peidro persisted.

"Not going to happen," Lyons said, "so let's move on."

Peidro realized he wasn't going to change the men's minds, so he sighed and quickly briefed them on the latest developments. He told them that, as expected, security had been tightened around the civic square. Along with an increased police presence, the barriers were being fortified and a coordinated effort was being made between the UOE, AMI and members of NATO's intelligence to both stake out and canvas an expanded five-block perimeter in hopes of intercepting the bombers before they could get within striking range of the conference.

"That leaves trying to get to them wherever they're holed up," Lyons surmised.

"We have teams looking into that, too," the officer told them. "But Barcelona is a big city, and we have a lot of ground to cover."

"I can see that," Blancanales said, eyes on a map of the city that Peidro had tacked to a nearby bulletin board. Colored pins marked the areas where the various agencies were taking action. The most pins, not surprisingly, were within a one-mile radius of the civic square, and though the concentration dwindled considerably out toward the far edges of the city, every area of the city, including the harbor, was clearly under some form of surveillance.

When he'd spoken to Hal Brognola shortly before they'd landed, Lyons had been told about the lead Hawkins had managed to sniff out by trolling the high-crime area of Pamplona. If they were lucky, he figured, maybe lightning could strike twice. "Where do the hookers and drug dealers do most of their business around here?" he asked Peidro.

Without hesitation, the man pointed out the lower stretch of the Las Ramblas district. "This whole area around Drassanes," he said. "It's just beyond the heightened perimeter, but, as you can see, we're giving it extra attention nonetheless. The BLM is made up of lowlifes, so it would make sense that they would feel most comfortable there."

That settled it for Lyons. He told Peidro, "Why don't you go ahead and stick another pin there?"

"THEY'RE BEING THOROUGH, that's for sure," Cristofer noted as he turned the corner and headed toward the entrance to the Barcelona civic center.

"Just not quite thorough enough," Guillermo Blanca replied. The BLM explosives expert was sitting next to Cristofer in the front seat of the police officer's squad car. He was wearing one of Cristofer's spare uniforms. It was a size too large for him, but it was unlikely anyone would notice.

In the back seat, the precinct's two bomb-sniffing German shepherd dogs, Sal and Pablo, sat obediently, panting lightly as they stared out the windows. Cristofer had worked with the dogs all week retraining them so they wouldn't respond to the scent of C-5 plastique, and the effort had paid off. Neither animal gave any indication of sensing the high-powered bombs concealed directly behind them in the car's trunk.

As he turned into the entryway to the civic square, Cristofer breathed a tentative sigh of relief. He recognized the armed guard stepping out of the security booth. During the week he'd made a point of engaging the man in small talk, establishing a rapport with this evening's fateful assignment in mind. When he'd found out the guard shared his passion for soccer, he'd gone so far as to lay a wager on this afternoon's game between Madrid and Seville. It was a lousy bet and Cristofer, as he'd hoped, had lost handily. After all, what better way to insure that the guard would be glad to see him that night?

Here, too, the ploy served its purpose. When another pair of armed sentries approached the squad car with hand mirrors and flashlights, intent on checking beneath the vehicle and searching its interior, Cristofer whispered a quick command to the dogs, and when Pablo and Salvador responded by baring their teeth and snarling, the guard waved the sentries off. Once the sentries had stepped away, Cristofer signaled for the dogs to be quiet. The dogs obeyed, but continued to stare out at the sentries as if ready to charge them at the first opportunity.

Cristofer stopped the squad car alongside the guard station and rolled down his window, grinning at the security guard.

"Sorry about that, Eduardo," he said, joking, "I guess they didn't get enough to eat for dinner."

"Not a problem," the guard replied, glancing back at the

animals. "As long as they don't try to bite me when I pick up that money you owe me."

"I was hoping you'd forget," Cristofer said, reaching for his wallet. "I should have known better than to make that bet with you."

"There's another game this weekend if you want to go double or nothing," the guard taunted good-naturedly as he handed Cristofer a log sheet attached to a clipboard.

"I don't think so." Cristofer chuckled, scribbling his name on the sheet. Before handing the clipboard back, he slipped a pair of twenty euro bills under the clip. "I'll just pay up and say I learned my lesson."

"Who's this?" the guard asked, glancing at Blanca.

"He's filling in for my partner," Cristofer explained nonchalantly. "You didn't hear about our crash this afternoon?"

"What crash?"

Cristofer quickly filled the guard in on Xavier Golato's supposedly ill-fated escape attempt on Seacoast Drive, concluding, "Nadra's milking the crash for all it's worth. He's staying at the hospital so he can talk to a plastic surgeon in the morning about his nose."

"Sounds like him, all right," the guard said. "You're here for the usual, I take it."

Cristofer nodded. "It has to be done, although I don't see how anyone could get past security with any explosives. Especially with this new gate they put in for you."

"It's pretty impressive, eh?" the guard said. "You're going to have to wait a minute while we move it."

The normal barrier used to restrict access to the civic center—an unimposing slab of yellow-painted redwood attached to a swing joint—had been supplemented at some point over the past few hours with a three-foot-thick, reinforced concrete slab that overlapped the similarly constructed barricades that now ringed the entire perimeter of the square. The slab was set on one-way rollers, but it still took Eduardo and the two other sentries all their strength to move it to one side.

Once he had enough clearance, Cristofer drove through, waving to the guard, then rolled his window back up. He reached beside him for a handful of dog biscuits and tossed them over his shoulder to Pablo and Sal.

"Nice work, boys."

Guillermo Blanca looked past the dogs and watched the guards sliding the barrier back into place, then turned back to Cristofer.

"That was easy enough," he said.

"You just have to know how to handle people," Cristofer said. "Now, of course, we come to the hard part."

ONCE THEY'D ENTERED the underground garage, Cristofer drove past rows of parked cars to the first power unit. He let the dogs out and put them on leashes while Blanca remained in the car, watching the nearby ceiling-mounted security camera. Cristofer went through the motions of having the dogs sniff the surrounding area until the camera had panned away from them. Then Blanca got out of the car and called out, "Now!"

Cristofer set down the leashes and ordered the dogs to stay put, then quickly circled to the rear of the squad car and popped open the trunk. Blanca joined him, and together they lifted out the first of bombs and carried it over to the power unit. There, Cristofer peeled the backing off the adhesive mounts while Blanca double-checked the timing mechanisms. Satisfied that everything was in order, the men carefully eased the bomb behind the unit and pressed it into place. The mounts held, and when the men stepped back to survey their handiwork, they were convinced that even in the unlikely event that someone noticed the bomb, they would mistake it for part of the power unit.

Blanco checked his watch. "Forty-nine seconds."

"Eleven seconds to spare," Cristofer replied. "Good work. Let's keep it up."

By the time Cristofer had reached the dogs and grabbed their leashes, the security camera was panning back their way. To anyone watching the surveillance footage, it looked as if the two men had just finished inspecting the area and were getting ready to move on.

With the same efficient ease, Cristofer and Blanca continued their rounds, planting another five bombs in their designated spots. Twice they crossed paths with security officers in motorized carts, but in both instances Cristofer had anticipated their rounds and made sure that he and Blanca were out with the dogs, conducting routine inspections on other parts of the garage.

It wasn't until they were about to set the seventh bomb that the men ran into a problem.

Cristofer had just opened the trunk and Blanca was helping lift out the bomb when they heard of faint squeal of a door hinge behind them. Twenty yards to their right, a janitor had just wandered out of the second-floor stairwell, carrying a bucket and several hand towels.

Christopher and Blanca exchanged a wary glance and quickly lowered the bomb back into the trunk. As they were doing so, Cristofer whispered a command to the dogs. Pablo and Salvador immediately turned to the janitor and bared their teeth as they lunged toward him.

Terrified, the janitor dropped his bucket and scrambled back to the stairwell, closing the door behind him.

"Hold off and wait for me in the car," Cristofer told Blanca as he closed the trunk. "Make it look like you're calling the dispatcher."

Blanca nodded. Cristofer moved away from the car, drawing his service pistol as he approached the dogs, calling out for them to be quiet. Pablo and Sal stopped barking and dropped to their haunches, awaiting Cristofer's next command.

"Nice job, boys," he whispered as he strode past them, leveling his gun at the stairwell door. He shouted to the janitor, "Step out slowly with your hands over your head."

There was a pause before the janitor responded, his voice filled with fear. "What about the dogs?"

"Do what I told you and you'll be fine," Cristofer assured the man.

"I can't open the door with both hands on my head," the janitor responded.

"I'll open it for you," Cristofer said, moving closer to the door. He stepped past the fallen bucket and slowly turned the doorknob, then yanked the door open. The janitor stood just inside the stairwell, hands over his head. Cristofer motioned for him to step out into the garage.

"I was just coming out to clean," the janitor said.

"You picked the wrong time," Cristofer said. He told the man to spread-eagle against the nearest wall, then moved forward and began frisking him. "We're checking for bombs. You startled the dogs."

"They scared me more than the other way around," the janitor protested. "I was just trying to do my job. I don't know anything about any bombs."

The man checked out clean. Cristofer stepped away from him and asked, "What needs cleaning out here?"

"I won't know until I look," the janitor said. "Usually the elevator doors and around the trash bins."

"Maybe you should just let it go for tonight," Cristofer suggested.

"If you say so," the janitor said. "Is there a bomb threat?"

"No," Cristofer conceded, "but we're not taking any chances. Go ahead and grab your bucket, then stay in the main building."

"Should I warn the other workers?"

Cristofer shook his head. "Just go about your business and let us do ours, all right?"

The janitor stared past Cristofer at the dogs, then picked up his bucket and headed back toward the stairwell. "Can you make a note of this?" he asked. "In case my boss yells at me for not cleaning up here?"

"Done," Cristofer said. "Now, go on, get out of here."

Once the janitor had disappeared inside the stairwell, Cristofer grabbed the leashes and led the dogs back to the squad car. He could see that the surveillance camera had filmed most of his encounter with the janitor and was now panning away from the power unit. Blanca was tracking the camera, as well, and he quickly bounded out of the car.

"Hurry!" Cristofer called out to him as he popped open the trunk again.

"Did he see anything?" Blanca asked.

"I don't think so," Cristofer said. "It's not like I could ask him."

As they carried the bomb over to the power unit, Blanca said, "I'm not sure we should have let him get away."

"What else could we have done?" Cristofer said. "Shoot him and stick him in the trunk? You don't think someone would notice he was missing?" Indicating the swiveling surveillance camera, he added, "Not to mention the fact that security would know we were the last ones to see him."

"Maybe so, but still, I don't like it."

They set the bomb into position and headed back to the car. "We have just one more bomb to set," Cristofer told Blanca. "After that, we'll leave. If anyone's suspicious, we'll be able to pick up something off the radio."

"And if it turns out they're on to us?" Blanca asked as he slid into the front seat.

"You have the remote detonators, right?" Cristofer said. "If worse comes to worst, we'll blow up the building early."

CHAPTER TWENTY-NINE

Pamplona, Spain

Rena Duli was standing amid the revelers outside the Plaza de Toros when she heard a deafening roar sound from within the arena. She guessed one of the bulls had just met its death and that the crowd was cheering the triumphant matador. Those around her picked up the cry and everyone carrying a flute, drum, whistle or anything else capable of making noise joined. Halfway down the street, someone set off a string of firecrackers, adding to the bedlam.

Before leaving the hotel, Duli had changed into a festive, revealing costume—a flowing skirt hanging low across her waist and a scanty, crimson-colored halter top—and she writhed seductively amid the revelers, crying out with seemingly drunken abandon. Men leered at her and some tried to move close and dance with her, but she was elusive, always on the move, as surefooted as her would-be suitors were clumsy. With tantalizing ease, she threaded her way through the crowd, making her way closer and closer to the thick, raised wooden fences of the outer pens where the remaining bulls were corraled while they awaited their fate in the arena. The pandemonium was making the beasts skittish, and they moved restlessly within their confines, snorting and pawing at the dirt with their sharp hooves, foam flecking the corners of their mouths. Now and then one of the bulls would butt its head against the fence. Guards stood around the barrier and two sets of gates separated the bulls from the street, and though they shouted for the crowd to keep their noise to a minimum, their warnings went unheeded.

Once she had made her way to the gate, Duli rose on her toes as she continued her dancing. Staring over the heads of those around her, she glanced past the street to the far hill leading up to the estates that rimmed the bluff. Dozens of festival goers had ventured up the grassy slope, hoping—in vain—to get a free view of the bullfights. Duli spotted Bansheh Abtaj and several of the other costumed Iraqis among them. They had just broken away from the others and were parading their way farther up the incline, headed toward the upright pylons that supported the terrace where Miguel Rigo had been spotted earlier. Flowering rows of bougainvillea rose up between the pylons, clinging to sturdy trellises and latticeworks. Back at the hotel, Abtaj's men had taken a good look at the latticeworks through their binoculars and determined that they would be strong enough to climb. All that was needed was a moment's diversion and the men would scale their way up to the patio and take the Basques by surprise.

Not all of the Iraqis were with Abtaj, however. Two of the men were following Duli, doing their best to keep up with her as she danced her way toward the gates. Two blocks away, another conspirator was perched atop the flat roof of a gift shop that had closed for the night. Duli couldn't see him, but she knew that he'd brought with him a portable launcher and a small supply of fireworks. She was waiting on his signal, and a minute later he came through, launching a single rocket into the air over the grassy slope.

The moment the rocket burst, filling the night sky with bright-colored streaks of light, Duli pirouetted one last time, then pretended to lose her balance, staggering into the arms of two young, drunken men she felt would likely try to take advantage of her.

She was right.

The two drunks were quick to keep Duli from falling, and they were just as quick to begin groping her with their hands. She let out a cry, telling them to stop, and halfheartedly tried to pull herself away, but they were reluctant to let go of her. She could smell liquor on their breath as they laughed and groped at her halter. Before they could expose her breasts, however, the two Iraqis who'd been trailing Duli came to her rescue, fists flying.

One of the drunks took a blow to the chin and dropped in his tracks, out cold. The other reeled backward, losing his grip on Rena and careening into those mingling behind him. He shouted a curse and staggered back toward his attackers, joined by a couple of his friends. Within seconds, a full-fledged brawl had broken out.

In the commotion, Duli and one of the Iraqis managed to extricate themselves to the edge of the crowd. As they'd hoped, the melee had drawn the attention of the guards. Blowing whistles and grabbing for their nightsticks, the sentries moved from their posts and quickly waded into the crowd, trying to restore order. Duli just as quickly beelined to the outermost gate and unlatched it, then stepped forward, pulling the gate open just wide enough for the other Iraqi to slip through. Once he was inside, Duli leaned against the gate, closing it, and looked past the brawling to the grassy slope.

The light from the rocket had already faded, but she could still make out the shadowy outlines of Abtaj and several other men as they began crawling their way up through the bougainvillea. Abtaj had shed the papier-mâché St. Fermin head he'd been wearing, and the others had torn off their masks, as well.

Everything was going according to plan.

Several seconds later, Duli heard a cry behind her. She glanced over her shoulder and saw that the Iraqi who'd slipped into the bullpens had climbed up onto the top of the inner fence. He was waving to her.

"Now!" he shouted above the surrounding din. "Now!"

The warning, it turned out, was unnecessary, because already Duli could hear a thundering of hooves behind her. The inner gate had been opened, and the bulls were headed her way.

With all her might, Duli flung the outer gate open, then moved to one side and pressed herself up against the fence. Seconds later, the stampede surged past her into the crowded street. A chorus of screams sounded the alarm as the first few bystanders were gored and trampled by the charging beasts.

The bulls were loose in Pamplona.

FOR THE THIRD TIME in as many tries, Timo Ibanez had botched the opening chords of his Rachmaninoff piece. He drew in a deep breath and closed his eyes a moment.

Concentrate, he told himself.

He wanted desperately to still his mind enough to focus on his piano playing. He knew if he could lose himself in the music, it would calm him. And, hopefully, that calmness would—as it had so many times before—allow his subconscious to provide him with a solution that had thus far eluded him.

Ibanez needed to figure out a way to escape from the estate. Now that he'd safely packaged the nuclear warheads for transport, he knew he'd become expendable, and any moment he feared that he would befall the same fate as Juan and Paulo. He'd been watching from a downstairs window earlier when Miguel had shot the men by the pool and had their bodies buried under the concrete of the guest house's foundation. He couldn't let that happen to him. There had to be a way for him to avoid his execution and slip away. But how? The estate was teeming with Miguel's henchmen. It seemed impossible to get past them, but somehow there had to be a way. There had to be. If only he could distract himself from his worrying for a few minutes, he was sure the answer would come to him.

Ibanez put his fingers to the keyboard once again and began playing. This time, finally, the music flowed, easing him into his desired reverie. Soon he was even able to block out the sounds of firecrackers and merry-making out in the city. He closed his eyes and slowly let his mind begin to drift.

Suddenly, Ibanez felt something close around his neck. Before he had a chance to react, his fingers left the keys and he felt himself being jerked up out of his seat. His windpipe was being blocked off, and he found himself unable to breathe.

Garrote, he thought, his mind reeling. Somebody had come up from behind and was trying to strangle him.

Frantic, Ibanez kicked outward, toppling the piano bench, and tried to reach behind him. He tried to cry out, but the garrote had closed too tightly around his neck. He could feel pressure building up in his temples, and flashes of light began to cloud his vision. He was losing consciousness.

"Give it up," Miguel seethed in his ear. "It's over for you."

Ibanez was about to pass out when a rocket erupted outside the den. It had gone off just above the terrace, filling the area with a blinding light. There were cries out on the patio, and in the aftermath of the explosion several of the den windows shattered inward. Ibanez heard Miguel curse, then, the next thing he knew, he had fallen to the carpet. Dazed, he clawed the garrote from his neck and gasped for air. When his vision cleared, he saw Miguel circling the piano, drawing his Walther pistol. Before he could bring the weapon into play, more windows shattered and more gunfire hailed into the den.

Terrified, Ibanez rose slowly to his knees and stared past the piano. Out on the terrace, he saw costumed gunmen climbing over the railing, firing submachine guns at Miguel's men. One of them was struck by return fire and toppled forward, knocking over the telescopes set near the railing.

Behind Ibanez, the door to the den burst open and several of Miguel's men swarmed in, guns at the ready. Ibanez slumped back to the floor and lay still, pretending to be dead. As he'd hoped, Miguel and the others were too preoccupied with their attackers to pay him any mind. They fired through the shattered windows, ducking for cover when shots were returned. The piano sounded eerily as several rounds pierced through framework and glanced off the strings. Ibanez cringed, lying as flat as he could.

Finally, he summoned his nerve and began to crawl away from the firefight. Once he was within a few yards of the door the other men had come in through, he rose to a crouch and lunged forward. Miguel spotted him and turned, leveling his Walther. With a burst of frantic speed, Ibanez dived into the hallway, bullets whistling over his head. He quickly bounded to his feet and raced down the corridor until he'd reached the basement stairwell.

The wine cellar, he thought. He would try to find refuge in there. Of course, that was where the bombs were being kept, but to Ibanez it seemed like his only hope.

"God help me," he murmured as he stumbled his way down the steps. "God help me, please."

"WHAT THE BLOODY HELL!" David McCarter exclaimed as he drove down the street toward the estate of Ruben Dupentiez. The rocket had just gone off behind the mansion, illuminating the grounds, as well those of the surrounding homes.

Rafael Encizo had seen it, too. He rolled down window and heard staccato blasts of gunfire. "Looks like somebody beat us to the punch."

Sitting behind the Americans in the back seat of the rental car, Raul Cordero scanned the night sky over the neighborhood. "I don't see our helicopter yet," he said.

"Must be the Iraqis," guessed CIA agent Trace Harper. He was seated next to Cordero and was already groping his holster for his pistol.

"Let's hope so," McCarter said. "It'll give us a chance to kill two birds with one stone."

By the time McCarter pulled up to the gate, which was closed, Encizo and Cordero had armed themselves, as well.

"I don't think this buggy's strong enough to bust through," Encizo told McCarter.

"Leave it to me," Cordero said. He swung his door open and climbed out. No one was guarding the gate, so he took his time aiming at the lock, then fired the grenade launcher mounted beneath his assault rifle. A resounding explosion obliterated the lock, as well as a section of the gate. Cordero charged forward and quickly swung open the gate. As he was doing so, a gunman rushed from the front entrance of the mansion, drawn by the sound of the explosion. He fired at Cordero, pocking the driveway with rounds from his carbine. Cordero dived to one side and rolled behind a planter box, then came up firing, driving the other gunman back inside.

Harper, meanwhile, slid out of the back seat and slammed the door shut behind him, yelling to McCarter, "Go for it!"

"Down in front," McCarter yelled to Encizo as he floored the accelerator.

Encizo crouched and braced himself as the rental car sped forward, clipping the gate and screeching up the driveway. Gunfire rained down on the car from a gunman firing from an upstairs window. Encizo's window shattered, and one of the rounds thumped into the headrest behind him.

McCarter kept his foot on the gas and veered the car from side to side as he drew closer to the mansion, finally rocking to a stop just short of the two other vehicles parked out front.

"Are you up for this?" he asked Encizo as he shut off the ignition.

"Hell, yes," Encizo replied, wincing as he slipped his left arm from his sling. "I'll go back into rehab tomorrow."

The two men got out of the car, dodging another fusillade from the gunman on the second floor. Encizo took cover behind one of the other cars and peered up over the trunk. He saw the sniper framed in an upstairs window and started to draw a bead on him. Before he could fire, however, a grenade from Cordero's M-203 struck the outer wall ten yards from the window, filling the air with shrapnel. The gunman had either been hit or knocked off his feet, because he disappeared from the window.

"You two go around back!" Harper called out as he sprinted

across the grounds toward McCarter and Encizo. Cordero was close behind. "We'll take the inside!"

McCarter nodded and motioned to Encizo that he would go around the right side of the house. The Cuban acknowledged, then headed the other way. His shoulder was throbbing but he wasn't about to go back to using the sling. Gritting his teeth, he dodged past a row of hedges and rounded the house just as three BLM gunmen were emerging from the side entrance. Encizo quickly brought down one of the men, then sidestepped the return fire from the others, taking cover behind a small bulldozer the workers had been using for work on the backyard. Bullets sparked off the framework.

Encizo dropped flat on the ground and crawled to the front of the bulldozer. He saw one of the gunmen crouching behind a stack of lumber and waited for him to move and make himself a larger target. The man stayed put, however, content to fire blindly Encizo's way. Rounds clanged off the front scoop with a sound like muffled chimes.

The surrounding grounds were faintly lit by a sensor light mounted high above the side entrance, and the glow saved Encizo's life, betraying the moving shadow of the second gunman, who'd reached the bulldozer and had climbed up onto the roof. The Cuban rolled clear as the man fired his way, putting a slug into the ground beside him. Lying on his back, Encizo raised his pistol and fired up at the silhouetted figure looming over him. With a groan, the gunman pitched forward, landing in the grass to Encizo's right.

Encizo hadn't been counting his shots but he figured there was more ammo left in the other man's gun, so he took it, then rose to his feet and climbed up into the driver's seat of the bulldozer, taking care to stay clear of the windshield. As he'd

hoped, the key was still in the ignition, so he started up the
earthmover, then worked the controls and raised the scoop off
the ground until it was blocking his view of the way before
him. That was fine with Encizo, as it also shielded him from
any shots being fired by the man behind the lumber stack. He
put the bulldozer into gear and eased it forward. Once he was
sure the machine was headed in a straight line, he grabbed a
toolbox from the floor and laid it on the accelerator.

"This better work," he muttered.

The bulldozer groaned its way along the grass, and once Encizo felt it was about to collide with the woodpile, he sprang from
the driver's seat. He landed on grass at the same moment the bulldozer crashed into the lumber. When the gunman who'd been
using the stack for cover leaped wildly into the open, Encizo was
ready for him and took him down with a blast to the chest.

The way before him finally cleared, Encizo stole his way
to the backyard. By now the chopper Cordero had summoned
was on the scene, hovering above the grounds as commandos
fired out the side doorway at gunmen out on the terrace. A
searchlight was mounted under the chopper's nose, and when
it swept across the lawn and fell on Encizo, he stopped running and waved frantically.

"Hold fire!" he shouted.

He saw a few commandos take aim at him, but before they
could shoot, one of the men apparently recognized him, because abruptly the soldiers turned their guns elsewhere and
the spotlight shifted away from him.

Relieved, Encizo headed toward the staircase leading up
to the terrace. Over his shoulder, he saw the chopper set down
on the freshly laid foundation for the guest house. The slab
hadn't yet fully hardened, and the wheels sank into the con-

crete. The commandos piled out and charged past the pool toward Encizo. He waved them on, then started up the steps. Halfway to the terrace, he came across the body of a slain gunman wearing a festival costume. One glance at the man's face and Encizo knew that Harper had been right: they'd stumbled onto a face-off between the Iraqis and the BLM.

The terrace itself had been turned into a death zone. No fewer than twelve men lay sprawled in bloody heaps, half of them Iraqis, the rest Basques. A fire had broken out near the far railing, sending smoke up into the sky. Moments later, McCarter appeared, heading up the staircase on the other side of the terrace. Encizo joined him and together they quickly surveyed the bodies.

"We can sort them out later," McCarter said, raising his voice over the sound of gunfire echoing inside the mansion. He pointed to the doorway leading to the den. "Sounds like the party's moved inside."

THE STENCH OF CORDITE filled the inside of the mansion, and as the surviving forces of the BLM traded shots with Abtaj's men, the smell grew stronger.

Miguel Rigo had retreated from the terrace moments after the first exchange of gunfire, and, room by room, he'd continued to back away from his attackers as they stormed the ground floor. By his count, he'd managed to bring down three of the costumed Iraqis, but there were at least that many still on the prowl, stalking him with slow certainty, felling more of his men along the way. He had no idea how many were left, but he didn't like the odds.

He'd circled his way to the stairs leading to the basement when he received some unexpected assistance from a pair of gunmen who'd burst in through the front entrance. At first he'd feared they were more of Abtaj's goons, but when they gunned down one the Iraqis and then shouted to one another in English, Miguel realized that he was caught in a cross fire between the Iraqis and an opposing force, most likely made up of Americans or NATO agents. The confrontation gave him fleeting hope. If he could lie low long enough, maybe they would kill off each other and he might yet escape the ambush.

Before Miguel could act on his intentions, a pair of bullets hurtled his way. One smashed a ceramic vase set on a teak stand near the basement stairway; the other bored into his left forearm, shattering his ulna. Grimacing in pain, Miguel dropped to the floor and crawled to the stairs, then lunged headfirst down the steps. He somersaulted once, then cleared the last few steps and landed hard on the tile floor of the basement, striking his head against the side of a hardwood cabinet. A burst of light, brighter than the exploding rocket, flashed before his eyes. Then, just as quickly, his world went dark.

BENSHAH ABTAJ DUCKED away from a volley of shots fired his way. Crouched in an alcove in the ground-floor hallway, he quickly reloaded his pistol, cursing to himself. He couldn't believe what was happening. During the first moments after he and the others had stormed the terrace, he'd felt certain the raid would be successful. They'd gunned down every Basque in sight and had driven Miguel Rigo and his surviving followers back into the mansion, and Abtaj thought it would be an easy matter to track them down and finish them off, then secure the warheads. But then this other force had arrived and quickly neutralized the Iraqis' advantage. Where had they come from? he wondered. There was no way they could have shown up as quickly as they had if they'd been merely responding to the initial assault. No, somehow they'd been tipped off; it was the only explanation. But by who?

There was no time to dwell on the possibilities. Abtaj was now fighting for his life. A few of his men were scattered around the ground floor, keeping the other invading force pinned in the foyer with a steady barrage of gunfire. But no doubt reinforcements were on the way to aid the interlopers, whereas Abtaj knew that even if his Iraqi colleagues down in the city realized the raid had gone awry, they would never be able to reach the mansion in time to be of any help. Like it or not, Abtaj was going to have to make a stand with the depleted force already inside the house.

Unless, of course, there was some way to slip through the cracks.

When Abtaj saw Miguel Rigo crawl across the hallway floor and disappear down a staircase leading to the basement, he figured the Basque was trying to get away. Maybe there was some sort of secret passage in the basement. True, it was a long shot, but Abtaj felt it was his best chance.

A pair of grenades was clipped to the belt he wore beneath his costume. Abtaj and the others had refrained from using grenades so far, wary that neighbors who might have mistaken gunfire for the rattle of firecrackers would not be so easily fooled by an all-out explosion. At this point, however, there was no point in trying to be discreet.

Abtaj waited out another round of gunfire from the foyer, then pulled the pin on one of the grenades and flung the bomb down the hallway toward the front entrance. The projectile clattered twice across the marble floor, then exploded with a force that shook the surrounding walls and ceilings, bringing down plaster and toppling various objets d'art.

The Iraqi was already on the run when the grenade went off, and several bits of shrapnel slammed into him as he rushed toward the basement stairway. He lost his balance but managed to stay on his feet. Blood began to stream down his leg and right side as he bounded down the steps, taking them two at a time, his gun held out before him. When he spotted Miguel Rigo lying on the basement floor, he took aim and began to pull the trigger, then caught himself and held back.

Clearing the last few steps, Abtaj leaned over Rigo and dragged him away from the staircase. When the Basque stirred and began to regain consciousness, Abtaj let go of the man and crouched alongside him, pressing the barrel of his pistol to Miguel's forehead. He waited for the man to open his eyes, then whispered, "We can settle our score later, but first we have to get out of here alive. Do you know a way?"

Miguel groggily stared down the barrel of Abtaj's gun, then glared up at the Iraqi. In the background, gunfire continued to sound from the ground floor.

"You brought this on," Miguel stated. "You with your greed. You thought—"

"There's no time for that!" Abtaj interrupted, grabbing Miguel's collar and shaking him. "We need to get out of here! Now!"

Before Miguel could respond, a door swung open behind the men. Timo Ibanez charged out of the wine cellar, brandishing a fire extinguisher. As Abtaj whirled to face him, Ibanez triggered the extinguisher, spraying the Iraqi with foam. Abtaj cried out as the chemicals engulfed his face and eyes. He fired his gun blindly, missing Ibanez and shattering the mirrored door to the wine cellar.

Miguel took advantage of the distraction and kicked at

Abtaj, striking him squarely below the knees. The Iraqi reeled to one side, grabbing for a nearby cabinet. He missed and fell to the floor. Miguel was on him in an instant, grabbing for the Iraqi's gun.

As the other two men fought over the weapon, Ibanez switched his grip on the fire extinguisher and began using it as a club. He swung down hard, aiming for Miguel but not caring which of them he struck. He was in a state of rage and flailed the makeshift weapon repeatedly, ignoring the men's attempts to stave off his blows.

So focused was Ibanez on his attack that he didn't notice Rafael Encizo bound down the staircase.

"Stop!" Encizo shouted, taking aim at Ibanez with the submachine gun he'd taken from one of the slain Basques. When Ibanez failed to respond, Encizo repeated the command, this time in Spanish. Ibanez glanced up momentarily, then continued to strike the two men lying on the floor. Abtaj had been knocked unconscious, but Miguel continued to put up resistance, however feeble.

"I want you dead!" Ibanez seethed, battering Miguel across the forearms.

Miguel fended off the blows, then managed to grab hold of Ibanez's wrist and pull him off balance. While Ibanez staggered and tried to regain his footing, Miguel snatched up Abtaj's pistol. He was about to fire at Ibanez when Encizo put him down with a 3-round burst from his submachine gun. Miguel dropped the gun and twitched a few times, then slumped to the floor, dead.

Ibanez stared at the slain man, then looked up at Encizo and raised his hands.

"He tried to strangle me," Ibanez said.

Encizo cleared the bottom step and approached the fallen

men. He recognized Miguel Rigo and suspected that the downed Iraqi might well be Abtaj. He looked up at Ibanez, realizing he was the tank expert wanted for his part in the theft of the FSAT-50. He couldn't believe his luck.

"Where's the tank?" Encizo demanded.

"I don't know," Ibanez responded. "But I can show you the warheads."

WHEN THE GRENADE had gone off, David McCarter had been on the second story of the mansion, caught up in a standoff with one of the BLM gunmen. The force of the blast had shaken the entire floor, but McCarter, positioned toward the rear of the house, had been spared the worst of it. Not so his opponent. The Basque had been firing at McCarter from the front end of a hallway located directly above the foyer, and the explosion had not only knocked the gunman off his feet, but it had also left a gaping hole in the floor, trapping him in place. He'd done his best to keep fighting, shooting at McCarter through the smoke and cloud of dust rising up through the hole, but with little cover and no place to go, it was only a matter of time before he ran out of ammunition and found himself at the Briton's mercy.

As McCarter advanced down the hall, he kept his carbine trained on the separatist and shouted for him to put his hands up. The gunman either didn't understand English or wasn't about to follow the command. He rose slowly to his feet, glaring through the smoke at McCarter. He tossed his gun aside, and when it dropped through the hole in the floor, he decided to follow suit. McCarter saw what he was about to do and quickly fired, nailing the man with three rounds to the chest that sent him staggering backward, away from the cavity. When the man's legs gave out from under him, he collapsed onto the floor.

McCarter kept an eye on the man until he was sure he was dead, then stealthily searched the rest of the second floor for other gunmen. The only one he found was the sniper Harper had drilled earlier.

Satisfied the area was secure, McCarter took the stairs to the ground floor. Out of the corner of his eye, he saw a costumed Iraqi darting through the den toward the terrace. He gave chase but held his fire when the man was brought down by UOE commandos who had circled around the mansion after disembarking from the helicopter.

More troops had charged in through the side entrances, and there was a brief exchange of gunfire as they finished off the last two enemy gunmen still standing inside the building. Once the men had fallen, an eerie silence filled the mansion.

McCarter cautiously made his way to the foyer, sidestepping several bodies lying in pools of blood. Another two more men lay dead amid the debris in the entryway, and as McCarter drew closer, he felt a tightness in his chest.

Raul Cordero and Trace Harper had both been killed by the grenade blast. From the looks of it, they'd gone out fast. Cordero's right arm had been blown off and he was barely recognizable through all the blood seeping from his shrapnel wounds. As for Harper, his head lolled at an odd angle where he lay; it had been nearly severed from his neck by the explosion.

McCarter turned away from the carnage and walked past the commandos crowding the hallway.

"Rafe!" he shouted. "Rafe! Are you okay?"

"Down here!" Encizo called back.

McCarter traced his colleague's voice to the basement stairwell and hurried down the steps. There he found Encizo and Ibanez standing before the shattered wine cellar door.

Ibanez was carrying the two containers he'd just retrieved from the cellar.

"They got Harper and Cordero with that grenade," McCarter told Encizo.

Encizo cursed, then said, "Well, at least they didn't die in vain."

McCarter eyed the containers Ibanez was holding. "The nukes?" he said.

"Yeah," Encizo replied. Pointing to his right, he added, "And there's Miguel Rigo and the Iraqi who was trying to get his hands on them."

McCarter eyed the two men. He saw that Abtaj was dead and that Miguel was close to it.

"If they've got that damn tank stashed away in the garage, we'll be able to wrap things up," he said.

"No such luck," Encizo said. Indicating Ibanez, he went on, "He says it's still out there somewhere between here and Barcelona. Not only that, but he says he overheard Miguel talking to his sister and they're still planning to blow up that convention center, with or without the tank."

"Not what I wanted to hear," McCarter said.

"We're not out of the woods yet," Encizo agreed. "Not by a long shot."

CHAPTER THIRTY

Stony Man Farm, Virginia

"...and from what we've gathered, it looks like they let the bulls loose to keep the local *federales* busy while Abtaj and his goons raided the mansion," Aaron Kurtzman said, pointing at a computer printout with a photo of Rena Duli, as well as the two Iraqis who had been arrested in the aftermath of the disruption outside the Plaza de Toros in Pamplona. Kurtzman was at his workstation, briefing Hal Brognola and Barbara Price on the latest developments in Spain.

"How many people did the bulls get?" Brognola wondered.

"Two dead, fifteen hospitalized," Kurtzman said. "It probably could have been a lot worse."

"So we've got some low-level Iraqis in custody but no one from the BLM, right?" Price asked.

Kurtzman nodded. "They were all taken out in the raid. Miguel Rigo's out of the picture, but his brother and sister are still unaccounted for."

"The sister has to be in Barcelona," Brognola ventured. "And my guess is the younger brother's with the tank, wherever that might be."

Price glanced over at Huntington Wethers, who was

hunched over at his cubicle a few yards away, his eyes fixed on his computer screen. "Are you making any headway?" she asked him.

"Give me another second," Wethers replied.

For the past few minutes, the cybernetics expert had been trying to pinpoint locales between Pamplona and Barcelona that were within transmission range of the server linked to Miguel Rigo's cell phone. It would take hours to tap into the necessary phone logs and get a record of any calls the ring-leader had made before the raid on the Pamplona safehouse, but the theory was that if his younger brother was indeed with the missing tank, Miguel would likely have been in com-munication with him at some point while the FSAT-50 was being transported to Barcelona. By figuring out which areas along the route were capable of raising a signal, it was hoped that the search for the tank could be narrowed.

Wethers swept his cursor across the monitor screen, then clicked to call up another window. After tapping out a series of commands on his keyboard, he reported, "I've got it nar-rowed down to two possibilities."

"Let's have it," Brognola prompted.

Wethers transferred the image on his screen to one of the large monitors on the far wall, then used the cursor to point out the areas in question. "There's a mountain relay tower here in the Pyrenees and another farther south in Zaragoza," he re-ported. "From the looks of it, there are viable routes to Barcelona in both areas."

"So where does that leave us?" Brognola wondered. "With a coin flip?"

"Pretty much," Wethers said. "They'd have more water options traveling south, but the way's quicker along the mountains and there's more cover, especially if they took to the ground."

"Is there a way to intercept any calls being made from either area?" Price asked.

"It'd be a little tricky," Wethers said, "but if I can tap into their sat-link I could probably get something."

"Even if you can," Brognola interjected, "won't there be a ton of calls to sort through?"

"Not if I focus on the more remote areas," Wethers countered. "And that's likely to be where they'd be moving the tank."

"Go ahead and do it, then," Brognola said. "And if there's some way to weed out any calls that aren't coming in from Barcelona, that might help, too."

"Good idea."

While Wethers launched into the task, Kurtzman eyed the map of northern Spain and suggested, "If David and the others can grab hold of a chopper, it might be a good idea to have them start out and just split the difference until we have more information."

"What do you mean?" Brognola said.

"Have them fly a course between the two areas," Kurtzman suggested. "Then once we have something, they can veer one way or the other and close in."

"It's worth a shot," Brognola said. "Meanwhile, let's cross our fingers and hope Pol and Carl can sniff out this bomber they're trying to use in Barcelona."

Barcelona, Spain

INCHING THROUGH TRAFFIC in the Drassanes district, Carl Lyons and Pol Blancanales saw that the area was indeed under heightened security. Already they'd passed four police cruisers, and there were additional officers patrolling the downtrodden neighborhood on foot and bicycle. If not on the lookout for terrorists, the lawmen would have had no trouble keeping themselves busy, as the street teemed with likely criminals. Besides the obvious streetwalkers and drug peddlers, there were petty thieves on the prowl. Lyons and Blancanales had seen two cars being broken into, and as they idled at a stoplight they saw a footrace between a young purse snatcher and the victim's boyfriend. The boyfriend won the race, tackling the thief and pummeling him mercilessly until bystanders intervened.

"Something tells me they leave this neck of the woods off the tourist maps," Blancanales observed, watching the skirmish.

"You got that right," Lyons said.

As the light changed and Lyons drove through the intersection, Blancanales said, "What do you think? Should we keep cruising or park and start looking around on foot."

"If we park, there won't be anything left of the car when we get back to it," Lyons replied. "I say we keep rolling."

The men detoured onto a side street. Traffic was still slow, and several times they were approached by prostitutes and hooded teenagers selling crack and marijuana. Blancanales had photos of Angelica Rigo and Guillermo Blanca with him, and after passing on any offers of drugs or sex, he countered by saying he'd pay for a lead on the whereabouts of the two separatists. The only promising response came from one of the prostitutes, who eyed the photos and said she might know where they could find Angelica. But when Blancanales pressed for specifics and said he'd only pay up if the lead panned out, the woman cursed at him and stomped off.

"She was lying, obviously," Lyons observed.

"No kidding," Blancanales said.

The men circled the block, then tried the other side of the avenue, with no better results. As Lyons pulled up to a stoplight two blocks from the Drassanes subway station, Blancanales grabbed his cell phone and said, "Let me check in with Jack and see if he's having any better luck."

"Go ahead," Lyons said, "but I think we'd have heard from him if he did."

Grimaldi had split off from the others back at the hangar after learning there was an available MD Defender recon chopper. His plan had been to take a spiral course, starting at the civic square and working his way outward until he'd reached the coast.

While Blancanales tried to reach their ace pilot, Lyons glanced to his right and saw a police cruiser idling in a back alley. He didn't think anything of it at first, but as he was about to look away, a woman and two men emerged from the shadows and got into the car. Lyons was too far away to get a good look at them, but something told him that Fate had finally cut him a break.

"Green light," Blancanales told him just as the driver behind them leaned on his horn.

Lyons suddenly jerked the steering wheel hard to the left and leaned on the accelerator. The rental car lurched across the median, just missing an oncoming car.

"What the hell?" Blancanales shouted, nearly dropping his cell phone.

"Got a bite!" Lyons told him, veering into the alley. Up ahead, the police car had begun to pull away, and as Lyons drew closer, the cruiser suddenly sped up. Lyons followed suit.

Blancanales told Grimaldi he'd get back to him, then clicked off the cell phone and asked Lyons, "What did you see?"

"Cop picked up two men and a woman," Lyons said without taking his eyes off the car ahead of them. "I can't be sure, but it might be our gal."

As they raced down the alley, Blancanales glanced out and saw they were passing the rear entrance to a small sheet-metal plant. A security guard was moving away from the rear entrance, drawing a handgun.

"That where they came from?" Blancanales asked, grabbing his pistol as he rolled down his window.

"Yeah, I think so," Lyons replied.

"Incoming!" Blancanales shouted, ducking in the seat. A second later, a bullet crashed through the back window and lodged in the rearview mirror.

Lyons instinctively floored the accelerator. Blancanales, meanwhile, turned in his seat and took aim through the shattered window, firing back at the security guard. Before he could see if he'd hit the man, Lyons turned sharply, clipping a trash can on his way back out to the side streets. Blancanales whirled back around and saw the police cruiser veering through traffic up ahead, trying to distance itself from Lyons. The Able Team leader kept up the chase, nearly sideswiping a slow-moving truck.

"Get Jack back on the horn and get him over here," Lyons told Blancanales. "I think we're onto something."

"WHO ARE THEY?" Cristofer exclaimed, sneaking a glance in his rearview mirror after veering around a bus and taking a sharp turn on Carrier de Santa Monica.

Xavier Golato peered through the back windshield. "I can't tell," he said, "They're too far back."

"Keep moving!" Angelica told Cristofer. "Whoever they are, we need to lose them!"

Cristofer gave the police cruiser more gas and sped past St. Joseph Hospital toward the heavy congestion of La Rambla. The other car was doing its best to keep pace, but it was clear that the driver was no match for Cristofer's reckless daring behind the wheel. By the time he reached the main boulevard, the officer had a good fifty yards on his pursuers.

Guillermo Blanca was sitting in back next to Golato. He drew his gun and thumbed off the safety as he rolled down his window. "If they start closing in I'll make them regret it," he said.

"They won't catch up with us," Cristofer said confidently. He flicked on the cruiser's roof lights and sounded his siren as he turned south on La Rambla. Cars began to pull over, giving him a clear run in the left lane. Pedestrians on the sidewalk stopped to watch Cristofer speed by. So did those strolling the grassy parkway that separated southbound traffic from the lanes heading north into the heart of the city.

"I'll bet this is the first time they saw somebody chasing the police instead of the other way around," Angelica said.

"Hang on," Cristofer interrupted. "I'm going to cut across."

Once he saw his opening, the officer cut sharply to his left, leaving the road and speeding up the passenger crosswalk onto the parkway. Pedestrians screamed and scattered, trying to get out of the car's way. A young couple walking arm-in-arm were too slow to respond, and Cristofer clipped them with the front end of the cruiser. The woman reeled into the grass while her boyfriend bounded up onto the hood and caromed off the windshield, obscuring the officer's view. Cristofer was forced to slow down momentarily, but as soon as the other man was thrown clear, he hit the accelerator again. The cruiser's tires chewed up the grass as Cristofer zigzagged around a trinket kiosk and vendor's cart. All the while he kept his eyes on the northbound lanes, looking for a break in traffic. Once he saw his opportunity, he cut sharply again, plowing through another crowd of pedestrians. A terrified mother barely managed to snatch her baby out of its carriage before Cristofer slammed into it. The carriage collapsed under the wheels and snagged the underside of the cruiser's chassis for a few yards before working free. It lay on the sidewalk in a mangled heap as the cruiser leaped the curb and headed the wrong way down the northbound lane of the boulevard. Oncoming cars swerved wildly to get out of Cristofer's way, and he narrowly averted a head-on collision before screeching into the parking lot for the Museu de Cera.

The museum was closed for the night, and only a handful of parked cars remained in the lot. Cristofer easily maneuvered his way around them, then crashed the cruiser through a flimsy wire gate blocking the rear exit to Carrier de Salve, a dark, narrow side street. It was only then that Cristofer shut off the siren and roof lights and began to slow down.

The others in the car had been thrown about in their seats during the course of the chase. Angelica rubbed her shoulder where she'd banged it into the door frame, and Blanca groaned faintly in the back seat, having struck his head against the roof when Cristofer had jumped the curb.

"Well, you nearly killed us, but you managed to lose them," Xavier Golato called out to the officer as he kept an eye on the street behind them. "At least for now."

"All we need is enough time to get to the marina," Cristofer said. "If we can reach the boat, there's no way they'll be able to catch us."

CARL LYONS HAD given up the chase back at La Rambla. The risk to innocent bystanders was just too great. He brought his car to a stop near the man who'd been struck by Cristofer's patrol car. The man's girlfriend was kneeling over him, screaming hysterically. The man wasn't moving.

"I'll see to him," Blancanales said, handing Lyons his cell phone. "Here's Jack."

Lyons got on the line with Grimaldi. Blancanales bounded out of the car and pushed his way through the crowd that had gathered around the injured man.

"He's not breathing!" the man's girlfriend wailed, tears streaming down her face. "They killed him!"

Blancanales shouted for the onlookers to move back, then gently put a hand on the woman's shoulder and eased her to one side. "Let me see if I can help," he told her.

"He's my fiancé," the woman sobbed. "We're supposed to be married next week."

"Don't lose hope," Blancanales told her.

He knelt over the man. A thin trail of blood seeped from his left nostril but otherwise he showed no visible sign of injury. When Blancanales checked his wrist and neck, however, he wasn't able to detect a pulse. Once he confirmed that the man had stopped breathing, as well, he began CPR. He tried to tune out the noise around him so that he wouldn't lose count when he was making his chest compressions, but it wasn't easy. The man's girlfriend continued to sob disconsolately, and over the sound of the gathering crowd the Able Team commando could hear the sirens of approaching police cars. One cruiser veered out of northbound traffic and rolled onto the parkway. Two officers climbed out and began shouting to the crowd, trying to clear the way for an ambulance that appeared moments later.

Blancanales continued to work on the man until the paramedics arrived and motioned him away. They had portable defibrillators with them and quickly ripped open the man's shirt so they could apply the paddles to his chest. The injured man's girlfriend shrieked when an electrical charge caused the man to jolt. She moved forward, screaming for the paramedics to stop, but Blancanales pulled her away and assured her, "It's his best chance."

It took another two charges, but finally the paramedics were able to raise a pulse and bring the man's heart to a normal rhythm. Blancanales left the woman in the care of the bystanders, then headed over to the rental car.

Lyons was standing spread-eagled outside the car, being frisked by the police, who had already confiscated his cell phone and handgun. When he spotted Blancanales, Lyons called out, "Obviously, my Spanish sucks. Help me out here, would you?"

Blancanales tried to intervene, but before he could offer the police an explanation, they had him up against the car and were frisking him as well. He continued to plead their case, but the police weren't buying it. Blancanales couldn't blame them. Given the high-security alert, he was sure that the men were under orders to detain anyone who seemed to pose a threat to the NATO conference.

"This is wonderful," Lyons groused. "We wind up hog-tied while the real perps make their getaway."

"Did you get a chance to talk with Jack?" Blancanales asked.

"Yeah," Lyons said. "I got as far as saying the squad car's probably got a dinged-up front end, then our buddies here showed up."

"Looks like it's up to Jack, then," Blancanales said. He glanced up, looking skyward for a trace of Grimaldi's chopper. All he could see, though, were the tops of the evenly spaced palm trees that lined both sides of the parkway.

Once they'd been frisked, Lyons and Blancanales were escorted toward the nearest patrol car. On the way, they saw the paramedics transferring the wounded man onto a stretcher. His girlfriend was standing close by, holding his hand. Blancanales saw that the man's eyes were open and he was talking to the woman.

"At least I got my good deed of the day taken care of," Blancanales murmured.

He and Lyons were about to be herded into the back seat of the patrol car when an unmarked coupe pulled up and a man shouted for the police to hold up. Blancanales immediately recognized the voice as that of Detective Etixa, the man he and Lyons had conferred with earlier in the day during the interrogation of Xavier Golato.

"Talk about the nick of time," Lyons muttered to Blancanales.

Etixa quickly vouched for Lyons and Blancanales. The officers released the men and apologized for the misunderstanding. Blancanales assured them he knew they were just doing their job and said there were no hard feelings.

Lyons was more to the point. He told Blancanales, "Tell them to give me back my gun and the damn cell phone."

Blancanales passed along the request. The police quickly obliged, and while Lyons was getting back in touch with Grimaldi, Blancanales filled in Etixa on the short-lived chase. The detective was visibly upset by the news that a member of the force seemed to be in collusion with the BLM.

"It helps to explain a few things, though," he conceded.

When Blancanales told him they had a chopper trying to track the patrol car from the air, Etixa gestured at the southbound traffic on La Rambla and said, "I'll close the lanes off here so we'll have a clear way once we find out where they're headed."

"Good idea," Blancanales told him.

While Etixa went off to set up the roadblock, Lyons finally got back in touch with Grimaldi. The two men spoke briefly, then Lyons clicked off and told Blancanales, "He's on them. They're headed for the marina."

CHAPTER THIRTY-ONE

Barcelona, Spain

The first thing Angelica Rigo noticed when she stepped out of Cristofer's squad car was the helicopter. It was hovering in place above the Palau de Mar and Museu d'Historia, which they'd passed only moments before on their way to the parking lot at the end of the marina.

"Is that one of yours?" she asked Cristofer.

The renegade officer glanced skyward as he got out of the car. "No, I don't think so," he said. "It might be the military."

"What if they're looking for us?"

"If they were looking for us, they'd have followed us with their searchlights on," Cristofer said.

"Quit staring at them," Blanca interjected as he emerged from the car. "You're just drawing attention our way."

"You're right," Cristofer said. "Let's get to the boat. If we don't act suspicious we should be fine."

Xavier Golato was the last one out of the car. He glanced at the boats moored in the marina and asked, "Which one is ours?"

"Right over there," Cristofer said, pointing toward the closest slip. "The first speedboat facing us."

The boat belonged to one of Cristofer's underworld connections, who used it to help with smuggling operations out of the nearby port. Cristofer had made arrangements earlier to borrow the craft. The plan was to head down the coast a few miles to Gava, a small fishing village where they would set anchor and wait for morning. If for some reason the timing devices on the bombs at the civic center failed, Blanca had already determined they would still be within close enough range to trigger the explosives by remote control. Blanca had the remote with him and slipped it inside his coat as the group headed for the docks.

The marina was quiet. Only a few boats were out in the water. The rest were tied down for the night and bobbed faintly at their moorings. As she followed the others up into the speedboat, Angelica Rigo stole a glance at the helicopter and was relieved to see it had circled away from them and was now drifting over Moll de la Fusta toward Port Veil.

"Looks like we're in the clear," she murmured.

"So far, so good," Cristofer said. Crossing the aft deck, he unlocked the cockpit freezer, as well as the sliding door to the boat's cabin. "I'll feel better once we've pulled out of the harbor."

While Angelica and Blanco followed Cristofer into the cabin, Xavier Golato untied the mooring lines, then remained outside and flipped open the lid to the cockpit freezer. He tilted up a bait tray, exposing a cache of weapons and ammunition. He opted for a 12-gauge Winchester 1300 loaded with three-inch Magnum shells. The shotgun was cold in his hands, and he had to keep shifting his grip to keep his fingers from going numb.

Moments later, the boat's twin four-hundred horsepower engines came to life, causing the floorboards to vibrate faintly under his feet. Above the heavy rumble he also heard the chirping of Angelica's cell phone inside the cabin. He figured it was Miguel calling from Pamplona about the transaction with the Iraqis. He hoped things had gone well. After the following day, the BLM would need all the money it could get its hands on to capitalize on their newfound notoriety.

As the speedboat began to slowly back out of its slip, Golato heard Angelica let out a wrenching scream.

"No!" she cried out.

Alarmed, Golato swung open the cabin door and rushed in. Angelica stood next to Blanca, her face ashen, tears already beginning to stream down her face.

"Miguel is dead!" she sobbed, lowering the cell phone. "They ambushed the safehouse and killed him!"

"The Iraqis?" Cristofer asked, looking away from the control console.

Angelica didn't answer him. "They killed him!" she repeated.

Golato set down the shotgun and moved forward to comfort Angelica. As she moved into the man's embrace, Blanca gently took the phone from her. He spoke to the person on the other end while Golato stroked Angelica's back. Once he had more information, Blanca told the others, "It's Jacque. He just heard there was a raid on the safehouse in Pamplona."

"Was it the Iraqis?" Cristofer asked again.

"Yes, but apparently there others, too. UOE and some Americans. They have the warheads now."

"Damn them!" Golato muttered.

Cristofer shifted gears and turned the steering wheel, pointing the speedboat out toward the open waters leading from the harbor. As he did so, Angelica reined in her grief and pulled away from Golato. Her expression had changed from sorrow to rage.

"They'll pay for this!" she vowed. Turning to Blanca, she said, "Trigger the explosives!"

Blanca was hesitant. "Angelica, I don't think—"

"I said trigger the explosives!" she shouted, cutting him off. "Now! Let's take down that center and everyone in it!"

Cristofer idled the boat's engines and tried to calm the woman. "It will be better if we stick with the plan," he told her. "I know you want to strike back, but if we wait, we can—"

"I don't want to wait!" Angelica interjected angrily, grabbing the cell phone back from Blanca. "I want to do it now! We need to make them pay for what they've done! We need to show them we're prepared to strike back with full force!"

Blanca glanced at Cristofer and Golato. The officer shrugged. Golato slowly nodded. Angelica, meanwhile, raised the phone back to her ear and told her younger brother, "Jacque, get the tank ready to fire. Once you have a jetliner in your sights, take it down! I don't care who's on it!"

Cristofer put his hands back on the boat's throttle and glanced back at Blanca. "Can you do that while we're moving?"

Blanca glanced up from the remote control and nodded. "Yes, go ahead. I'll need a minute to override the timers anyway."

"Good," Cristofer said, "because we need to get the hell out of here!"

The officer stared out the cabin windshield and was about open up the throttle when he suddenly stopped and cursed.

Out across the water, the helicopter they'd seen earlier had apparently doubled back toward them. Once it had rounded the peninsula that separated the marina from the shipping port, the chopper drifted low over the water, placing itself directly in the path Cristofer had planned to take out of the harbor. Before he had a chance to react, the chopper's high-intensity searchlight suddenly flashed on, flooding the cabin with its harsh glare. Cristofer instinctively glanced away, but it was too late: the light had left him half-blind.

Similarly stricken, Golato staggered to one side and groped for his 12-gauge, shouting, "They're on to us!"

Cristofer and Golato weren't the only ones in the cabin left incapacitated by the searchlight. Blanca had nearly finished programming the remote control to detonate the explosives beneath the civic center when the light caught him by surprise, obscuring his vision with starlike flashes and the afterimage of the harsh beam. No longer able to make out the LED readings on the remote, he was forced to abort the detonation.

Angelica had been facing away from the light when it first poured into the cabin. She knew what was happening, however, and instinctively crouched, fearing that at any second gunfire would begin pouring in through the windows. She quickly finished speaking with her younger brother, then clicked off the cell phone and shouted to Cristofer, "What are you waiting for? Get us out of here!"

"How?" Cristofer countered. "I can't see a thing!"

"Then move aside!" she retorted, crawling across the floor to the control console. As she hoped, there was a pair of sunglasses in the catch-all, and though they didn't block the glare of the spotlight entirely, they allowed her to see the way before her. She nudged the officer to one side and took his place at the controls, telling him, "When your vision clears, get up on the bridge with some kind of rifle and take out that spotlight!"

"Are you sure you can navigate past the helicopter?" Cristofer asked.

"It can't get down into the water to stop me, now, can it?" Angelica stared defiantly at the chopper and vowed, "They won't have as much luck killing me as they did Miguel."

As he followed Detective Etixa's sedan into the marina parking lot, Carl Lyons could see the helicopter hovering above the water. Sitting beside him, Blancanales was on the two-way with Jack Grimaldi. Once the chopper pilot had filled him in, Blancanales turned to Lyons.

"Jack bought us some time with the searchlight, but it looks like they're going to try to make a run for it."

"How soon before we get an attack chopper on the scene?" Lyons wondered.

"Not in time to keep them from getting out of the harbor," Blancanales reported. "And there's still no word on how quick the coast guard can get a boat over here."

"Kinda leaves it up to us, then, doesn't it?" Lyons said.

By now they were nearing the end of the parking lot. Both men could see Cristofer's parked squad car, as well as the speedboat Grimaldi was trying to hold at bay with the searchlight. The boat was idling twenty yards out in the water, but if Grimaldi's assessment was right, any second they could expect the craft to pull away. Up ahead, Etixa's car was screeching to a halt, and Lyons suspected the detective was going to get out and try to fire at the boat in hopes of taking out its pilot. Lyons doubted he'd be able to pull it off. There seemed to be only one other option. It was a hell of a lot riskier, but Lyons figured he had to go for it.

"Hang on," he told Pol, flooring the accelerator.

As the rental car sped forward, Lyons jerked the steering wheel, swerving past Etixa and crashing through a wood-rail fence separating the parking lot from the docks. Blancanales realized what his partner was up to and shook his head in disbelief.

"You're nuts, Ironman!" he cried out, bracing himself. "It'll never work!"

"Never know till you try," Lyons countered, keeping his foot to the floorboard. Soon they were racing diagonally across the docks, headed straight toward the speedboat, which churned up a wake as it began to pull away.

"Oh, no, you don't," Lyons muttered. He veered slightly as he neared the edge of the dock, aiming the car between two of the concrete pilings supporting the dock railing. It seemed doubtful that the car could thread the gap, but Lyons refused to back down. He eased off the gas for only a split second, then floored the accelerator again, building up a surge of speed as he crashed into the railing. The rails burst free on impact, as did both of the car's side mirrors, and the car went airborne out over the water. Clenching the steering wheel, Lyons stared out the windshield at the retreating speedboat and shouted, "Special delivery!"

STANDING ON THE AFT DECK of the speedboat, Xavier Golato had been preparing to fire his shotgun at Detective Etixa when he spotted Lyons speeding across the docks. He quickly shifted aim on his new target. When, to his amazement, the car plowed through the dock railing, he squeezed the trigger. A 12-gauge round blasted its way through the front grillework and wreaked havoc on the engine compartment but did little to stop the car's airborne momentum. He worked the Winchester's pump action, but before he could get another shot off, the car crashed into the rear of the boat, obliterating the upper half of the gunwale, as well as much of the deck Golato was standing on. The shotgun flew from his grasp and he was thrown forward, striking his head sharply on the gin pole. Knocked out, he tumbled limply over the crumpled hood of the rental car and splashed into the cold water of the harbor.

Inside the cabin, Lyons's crash landing had sent Angelica reeling back from the control console. When she crashed into Guillermo Blanca, the explosives expert dropped the remote control and together they tumbled to the deck, landing alongside Cristofer. The police officer was dazed and bleeding where he'd been struck by flying shards of glass from the shattered windows.

"What happened?" he moaned.

"I don't know," Blanca said. "A grenade or a missile, I think."

Angelica pulled herself away from Blanca. When she tried to stand, she realized the boat was listing sharply to one side. The engines had died, as well, and a faint smell of fuel wafted up through the floorboards. She could also smell smoke.

"We need to get out of here," she said. The chopper's searchlight was still flooding the cabin, and when she spotted the remote control, she grabbed it and handed it Blanca. "But first set off those explosives at the civic center!"

Blanca nodded weakly and took the remote.

"There's no time for that!" Cristofer said, wiping at the blood that streamed down his face. "This tug's about to blow!"

Angelica ignored the officer and told Blanca, "Do it!"

Blanca's vision had finally cleared enough for him to be able to read the remote's LED display. As he started to reenter the detonation commands, Angelica awkwardly crawled to the rear of the cabin.

"Xavier!" she called out, looking for Golato.

Cristofer drew his gun and lurched past the woman, pushing her aside in his haste to flee the cabin. When he stepped outside, he saw the rental car imbedded in the aft deck, weighing the rear of the boat below the waterline. Inside the vehicle, he spotted the same two Americans who'd been on in the loft raid and had later tailed the motorcade leading Golato to the airport. They were struggling to push aside their air bags and get out of the car.

Seething with rage, Cristofer took aim at Lyons and was about to pull the trigger when a gunshot echoed across the marina. Cristofer grunted as a 9 mm slug from Etixa's pistol punched its way into his chest cavity. He fired wildly and toppled forward, landing next to Golato's fallen shotgun. A few feet away, flames began to poke up through the smoke rising from the boat's engine compartment. Fear registered in Cristofer's eyes, but after crawling a few inches away from the flames, he collapsed. With a piteous groan, he let out one final breath and went limp.

Crouched in the cabin doorway, Angelica stared numbly at the blood seeping from beneath Cristofer, then shouted frantically over her shoulder, "What's taking you so long?"

"Almost ready," Blanca shouted back. He'd just finished overriding the timers on the explosives at the civic center and was about to enter the final commands to set the bombs off. Before he could finish the sequence, however, the boat itself was wrenched by a violent explosion. A fireball shot up through the floorboards and engulfed the cabin with such quick, fiery intensity that the remote was already aflame and had been rendered inoperative by the time Blanca dropped it. He was thrown off his feet by the force of the blast and careened into Angelica, knocking her out onto the deck. Their clothes were on fire and they both screamed in agony as the rapidly spreading flames seared their flesh. In a matter of seconds their cries were silenced along with their hopes of destroying the civic square.

CARL LYONS and Rosario Blancanales were both still trapped in the car when the boat exploded. The front end took the brunt of the blast and was wrenched free of the aft deck with so much force the car flipped upside down as it was thrown clear. The windows had blown out, and the moment the car splashed into the marina, water began to surge into the passenger compartment. Neither man had been knocked unconscious, but they were both shaken up and by the time they regained their bearings, they found themselves underwater. The car was still upside down and they were both lying on the ceiling, with the air bags undulating eerily beneath them like ghostly sea creatures.

Blancanales was the first to orient himself. Reaching out through the cold water, he tapped Lyons's arm, then put a finger to his mouth and pointed up toward the floorboards. Lyons nodded and followed Blancanales's lead, contorting around the air bags and the front seat and extending his body upward until he reached a trapped air pocket just below the dashboard. Both men were gasping for air when the car landed with a gentle thud at the bottom of the marina. Fortunately, they were less then twenty feet down and there was no problem with the water pressure.

"You all right?" Blancanales asked Lyons between breaths.

"Yeah, I think so," Lyons said. "So much for my Evel Knievel impersonation."

Blancanales forced a grin. "That was some stunt, all right. Next time I'll watch from the cheap seats, though."

"I hear ya," Lyons replied. "Now, let's get out of this bathtub."

"Right behind you."

Once the men had filled their lungs, they turned around and worked their way back down to the ceiling, then wriggled their way through the side windows. The water was dark, but as they swam upward, the men could see bits of debris sinking past them. At one point Lyons had to veer to one side to avoid what he thought was a large chunk of the boat. As it drifted by him, however, he realized it was the half-charred body of a dead woman. The fireball had spared enough of her face for Lyons to recognize Angelica Rigo. Her lifeless eyes stared outward at Lyons, sending a chill down his spine. He quickly swam away from the body and continued upward toward the surface.

As the two men neared the surface, a bright shaft of light penetrated the water twenty yards to their left. They shifted course and swam toward the light. Once they reached it, they quickly surfaced, then closed their eyes briefly against the intense glare. They both knew it had to be the spotlight from the helicopter. When they heard someone calling out to them, the men blinked their eyes and saw a UOE commando reaching out from the lower rungs of a rope ladder suspended from the hovering chopper. Lyons was closest, so he grabbed the man's hand first. Once his fingers had closed around one of the ladder's rungs, he let go of the man's hand so that he could help Blancanales up, as well.

Once both men had climbed free of the water, the commando called up to another soldier poised in the doorway of the chopper. The other soldier, in turn, signaled Grimaldi, who took the chopper out of its holding pattern and drifted slowly toward the docks. There, Lyons saw Etixa, drenched and half-submerged in the water, clinging to a ladder with one hand while he used the other to prop someone else's head above the waterline.

"Golato!" Lyons exclaimed.

Etixa nodded and called out, "I fished him out. Looks like he pulled off an escape back up the coast after all."

"Is he alive?" Lyons shouted.

"Yes, but he's unconscious," Etixa responded. "Which is more than I can say for whoever else was on that boat."

Once the chopper had carried them over to the docks, Lyons and Blancanales let go of the ladder and collapsed onto the planks. The commando did the same, then went over to the ladder and helped Etixa haul Golato up. The terrorist was still unconscious, and it would likely be some time before he could be interrogated, but Etixa had already guessed how he'd managed his escape. As he joined Lyons and Blancanales, he pointed to the squad car that had brought Golato and the others to the marina.

"That's Officer Cristofer's car," he told the men. "He's the one who drove into the guard rail while taking Golato to the airport. He must have been in on the setup."

"If that's the case, he must have been aboard the boat," Lyons surmised, glancing over his shoulder at the bits of debris still floating on the surface of the water.

"He got what he deserved," Etixa said.

Blancanales nodded, then said, "Now we just have to figure out what they were up to."

CHAPTER THIRTY-TWO

Stony Man Farm, Virginia

Blancanales didn't have to wait long to find out how the terrorists in the speedboat had planned to disrupt the NATO conference.

Within ten minutes after he and Lyons had been fished out of the water, Aaron Kurtzman was in touch with the men, calling over a secure line. The Stony Man cyber team had managed to intercept the tail end of Angelica Rigo's frantic cell phone conversation with her younger brother. Kurtzman had heard enough of the exchange to realize the BLM had managed to plant explosives somewhere inside the civic center.

"...and the last thing we heard was her telling somebody to set them off," Kurtzman concluded. He was seated at his workstation, talking with Blancanales on a speakerphone while he continued to peck away at his keyboard. Hal Brognola and Barbara Price stood close by, eavesdropping on the conversation.

"In that case, we're in luck," Blancanales responded. "Whoever she was talking to went down with the ship here, and if the civic center's still standing, you've got to figure they were deep-sixed before they got a chance to trigger the explosives."

"Let's hope so," Kurtzman replied. "But I'd suggest you get some people over there quick to check over the place."

"Will do," Blancanales promised.

"Good work, Pol," Brognola called out. "And tell Ironman that if he keeps driving like that we're going to have to take away his license."

"As if that would stop him."

Once Blancanales clicked off the line, Kurtzman exchanged a glance with Price and Brognola. "Hopefully that's one less calamity we need to avert."

"Thank heaven for small favors," Brognola murmured. He turned his attention to the far wall, eyeing the monitor screen filled with a topographical map of the rambling border between Spain and France. "We've still got this missing tank out there somewhere looking to bring down the next jetliner it gets in its sights."

Kurtzman looked over at the rest of the cybernetic crew and asked, "Are you guys making any headway?"

"I just spoke to David," Wethers responded. "They're veering off toward the target area."

Wethers accessed the monitor screen and highlighted the area in question, a ten-mile stretch of the Pyrenees between the mountain villages of Monzon and Alfarras. It had already been determined that the cell call between Jacque and Angelica Rigo had made use of a relay tower servicing both towns. Assuming Jacque had been calling from the tank, it seemed a safe bet that the FSAT-50 was in the vicinity.

"I'll call the White House and see if they can arrange the grounding of all flights heading over the Pyrenees," Brognola suggested.

"Good idea," Price said, "but it's going to be too late for any flights that are already headed that way."

Kurtzman called out to Tokaido. "Akira, you got those co-ordinates yet?"

Tokaido nodded as he raced his fingers over his keyboard. "Just entering the last ones," he said.

Once he'd finished, Tokaido networked the information to the monitor on the far wall. As the others watched on, three brightly colored curved lines were transposed onto the topographical map, indicating the flight paths for three different airlines whose Barcelona runs crossed over the Pyrenees within the suspected target range of the missing tank.

"The red and yellow lines are commercial flights," Tokaido explained. "British Airways and Air France. The good news is if they're on schedule and they've already passed out of range."

"And the bad news?" Price asked.

"The green line," Tokaido said. "It's a charter flight out of Paris carrying EU delegates to the NATO conference. Their takeoff was scheduled for forty minutes ago."

Price didn't need to do the math to realize the gravity of the situation. She stared bleakly at the map and whispered under her breath, "They're heading into the line of fire."

East Navarra Province, Spain

FIFTY MILES NORTHEAST of Zaragoza, David McCarter guided the UOE's Galicia helicopter over a tributary of the LaTrousse River. The chopper's pilot had been killed during the raid on the safehouse in Pamplona, leaving McCarter to take the controls. Rafael Encizo rode beside him in the gunner's seat. T. J. Hawkins was back in the rear cabin along with five UOE commandos. They'd been up in the air close to two hours, combing the rolling foothills and waterways for a trace of the missing FSAT-50. So far they'd come up empty, and as the tributary gave way to a series of shallow streams incapable of concealing anything the size of a battle tank, it was clear they'd come up against yet another dead end.

"Great," McCarter grumbled, pulling the chopper up through a thick bank of fog and heading north over a small mountain range.

Encizo checked the chopper's fuel gauge. "We're good for a couple more passes somewhere, then we've got to put down."

"Any suggestions?" McCarter asked.

The Cuban switched his attention to the map spread out across his lap. "Let's try to make it to Monzon," he said. "Looks like there's an airfield there."

"Sounds like a plan," McCarter said. "We'll check in and see if Bear's got anything out of those sat peepers yet."

While McCarter set a course for Monzon, Encizo put a call in to the Farm. Kurtzman had told the men earlier that he was trying to get a pair of NSA spy satellites to hone their sights on the area surrounding the relay tower Jacque Rigo had used for the cell phone call to his sister. When Encizo got back in touch with him, Kurtzman reported that the sat cams had been repositioned and were transmitting a steady stream of images. So far, however, none of them had included a view of the missing tank.

"What about a heat signature?" McCarter asked once Encizo had passed along the update. "If the tank's on the move somewhere, it seems like they'd be able to get at least some kind of read with their infrareds."

"Good point," Encizo conceded, his attention back on the

map. "But a ten-mile radius is still a lot of ground to cover. Maybe they just haven't panned over the right area yet."

"Okay, I'll buy that."

Encizo continued to scour the map. Suddenly he blurted out, "Then again, maybe there's another explanation."

"Such as?"

"Check these out." Encizo held out the map and pointed to a specific area. McCarter shifted his gaze and checked it out.

"A couple small lakes. So what?"

"Not lakes," Encizo said. "They're hot springs. As in hot enough to mask the tank's heat signature."

McCarter was skeptical. "You really think they've got their act together enough to think of that?"

"What else do we have to go on?" Encizo countered. "I think it's worth a shot."

"Okay, okay," McCarter replied. "You're on."

Alvaro Hot Springs, Pyrenees Mountains, Spain

THE LATE Luis Manziliqua wasn't the only BLM underling with a distaste for sentry duty. Felipe Buvar, a twenty-year-old Pamplona native who'd joined up with the separatists six months earlier with visions of Che Guevara dancing in his head, had spent five of those months, like Manziliqua, exiled to remote mountain peaks with a pair of binoculars and his daily rations, assigned to keep an eye open for whatever the Rigos happened to be looking for at any given time.

This night, of course, it was jetliners.

Buvar stood atop the peak of Mt. Alvaro, two hundred yards uphill from the hot springs, staring northward at the night sky through his field glasses. He'd been at his post more than twelve hours now, and he had a crick in his neck from all the time he'd spent tilting his head backward. He briefly took one hand off the field glasses and massaged the base of his skull. He'd be glad when this was all over and he could climb down and join the others. He'd finished his food rations a couple hours earlier and there was only a little water left in his canteen. He wanted nothing more than to fill his stomach and crawl into his sleeping bag and doze off until morning. Of course, if they succeeded in bringing down a jetliner, there would be no sleeping. They would have to flee the area, with or without the tank. Most likely the latter. The last time he'd looked, the FSAT-50 was still mired in the hot springs like a fat man stuck in a bathtub. What a joke! All that time and effort put into stealing the tank, and for what? A chance to shoot a plane out of the sky? That could be done with a black-market surface-to-air missile mounted on the back of a jeep, or even his shoulder, for that matter.

"*Viva la revolución,*" Buvar muttered to himself cynically.

After a few minutes of picking out constellations, he saw a shooting star and made a quick wish for the day this was all behind them. When that day came, he decided, he would take his pay and bid the BLM adios. He'd go back to Pamplona and celebrate like he'd never celebrated before. Women, wine and more women. Let somebody else fight the war for Basque independence.

Buvar was elaborating on his fantasy when another flicker of light appeared on the northern horizon. This time it wasn't a shooting star, however. Buvar focused his binoculars and tracked the light for a few seconds, then reached for the walkie-talkie clipped to his belt. A tingle of excitement dispelled his boredom and discontent as he patched through a call to Jacque Rigo.

"A jet is coming," he reported. "Get ready."

"NOT A MOMENT TOO SOON," murmured Geraldo Carreon, wiping the sweat from his face as he hunched over the FSAT-50's weapon controls. Even with the hatch open, the temperature inside the tank had continued to rise. And the heat was the least of his concerns. Yet another seal had given way an hour earlier, and water from the hot springs had begun to seep up through the floor. It was ankle deep now, and behind Carreon, Jacque Rigo was using a meal tin to methodically scoop up the water and pitch it out through the open hatch. Rigo had stopped momentarily, however, when the call had come in from Buvar.

"Are you sure we can do this?" he asked Carreon.

Carreon nodded as he prepared to launch the tank's surveillance drone. "The controls are all well above the waterline," he assured Rigo. "As long as we have power, everything will be fine."

"I hope so."

Jacque resumed bailing the tepid, oily water pooling around his ankles. He kept his back turned to Carreon so that the other man wouldn't be able to see the tears he'd been fighting back since hearing the news of his brother's death. He was concerned, as well, about what had happened to his sister after their hurried call. From the sounds of it, the authorities were closing in on her and the others, and he had his doubts they would bother taking prisoners. If Angelica was dead, that would leave him without a family, the only one not brought down by the enemies of the BLM. The notion filled him not only with grief, but also rage. As with his sister in Barcelona, he was determined not to go down without a fight. He would have his revenge or die trying.

Rigo emptied another load of water outside the tank, then leaned over to refill his tin. Nearby, the walkie-talkie crackled again. It was Buvar. There was urgency in his voice.

"I just spotted a helicopter," he reported. "It's headed this way!"

"THERE THEY ARE!" shouted Rafael Encizo, using his uninjured arm to point out the windshield of the helicopter.

McCarter peered through a break in the fog bank they were flying through and spotted the leaf-draped FSAT-50, as well as a handful of men scrambling through the grass alongside the hot spring.

"Nice hunch, Rafe," he told Encizo. "You win a bloody Kewpie doll once we're out of this."

"Why didn't you say so in the first place," Encizo wisecracked, grabbing a pair of night-vision goggles. "I would've found the damn tank sooner."

McCarter pressed the intercom linking the cockpit with the rear cabin. "Ready yourselves, lads," he told T. J. Hawkins and the Spanish commandos. "We're in business."

"We see them, too," came Hawkins's quick response over the console speaker. "Ready when you are."

Once Encizo had donned the goggles, he took a closer look at their target. "They've spotted us," he warned McCarter. "You might want to mix it up a little as we close in."

"Will do."

McCarter executed a quick series of evasive maneuvers, weaving in and out of the fog bank as he circled the hot springs. Encizo kept an eye on the ground troops, as well as the FSAT-50. A few of the tree branches draped over the tank fell free as the turret's cannon tilted upward and began to pivot to one side.

"The tank's aiming away from us," Encizo reported, "but a couple gunners are drawing a bead on us. One of them's got some kind of shoulder launcher."

"Stinger?" McCarter asked.

"I don't think so," Encizo replied. "It looks more like a bazooka. Keep up the bob-and-weave till he fires, then hold steady while I try to nail him."

"Affirmative."

McCarter banked away from the enemy, retreating farther into the fog bank. Then he dropped low and swung sharply to the left.

"Hey, what's with the thrill ride?" Hawkins called out through the console two-way.

"Sorry," McCarter told him. "We're trying to dance our way out of a turkey shoot."

The Briton pulled the helicopter back up and to the left. He'd just finished the turn when there was an explosion in the air forty yards above them.

"That's your cue, big guy," Encizo told McCarter.

McCarter nodded and straightened the warship's course. Encizo turned his focus to the gunner controls, readying the Galicia's nose gun. The moment they emerged from the fog bank, he started firing.

Tracer rounds streaked in the direction of the hot springs, and as the deadly spray stitched its way along the ground, the BLM gunner with the bazooka reeled to one side and fell to the grass, dropping his weapon. Another two men crumpled alongside him. The others raced madly for the nearest cover.

"Thinned the herd," Encizo said.

"Should we try for the tank?" McCarter said.

"We'd be wasting ammo," the Cuban replied, glancing toward the mired FSAT-50. "You saw the spec sheets on that sucker's armor. Anything we throw at it's just gonna bounce... Hold on, maybe not."

McCarter was too busy minding the controls to look at the tank. "What?" he called out.

"Pull up!" Encizo exhorted. "They've got the hatch open. It's a long shot, but maybe we can put a three-pointer through the hoop!"

"Going up," McCarter murmured.

As the Briton eased the Galicia upward, he heard a faint sound like drumming on the chopper's roof. Encizo heard it, too.

"Somebody's firing down at us," he guessed. "Back off and let me have a look!"

McCarter complied. Encizo yanked off his goggles in favor of a pair of binoculars and peered up the side of the mountain overlooking the hot springs.

"Sniper on the peak," he called out. "Rifleman, I think."

"Want me to go after him?"

"No," Encizo said. "He's just bee-stinging us. Let's keep our eyes on the prize."

"Are you sure?" McCarter said. "I've been through my ration of chopper crashes for this week."

Before Encizo could respond, Hawkins piped up over the intercom again. "Looks like they're ready to go for a jet, guys!"

Encizo glanced back down at the tank. Hawkins was right. The FSAT's turret had stopped swiveling and its cannon was fully angled toward the night sky. And that wasn't the only cause for concern. Someone had just closed the main hatch and opened a second, larger panel beside it. Slowly, the tank's retractable missile launcher had begun to rise into view. It was aimed in the same direction as the turret gun.

"Looks like they're going to use a one-two punch," Encizo muttered.

"Missile and cannon?"

"I think so," Encizo said. "If the plane's close enough, they can bring it down with either one."

McCarter jockeyed the chopper around so that he could get a better look at the tank. As he did so, more gunfire rattled off the framework, not only from the sniper on the peak but also a few gunmen on the ground. He did his best to ignore the fusillade and stayed focused on the larger threat posed by the FSAT.

"Okay, maybe we can't take out the whole tank," he told Encizo, "but we should be able to at least neutralize the launcher with our TOWs."

"I'm on it!" Encizo said, grabbing at the controls for the chopper's submounted pod missiles. "This is gonna be close!"

THIRTY THOUSAND FEET above the Pyrenees, Captain Anton Gerard ran a cursory check on the instrument readings of his Boeing 767, then sat back in his pilot's seat and calmly sipped a cup of coffee one of the flight attendants had just brought him. Charter Flight 385 out of Paris was on schedule and due to begin its descent toward Barcelona in less than half an hour. So far the flight had been routine, and once he finished his coffee, Gerard planned to turn things over to his copilot so he could take a stroll through the cabin. In his thirty years of flying, he'd carried his share of high-profile passengers—everyone from movie celebrities and sports legends to business tycoons and touring rock-and-roll stars—but this night was a highlight in his career. Two heads of state, four ambassadors and enough other high-ranking political figures to make the plane the equivalent of an aerial UN. He wanted to see how many of them he could meet, and he was particularly interested in getting a chance to shake hands with the French prime minister. He'd already seen to it that one of the flight attendants had a camera ready to record the moment so that he could add the photograph to the collection he had mounted on the walls of his den back home in Calais. It wasn't just a matter of propping up his ego. He'd found over the years that the photographs worked like an aphrodisiac on the women he brought home for drinks. All it took was a few minutes of spinning anecdotes while showing off the photos and the women would be like putty in his hands. It was as if some of the charisma and power of these potentates was passed on to him, making him more desirable. A friend of Gerard's had once ventured that the women were likely less interested in him than fantasizing about the men he'd shaken hands with, but that didn't bother him. As he'd told his friend, "Hey, whatever works..."

Gerard was finishing his coffee when a call came in from the EUAA. The copilot took the call over his headset. Gerard saw the man's face turn white as he listened to the message.

"What's the matter?" he asked once the copilot had finished the call.

"We need to turn back," the other man responded, reaching for the plane's controls.

"Why?"

"There's no time to explain!" the copilot responded. "We're about to be attacked!"

"I'LL SEND THE DRONE up first," Geraldo Carreon told Jacque Rigo, "then the surface-to-air missile. The missile has its own guidance system, so it will lock in on the jet while the drone sets up coordinates for the cannon."

"I don't care how you do it!" Rigo said. "Just bring that plane down!"

Jacque sloshed through the water rising up around his ankles, pacing as best he could within the tight confines of the tank. With the hatch closed, the air around him was as stifling as it was hot. He tugged at the collar of his shirt. His heart was racing and his eyes stung from the perspiration. Everything was happening so fast. It was all he could do not to give in to the panic gnawing at him. He tried his walkie-talkie but was unable to make contact with any of his men outside the tank, so there was no way for him to see if they'd been able to do anything about the helicopter that had come up on them. Why did it have to show up now, when they were so close? All they needed was a few more seconds.

Carreon was about to launch the drone when he suddenly cursed aloud and thumped his fist against the radar console.

"The plane's changing course!" he cried out, eyeing a blip on the screen. "It's turning back!"

Jacque stared over Carreon's shoulder at the radar. "It's still within range, though, isn't it?"

"Yes, but—"

"Then go ahead with the launch!" Rigo demanded. "You just said the missile has a guidance system! The jet can run, but it won't be able to hide!"

Carreon drew in a breath, trying to settle his nerves. He thumbed a few switches, then flipped the protective cap from the launch button and pressed it. The tank shuddered faintly.

"The drone?" Jacque asked.

"Yes," Carreon said, glancing at the radar. "It's on its way."

"How long to fire the missile?"

"Ten seconds," Carreon responded. He quickly reprogrammed the launch commands, continuing the countdown. "Nine...eight...seven...six..."

"DAMN, WE'RE TOO late!" David McCarter swore, staring at the dissipating tendril of smoke trailing from the tank's retractable launcher.

"No, that was just the drone!" Encizo said. "We've still got a chance."

"What are you talking about?" McCarter asked. "The drone lines things up for the bloody cannon, doesn't it?"

"Let me get the SAM, then we'll worry about the cannon!" Encizo shot back, eyes on the tracking system for the helicopter's TOW missiles. "Now, hold this sucker still!"

While McCarter hovered the chopper in place, Encizo aligned his sights on the FSAT's launcher, then squeezed the trigger operating the left pod missile.

Both men held their breath as they stared out the windshield. As they watched on, an explosion briefly lit up the area around the hot springs, replacing the SAM's contrail with a widespread puff of smoke. As the smoke began to clear, McCarter traded high fives with his colleague.

"Bull's-eye!"

Down below, there was nothing left of the tank's missile launcher but a stub of twisted metal. The turret itself, however, had withstood the impact.

"We're not out of the woods yet," Encizo reminded his teammate. "We might've shaken them up a bit, but once they get their bearings, they can still get a shot off with the cannon."

"Then fire the other TOW!" McCarter said.

"Hold on, hold on," Encizo said. "We've only got one shot left, and I don't think we can even put a dent in the cannon. There's got to be a better way."

There was only one other option McCarter could think of, and it amounted to suicide. Still, it seemed like a price they would have to pay to keep the tank from bringing down the jet.

"We need to get in the line of fire," he said grimly.

Encizo looked at McCarter and nodded gravely. "Yeah," he said flatly. "Let's do it."

McCarter was about to open up the throttle when the doorway separating the cockpit from the cargo bay opened and Hawkins poked his head in. "What's the holdup?"

McCarter quickly explained the situation.

"That sucks," Hawkins said. "And, hell, once they've taken us out, what's to stop them from firing again and—?"

"Wait, wait!" Encizo suddenly blurted out.

McCarter saw that Encizo was staring out the front windshield. He followed the Cuban's gaze and saw a pile of fallen rubble building up at the base of the mountain near the hot springs. Some of the loose rock tumbled off the growing heap and splashed into the nearby hot spring.

"The TOW set off a landslide," Encizo said. "And from the looks of it, there's more where that came from."

"Bring the mountain to Mohammed?" Hawkins said.

"Just might work." Encizo turned back to McCarter. "Tilt her up a little and throw some light on the mountain."

"Gotcha!"

McCarter worked the controls with one hand and used the other to shine the chopper's searchlight on the mountainside. More than halfway up the slope, the light fell on the spot where the landslide had started. There was a huge indentation where part of the mountain had given way. A large chunk of rock protruded directly above it, all but begging for gravity to bring it crashing down.

"There you go," McCarter said. "Punch it a good one."

Encizo closed his fingers around the grip working the second TOW missile, then squeezed the trigger.

LYING PRONE at the edge of the mountaintop, Buvar peered downward through the scope of his rifle. His hands were trembling. Now that he found himself thrust into the kind of action he'd dreamed about, he was overcome with terror. There were no thoughts of glory or the triumph of his cause; his only instinct was to stay alive. So far his shots had glanced harmlessly off the chopper hovering below him, but now the Galicia had turned and offered him an unobstructed shot through the cockpit windshield. He couldn't see past the reflection of the glass, but he was sure he had the pilot in his sights. One well-placed shot would bring down the chopper.

Buvar was about to pull the trigger when a TOW missile roared out from beneath the chopper. There was a deafening blast as the warhead slammed into the mountain, quaking the ground beneath the sniper. He fired but the quaking had thrown off his aim and the bullet glanced off the chopper's nose. Buvar cursed and quickly worked the rifle's bolt action, hoping to get off a second shot before the Galicia changed its position.

Suddenly, however, the Basque sniper felt the ground giving way beneath him. Before he could make sense of what was happening, Buvar found himself falling, dragged down by the collapsing side of the mountain. He let out a cry that was quickly silenced as he was sucked into the avalanche that thundered its way down toward the hot springs and the immobile FSAT-50.

McCARTER BACKED the Galicia away from the showering downpour of rock and stone, then quickly set the chopper down on the grass. Hawkins and the UOE commanders stormed out from the rear cabin, ducking to avoid the gunship's rotors. Encizo quickly joined them, and once McCarter had shut off the engines, he grabbed a carbine and brought up the rear.

A few surviving BLM fighters fired at them from cover in the nearby foothills. The Basques were outnumbered, however, and within a matter of minutes after fanning out from the chopper, the members of Phoenix Force and the UOE troops had pinned down the gunmen and finished them off. The last to die was Salvador Jobe, who'd managed to reach his truck but was taken out before he could so much as start the engine.

By then, the avalanche had done its work. As McCarter and the others headed back toward the chopper, they saw a last few boulders tumble onto the heap of loose rock and stone at the base of the mountain. The pile had spread out across the hot spring, burying the entire pool as well as the trapped FSAT-50. Thin ribbons of steam rose up through gaps in the slagheap, but there was no trace of the tank.

"I don't think we need to bother digging it out," McCarter said. "Unless that thing can burrow, it's done for."

WHEN JACQUE RIGO came to, he was lying on the floor of the tank, his head a few inches above the rising waterline. It was pitch-black and silent inside the tank, and it took him a moment to remember where he was. Groaning, he slowly sat up.

"Geraldo?" he called out.

"I'm here," Carreon responded. He was only a few feet away, but Rigo couldn't see him. He groped through his pockets for a cigarette lighter. It took several flicks to get it to work. In the dim light, he saw that the cabin was still intact, but a number of things had been knocked loose and several of the wall cabinets had been jarred from their brackets and toppled onto their sides. Carreon sat wearily at the tank's controls, rubbing the side of his head.

"What happened?" Jacque asked.

"They brought part of the mountain down on us," Carreon said. "I already tried the hatch. We're trapped."

"There's no power?"

"I shut it off," Carreon said. "The water's too high. I didn't want us to be electrocuted."

Jacque staggered to his feet and kicked at the water around him, laughing bitterly. "Electrocution would be better than drowning or suffocating!"

Carreon thought it over. "We could try the radio," he suggested. "If we told them we surrender, maybe they—"

"Surrender!" Jacque shouted. "Never!"

"What do you suggest, then?" Carreon snapped back. "I told you, we're trapped!"

Rigo propped the lighter on one of the overturned cabinets and checked the hatch for himself, unlocking it and pushing upward. It wouldn't budge.

"I told you—"

"Shut up!" Jacque screamed at Carreon. "Let me think!"

Carreon shrugged and fell silent. Rigo paced. The lighter soon began to run out of fuel and the enclosure grew darker.

"The cannon," he finally said.

"What about it?"

"Fire it," Jacque said. "Maybe we can clear out an opening."

"I doubt it."

"Try!"

Carreon sighed, then cringed as he reached for the auxiliary power switch. When he turned it on, some of the instrument panels lit up without shorting or electrocuting him. He felt a prick of hope, but it was quickly dashed when he checked the weapons system monitors and saw a bank of warning lights flash.

"The cannon is inoperable," he reported. "There's probably debris in the barrel. That or it's been dented."

The cigarette lighter went out. Rigo swatted it aside and glared at Carreon. "We need to try it anyway!"

"Don't be an idiot!" Carreon shouted back. "If it misfires, we're dead for sure!"

Jacque drew his gun and aimed it at Carreon's head. "Fire the cannon," he said coldly. "I won't ask you again."

Carreon stared past the gun and saw the look of intent in Rigo's eyes. He knew there was no use trying to talk sense to him. Resigned, he turned back to the console and reached for the cannon's firing switch.

"This is madness," he murmured.

THE MEN HAD clambered back aboard the chopper and David McCarter had just fired up the engines when an explosion sounded deep within the pile of fallen rock and stone that had entombed the tank. A few bits of flying stone pelted the helicopter, cracking the windshield and clanging off the rotors. The heap shifted slightly, creating a faint crater that quickly filled in as the loose rock fell back into place. Smoke seeped up through the debris, but the tank remained hidden from view.

"Their last hurrah," McCarter muttered to Encizo, who was seated beside him.

"I think so," Encizo replied. "Let's get out of here."

EPILOGUE

Santa Maria Hospital, outskirts of Bilbao, Spain

The hospital doors swung open and Calvin James squinted in his wheelchair as the morning light shone on his bandaged face.

"A beautiful day," he said.

"That it is," T. J. Hawkins agreed as he pushed James out toward the curb, where two cars were waiting. David McCarter was behind the wheel of the first vehicle. Gary Manning sat up front next to McCarter, and Rafael Encizo was in the back seat. Hawkins would be driving James to the airport in the second car.

James suddenly clamped both hands on the wheels of his chair. "Hold on," he told Hawkins. "I want to walk the rest of the way."

"Are you sure you're up to it?" Hawkins asked.

"Hell, yes," James replied. "We're talking a few yards, for crying out loud, not the Boston Marathon."

James slowly got out of the wheelchair, wincing with each movement. He knew his recovery was going to take a while, but he wasn't about to pamper himself any more than necessary.

Once James was on his feet, Hawkins pushed the wheelchair aside, then helped steady his colleague as they headed for the second vehicle.

"When's our flight?" James asked.

"As soon as we get to the airport," Hawkins told him. "Carl and Pol just got in from Barcelona."

"Good," James said. "We can catch up on all our war stories."

"That'll be the day," Hawkins replied. "You know the drill, Cal. As soon as we get back to the Farm, somebody else is gonna step outta line and we'll be back at it. The war never ends, and neither do the war stories."

"How true," James conceded. "How true..."